PRAISE FOR

A Spanish Sunrise

"Walker dazzles in this heart-wrenching tale about a grieving father's restorative trip to Spain with his daughter . . . Transporting descriptions of Ester's farm bring the setting to life, the characters all earn the reader's emotional investment, and the pacing is perfect. Readers will fall in love."

—*Publishers Weekly* (starred review)

An Unfinished Story

"Walker's attention-grabbing and surprising plot highlights the engaging characters in this tale of second chances. For fans of women's fiction such as Nicholas Sparks's and Kristin Hannah's work."

—*Library Journal*

The Singing Trees

"Walker's (*An Unfinished Story*) beautifully written coming-of-age novel is set during the Vietnam War . . . Ideal for book groups and for readers who enjoyed Taylor Jenkins Reid's *Daisy Jones & the Six*, Susan Elizabeth Phillips's *Dance Away with Me*, or Nicholas Sparks's novels."

—*Library Journal* (starred review)

"A heartwarming read."

—Historical Novel Society

THE
STARS
DON'T
LIE

OTHER BOOKS BY THE AUTHOR

A Spanish Sunrise
The Singing Trees
An Unfinished Story
Red Mountain
Red Mountain Rising
Red Mountain Burning
A Marriage Well Done

Writing as Benjamin Blackmore

Lowcountry Punch
Once a Soldier
Off You Go: A Mystery Novella

THE
STARS
DON'T
LIE

A Novel

BOO
WALKER

LAKE UNION
PUBLISHING

Published by Lake Union Publishing, Seattle

www.apub.com

Amazon, the Amazon logo, and Lake Union Publishing are trademarks of Amazon.com, Inc., or its affiliates.

ISBN-13: 9781662513619 (hardcover)
ISBN-13: 9781662508783 (paperback)
ISBN-13: 9781662508776 (digital)

Cover design by Ploy Siripant
Cover image: ©KenCanning / Getty; ©USBFCO / Shutterstock;
©jaboo2foto / Shutterstock

Printed in the United States of America
First edition

*For Leila Meacham and all the other teachers out there
changing the world, one student at a time*

Chapter 1

So Far from Perfect

I didn't put stock in the stars anymore. To lazily look up at the sky and seek some sort of epiphany . . . who had time for such frivolity? If anything, the stars had crashed down around me, and the only way I'd get my life back together was if I picked them up, one by one, and placed them exactly where I needed them to be.

The secret to life was simple: you put your nose to the grindstone and got things done with an impenetrable resilience. That was how I'd made something of myself. My father said my drive comes from a need to fill a void in my life. Since when did the reasons we worked hard matter? They didn't put your motivations in your obituary, only your accomplishments.

Three years ago, I'd borrowed every penny I could to open a veterinary practice in the Blue Ridge Mountains of Asheville, North Carolina. Though I still remembered the pride of opening our clinic's doors for the first time—realizing a nearly impossible-to-achieve dream I'd had since I was eighteen—I couldn't wait to take the next step in growing what I somewhat jokingly called "my empire." I'd come into a good deal of money in December because of a surgical patent I'd sold, and a portion of the proceeds was going into the construction of a state-of-the-art practice a few miles away.

We shared our current space with a group of attorneys, who had been happy to hear we would be moving out soon. Not only were they trying to expand, but I'm sure the animal noises were getting to them. They weren't as happy as I, though, because the building that had once housed the pinnacle of a dream now felt outdated and cramped—especially where I was now, in the rather drab lobby, with its cracked linoleum floors and drop ceiling.

The cramped feeling was exaggerated by the fact that all eight of my staff had ambushed me with a cake and were currently singing a "Happy Birthday" that was surprisingly jolly for so early in the morning. Even the dogs in their kennels had joined in and barked at the commotion.

My office manager, Mary Beth, held a cake decorated with plastic animals. "Happy Birthday, Dr. Livingston" was scrawled across the top in red lettering. Having recently recovered from breast cancer, Mary Beth always wore a hat or scarf on her head. Today she wore a lime-green baseball cap. Considering what she'd been through, her smile was all the more infectious.

I stood with my hands clasped at my waist, waiting eagerly for the end of the song so I could blow out the candles and escape. I was so much better suited for the company of animals. But the other side of me, the veterinary surgeon who'd led this group standing before him, wore a big fat forced smile. I showed so many teeth I probably looked like I was auditioning for a toothpaste commercial. Not that I wasn't appreciative of their gesture, as that kind of camaraderie among colleagues was special.

Mary Beth was the only one in the office who'd cross the professional line into a more familiar and friendly zone, a slow play she'd worked on for years, like a prisoner chiseling away at a tunnel—a little every day and you'll get somewhere. Knowing me so well, she loved to see me squirm at all the attention I was getting. Her lips curved upward in amusement as the staff finished the song.

"You guys are too good to me," I said, finding everyone's eyes, then giving a playful glare to Mary Beth.

As I drew in a deep breath to blow out the candles, I noticed Jenny Post, a longtime client and mother of four boys, racing across the parking lot toward the entrance. She held her pug puppy close to her chest.

Though I never liked to see a patient and his owner in distress, I welcomed the opportunity to escape all the attention. Addressing the team around me, I said, "Back to work, folks." And though I could have used one, I blew out the candles without a wish.

I met Jenny at the door and quickly unlocked it. The running had caused her headband to break free, and she pulled it from her curly hair as she breathlessly pleaded, "Please help, Dr. Livingston. I thought he just wasn't feeling well last night, but I think something's wrong—like bad. He can't hold anything down, isn't eating . . ."

I observed her pug—his light-brown fur and black face—and recalled his name was Sam and that he was six months old. We'd done his initial shots, and if I remembered correctly, he was two weeks away from his orchiectomy—or neutering.

"What's going on with you, buddy?" I lifted him up out of her arms. His eyes appeared glazed, and the dryness in his gums indicated dehydration.

I looked back at Jenny, and she elaborated with a staccato burst of information. "He was lying around most of yesterday afternoon and didn't even touch his kibble last night. I thought he might have picked up a bug. This morning, he threw up in the kitchen. I tried to call but got the voice mail."

I probed her with the standard questions, then said to Susan, my approaching assistant, "Please take care of Jenny, get her something to drink, and set her up in one of the patient rooms. I'll take Sam back to room four." I turned back to Jenny. "We'll figure out what's going on with your little guy. Let me take some X-rays, and we'll go from there."

Tiffany, the most technical of my technicians, joined me as I carried Sam to the back. "Patient is exhibiting inappetence and lethargy," I said, "along with bouts of diarrhea and vomiting. I'm guessing he's ingested something." I set him on a metal table that lined a wall of the window-less room. The fluorescent bulbs overhead offered ample lighting.

I rubbed behind his ears, and he looked at me with helpless eyes. "Poor puppy. You'll eat anything at your age. Don't worry, I gotcha."

To Tiffany, I said, "No need to sedate him. Let's get a lateral and VD of his abdomen. And don't miss the diaphragm, please."

~

Twenty minutes after she'd arrived, I found Jenny sitting in a chair in one of the patient rooms, picking at her fingernails. On the side table were a jar of treats and a copy of *Dogue* magazine.

I sat in the chair facing her. "The radiographs show a large amount of gas distension of the small intestine, which is consistent with an obstructive pattern, likely from foreign-body ingestion." I pulled back from the vet-speak. "In other words, I think he ate something he wasn't supposed to. Happens all the time with these pups. I'll have to make an incision in the intestine to get in there, but I'm hopeful."

Tears spilled from her eyes, and I did my best to make her feel better, explaining that I performed this type of surgery on a weekly basis. "I know it's scary, but he has a strong chance at a full recovery."

Before the tech even went over the costs of surgery, Jenny said, "I don't care. Please help him."

I knew the feeling. Six months earlier, after trying everything I could to keep my German shepherd, Penelope, alive, I'd been forced to put her down.

I wasn't about to promise Jenny that Sam would be okay, but I told her the truth, that I would do everything in my power to bring him back to normal. She whispered a thank-you.

My team and I spent the next hour correcting his hydration with shock doses of intravenous fluids. Immediately it had a reviving effect, and right before we gave Sam his anesthesia, he was wagging his little stump of a tail.

Ready to begin, I cut Sam's abdomen open with an electric scalpel, and the smell of burning flesh and sour stomach acid rose into the air. Ironically, this was my happy place and what I did best—almost second nature to me. I liked the bright lights and the energy found in an operating room, and the feeling of confidence that washed over me, knowing I'd trained hard for this moment.

Give me this situation all day long over being the target of a birthday song.

I located the problem area, clamped off the intestines with forceps on either side of the obstruction, then triple ligated and transected each vessel, which allowed me to remove the necrotic piece of intestine along with its compromising foreign material.

Fourteen minutes from start to finish. A new record for me. Little Sam would recover nicely. I just had to figure out how to tell his owner what I'd pulled from him without cracking a smile.

After giving Jenny the good news that the surgery had gone well, I asked her to return later in the afternoon so I could monitor her pooch. I didn't mind that it was a Friday. A day in the life of a vet, right? All that mattered was that Sam would go on to live the glorious and carefree life of a canine.

"I had to put my best friend down over Christmas," I said to Sam, who slept beside me on the couch in my office.

It was a quarter after six, and everyone else in the office had gone home. He lay against my leg, the cone around his neck preventing me from seeing his face. He was certainly coming in and out of consciousness due to the anesthesia lingering in his system.

"Penelope was her name," I said, looking out my window at the fenced-in grassy area where she used to play while I worked. "A big beautiful German shepherd." I felt Penelope's fur in my fingers as if she were still there beside me. "Her kidneys began to fail, and I tried everything. Kept her alive maybe longer than I should have. Though a piece of me dies every time I euthanize an animal, it's a part of my job. But with Pen, I . . . I was leveled."

I reached for my phone—to distract myself more than anything else. I certainly wasn't eager to leave. Had I been home, my extremely nice and outgoing and a bit overbearing neighbors, the Tacketts, would probably knock on my door with another cake and their own rendition of "Happy Birthday." The couple sang in their church choir and took any opportunity to break into song. I'd moved into my house at Christmas three years prior, and they'd welcomed me with sugar cookies and a duet of "Baby, It's Cold Outside." Nice people, but Tony Bennett and Lady Gaga they are not. Great bakers, though.

I thumbed my way through my ever-growing inbox, thinking I should block an hour out of my schedule to unsubscribe from half the junk pouring in. My head dropped when an email from Bree Arsenault caught my eye. If only her emails had an "Unsubscribe" button. Apparently the woman had nothing going on in her life until she'd been tapped to run our twenty-year high school reunion, which was two weeks away.

She was like one of those people who sat on the board of directors of the condo association and took it as seriously as if they were working at the White House. Her entire mission in life seemed to be to get as many as possible of our class to the reunion, and she'd been relentless in doing so. It was like someone had offered her a sizable cash bonus if she could get 70 percent of Teterbury High's class of 1999 to attend. I would have doubled it if she'd left me alone. Who in their right mind would want to go back to that small-minded backwoods colony where dreams died a slow death?

I started to read her latest transmission, expecting something along the lines of the calendar of events, perhaps a morning hike, followed by breakfast at the hotel, then who knows what? A sack race? A cheddar and maple syrup sampling? What do people do at high school reunions in small-town Vermont?

Once I'd caught the gist of her email, my sarcasm and humor dissipated. Twenty years had gone by, and one simple message could stir it all up, like jabbing at the ashes of the previous night's fire and getting it to spark up again.

I reread her words, and my heart picked back up with a vengeance, thumping so hard I could hear it. She had asked if I'd be interested in speaking at the reunion and talking about my path to success. Without intentionally doing so, I imagined the email going out with the finalized program for the evening, and I saw in my mind's eye my name listed near the top.

What would it say about me? *Dr. Carver Livingston will speak about his life as an innovative surgeon who recently sold a patent to the biggest player in veterinary medicine.*

For a moment, that felt pretty good.

Fear soon followed, and my fingers and toes tightened. "There is absolutely no way in hell I'm going back home."

Responding to Bree, I typed: I'm so honored you'd ask, but I'm about to break ground on a new building, and there's no way I can get away. I'm really bummed, as I would love to see everyone. Was that the lie of the century or what?

No sooner had I sent the message than my phone lit up with an incoming text. Don't say no yet, Carver! Please consider it. I ran into your dad yesterday, and he said it was about time you came home. He also gave me your number. Hope it's okay I reached out.

No, Bree. It's not okay.

I set down the phone. My dad. My dear old cowboy father. Of course he had told Bree it was about time I came home. He'd been telling me that for two decades.

I turned to Sam. "You're lucky to be a dog, trust me. The shit we humans have to deal with is ridiculous." I saw a quick flash of a teenage me slamming my fist into the wall of my bedroom.

Looking toward my stand-up desk, I settled my gaze on the birthday cards the office staff and our clients had given me. What had I learned in the past twenty years? If I were to give advice to my younger self, I knew what it would be. I'd say, "Young Carver, put your head down, avoid heartache at all costs, work your tail off, and don't look back." So I wouldn't scare him (because he was a fragile guy), I would not tell him the whole truth, that the past was a vampire that wanted your blood.

The front door chime announced Jenny's arrival. She and her husband, Wes, were waiting in the lobby when I entered from the back with Sam in tow. Wes was about her height and wore a flat-billed Patagonia hat that looked so new he might have bought it earlier in the day.

Jenny fell to her knees when she saw her dog. "Sam!"

I let go of the leash, and he waddled over.

She stuck her head in the cone and let him lick her face. "He seems like he's as good as new."

"I'd say so. What a great pup."

Barely lowering himself, Wes gave him a quick pat on the head, making it obvious who Sam's true caretaker was. "I don't want to know what you cost me, do I?" he asked with a smug grin. Then to me: "What was it, anyway? What did he eat?"

That was the question, wasn't it? I produced the Ziploc-bagged object from behind my back and held it up in the air like the missing piece to a puzzle. Right there for all to see was an intact, slightly discolored red lace thong.

I held it toward Jenny. "I think he got into your fabrics."

She took the bag from me and held it up for a moment, perhaps wondering why Sam would want to eat them.

The air in the lobby suddenly felt suffocating.

Realizing something was off, I turned my head to Wes's yellowing face as his wife said to him through gritted teeth—a long, angry pause between each word—"These are not mine."

Even Sam froze.

Wes cut a look at me that could have lasered through glass, and it got under my skin quickly. As if I had anything to do with whatever it

8

was he'd done. I knew exactly what she felt like—knew exactly the pain that would never truly go away.

This Wes guy would get no sympathy from me. He was worried about how much Sam would cost him. It looked like it would be far more than a vet bill.

A second away from taking that flipping hat off his head and hitting him with it, I swallowed what I wanted to say to this asshole and turned to Jenny. With empathetic eyes, I gave her Sam's discharge instructions and told her I'd be available if she needed me.

Back in my office, I collapsed onto the couch. What a long week, capping it off with a woman whose heart had been broken. Hell yes, I'd been there, and I could only imagine what lay in store for Jenny in the future.

I thought of Bree's email—her invitation for me to speak. Was it any wonder I didn't want to go home? No, not home. Teterbury, Vermont, wasn't home. That town was a cesspit of everything wrong with the world, and it was far more than a broken heart that kept me away.

Chapter 2

Double Whammy

My house stood halfway up an east-facing slope of Coyote Mountain two miles north of Asheville. My real estate agent had called it mountain chic. With its modern accents, the repurposed beams running along the tall ceilings, and the enormous windows offering dramatic views, she'd captured the idea well. It was one of the sharpest houses I'd seen in a year of looking and was only a short walk away from the Grove Park Inn, the stunning mountain resort the Vanderbilts had constructed more than a century earlier. I had a membership to the sports complex and got over there at least four days a week to swim laps, lift weights, or do the occasional yoga class to stay limber.

I plugged in my car and took my brown bag of sushi up the stairs to the main floor. Even after six months, I still anticipated that Penelope would be waiting for me on the other side of the door, as if losing her had been nothing more than a nightmare. The house was eerily silent, a heartbeat forever missing.

A shower and a change of clothes didn't help to clear my mind. I couldn't stop thinking about Bree's invitation and all the heavy things that came with it. After spreading my meal out on a kitchen island that was big enough on which to land a plane, I flipped on the evening news. They could have been discussing a UFO encounter, and I wouldn't have known. Slowly stirring my miso soup, I stared into it, the small pieces of dried kelp eerily surfacing like tails of lake monsters.

More than anything, I hated that I'd let it get to me. I'd gotten good at forgetting, but the uncomfortable memories were forcing their way in today.

I poured some sake in a Riedel wineglass and spun it around. The local news and a plate of nigiri and sashimi paired with a Junmai Ginjo was my idea of a good birthday. I took the first sip and followed it with a bite of uni.

"To speak at your high school reunion," I said with Shakespearean command, as if I stood on the stage. "To attend your high school reunion. To even venture over those borders into Teterbury again." Aware I sounded like I might be unraveling, I took another long sip of the sake and let it soothe me. I used to speak to Penelope, and when she was gone, I kept talking.

Back in my regular voice, I said, "Everyone leave me the fuck alone."

With chopsticks hovering over my next bite, I watched the end of a commercial I'd seen a couple of times lately. A man climbed out of a Subaru Forester parked at the edge of a high cliff that looked out over the dark night, only a few lights twinkling in the valley below. He lifted his head, and the camera panned up to the night sky to follow his gaze.

With a voice that might come from Thomas Haden Church—the actor from *Sideways* and *Wings*—the man asked excitedly, "What do the stars say to you?"

The camera showed several of the stars twinkle from up high. Then the actor grabbed the camera and aimed it at his face. He was handsome, chiseled even.

He jabbed his finger at the audience. "And remember . . . the stars don't lie."

It was exactly something Mrs. Cartwright might have said. My high school English teacher had been a stargazer, perpetually preaching the importance of lifting one's head to the sky, assuring us that every answer we needed waited for us up there. Even after all this time, I could see her plump form, wearing a dress and tennis shoes, her right arm raised with a stick of chalk between her fingers, and her wise and caring eyes staring at me, demanding the best.

Though some of her teaching might have leaned toward the romantic, there was no way to gainsay the impact she'd had on my life. Of all the teachers through the years, in Teterbury, at Wake Tech Community College and Davidson College, and then at NC State for vet school, she'd been the best. No question. And she'd been far more than that too. She'd gone well beyond the duties of a teacher to be there for me when I unraveled halfway through my senior year.

I raised a silent toast, grimacing at how I'd lost touch with her. God, I hoped she understood why I'd disappeared.

Teterbury was coming at me from all sides right now, and the memories twisted and turned in my gut. I'd done a lot of bad things back then, walked out on a lot of people, but I felt like I'd done my time. I was tired of beating myself up for it all, tired of reliving all that pain, spinning endlessly in the guilt. Here I was still alive; there was something to be said for that.

A ringing phone rescued me from the darkness.

I knew it was my parents before I looked at the screen, as they hadn't yet wished me a happy birthday and never missed it. I shook off the dark thoughts and accepted their FaceTime call. "I had a feeling," I said, seeing my mother's head fill the screen.

"Of course you did."

I'd inherited her thick wavy hair, but hers was a honeyed blonde to my dark brown bordering on black. She'd chopped off most of hers recently, so it wasn't much longer than mine.

She stretched her endearing smile. "Happy birthday, Mr. Thirty-Eight." She backed away from the phone to show my father standing behind her. He'd been the unlucky one when it came to hair, as he'd lost it when he was in his thirties.

"Happy birthday, son," he said.

Before he could get another word in, my mother jumped into her time machine. "I feel like I was changing your diapers yesterday."

"Oh, good, thanks for bringing that up." The sushi lost its appeal.

They were in their kitchen and had propped up my mother's phone on the counter. She said something about my cute, dimpled baby butt, and I stopped listening for a few seconds. Only a mother could get excited about such things.

My mother, I pondered, hearing her go on in chronological order through the years. She was always my biggest champion. I'd inherited my drive from her. Sixty-four years old and she was still branch manager for the Teterbury Bank of America, working like she was fresh out of college and scrambling for a promotion. She was the one who'd always pushed me, cheering me on as I broke records on the track field and sailed my way toward valedictorian of my class. She'd even been there for me after I'd screwed up, encouraging me to get back onto my feet and fight. Couldn't say the same for my father.

About the time she reached eighth grade in her recounting of my history and was talking about my first girlfriend, I said, "All right, you've embarrassed me enough. Thank you, Mother, for all the love."

"I could go on and on and on."

"I know you could."

"Any big plans, dimple butt?"

I chose not to acknowledge the nickname, because that would only encourage her. "You know me." I sat up on the stool and took a swig of sake. Then another. "Catching up on some work and the news, then crashing early so I can get a good ride in nice and early before a meeting with the contractor for the new—"

"You don't slow down, do you?" my father asked in the drawl he hadn't shaken from his Wyoming youth. He talked like he'd come in from roping a bronco, an accent New Englanders always called adorable. It was my mother who'd thrown a lasso around him, convincing him to leave Cheyenne, Wyoming, for Teterbury after a love affair sparked by a random encounter in Boston. He'd been visiting a friend who was attending BU, and they'd sat next to my mother at a

BU versus Harvard hockey match during the Beanpot tournament at Boston Garden.

"You'll be turning sixty before you realize you missed it all," he said. "Boy, if I was in your shoes, I wouldn't work another day in my life."

I shook my head in exhaustion, already weary of my father's endless spouting of supposed wisdom. Hell, I was still tired from the last time we'd spoken—and the time before that. He'd taught me a lot over the years, but it had gotten to where he'd become a windup dad ready to offer unsolicited advice anytime he felt my failures had pulled the string dangling from his back. Truth was, he was sad, and when I was around him, I felt sad.

A long pause draped over the moment, something the three of us were used to. As much as we loved each other, there'd been something missing for a long time. Every year I didn't go back was another hammer strike on the wedge of our growing divide.

Our words collided with one another as we scrambled to fill the silence. I raised the volume of my voice and repeated my question. "Warming up over there?" The weather was safe territory for the Livingston family.

My dad should have been a meteorologist. I thought all cowboys were that way, even the transplanted ones. Though he was a retired mechanic who'd been living in New England for a little longer than I'd been alive, he was still stuck in Cheyenne, still saddling horses, herding cattle, and fixing farm trucks.

"You know, son, this has been the dandiest early June I've ever seen. Not a lick of rain yet, and we've been sitting right in the upper sixties every single day. I'm watching that system move in from the coast, but I don't think it's gonna hit us."

"And, Mom, how's your ankle?" She'd hurt it a few weeks earlier and gave me an update. The other thing we could talk about ad nauseam was the plight of age.

Before my dad could recount his latest bout with shingles, I said, "Mom, you're quiet. What else is going on with you?"

"Everything's great, sweetheart. Everything is just great." What I saw was the same smile I'd shown when my staff had sung me "Happy Birthday" earlier that day. Everything was not "just great."

"What's going on?"

My mother and father both looked away for a moment.

I sat up and pressed my hands against the counter. "Seriously, what's happening?"

"Not on your birthday," she finally said, shaking her head.

"What do you mean, 'not on my birthday'? I'm not ten years old. Is everyone healthy?" As much as they frustrated me, their mortality scared the shit out of me.

"Everyone is healthy," my mom said. "Well, sort of."

"Dammit, Mom, what's going on?"

She finally let it out. "Your father has dementia."

"Christ, Lisa." My father backed away. "Don't make stuff up."

She side-eyed him. "I'm not making stuff up, Ben. You're showing early signs of dementia."

He approached, his wrinkled forehead covering most of the screen. "What it is, Carver, is that I'm curious. I want to go out and do things."

My mom squeezed back into the frame. "Carver, people who get dementia don't know that they're getting dementia—that's not how it works."

"He doesn't sound like he has dementia," I said. "What's really happening?"

"You want to know?" my mother asked, both the pitch and volume of her voice rising. "Why don't you tell him, Ben?"

"Carver," my dad said, clearing his throat, "your mom and I are getting a divorce."

The word slammed into me. "A divorce?"

She pointed to him. "*He* wants a divorce. This is all your father."

He didn't disagree.

"Where is this coming from?" I asked. I poured myself another glass of sake and gulped it down, thinking Japan didn't make enough

15

sake to soothe me. Why did they have to put it in such small bottles, anyway?

My father shook his head. "I don't know that it's your business."

"I don't understand."

He raised his hand to wave. "I'm gonna sign off now, Carver. I know it doesn't feel good, but it's what's happening. You want to come home and talk about it, you know where to find us."

He wished me a happy birthday again and walked away. In the following silence, I could hear my mother's weeping, a sound that had always crushed me more than any other. She'd often cried my senior year because of what had happened. Though she'd tried to hide her breakdowns as best as she could, I still knew. I could see it in her worn-out eyes after she'd emerged from her room. I could tell by the wadded-up tissues in her purse. And her tears flowed into me like a river of guilt, because I'd played no small part in everything that had gone wrong with my family.

The way she'd still stuck with me hurt even worse. Maybe it would have been easier if she'd treated me like my father had, stopping shy of giving up on me. I could still see the disappointment in his eyes as I walked out the door to school each day toward the end of my senior year. I'd broken him like he used to break horses, and he'd set out to make sure I knew it.

"So sorry, Mom," I said, thinking she'd always deserved better. Yes, I might have been the one who'd ruined him, but he'd taken it out on my mom too. I'd forever judge him for that.

She sniffled as she took the phone into her hand. A shiny new fridge that had been part of their recent renovation stood behind her. "I didn't want to tell you on your birthday."

"I don't care about my fu—" I caught myself; she hated it when I cursed. "Forget about my birthday. What is he thinking?"

Her sigh revealed something that sounded like giving up, and that was new for her. "I don't know if it's dementia, but he's losing his mind. A couple of days ago he came home pulling a rickety old canned ham."

"A canned ham? What are you talking about?"

"He bought a vintage camper, Carver. Like an RV. I guess some of the aficionados call them canned hams because that's what they look like."

"I'm having a hard time processing what you're telling me."

She wiped off a tear. "Your father bought a nineteen-sixty-two Shasta camper he's calling Clementine. That's where he's sleeping. All he does is work on it—her," my mother corrected herself with disgust. "It's like a cult, these people who restore old Shastas. He's constantly reading forums and chatting with people online. He says he wants to"— she changed her tone, impersonating my father if he were running for election—"go see our great country." She laughed darkly. "He didn't even ask me if I wanted to go . . . not that I do. When I asked what that meant for us, he brought up the D-word."

I put the D-word on hold for a moment and tried to picture my dad pulling a Shasta trailer. He certainly had the truck for it, a big four-wheel drive that could pull anything, but he wasn't a canned-ham person. Was he? Hell, I didn't even know him. Other than the times I'd flown my parents down to Asheville, I couldn't think of the last time he'd left Teterbury.

"He wants to go see all the sights: the Grand Canyon, the Badlands, Little Bighorn."

"The homebody of the century suddenly wants to leave. I don't get it." Had I been a submarine, I would have been hearing a torpedo alarm. "When is this supposed to happen?"

"Whenever he's done fixing it up. He's shooting for Wednesday. He's barely talking to me, Carv. Sleeps in there at night. He's camping in our yard, cooking on the grill. He comes in to use the bathroom, and that's about it. Our house is basically a KOA campground now."

A trailer. In our yard. My father camping out in our tiny yard amid our neighbors. My parents divorcing.

"I need you to come home, honey."

There it was, the torpedo strike. Direct hit, shaking my foundation.

"Come home?" I said. "I . . . I . . . I can't come home." I said it like she'd suggested I swallow a glass of bleach.

She brought the phone closer. "Your father listens to you. You need to talk some sense into him."

"My father listens to me? Since when?"

"You haven't always realized it, but he loves you. He's so proud of you, tells everyone about what you're doing. He keeps the article from the newspaper on the fridge. See?"

"Why don't you guys come here?" I asked as she gave me a close-up of the article. "I'll fly you first class. The weather's great. We can sit down and talk about it."

"I already tried that," my mom said. "Look, I know you hate the idea of coming home, but I need you. He needs you."

I dropped the phone like it had turned to a hot stone. My mother's pleading voice rose from the speaker into the air, but I didn't know what she was saying. Because I was drowning. Teterbury was nothing more than a reminder of the broken boy I'd once been. I wanted nothing to do with that kid or those feelings or that awful town.

A good thirty seconds later, I picked up the phone. "Here's the thing. I have this darn twentieth reunion coming up two weeks from tomorrow. They want me to speak. I can't show up a few days before. I already said I was busy with the new building. They'll know I was lying."

"They don't have to know you're home. I won't tell anyone."

I paced again. Not once—not *once*—had she ever asked me to come home. She'd always understood.

"Let me talk to Dad," I said.

"Hold on."

The view through her camera was shaky as she crossed the house. She opened the front door and then switched the screen so I could see the trailer. No kidding, it stood in the front yard, a vintage blue-and-white canned ham. Holy ever-loving God.

My mother yelled, "Ben, he wants to talk to you!" I winced at the idea of the neighbors hearing.

Though I couldn't see him, I could hear him grumble something back. As soft as he could be—a pushover when it came to my mom—he had a hardheaded streak that surfaced occasionally.

My mom was no pushover at any moment ever that I could remember, and she went after him. "Your son wants to talk to you, and it's his birthday and . . ."

I put the phone down. This. *This* was one of the million reasons I hadn't been home in twenty years. All this bickering and odd behavior hadn't existed until the winter of 1998. Though it was hard to imagine, we had been incredibly happy and stable together for a lot of my childhood.

Teterbury was a thousand miles away, yet I couldn't escape its vast reach. Bubbling up out of nowhere came a desperate hate for my hometown and for my teenage years and my father and . . . and maybe even for myself too.

I raised the phone to my face. "Mom, I don't know what to say—"

"He's done talking. Says I'm trying to get you to do my dirty work now. I'm telling you . . . please come."

Had twenty years of my self-imposed exile not made it clear? "That's not an option, Mom, and you know that." Even she couldn't understand what it had taken for me to climb out of the hell that became my life back then. I had it all and let it slip away, all in one cataclysmic and unbearable public decline.

"Let me talk to him tomorrow," I said, trying to speak with compassion. Her sniffling was breaking my heart. "He's always better in the morning."

Her face showed a bit of hope. I felt it too.

"He's having a momentary lapse of reason," I said. "He'll come around."

"I don't know."

We ended the call, and I stood in the middle of my kitchen staring off into the middle space, letting the conversation settle. What was it with life? Inevitably, the moment you got to the top, or somewhere close to it, strange forces came after you, standing between you and the finish line.

I pictured my father's face, hearing that slow cadence of his voice as he tried to be a good father. From where I was now, I saw it as all lies, every piece of advice he'd ever offered. Sure, we'd had some great times, and he'd taught me some good lessons, but when it mattered, when I'd really needed him, he wasn't there.

My mother could have had anyone, but she chose him. He should be grateful she had somehow put up with him for another twenty years, despite how he'd checked out. He should consider himself the luckiest guy alive. But no. Forty-three years later, he'd decided he was too good for her.

How could I not hate him for that?

Chapter 3

Never Stop Chasing

Early the next morning, dressed for my Saturday bike ride, I sat in a chair in my living room and tossed back two K-Cups of coffee while blazing through Asheville's *Citizen-Times*, the *Wall Street Journal*, and the *Washington Post*. Per the usual, I spent longer on the business sections, where I enjoyed reading about successful entrepreneurs like myself.

Then the moment of truth came, and I called my father on his cell. To my surprise, he actually answered.

"How did I know?" he said, as if he were some wise sage whom I'd tracked down in the forest, the Yoda of Teterbury.

I stood from the chair and faced a window that overlooked the Asheville skyline. The sun had burned off the morning fog, revealing the mountains surrounding the city, a view I'd paid for and should enjoy more. "You slept in the trailer last night?"

"I did indeed," he said proudly. "Now I've got a fire burning, drinking my coffee, listening to the doves."

"In the front yard?"

"Sure, why not? Clementine looks good out here."

Clementine. Had he really named his Shasta? I was beyond embarrassed for the whole family. We'd all learned the hard way how "New

England small town" Teterbury was, how news could travel and twist into the steamiest of gossip.

How many people in my hometown were making assumptions about Ben Livingston being kicked out of the house and now living in the front yard? I could hear someone saying, "Carver took it all out of them after what he did."

"Is it even legal to live out there?" I asked. "I didn't think you could create additional living space without a permit."

"No one has said anything to me yet." Proud defiance rang in his tone.

I could have asked him about Clementine and lured him into a genuine conversation, but I didn't have the patience or the time, so I jumped right into it. "Dad, what are you doing to Mom? You're killing her. Can't we fast-forward through this late-life crisis and get back to normal? We both know you're not leaving Teterbury."

"Back to normal?" my dad said loudly, sarcastically. "I'm not looking to be normal right now. I'm looking for the opposite."

I let my eyelids fall, feeling like nothing I could say would make a difference. "You can't do that, Dad. You're sixty-four years old. Your best friend is in there lonely and . . . devastated. You leave her, and you'll regret it for the rest of your life."

"Who knows what's coming? Of course I wish her the best. But, Carver, your mom and I are getting a divorce, and nothing will change that. We've each spoken with an attorney. She's getting most everything. I just need enough cash to get by."

"What are you going to do?"

He gave a quick laugh. "That's the fun of it. I have no idea."

A wild turkey appeared at the edge of the tree line in my backyard and waddled into the grass.

"Carver," my dad continued, "one day you'll realize you worked your whole life to get to a point where you can start living, and the one regret you'll have is you could have been living all along."

With my eye on the turkey, feeling a bit like a turkey myself, I said, "That's a nice thing to say, Dad. My mom and I appreciate that we don't matter enough to make your life worth living."

"You know that's not what I mean," he responded quickly. "There comes a time when a man needs to rise up. I'm rising up."

"What does that even mean?" Maybe my mom was right about dementia. Desperate for some fresh air, I opened the window and drew in a deep breath. Startled, the turkey spun around and disappeared back into the woods. I wished I could do the same. No matter how far I'd run from Teterbury, there was no way to escape the truth of what I'd done to my parents.

As if reading my mind, he said, "Carver, this has nothing to do with you—or what happened before you left. This is about me wanting to live my last years differently. It doesn't mean I love you or your mom any less."

The pain of my past tried to sneak its way up my spine, causing a burning sensation in my lower back.

"I gotta go, Dad."

"Carver, I love—"

Not letting him finish, I ended the call. Why couldn't everyone stay in their lanes? Why did my parents have to keep reminding me that I'd destroyed each one of us individually and as a family? I'd done a pretty damned good job of moving on. Why hadn't they?

Ten minutes later, I was digging into the pedals of my mountain bike. I'd learned physical activity could almost always allay the darkness when it flowed through me. Yes, I'd cut a lot of people out of my life. That was the only answer I'd found, the only way I could let go of the guilt and shame and heartache. Up and down the hills I rode, navigating the technical parts of the single track with all I had, doing everything I could to shake the demons that clung to my ankles.

No, I didn't want to think back to my time in the hospital, me lying in the bed, staring up at my parents shortly after I'd awoken, seeing in their eyes how sure they were they'd failed me. No, I didn't want to revisit the shame that hid behind every corner, the kids in the hallways staring at me upon my return to school, seeing me at my absolute weakest. I didn't want to feel the scars on my body that already itched again, making themselves known.

I wasn't that person anymore!

When I reached the top of a peak, I came to a stop at the edge of a rock cliff that looked west toward Black Mountain. The cliff reminded me of the Subaru commercial I'd seen. *What do the stars say to you?* I looked up to the sky and couldn't see anything but a brushstroke of bleak clouds.

"Even whatever's up there can't fix this one," I said.

⌒

Thoughts of my parents divorcing distracted me while I met with the contractor. It wasn't hard at all to connect what had happened in 1998 with the fallout now. If only I could have made better decisions.

When I returned to the house, I walked around aimlessly, straightening pictures, tidying up the garage, hosing off my bike. Anything to shake the poison that pushed its way through my veins.

It must have been a little after ten when I realized I'd been caught in some sort of trance. I opened my eyes and found myself sitting crosslegged in the center of the third bay of the garage, the one space that was open. I'd kicked off my cycling shoes but still wore my pants and jersey. The garage door opener was in my hand, and it occurred to me that I'd been mindlessly raising and lowering the door for a while, lost in thoughts, torn by my mother's request.

I set the opener down on the ground next to me and lay on my back, stretching out and feeling the cold of the concrete against the bare skin of my calves and forearms. Had twenty years of my absence not underlined how serious I was about not returning? Teterbury pulled at me, but I couldn't let it win. There had to be a better way.

I wanted to think that my dad would come around, that I'd get a call at any moment saying he'd been confused and he'd straightened himself out. If not, what was there to do? What could *I* do?

My pulse quickened as the past tugged me backward through the years . . .

Shannon.

I could see her face as if she still lay next to me. The pain of missing her filled my body. Oh, to still have her in my arms, to feel her hair fall across my chest, its flowery scent still dizzying me. Lying there on the cold concrete, my imagination went into overdrive. I could feel Shannon's soft skin against mine, warming me. I could taste her strawberry lip gloss as she touched her lips to mine. I'd once been a believer in destiny. Even now I knew there was something wrong—something incredibly unjust—with how she'd been taken away from me.

As sad as it was to admit, not many days passed where I didn't think about her, if only for a few seconds, until I was able to usher those thoughts away.

A song came alive in my head, our song: Aerosmith's "I Don't Want to Miss a Thing." Chills rose on my skin as I heard in my head the orchestra setting up the tune and then Steven Tyler stepping in with his haunting vocals. I felt Shannon take my hand and pull me toward her, then hook her arms around my neck. Those lyrics wrapped around us as we sang them to each other, knowing that we were meant to be together forever.

It came out of the blue, her liking me. As anyone who'd seen my high school yearbook photos would attest, I'd become more handsome later in life. As a teen, I had acne issues and was too skinny. Though I ran track and loved mountain biking, I was far from a jock. I suppose I was a borderline geek, more than anything else. Point being, I wasn't dating many girls, and the ones I did date didn't look like Shannon. She was so stunning a poet could not have painted her with words, the kind of beautiful that made me quiver. That was why, when she first kissed me, it took me a while to believe it was happening. In those moments afterward, she gave me wings, turned me into a prince after a youth spent as a frog.

"No. I can't." I pressed my hands on the cold concrete and sat up, shaking my head. It did me no good to dwell on what could have been or how I could have done things differently. All I could do was get my body moving and stop letting the madness come after me. Everyone was haunted by their pasts, and only the best of us could move forward. Thank God I'd figured it out.

~

I had the same stand-up desk in both my work and home offices. I raised the one at home to my preprogrammed height and stepped onto the cushioned mat. After plugging my laptop into the big screen, I allowed myself a few moments to scan the local animal shelter websites, looking for a dog in need of a home. A one-eyed husky kept drawing me back. His name was Memphis, and he liked peanut butter and chasing tennis balls. I also revisited the profile of a two-year-old yellow lab mix named Althea, who'd been saved from a kill shelter in Alabama.

Several other dogs also pulled at my heartstrings, but I still didn't feel like I'd found *the one*. I looked up on the wall at Penelope's framed paw print, which I'd had taken before her cremation. She would be a hard act to follow. Maybe I wasn't ready.

NEVER STOP CHASING, the words written on the whiteboard next to her paw print, reminded me to get back to work. Though breaking ground on the new clinic, complete with a specialty and ER practice, had dominated my mind, I was already looking to the next part of the plan. Within three years, I would expand to four practices total, one in Asheville, Charlotte, Greenville, and Spartanburg. That level of ambition required a seven-day workweek.

Prepared to get an earful, I dialed Mary Beth's number. "I know, I know. It's Saturday." She didn't like it when I called her on Saturdays. Not so much because I was disturbing her, more because, along with being my office manager, she'd become my North Carolina mother. Of course, I wouldn't have called her that to her face, as she would have jokingly responded with, "I'm not old enough to be your mother!" She was, though.

"That's exactly right," Mary Beth admonished. "And what do we *not* do on Saturdays?" Her voice reminded me of Julia Child when she spoke, though I'd never tell her that either. What I *had* told her, as if she didn't already know, was that I couldn't survive without her. She picked up the balls I dropped; she listened and asked the right questions when I faced a dilemma; and she sometimes had better ideas than I. I'm ashamed to admit how many times I contacted her for help while she was in the hospital or in recovery at home.

Like most of us in the field, the thing we most shared was our love for animals. That was the glue that bound us and why I'd get her to talk to me on a Saturday. After a quick chat about some staff drama, I brought up a new candidate who'd applied to spearhead the expansion. While I had her, we discussed a few lingering issues regarding the new building, mostly about equipment I wanted to get on order and the dilemma of where we'd store it. Prices were rising, so we were better off making purchases now.

Then I made a mistake. She asked if my parents had given me the obligatory birthday call, and in a moment of weakness, I vomited what they had told me into the phone.

"My mom wants me to come home," I said. "As if I can fix it." I shook my head at the absurdity of my mother's request.

Though she was aware of the reasons I hadn't gone home in so long, Mary Beth did not validate me. Instead, in a stern mothering tone, she said, "You have to go home, Carver."

I pulled off my computer glasses and set them on top of a motivational book. "Mary Beth, I'm no divorce counselor."

"Your mother needs you."

"I know." I stopped short of cursing and let the silence ease me.

"You know I'm not one to butt into your business, but—"

"But you're going to." She actually *was* one to throw herself into my business, if truth be told.

"When I lost my dad last year," she said, "I didn't realize how much it would hurt until it came down on me. I should have seen him more while I still had the chance. Then, with my cancer, I was painfully reminded how little time we have. I get you don't ever want to go back, but you may regret it the rest of your life if you don't. Your mom and dad won't be around forever."

I calmed myself with steadying breaths. "I know . . . and I've told them I'd fly them down here. If they need me, they know where to find me." I could hear my father's words in my own voice.

"Carver Livingston. Get over yourself and book a ticket home."

I set my hand on the computer mouse and clicked around haphazardly on the screen. "And let everything back here fall apart?"

She laughed out loud. "I think we could handle you being gone for a few days. If I'm being honest, it might be a pleasant break."

My head swiveled back and forth. Though she knew the truth, the idea of going home jarred me more than she could know. Actually, outside of various tradesmen and women—electricians, handymen, etc.—Mary Beth was the only one who'd ever been to my home.

It was the day after I'd put Penelope down, and she'd shown up without invitation, a framed picture of Penelope and me in hand. Distraught as I was, I invited her in, and we talked by the fire as the snow fell outside. In that state of vulnerability, I'd told the whole tale of my senior year of high school, how a girl I'd thought I would spend the rest of my life with had sent me into a tailspin of heartache that nearly killed me—in the most literal sense. I'd told her I wasn't sure what hurt worse: having lost my soulmate or having the whole town watch me fall apart afterward.

There had been only one other person in my life who listened like her, and that person was my former teacher, Mrs. Cartwright. Perhaps it was in their similarities that I found comfort sharing such a giant piece of me.

I made circles with the mouse. "It's not that easy."

"Since when is anything easy?" she argued.

I had nothing to say so there was quiet for a while. A car crunching gravel broke the silence as it climbed my neighbor's driveway.

Turned out she wasn't done. "Carver, going home will be good for you. I know it."

"I'll think about it," I said, silently disagreeing. Maybe it's what I had to do, but it wouldn't be good for me at all. It would be a distraction when I needed complete focus.

"Don't make me book you a ticket," she said.

"Sorry to bother you on a Saturday."

I could sense her rolling her eyes. "You say that every Saturday."

"Yeah, I know."

After saying goodbye, I considered my options. As if there were any. The one fact I couldn't let go of was that, unlike my father, my mother had always understood why I hadn't returned home, and she'd supported my decision.

Until now . . .

Why did Mary Beth always have to be right?

I lowered my desk and sat down in the chair. Maybe there was a way. What if I got in and out of Teterbury with no one besides my parents knowing? I played a drumroll with my fingers on the desk, feeling reinvigorated. "No big deal," I said. "In and out."

My phone stared at me, waiting for me to call her. Finally, I caved. "Mom, I'll come home on one condition. You and Dad can't tell anyone I'm coming."

"Really?"

"Let me look at my schedule."

"Could you catch a flight out today?" she asked.

"Today?" I said, thinking I would need time to prepare, not only apropos of work. I needed time to mentally equip for my return.

"Honey, I need you now," she said. "Please see if there's any way to get here this afternoon."

The darkness rose around me, refusing to let me escape. No way I could bail on her again.

Chapter 4

In Disguise

A last-minute flight out of Greenville-Spartanburg International Airport delivered me to Burlington, Vermont, a few minutes before five. I wore a hoodie that I had pulled over my head. Dark shades hid my eyes, and though I didn't realize it until thinking about it, I rode low in the seat of my rented blue Audi sedan. My mission: sweep into Teterbury, save a marriage, and get the hell out before anyone knew I was home. "Secret Agent Man" played in my head.

The mountainous terrain around Asheville wasn't that different from this part of Vermont. Unlike the tall, sharp peaks in my father's Wyoming, these tree-covered mountains had been rounded by climactic events for thousands of years. The highway, which was in much better shape than I remembered it, wound effortlessly through, offering views I'd long forgotten.

Taking the exit to downtown, I sank even lower into my seat, as if they (whoever "they" were) had scouts out searching for my face. A wooden sign read: WELCOME TO TETERBURY. WE MIGHT JUST SURPRISE YOU.

I chuckled to myself. "I highly doubt it."

The men and women who'd settled the town in 1804 never would have believed the growth. They'd come for Teterbury's prime location on the Tye River and the area's abundance of lumber. The town had continued to grow, finding good use of the fertile land by farming, and raising sheep and cows, and then it had grown even more when the Central Vermont Railway laid its tracks. By 1850, two thousand people made their living in this town. These were my mother's people, who'd come from England and Ireland to Boston and then sought more land and greater opportunities. If the stories were true, my maternal grandfather, a few generations back, had a hand in dumping a chest of tea into Boston Harbor in 1773 before joining other settlers up here.

I'd read the day before that the tourism boom of the last ten years had added another thousand to the count, making Teterbury home to 3,012 people. The growth was evident. Brick buildings that had once been used for industrial purposes a century earlier had been repurposed into coffee shops, restaurants, and art galleries. Remnants of the past lingered, though. Luke's Dairy, the ice-cream shop where my friends and I had gathered after school for years, still stood on the corner of James and Dagger. I could taste the maple walnut I had religiously ordered, remembering how eagerly we would wait for the shop to open at the beginning of May each year.

We'd eat our ice creams in the main square, where a fountain and a statue of one of the founders stood in the center. Then the boys would show off to the girls on our mountain bikes and skateboards as we attempted our jumps and rail slides. Those were good times, the days before I'd learned the hard truths of life.

It was Saturday afternoon, and the tourists swarmed the sidewalks. People with cones and cups stacked high with their favorite flavors filed out of Luke's like it was a train station. A man on a ladder painted the brick of a restaurant black. On the other side of the street, in a tattoo parlor, a young woman was making a potentially grave decision. Had I the time to be charitable, I would have pulled over and popped my head in to say, "I know this makes sense to you now, but there will be a day, trust me, when you'll regret it."

I'd gotten one on my back right shoulder in the old days, and it was unquestionably a bad decision. During college, I'd had it removed, and only a scar that in some ways was worse than the tattoo remained. I wondered if Shannon had regretted hers.

At the red light before I swung a left toward my parents' place, I casually scanned the crowd and then froze as a familiar face appeared. There before me, twenty years older than I'd last seen him, was my old best friend, Elliot Baker. I couldn't believe it. Less than five minutes in town.

Guilt crashed over me. There was no denying that when Shannon and I had started dating, I'd suddenly found myself way too cool for him. The last time I'd wronged him was by skipping his wedding, in which he'd asked me to be his best man. Even worse, I'd turned him down via text message.

I readied my foot on the gas pedal and waited for the light to turn green like a jockey waits for the firing of the starter pistol. Looking at him from the far corner of my eye, I wondered how his life had turned out. Not one for social media, the little I knew about anything Teterbury related had come from my parents.

It was my dad who liked to sneak into our phone calls something like, "You know Elliot had a second boy." I could read right through the lines. That meant, "Your former best friend could use a phone call. That's what friends do." I faulted my dad for a lot of things, including burying me with reminders of my failures, but he had integrity when it came to that kind of thing, being a good friend.

Actually, he'd lost his best friend in March, a navy vet everyone called Romo. They'd bonded over a love of muscle cars. Switching between their two houses, they'd hosted a weekly poker night for their group of buddies for the better part of twenty years. His doctor had diagnosed Romo with throat cancer the year prior and had given him six months to live. Tough as he was, Romo made it seven. His funeral was another event that had tried to pull me home unsuccessfully.

All the way to the bitter end, my father had sat with Romo at his house—every single day telling stories and trying to draw the last laughs out of his dying friend. Yeah, my dad knew a thing or two about being good to people. I just wished he'd known how to be good to my mom and me. I'd never understand it.

The Audi's tires squealed as I swung left to safety. Then the steel bridge that crossed over the river came into view. Every spring, the water would be high enough to jump into it from the bridge, though our parents never allowed it. But that didn't stop us. As we got older, we'd drink beers down on the riverbank, and inevitably someone would make the first climb. The jump wasn't far, maybe thirty feet, but you had to avoid the boulder we all knew was there even though the higher water from the spring runoff had covered it up. As I crossed over the bridge, I could hear my friends cheering on a younger Carver the first time I'd jumped. For a geek like me, that was maybe the most self-confident I'd ever felt to date, only to be topped by the first time Shannon had pressed her lips to mine.

Wherever I turned, her memory waited. I'd more than once wondered what she would think of me now, if she might regret leaving me. I could still see that bastard Trey giving me the finger as he slipped his arm around the girl he'd stolen from me. The darker part of me hoped he had turned out to be a lousy husband and that she'd spent her lonely nights dreaming of me, wondering what it might have been like to follow me to North Carolina. Surely she'd read about me in the local paper or had at least heard about the impressive things I'd been doing.

The bridge connected the somewhat bustling town with the quiet residential area, where all the houses had been built around the turn of the twentieth century—gorgeous gems that were an expensive nuisance to keep up with. I knew their burden well, because my mother often complained about the issues that would come up with ours: the rickety doors that wouldn't close, the cold spots because of the lack of insulation, the humidity issues in the basement. She'd always wanted to build something outside of town in one of the newer neighborhoods, but my father dearly loved the house and begged my mother to find a way to be happy there. Trying to be a good partner, she'd given in, her only win being she'd occasionally try to get under his skin by calling the house "the enemy."

At breakfast on Saturdays, she'd say, "Honey, I need some help battling the enemy today." I'd look up from my bowl of Frosted Flakes and find my father glaring at her. They'd both smile, though, and looking back on it, that had been my mother's way of flirting.

My father called the house a Rolls-Royce that "needed a little extra love." I suppose that was what all these houses were, a middle ground between Rolls-Royces and pains in the ass. Though the downtown had changed, so much of my neighborhood had stayed the same. The houses shone brighter with fresh paint and a few had additions, but they were the same houses Elliot and I had passed by on the way to school every morning.

It was tough to recall the good times I'd had growing up here, though I knew there were many. All the way up to my senior year, I'd known only a normal existence. Elliot's folks called us the Cleavers, a reference to a show I'd never seen called *Leave It to Beaver*. My mom had proudly explained what that had meant. Elliot would often tell us that was why he hung around our house, because everyone was so happy all the time.

A few blocks away from my parents, my phone buzzed, and I instantly tensed, worried it would be Elliot or someone else who'd somehow heard I was in town. I'd been careful at the airport to move quickly. Of course I'd drawn some stares from the TSA, who apparently didn't like glasses and hoodies. "I'm a doctor, for God's sake," I'd wanted to yell at them.

Nope, it was my contractor, probably calling to . . .

I didn't see the dog until it was almost too late. A flash of white, black, and brown came out of nowhere, past a tree and then the sidewalk and right out in front of me. I slammed on the brakes, and my head flew forward as the tires screeched to a halt.

Letting out a string of curses my father probably could have heard from his front yard, I threw the Audi into park and raced out of the car. Someone yelled at me as I rounded the front of the vehicle and looked under the bumper. A Jack Russell, probably two years old or so, sat on his haunches breathing heavily, his black eyes tucked into a light-brown mask like two jewels.

Thankful I hadn't hit him, I knelt and reached down. "Hey, you okay, friend? I'm so sorry."

He lunged at me. Though I let out a startled yell, I forgave him quickly, considering the circumstances. I'd about turned him into a pancake.

As I stood, he glared at me and let out a vicious growl.

A sharp voice came from behind. "What are you doing driving that fast down this road? You nearly killed him." She was angrier than he was, and her bark might have been worse too.

I turned with one hand going up, as if whoever owned that voice might come after me, but I realized she wasn't a threat—at least, not physically. She was older than my parents, probably midseventies, and wore a lavender-colored bathrobe over her short and plump body. An ancient Red Sox cap was pulled over her unruly hair, giving her a disheveled look.

I apologized again. "He came out of nowhere."

She wagged a finger at me. "I suppose anything would come out of nowhere when you're driving sixty miles an hour in a twenty-five."

I glanced back at the dog, wondering if they were surrounding me, prepping to attack. They'd be the greatest unassuming duo in history. Something in her voice, though, I recognized.

"Sixty might be pushing it," I said, turning back to her. "I might have been going ten over."

"Ten over?" She came down from the curb to the road. "Oscar Wilde," she snapped, "get over here." She passed by me and stomped her way to the dog, barking out a string of orders. The dog wasn't taking it, though, and as soon as she got close, he took off running. I was half paying attention, because it had occurred to me I knew the woman.

Mrs. Cartwright.

As much as I loved her, I was not prepared to see her. I could still remember tossing away the last letter she'd sent me, the same way I had all the others over the years, deciding it would be best not to respond. To move on, I had to cut away every bit of the tumor that was Teterbury from my heart.

"Come back here right now." We both watched as the Jack Russell crossed the street and lifted his leg on the base of a tall oak.

"Let me see if I can get him." I followed him and used my "calm vet voice" to lure him in. "Come here, Oscar Wilde, you cute little puppy, you."

When I moved his way, he shot off toward the far side of the front portico of a gray house. Hearing Mrs. Cartwright yelling—possibly at both of us—I picked up speed and chased after him. The next few moments were part of a comedy hour, with me darting after Oscar as he continued to escape my clutches, only to stop close enough to lure me back to the chase.

Someone behind Mrs. Cartwright, a younger female, was laughing. That made me even more determined, as the whole thing felt incredibly embarrassing. I chased Oscar back and forth long enough for a pot of water to come to a boil, all the while being laughed at and yelled at simultaneously.

"Just pick him up!" Mrs. Cartwright commanded from the street.

I whipped around and unbecomingly said, "I'm trying to pick him up. Where'd you have him trained? Prison?" I felt like a real jerk then, raising my voice at her.

Apparently I wasn't as threatening as I had thought, because all I heard was more laughter coming from the younger one. I glanced over. A redhead with freckles painting her face stood looking at me. She wore gray jeans and a burgundy-colored silk blouse, rolled up at the sleeves, showing a dangly gold bracelet.

Oscar sniffed at some violets that had sprung up in a bed near the steps leading up to the gray house. As I approached him this time, I tapped into the focus I used for surgery and said with all the kindness in the world, "Come here, Oscar. Let's get you home."

Only then did I realize I'd never removed my hoody or glasses. No wonder the poor puppy was terrified of me and that my former teacher hadn't recognized me. A rush of embarrassment washed over me, knowing I must have looked like a fool.

Kneeling a few feet away from Oscar and removing my disguise, I whispered, "You see, I'm not so scary after all. Let's you and I make a deal. Make me look good right now, and I'll get you back. An antler, a big steak, a bully stick, whatever you want. What do you say?"

He looked at me like he knew exactly what I'd said. For a moment I thought he was about to slap his paw into my hand and accept my offer.

"There you go," I said, crawling to him, wishing him to come to me.

He growled again and then barked. So much for my stealthy entrance into town. Feeling a bit upset he wasn't going to work with me, I dashed forward and almost got my hands on him. My fingertips brushed his fur as he escaped once again, leaving me lying on my stomach while Freckles continued to laugh.

I heard footsteps and turned, or rather rolled over, to see her crossing the yard toward Oscar. My eye level was at her ankles, so I mostly saw her leather boots and the top of a sprinkler head poking out of the grass.

In a voice as soothing as her smile, she called out, "Oscar, want a treat?"

Oscar had inched his way closer to the house and sniffed the area close to a basement window. Upon hearing this woman's voice, he twisted his head. She repeated herself, and he darted toward her, nearly leaping into her arms.

She kissed his head. "I don't really have a treat. But we'll find you one in a little bit." Glancing my way, she whispered, "Oldest trick in the book."

I couldn't help but chuckle.

"Is that you, Carver Livingston?" Mrs. Cartwright called out from the sidewalk.

That I'd shut her out of my life threw punches at me. "I wondered if you'd recognize me."

"I never forget a student, especially *you*."

The way she said *you* didn't feel too much like a compliment. Nevertheless, I approached her, glancing up at the Red Sox hat that covered tufts of curly gray hair. Her husband had played for them before abandoning his position in left field to chase her to Teterbury. He'd given up his athletic dreams for the dream of family.

She squinted at me through her glasses, as if she was inspecting me. I wondered if I disgusted her. Hopefully she could understand I was young and making all kinds of bad decisions back then.

"I see you're still getting into trouble," she said.

"I'm still the hellion you knew, maybe a hair more civilized." The turquoise eyes I'd remembered had faded a shade. Recalling the many hours we'd spent together, both in school and out at her farm, I couldn't help but smile. "Time has treated you well, Mrs. Cartwright. You don't look a day older than last I saw you."

"Don't you give me that baloney." Back in the old days I could charm her, but she had an impenetrable barrier around her now.

Mrs. Cartwright introduced me to Freckles. "This is Ava, my physical therapist. She's trying to get my knee back to normal after surgery in March."

Ava reached out with her free hand. "She's days away from being as good as new. Good to meet you."

We shook. "Likewise."

"As good as new," Mrs. Cartwright mumbled. "Ava, Carver was one of my most . . ." She paused to think of the right word.

"Oh boy, I can't wait to hear what follows," I said.

Ava and I both grinned at each other until Mrs. Cartwright finally said, "Promising students."

I turned to Ava with a rush of emotions I wasn't expecting. "Mrs. Cartwright was the best teacher I've ever had."

"Aren't you supposed to be a veterinarian?" Mrs. Cartwright asked. "You can't even catch a harmless little Jack Russell?"

I turned back to her. "That dog is half beast."

"We can agree there," Mrs. Cartwright said.

"He's adorable," Ava argued, rubbing his face to the dog's great delight.

I directed my look at Mrs. Cartwright. "How are you? How's Tom? Why aren't you guys out at the farm? My parents didn't tell me you'd moved here."

"Back here, rather. Tom's and my first house together was right down the street on Terry, shortly after he left baseball." A black veil cast a shadow over her face. "He died last year."

"No." My heart sank as I pictured Tom's face the first time I'd met him out at their farm. Mrs. Cartwright had said they had work for me, so I'd shown up one day after school. I didn't think it was much warmer than zero degrees, and Tom had worn black Carhartt overalls over a T-shirt. Growing up in the winters of Vermont, I'd met some tough men, but he was tougher than all of them. I didn't believe him when he first told me he was an accountant, but he'd quickly proved it to me when I came to understand his ability with numbers—especially with baseball stats.

The Cartwrights had put me to work helping repair the barn and taking care of their growing collection of animals, beings that knew nothing of what I'd done and wouldn't have cared anyway. I had found refuge there, a place where I could escape the beady eyes of everyone in town, a place where I could move forward and not feel stalled out.

They hadn't made much money off the farm; it had been what they called a "labor of love." Mrs. Cartwright had grown up on a farm and had taught Tom a lot of what he knew about running one. They'd had four dogs, including a handsome black lab named Ted Williams, whom they'd bred every year, a ton of cats, chickens, a peacock, a hungry goat named Carol, a flock of merino sheep, and two horses.

Working with them, I had learned there was something so incredible about animals, a part of life I'd never known, since we'd not even had a gerbil growing up. Animals loved you no matter who you were or what you did. They loved you unconditionally, and I couldn't say that for a lot of people in my life back then.

I'd never forget when Mrs. Cartwright helped me deliver my first foal—a stunning Morgan horse who wowed me beyond belief when he first came to his feet on those skinny legs. After six months of being around their animals, I'd already found my love for them, but it had been that day when I knew I would be a vet. I'd first thought I'd serve larger animals, but my work in vet school had given me an even stronger love of dogs that ultimately won me over. Not that I wasn't a cat person. If Penelope hadn't wanted to eat every one she saw, I'm sure I would have had a couple back home.

It was also the day that I stopped being a victim. After doing a ton of research, I'd decided I'd apply to a community college in North Carolina and climb my way back, find a way into UNC or Davidson, maybe NC State. Full-on Rudy Ruettiger style, as more than one of my classmates had said. Enough hating myself for not being enough for Shannon, enough feeling sorry for myself for publicly falling apart in the second semester, giving up the race to valedictorian and losing every single scholarship I'd been offered.

"I'm so sorry, Mrs. Cartwright. No one told me." Tears filled the rims of my eyes. How had I been so selfish as to walk away without holding on to Tom and her, at the least writing a letter or making a phone call?

She merely lifted her eyebrows, as if to say, *It is what it is.* "The farm was too much for me to take care of on my own, so I sold it. Jack helped me pack up and talked me into moving here, so I'd be closer to everything."

"How is he?" I asked, referring to her son, whom I'd met only a few times. A car passed by and the driver waved. The imagined Navy SEAL in me felt like my position had been exposed. A voice yelled, *Take cover!*

"He's the one who gave me Oscar," she said. "He'd read widows do best with lapdogs and decided he'd surprise me with one. Found him at the shelter across town. Then he was off again, back to lawyering in Minneapolis."

I saw a lot of things in her eyes then, but the most powerful of it all was loneliness. This woman who'd pulled me out of the darkest moment of my life had lost her fire, and it was enough to break my heart.

I looked over at Oscar in Ava's arm. Was he all Mrs. Cartwright had? "He just needs some work. Not that I look like I know what I'm doing, but I had a German shepherd I had to put down a few months ago. We went through extensive training, and it was amazing how much better it made our lives. Maybe I could help."

"Or if you want to take him," she said without a glimmer of humor. "You're in North Carolina, right? He'd love it down there."

I gave her a dirty look, trying to draw a smile. She met me in the middle and stared right back. After a few long seconds, she let her lips curl. For that moment, it felt like all was right in the world. There she was, the way she used to be.

Then she broke eye contact with me, and I read in her body language that it was time to move on. Raising my hand, I said, "It's so great to see you. Ava, great to meet you. Please take care of her. She's one of a kind."

"Isn't that the truth?"

"You must be back for the reunion," Mrs. Cartwright said.

I slowed my retreat. "Um, no, not exactly. Sadly, I'm only in town for a few days."

"I see." She looked at me, sizing me up. "Are you still reading?"

I laughed out loud. "What a very Mrs. Cartwright question. No, not like I used to," I confessed. "How about you? Reading a lot of Phil Roth these days?"

She cut her eyes toward me, as if she were going to strangle me.

I smiled. "Still not a fan, I see."

Though she showed no sign of enjoying my humor, I suspected that some of her—even if it was only one measly atom—was glad to see me again.

She looked down at the grass between us. "Still not a fan, no. Either way, I'm dealing with some eyesight issues, so I can't read like I used to."

"That kills me. Have you tried audiobooks?"

She shook her head. "It's not the same, is it?"

"I suppose not." This poor woman. It was as if hope had abandoned her. I certainly had, and despite my wanting to hide while back in town, I was compelled to be there for her, to at least show her I'd not forgotten her. I hadn't forgotten her at all.

"I'm here for a few days," I said. "Maybe I could come back and visit?"

"She'd love that," Ava said, answering for her.

I kept my eyes on Mrs. Cartwright. "Okay, then. I landed an hour ago and have yet to see my parents, which is a whole other thing. Perhaps tomorrow?" I almost asked her not to mention my arrival but thought it might appear childish.

"Perhaps." Mrs. Cartwright turned away from me and started back across the street. I looked at Ava and frowned.

She gently smiled. "See you around."

"So long." Then I turned to my former teacher. "Mrs. Cartwright."

She stopped but didn't turn around. A book of pain was written on her back.

"Your letters meant the world to me," I said. "I just . . . I didn't write anyone."

She nodded but kept going.

Back to Ava, I asked, "She has the house on the corner there, with the blue shutters?"

"That's her. And though she might not admit it, she'd certainly like the company."

I won't abandon her again, I thought.

Then I looked at Oscar Wilde, deciding to keep my hands to myself this time. "Maybe tomorrow we'll get along, huh?"

He flashed his teeth and growled.

Chapter 5

A Bitter Homecoming

Mrs. Cartwright and her current state weighed on me as I climbed back into the Audi and drove the longest two blocks of my life to my parents' house. What kind of person hid from the good people who had saved him? And how had I not even known Tom passed?

Then my former home came into view, the house where I'd lived for the first eighteen years of my life. My whole body tensed, but I felt the resistance most in my gut, a sharp pain I reached for as I slowed to a stop out front.

Blurring my vision to avoid focusing in on my father's canned ham I wasn't ready to accept existed, I took in the sight of their white colonial home, a simple rectangle with a gabled roof and a chimney rising out of the middle. They'd recently replaced the shingles and finally added gutters, something my father had never wanted to do in fear of ice dams. Guess Mom finally won that one.

I lowered my eyes to the vintage Shasta trailer my father had parked in the front yard. The upper half of the trailer was painted white, the lower an awful baby blue. The window facing me showed flowery curtains heavy with white and yellow. On the back was a decorative silver wing, surely matching one on the other side. An awning stretched out from the trailer and shaded an area containing a red Coleman cooler and a blue camping table with two matching lawn chairs. He even had a potted plant under there. To the left, three plastic Adirondack chairs surrounded a firepit. A weak plume of smoke rose from the ashes.

No words in the English language could describe the humiliation I felt in that moment. This act of idiocy had surely reached far beyond the neighborhood and become the talk of Teterbury. He might as well string a line to the fence and hang his underwear out to dry. It wouldn't take Sherlock Holmes to deduce he'd either been kicked out of the house or lost his mind, one of the two.

Hadn't we, as a family, endured enough public scrutiny and humiliation? Did we really need to provide more fodder to the livestock that was this judgmental town?

My father appeared at the front door of the Shasta, drying his hands on a towel.

Five days, I thought, squeezing the Audi into the small driveway behind my father's dusty old Ford truck and my mother's white three-series Beamer.

"This is her," my father said, as I climbed out and faced the man who'd indirectly forced me back home. "A 1962 Shasta Airflyte. Found her down in Saugerties, New York, been sitting in a guy's barn for the majority of her life. Mostly original. Just needed a little TLC."

"Nice," I said. Was I supposed to be impressed? Usually I was kinder to him, despite his shutting me out in the months before I left this god-forsaken town, but I didn't have the patience for him in this moment.

Though he never wore a cowboy hat over his bald head, he rarely wore anything but his well-worn Levi's and Ariat boots. Cowboy hat or not, Wyoming oozed out of him. I hadn't seen him since he'd visited Asheville last Christmas, and it was evident by the sharp cut of his cheekbones and the extra slack in his belt that he'd lost some weight. As usual, a pocketknife in its sheath hung on his right hip.

Approaching, he said in the western drawl he'd never shaken, "How's it feel to be back?"

If he only knew. "Surreal, I guess." I had no intention of holding my tongue, so after a hug, I said, "What the hell has gotten into you?"

We both turned our attention to his ridiculous setup in the front yard.

He set his hands on his waist. "That right there is going to be the rocket ship that takes me to new heights."

"I don't even know what that means."

We both stared at the Shasta like we were looking at an old Porsche, only I wasn't dazzled. His pride in the purchase was clear in the tone of how he described the restoration. "I put a fresh coat of paint and new tires on her. Working on the inside now. I plugged a leak in the back and fixed a soft spot on the floor. Got the stove running yesterday. All the cushions are being reupholstered now. Should be ready tomorrow. Wanna take a look?"

He strode toward the door, but I stopped him. "No, Dad, I don't." I raised fisted hands. "I'm . . . I don't even know what to say. Is Mom right? Have you lost your mind?"

He let out a small smile. "All fifty states. I'm gonna hit every single one of 'em. Go see the national parks. See all the things I was too busy missing all my life."

"You're doing this without Mom?"

"You know as well as I do she'll never spend a night in there in her life. Where in the world would she keep her beauty products? And she likes her baths." He was right. She was far more particular when it came to travel.

I stared him down, shaking my head with disappointment.

His hands flew from his waist to the back of his hairless head. "Look, Carv, if you came home thinking you're gonna change my mind about the divorce, you wasted your time. I still love your mother very much, but it's time for us to move on. Losing Romo shook something loose for me, reminded me how short life could be. Let's have a nice few days having you back and not get into the nitty-gritty of it."

"My little boy," my mother said, coming out the front door and clapping her hands together. She stood there for a moment, apparently taking me in. "Oh, to have you home. What a dream."

"Look at you," I said. "You look great." She did too. Her svelte five-foot-ten-inch frame always reminded me to keep exercising and eating well, like she'd raised me to do. She and my father were both sixty-four years old, but she looked a decade younger.

I met her at the bottom of the steps for an embrace. Her bright-green eyes typically glowed with ambition and confidence, but something was amiss today.

"It's about time you came home." She hooked her short blonde hair behind her ears, revealing diamond earrings she'd bought herself a few years back.

"It's been a minute, that's for sure." I pivoted to include my father. "So how's this going to go? Are we splitting time? You get me on the weekends?" My sarcasm screamed through me.

My dad shook his head, not saying no to the question, only to my failed attempt to lighten the mood.

She crossed her arms. "Your father can do what he wants. That's the way with him now. As for you, you're staying upstairs in your old room. I turned the guest bedroom into an office."

I raised my eyes to the finished attic of the third floor, sensing the ghosts of my past haunting it. A giant part of me wanted to avoid going up there at all, but I didn't want them to see my weakness. I needed them to see I was well past all that had happened.

"I ran into Mrs. Cartwright on the way here. She lives right down the street."

"Does she?" my mom asked.

"You didn't tell me Tom passed."

They both looked down.

"You knew? Why didn't you tell me?"

My father let out a groan. "There's a lot that's happened since you've been gone."

God, it was going to be a long visit. I turned away from them. "Let me grab my bag."

As I walked back to the Audi, my father said as if he were being accused of something, "What?" Though my back was turned, I could sense the two of them silently arguing.

Welcome home, Carver.

⌐

One small step for man, one giant leap for Carver Livingston. Neil Armstrong spoke in my head as I crossed the threshold of Twenty-Seven Whitney Road. I felt seventeen again, could see the navy-blue snow boots I used to wear as my foot hit the beige mat. I could even hear my father yelling at me across the house to make sure I didn't track in any snow.

Casting a look around the foyer, I saw things hadn't changed much. Same old hardwoods, same long glass table on the right, same painting of my maternal grandparents, who'd passed away when I was young.

I could still feel my parents angrily gesturing behind my back and wanted to scream at them, but I resisted. My eyes went left to find a smashed printer on the ground. "What in the world?"

"Ben was supposed to take that out," my mother spat with a heavy dose of disgust.

"What happened?"

"This is how your father gets along with technology," she said, all three of us now collected in the foyer, staring at the printer. "He can take an engine apart, but when it comes to electronics, he's a caveman."

"I tell ya," he said, "there's a special place in hell for the people who make it so hard to set up the wireless on the printer."

He followed behind as my mother gave the tour, showing me the things they'd done in the last twenty years. "You remember that old dining room table, don't you? We finally upgraded."

"I liked the old one," my dad said, trailing behind us.

"You would," she said back.

"God, you guys bicker a lot now, don't you?" I looked for the best spot on the wall in which to ram my head. Was this the same couple Elliot and his parents had called the Cleavers? I would have asked what had happened, but all three of us damned well knew.

One thing that had certainly changed was my parents' tolerance for messiness. I'd grown up in an immaculate household, pushed by both of them to make my bed and to clean up after myself. Today I could have dragged my finger through a thick layer of dust on the end tables in the living room. The windows and mirrors begged for Windex.

In the kitchen, my mother showed me the details of their renovation. They'd finally ripped out the old cabinetry and put in something custom. A younger me stood up on my tiptoes to pull a granola bar from one of those shelves. They'd replaced all the appliances. They'd redone the island with a new slab of granite and painted just about everything a baby blue. I could only imagine how difficult my father had been during the process, especially when it came down to paint color.

"I don't get the . . ." I was having a hard time getting past the filth.

"What?" my mother asked.

"It's dirty in here. Don't you have a housekeeper?" Did I even know my parents anymore?

My mom gave a mean smile. "I canceled her. Who the fuck cares anymore? Your father sure as hell doesn't."

For a woman who rarely let a curse word slip, this one came out of her mouth like she'd been hanging around the pool hall all morning. Had they both lost their minds? The picture of their current state became clearer. It had been one thing to see them in Asheville when they came to visit. Perhaps they'd been on their best behavior. Seeing them now, like this, made me feel like their marriage had never recovered after . . . after that day.

"Jesus, here we go," my dad said.

"Guys, you can't live like this," I said. "Tomorrow, we're pulling this house together. I'll get you a new printer." I looked down at the floors.

"And a Roomba. We're going to clean. All three of us. Seriously. This is . . . this is ridiculous. You've been married forty-three years. Let's find some common ground here."

After a peek in the sunroom at my mother's new treadmill, which she resorted to in the cold months, we climbed the first set of steps, and my mother, who'd regained her composure, continued the tour, the new tile in the primary bath, the polished brass fixtures. I was still trying to reconcile her pride at what she'd done to the house mixed with the filth that she'd let invade it. Her excitement was obviously a facade, an effort—albeit a lousy one—to ease my return.

The next set of steps—these carpeted—led to my old room in the attic. I'd shut out my previous life so much that I'd neglected to ask over the years if they'd changed anything in my old room. The Guns N' Roses poster hanging by pushpins on the slanted ceiling at the top of the stairs gave me my answer.

We looked around the room as if we'd disembarked from our spaceship on Mars. The same gray carpet and same bunk bed were still there. A flash of my best friend, Elliot, launching a sneak attack with a water gun from the upper bunk leaped into my mind. He'd filled it with his own urine. Though we'd both thought it was funny, my mother told his mother, who grounded him for a week. If only I could have enjoyed those more humorous memories without being tugged deeper into darkness.

My faint smile melted as I remembered the broken kid curled up on that bed, wailing into the hollowness that swallowed him as he came to grips with his shattered reality. That bottom bunk was where, on November 23, 1998, I had dragged a razor blade up my wrist, hoping to end the unbearable hurt that had been drowning me.

The scar I hid behind a large watchband burned, as if I were summoning up the energy from those days. I reached for the pain. No way could I let my parents see me, Dr. Carver Livingston, twenty years past that nightmare, still struggling with it. Squeezing my scarred wrist tight and sipping in a sobering breath, I explored the room.

A lava lamp stood on the bedside table next to the phone where I'd made the call that had changed everything. A Radiohead poster inspired by the *OK Computer* album hung above the desk that had always been too small for me. My old boom box stood on the shelf, along with a stack of compact discs. I flipped it on and was surprised to see the light turn green.

I fumbled through the CDs. An R.E.M. album was the first on the stack. "So we left upstairs back in the nineties, huh?" I cringed at my weak attempt at using humor to put out the flames of my distress.

"We haven't gone up here much, honey," my mother said, stepping to the bed and fluffing a pillow.

"Might be time to open some windows." I was doing the best I could to keep it light in there.

She reached for the next pillow. "I came up to change the sheets, but we haven't had any guests in a long time."

It occurred to me that being up here might be as difficult for them as it was for me. If that was the case, why hadn't they gotten rid of all this stuff, all these reminders?

The air grew suffocatingly thin. I set my bags down by the bed, went to the window that faced east, unlatched it, and wiggled it open. Cool air rushed in and blew back my hair. The idea of everyone frozen in time came to me, as if Mr. Colby were still cutting the grass with a Manhattan in hand, or Matt and Joe Baskins were on their way to bring another tray of pistachio cannoli.

I looked at the closest neighbor's second-story window, where I'd feasted my eyes on my first pair of nonmaternal breasts. Mrs. Adley, who'd been endowed with the most glorious pair of melons, occasionally forgot to close the blinds while showering and would give me a show that would keep me standing at attention for a week. I could still see Elliot's mouth fall open when I'd shared my discovery with him. It was a sad day when a moving truck pulled up in front of their house. Mr. Adley had taken a job in Bangor, and he'd also taken away the greatest joy of my life. Little did Mrs. Adley know she'd single-handedly turned Elliot and me into men.

I looked back at my parents. My mother was busy straightening a curtain on another window. My father had his arms crossed and looked to be lost in thought.

The images came rushing back to me. Sirens wailed. A bottle of Jack Daniel's sat sideways in a pool of its own whiskey on the bedside table. The receiver for the phone hung by the cord, screaming that awful alert because I'd not hung it up.

Apparently my mother was talking to me, because I came out of it to see her waving her hand in my face. "Did I lose you?"

"Sorry, just thinking about . . . about something back home. A work thing."

Letting me get away with that lie, she smoothed her hands together and said, "I was saying I hope you're fine still sleeping up here. Had you given me more warning, I would have replaced the bunk bed." I could hear the worry in her voice.

"For my one visit home? I'll be fine." I felt my forehead wrinkle as I asked them both, "Have you heard from Elliot? How is he?" The words felt like betrayal in my mouth. I should have known exactly how he was. I should have kept up with him. I should know his wife and boys.

My mother lifted her hands, palms up. "I occasionally see him at Hannaford or at that new coffee shop on Dillard with the smoothies I like. He always asks about you and says hi. He's coaching his boys in baseball."

"They're that old?" I asked.

I returned to the window and could see Elliot and myself riding bikes on the street. When it snowed, we'd build snowmen and ice forts. He was there at the hospital, the third person I saw when I awoke after surviving my attempted suicide. Despite how I'd left him in the dust after I'd started dating Shannon, he had been there for me. And still, I'd barely returned his calls once I crossed the Vermont line in the August after we graduated. He came down to see me one time at Davidson, crashing in my dorm. Though I tried, I couldn't do it. I couldn't spend time with him. As kind as he was, as good a friend as he was, all he did was make me hate myself, hate that kid I'd been. I had to keep my eyes on the future and off the past.

"You should call him," my father suggested from his safe spot near the stairs.

"Yeah, we'll see," I said, still looking out the window.

I could sense my parents looking at each other again, and I didn't want to turn my head.

"I'm getting hungry," my dad announced. "I thought we'd take you down to Johnny Marelli's. You should taste their chicken parm. This town really has changed for the better when it comes to food."

Turning back to the room, I raised my hands in a WTF motion and looked at my mother for refuge and support. "I told Mom. I'm not going out." Back to my dad, I said, "Aside from going to see Mrs. Cartwright, I'm not leaving this house while I'm home."

He laughed like I'd told him the earth was flat. "You're not going out?"

I was absolutely appalled. "Mom, did you not tell him?"

She scowled at my father while saying to me, "I mentioned it to him."

"I thought she was joking," my dad said, giving me his own WTF face. "What are you? Five years old? First time you're home since high school, and you're not gonna check out how your hometown has changed? You're not going to see your friends?"

"Um, no. And I don't feel a need to explain myself either."

He shook his head and looked down at the carpet that had once had my blood all over it. "You still can't shake it, can you?"

"Shake what?"

"Shake your senior year."

"I think I've done a pretty good job," I said, glancing at my mother, who was letting it play out.

"You mean by becoming a doctor and inventing some bone plate? You've certainly been successful. But you're still running from that day."

I stepped toward him, not with the intent of hitting him, but to show him I was no longer a boy. I fought to keep him from seeing me shaking inside.

"Aren't you, Dad?"

"No, I'm not. Life's difficult, Carv." He unfurled his arms. "Quit beating yourself up. We all make mistakes."

I sighed, toying with the notion of a retreat to North Carolina. "Yeah, well, that was more than a mistake."

"Maybe so. But *you*"—he pointed at me—"need to let it go. Everybody else has moved on."

I wondered what it would feel like to nose-dive out the window. "Dad, I will join you at church in the morning if I need a sermon, okay?"

My mother finally intervened, stepping between us. Not that my father and I had ever come to blows, but there was always time. "That's enough, boys. We don't have to go out. I already planned on picking something up. He's had a long day of travel anyway. I'm sure he wants to relax."

"A long day of travel," my dad said. I readied myself for a comment about how he used to ride his horse through a blizzard to school. Instead, he said, "God, we raise 'em soft these days."

I was about ten seconds from pulling out my phone and booking a morning flight home. Who was I kidding? I wasn't going to swoop into Teterbury and rescue my parents' marriage. To do that, I'd have to rescue my relationship with my father, and even God couldn't do that in a few days. The way he'd changed after my suicide attempt, the way he'd looked at me, the disappointment, the shame . . . the way he'd let go of my mother, too, abandoning her when she needed him, putting it all on me, all the blame. I'd never forget any of it.

The room was increasingly and entirely too small for the three of us, especially with the added density of the past closing in on us like moving walls. Offering a ticket to freedom for all, I said, "Could I have a moment to unpack and change, and then maybe we can have a glass of wine downstairs?"

My dad got out of there so quickly I don't even think I'd finished the sentence before I heard his retreating boots hitting the carpeted steps. My mother lingered for a moment, and when my dad was out of earshot, she whispered, "You sure you're okay staying up here?"

I wanted to say, *I'm an adult now, Mom. Please don't treat me otherwise.* I didn't say that, though, because I knew she cared.

Looking into her fragile eyes, I said instead, "This will be good for me." I don't know where those words had come from. "Don't worry about me, anyway," I continued. "I'm home for you."

She approached me and patted my cheek. "I know you are, honey. I know."

Four more days.

Later that night, after a painful family dinner, I found my father sitting out in the front yard, poking a maple branch into the crackling fire in front of him. The crickets chirped from the bushes. Only a few lights glowed in the neighbors' windows. The street was deserted.

When he saw me approach, he said, "I was hoping you'd come out and visit."

"Don't you dare offer me a s'more."

He grunted. "No s'mores tonight. Got a Coke or a cold beer, though."

I sat in one of the other Adirondack chairs. "No, thanks."

He tossed the branch in the fire and sat back. "You're not coming out here to give marital advice, are you? We had enough of that at dinner." He was right about that.

"I want to know what happened to you," I said, smelling the burning wood and feeling the heat of the fire press against my face. "I don't remember you being this way. The man I knew would never have done something like this, putting himself first, running out on his family."

He tossed the stick into the fire, sending a few ashes up into the air. "Like son, like father."

I tightened my grasp of the armrests. "That's a low blow."

"You're right. I shouldn't have said that." He sighed, sat back, and rested his hands on his thighs. "I'm not running out on my family. Your mom and I have run our course. She knows it as much as I do, but she doesn't want to deal with the change. She doesn't want to have to explain it to everyone." He flapped his hand forward. "Who cares what they think? We all have our issues. I'm not afraid of talking about mine. *You*, on the other hand. Let's be honest. The only reason you're worried about our divorce is what it does to you."

I whipped my head his way. "That's not true. Jesus, Dad. Are you going to ride me the whole time I'm home?"

"Of course it's true," he shot back. "You don't want any more of your childhood to fall apart. Like your mom's and my relationship now has any bearing on you."

I made a show of looking at the surroundings: the Shasta and then the table under the awning and then the firepit. "Maybe you *should* be more worried about what others think."

He laughed heartily. "Why's that?"

I swallowed back my words.

"Ah," he said, a light bulb apparently going off in that bald head of his. "You think you're the reason your mom and I are getting a divorce? I should have seen that. All of you youngsters . . . everything is about *you*."

"Your insults cut just as deep on the phone. I don't need the live version. Either way, you and Mom changed after what I did. Don't tell me you didn't."

He pondered my assertion before finally saying, "Yeah, hell yeah, we changed. Your kids change you. Every day they do. Sure, it hurt. We both felt like we'd failed you. We blamed each other. But that was a long time ago, Carver. Look at you. You turned out great. You're living the life, more successful than anyone else we know. Who else offers to buy their parents cars and a house? No, we're not worried about you, and I can say confidently that what happened pushed us all to be stronger, and we came out better for it."

My eyes welled with tears.

He nodded toward the house. "Your mom is looking out the window."

I looked in time to see her as she pulled away. Poor thing. Was she relying on me? Helping her right now was the one thing I couldn't do.

My father sighed, and I could hear years of frustration pour out of him. "I wish, son, that you could let that day go."

"I have. I don't think about it."

He faked a smile. "I half believe you."

"I know. I should be enjoying an early retirement with all my—"

"Not if you like what you do," he interrupted. "I get it. You're a good vet. You found your calling. What you do matters. I wouldn't take that away from you. I do question how much living you're really doing down there."

The rising smoke looked a lot like my parents' marriage. "I want you to take care of Mom. Don't worry about me."

"You know what, son? I think me leaving will be the best thing that could ever happen to your mom."

I slid my eyes to him. "I don't know why you'd say that."

In the way he looked back at me, I wondered if there was more to it. Was he sick? Was there someone else? What wasn't he telling me?

Chapter 6

Guilt River

My mother's footsteps woke me early the next morning. "Coming up," she announced, only after she'd pushed open the door.

"That time already?"

Wearing brand-new flashy New Balance sneakers, my mother came into the room with eyes blazing. She'd probably already had her morning smoothie. Almost thirty years my senior and she still had more fire in the morning than I. How many times had she woken me for a run like this back when I was a boy? She'd run track for Boston University and had pushed me since I was a young child to do the same. By the time I joined the middle school track team, the others didn't stand a chance against me.

"What time is it?" I asked.

"Five." She grabbed one of her wrists and stretched. "I let you sleep in. Still wanna join me?"

As if I were going to bail on her. I figured it was too early to risk being seen anyway. "Give me a minute."

Downstairs, she handed me a peeled tangerine, and we headed out the door into the early morning. My dad's infamous snore tumbled out of the open windows of the Shasta as we passed by it.

"At least you're getting a break from that," I said.

"You know," she started solemnly, "his snoring used to irritate the heck out of me, but now that he's gone, I miss it."

That was the saddest thing I'd heard in a long time.

We veered onto the sidewalk and strolled for a moment as I ate my tangerine. The rising sun cast a violet hue over the horizon, but it hadn't brought any warmth yet. I shivered, remembering how New England could be chilly in June. Though I didn't see any lights on in the houses, the birds had begun their day.

"How'd you sleep?" asked my mother, glancing over at me.

"Not bad," I said, lying through my teeth.

"I should have replaced the bunk bed, I know."

"Mom, don't worry about it."

"Okay." It was a whisper. She was brittle, a side of her I didn't know well.

I attempted to be the best of myself, the son she needed. "Thank you, though. Thank you for caring."

It was a charming neighborhood, constructed in a time when people weren't in a rush and the homes were custom built. I couldn't pass by them without thinking about all the people—all the generations who'd lived in them. That was something special about this insignificant blip on the map of New England. These houses and this town had been here long enough to have created a certain feel, a sense of deeply rooted community. I could see Teterbury's settlers building these homes, planning their town, constructing the church and the town hall. All gathering in the square for the weekly farmers' market on Saturdays. This would have been before automobiles were here; they'd used horses to pull building materials. I couldn't deny the appeal of this place, especially for someone clueless to its inner workings.

The stunning trunks of the trees pushed high into the air, forming marshmallow canopies that rose over the roofs, as if protecting everything and everyone below. *As if,* I said to myself. The leaves were a deep green, so healthy and full of life, and the branches up high whooshed back and forth in the wind. The birds and squirrels darted around like sentinels keeping watch.

"What did you and your father talk about?" my mother asked.

That question said it all. Of course she was fragile. Even she, my glorious hero of a mother, wasn't bulletproof. That was a hard concept to digest. After my suicide attempt, she'd been the strong one, hiding her struggle while continuing with work, setting an example for the rest of us, showing us life would move on. She smiled even when my father pushed her away.

I popped the rest of the tangerine in my mouth and pulled the hood up over my head. "Let's get going," I said.

As always when we ran, we fell into an instant rhythm, like two dancers picking up where they'd left off. As we worked our way through the neighborhood toward the river path, I said, "Are you sure he isn't sick? He's lost some weight."

"I don't think so. He'd tell me."

"What else could it be? You don't up and do something like this. Maybe when you're forty and going through a midlife crisis, but not now."

"Now hold on," she said. "Being in your sixties brings a whole new set of crises. Don't let yourself think your age group is alone in trying to figure life out."

I silently pointed to a big crack in the sidewalk, and we both took strides to avoid it. "Dad's introspection is nothing new. I know you were exaggerating about the dementia. What aren't you guys telling me?"

She seemed to want to say something but held back. I didn't want to push, for fear my prying might do more damage than good.

We were quiet for a while as we reached the paved path, a seven-mile loop that followed the rushing river into the woods. The misty air smelled like pine and morning dew. The rising sun hid behind clouds and projected a soft light over the day.

"What happens next, Mom? If he doesn't change his mind."

"Who knows?" She ran like a gazelle, barely touching the ground.

"What if you moved down to Asheville? Come live with me."

She offered a smile and a quick glance back at me. "That's sweet of you to offer, but I don't want to leave. I might sell the house and find

61

something more modern on the east side, but Teterbury is my home. I like knowing the people around me, watching everyone's children grow up."

"I don't know how to help you, Mom. I'd do anything for you, but I don't know what that is."

She slowed to a stop, and I did the same. We were both out of breath, and I welcomed the pause. Up ahead, the river grew wider and deeper. No more rocks punched up through the surface. Several birds floated on the top, searching for fish.

"Having you around is all I need. This feels very—I don't know. This whole thing with your father is not something I ever thought would happen, and I already feel lonely. I have my sister and your cousins, but they're busy. And it's not the same."

I bent down to touch my toes. "This is why you should move to Asheville. That way you don't have to be reminded of him. Screw him if he doesn't see how lucky he is. Move to Asheville and find someone new."

She laughed. "At my age? Why don't you move up here?"

The question came out like she'd been waiting for the right moment to ask it. I came back to a stand. "Is this why you wanted me up here? To see if I'd move?"

She shrugged and then nodded down the path, her signal to get back to it. As we started to run again, I said, "Mom, my work is in Asheville. There's no turning back. I'd do about anything for you, but I can't do that." Realizing I was sounding a lot like Meat Loaf ("I would do anything for love, but I won't do that"), I said, "My whole life is back there."

"Not your whole life," she said in a melancholy tone.

"You know what I mean."

Apparently, she wasn't going to give up so easily. "It's not like there aren't animals here. You could always open a practice in Teterbury. You and Elliot could make up for lost time."

Even if I wanted to come back, which I didn't, I wouldn't because of Shannon. What? So I could run into Trey and her at the store? So I could be reminded what it was like when I returned from Christmas break to see them all over each other? This town was *way* too small for the three of us.

I wanted to ask my mother about her, but I didn't want to rip open the wound either. It took another hundred yards before I decided I had to know. I asked as casually as I could. "You ever see Shannon?"

The quiet between us was charged.

"You're not still thinking about her, are you?"

"No, of course not. Not really. I mean, it's hard to be back and not wonder about her."

She paused, and I could tell she was scrambling, trying to figure out what to say. "Don't get all excited, but she and Trey divorced. I didn't want to tell you."

I stopped like I'd run into a tree. "What?"

She slowed to a stop herself and turned back to me. Tall trees reached up around us, leaving us in the shade. "I don't want you reconnecting with her, you understand? She's not good for you, Carver."

"Who says I'm reconnecting? Just wondering what happened."

"She left Trey a year ago, and I don't know. She's been seen around town dating."

"Been seen around town?" I said, still trying to process the news.

"She's kind of . . . ugh, I don't know. You can do better." She motioned for me to keep running, and we both picked back up to a jog.

As much as I didn't want to think about it, I had to ask, "Why did they get a divorce? What happened?"

Our feet hit the pavement in perfect rhythm. "You know Trey," she said. "Rumor is he ran around on her. Or maybe she did to him. I don't know. Everyone speculated for a while."

That news hit a nerve. She was either leaving a path of damaged males in her wake, or she'd been served a proper dose of her own medicine.

"Do they have children?" I asked.

"I don't think so."

Thinking about the end of Shannon and Trey made me feel admittedly giddy inside. It was healing to know she'd chosen the wrong guy. I was suddenly desperate to know if she'd read about me in the *Teterbury Times*. If so, had she second-guessed her decision to leave me? Guilt sideswiped me for thinking that.

Speeding up ahead of my mother, I lost myself in what my life might have looked like had Shannon still been in it. Would I have still gone south? No, not at all. She and I had plans. We both would have returned to Teterbury after college. I'm not sure I would have ever connected with Mrs. Cartwright and her husband like I did, which meant I might not have become a vet. What would I have been then? Vet or not, we'd have several kids and live north of town in one of those larger mountain houses. We'd be the power couple of Teterbury . . .

I winced at the thoughts circling my head, the worst of which was how badly I wanted to shake a finger in Trey's face and make sure he knew I'd won. He may have stolen her from me in high school, but I'd gone on to be someone. What was he now? A divorcé trying to pick up the pieces. Served him right.

What about Shannon? I wondered, half realizing I was at a full sprint, running faster than the water. Up ahead, I could see the bridge that marked the halfway point. Was I happy she'd learned her lesson? Was I happy she had to endure the pains of divorce? Through my parents I saw what it did to people firsthand, so no. She was young, and she'd picked the wrong guy. She'd spat in the face of destiny, ripping apart a love like this town had never seen, but she'd been so young, so . . . so impressionable. Most of the fault lay on Trey, and perhaps on me, for not yet realizing my potential. Had she known who I would become, she never would have left me in the first place.

"Don't take this the wrong way," my mom said, "but I saw her not too long ago, and she told me to tell you hello."

My face contorted. "What? You're telling me this now?"

"People tell me to tell you hello all the time." She shrugged. "I can't report back to you on each occasion. Take this as a collective: *Everyone in Teterbury says hi.* I'm sure there's a handful of women far better than Shannon who would love to see you while you're back. What about Sadie Mendelson . . . Wasn't she . . . ?"

I had purposely not asked about Shannon for this very reason. I didn't want to feel this way, like I was seventeen years old and madly in love, only to be destroyed to the core of me. Some things were unquestionably better left with the lid on.

Chapter 7

THE CARVER SHUFFLE

As a peace offering, I cooked my parents breakfast: eggs, bacon, and potatoes. I'm not sure my father had skipped his morning bacon since he was a baby. His parents, who had both succumbed to old age, had owned a meat and dairy ranch in Cheyenne, and my father never missed a chance to compare a cut of steak or pork to the tastes of his childhood.

Nary a word was spoken among the three of us as we sat around the table. My mother barely ate. Afterward, she disappeared upstairs, and my dad went to church. I jumped onto Amazon and ordered a Roomba, a new printer, and a stronger Wi-Fi router with a satellite. It was time I brought them—or, at least, my mom—into the twenty-first century. In the following two hours, I started cleaning. If I couldn't help save their marriage, I could at least show them they were still loved and save them from this mess.

Midmorning, hood pulled over my head, I walked two blocks down the road to visit Mrs. Cartwright. I hoped the chances of any-one else seeing me were slim, but for my mentor's sake, I was willing to take the risk. A couple of neighbors said hello, but they were new faces to me.

In the driveway of her light-gray house with royal-blue shutters were two vehicles: a smaller Ford SUV and an older Chevrolet truck sparkling with a fresh coat of teal paint. I'd seen them both yesterday, which meant Ava, the physical therapist, was there again.

Had someone been looking out of the window, they would have seen me do a jig to the tune of the Clash's "Should I Stay or Should I Go?" I stopped and pivoted, then looked back toward my parents' house. That Ava seemed like trouble, for some reason. I pivoted again, glancing at the truck and then at Mrs. Cartwright's house. Another pivot, a twist, a shuffle.

If I could change one thing about myself, it would have been my indecision. I don't know where I'd gotten the trait, but it hung over me, frustrating me to no end. A colleague once told me that highly intelligent people could often be indecisive because they liked to think things over and debate them ad nauseam. I was certainly that way, and even with that awareness, I couldn't change it.

Get over it, Carver, I finally said to myself. *Who cares? You're gone in a couple of days. Ava is not a threat.*

Mortified at the sudden idea of someone bearing witness to my lunacy, I diverted my gaze to the sidewalk and pretended to be looking for something on the ground. Once I'd found the imaginary object, I scooped it up, slipped it into my pocket, and carried on toward the house as if all was well. What a kook I could be.

Mrs. Cartwright's one-story home was about half the size of my parents'. Cushions cross-stitched with spines of books sat on each side of a bench swing. Several pots flanked the front door—all of them empty, which Mrs. Cartwright would have called a crime the last time I'd seen her, a day before I left for the fall semester at Wake Tech. Along with her extraordinary garden and colorful landscaping around her house on the farm, she'd also decorated her wraparound porch with dozens of pots spilling over with plants and flowers. What a change this was to see.

I rang the bell and stepped back. On the other side of the door, Oscar Wilde launched into a barking fit as he raced toward the unknown visitor. I soon heard the desperate scratching of nails.

Mrs. Cartwright's voice cut through his barking. "Settle down, Oscar. Good heavens." She was at the door a moment later and cracked it open a couple of inches. "You stay where you are."

I started to raise my hands, as if she might have a shotgun and was about to warn me off her property, but then I realized she was speaking to him, not me.

"Good morning, Mrs. Cartwright," I said above Oscar's yapping. Through the tight aperture from the crack in the door, I saw she was dressed up with slacks and a matching sweater. "I thought I'd come say hello, but it looks like you might be headed to church?"

She peered at me through her glasses. *Church?* If the good Lord hasn't made His decision by now, then there's not much I can do."

"I suppose I can't use the same excuse, can I?" I recalled some of the countless Sundays that I'd tried to get out of going with my parents to Advent Episcopal in town. Shannon's presence was the only reason they sometimes won out. Though I figured I had no chance with her, it was still a gift to simply set eyes on her.

"Come in, Carver," she said. "Just watch him, though. He's been insufferable this morning." She opened the door farther, and I slid in with one hand down low to keep Oscar from leaving. He growled aggressively as he inched backward on the oriental rug that stretched out across the foyer. His whole body trembled in fear.

"I brought you a treat," I said, staying low so as not to intimidate him.

Oscar's ears perked up. I produced a baggie with a few carrots I'd cut up into small bites. He moved skeptically, approaching the carrot while keeping a clear eye on me. Finally, he took his reward and backed away.

"He's terrified, isn't he?" I watched the poor dog continue to shake as he chewed on the carrot. Beyond him I recognized a grandfather clock in the corner. Even as a teenager, the Cartwrights' antique furniture had impressed me. If you wound her up, she could talk for an hour about a British corner cupboard she and Tom had found in an antique shop in the middle of some nowhere town in Vermont or Maine.

She wore a necklace of pearls, a gift I remembered Tom had given her. Her curly hair rested high on her head. The bronze tint of her lipstick matched her sweater. "He was attacked by a dog down the street a couple of months ago," she said, "and he's been behaving like this ever since. A complete bedlamite. I never know which dogs or people he'll go after."

"That must make it hard to walk him," I said.

"I rarely do anymore." She gestured behind her. "Anyhow, I need to sit back down. Ava's making coffee."

I followed her into the living room. Noticing her unsteady step, I offered a hand, but she shrugged me off. The old hardwoods creaked, and the china in the cupboard shook as we came into the room where she clearly spent most of her time. A stale smell not unlike that of my old bedroom hung in the air.

Again, I tried to offer Mrs. Cartwright a hand as she sat in the baby-blue recliner that was, as illustrated by the impression left in the seat, clearly her go-to spot. She swatted at me as if I'd insulted her, so I retreated to the couch with too many pillows to count. The one that caught my eye had a big "B" on it, the Boston Red Sox logo. She'd obviously made that one herself.

I watched as she lowered into the chair with obvious pain. On the table next to her was a basket filled with various colors of yarn, and I could easily imagine her hypnotized by the rhythm of the needles as she knitted the days away. Without her farm, she must have had so much more time on her hands.

Still keeping his distance, Oscar sat on his haunches and watched me, waiting for another carrot. I tossed one to him, and he took it to a safe place near his owner to enjoy.

Having neutralized the threat, I took a moment to look around. Curtains covered the windows, and only a slice of sunshine had found its way in. Most of the light came from the floor lamp with a jeweled shade. The recliner, the couch, and another chair faced a small television that rested on a fancy mahogany table in the corner. Books spilled out of the built-in floor-to-ceiling shelving that nearly covered an entire wall. The ones I recognized right off were an entire slew of Diana Gabaldons, surely the entire Outlander series, and the spines indicated they'd been read more than once. She and my mother shared that love and could probably chat about Jamie until the sun rose.

Staring at her turntable in the corner, I said, "I remember enjoying your turkey sandwiches on the porch after the morning's work. And you always had your show tunes going." A part of me could taste the way I was coming alive back then, that small morsel of hope returning to me. Why was even simply being around my former teacher so elevating, even when she was in such a dark place? I suppose that was the impact she'd had on my life, a piece of me forever changed, that piece of me lodged deep within, never truly going away.

She gave a weak smile and rested her hands on her lap.

"It must have been hard to say goodbye to the farm," I said soberly, wishing I could take her back in time and show her the Mrs. Cartwright I remembered, the woman who would chase the sheep with her dogs, or take Tom's hand and dance on the porch without a second thought about it, not shy at all that her student was there. In a way, they became my heroes, people I wanted to be like as I grew older.

She inclined her eyebrows. "As my son says, it made the most sense. Less driving, especially at night. I'm closer to the medical center, the grocery store, all the necessities of one's descent into the grave."

I felt determined to break through this icy shell she'd donned. "What do you do for fun now?"

Her eyes expanded. "Fun? You don't have fun at my age. You just try to keep all your parts from falling off."

"C'mon. This doesn't sound like you at all."

She waved a hand through the air. "Never mind me, tell me about you. I would welcome the distraction. What's going on with your parents?"

I sighed. It didn't feel like a betrayal when I said, "They're a disaster over there. Have you noticed the trailer in the front yard?"

She shook her head with her bottom lip jutting out. "I never go that way."

I tossed Oscar another carrot. "My father bought a 1962 Shasta trailer and is keeping it in the front yard." I caught her up, unable to recount the details without a maniacal smile rising out of me. I admitted, "I'm still in shock over the idea of them getting a divorce."

"I'm so sorry, dear," she said.

I recognized the old Mrs. Cartwright in the way she looked at me with her sympathetic eyes. No one had ever been a better listener. How many times had we strolled through her property, chatting about life? She'd been so patient with me, listening without a shred of judgment as I tried to make sense of losing the love of my life and then letting that destroy the future I'd been working to create.

I scratched at the material of the couch, thinking Mary Beth was the only one in a lot of years I'd ever shared with on this level. It was as if I'd been unconsciously longing for Mrs. Cartwright and had found in Mary Beth a piece of her.

"I don't know why it's affecting me so much. It's like they're knocking down the foundation of our family. Even though I don't see them that often, they've always been there, you know. My blood."

The creaking floors from the hallway warned me that Ava approached, so I waved the conversation off. "I don't mean to dump it on you."

Ava came into the room carrying a tray with three mugs of steaming coffee. "I thought that might be you at the door."

I stood and said hello as the smell of freshly ground coffee filled the room.

Wavy red hair fell down her back. Her olive-green sweater made it look like her gingerbread eyes had a hint of green to them as well. Her unzipped sweater fell open to show a V-neck T-shirt.

"He was explaining," Mrs. Cartwright started, clearing her throat, "that he's having a hard time with his parents. Coming here is his escape." She looked at me. "Don't worry, she's a transient. Your secrets are safe here."

"A transient?" I asked.

"That's what she calls me." Ava set the tray down. "I'm only here a few more weeks."

"I see," I said, deciding Ava wasn't a threat at all.

"She's a traveling physical therapist," Mrs. Cartwright added. "And a poet."

"A poet," I echoed, lowering back to my seat. "That's . . . interesting." *Interesting*, I thought. *Way to hit them with your best word, dumbbell.* I was surprised Mrs. Cartwright didn't throw something at me. Maybe a thesaurus.

Ava's cheeks reddened beneath her freckles as she set one mug on the small table next to Mrs. Cartwright. "I put in only a dash of cream, okay?"

Mrs. Cartwright rolled her eyes, looking like she wanted to give Ava an earful.

"Good coffee doesn't need any more than that," Ava responded.

What was that all about? Was Ava helping her with her diet?

Ava crossed the room to the windows. "It's darker than the inside of a pocket in here." As she drew open the curtains, light spilled in, and a view of the front yard with a lone sugar maple unveiled itself.

Coming back my way, she sat at the other end of the couch. "I'm a great physical therapist but a hack of a poet," she said.

"That's not true at all," Mrs. Cartwright disagreed. "Why don't you read him something?"

"Please." I reached for the mug she'd poured for me.

A shy streak showed in Ava's eyes. "Thank you, but no thank you. She's been trying to get me to write more, which has been fun."

Mrs. Cartwright raised her hands. "What are words if you don't share them? I'm sure I have some of Carver's poems in the back room somewhere."

I smiled, unable to remember a time when I wrote poetry. "Please tell me you didn't keep all that stuff."

"She did," Ava said. "I've seen them. Boxes and boxes of her students' papers."

The picture of her loss became clearer. Her profession. Her husband. Her farm.

"It must be hard being retired," I said, feeling her loss like it was my own. "You were such a wonderful teacher."

Mrs. Cartwright set down her coffee. "Leaving was bittersweet. The new principal. He was happy to see me finally relent."

"You were certainly never afraid to push the limits. Dare I call you a rebel?"

"Was she?" Ava asked.

I was taken back to those days when Mrs. Cartwright would step in front of the class. "She would do whatever it took to get us to read. Even if that meant straying a long way from the curriculum."

Mrs. Cartwright fought off a glow on her face as I continued.

"I'll never forget the time you had us read James Bond. Who wrote those—"

"Ian Fleming," Mrs. Cartwright said.

I slapped my knee. "Ian Fleming, that's right. Not exactly on the reading list for high school seniors."

"But did you read it?" she asked, knowing I did.

"Every single person in the class did," I replied.

Mrs. Cartwright smiled with satisfaction.

"You bought them for everyone with your own money, right?"

She crossed her arms with a bit of sass. "The state of Vermont sure wasn't going to pony up for the bill."

As we enjoyed our coffee, I told a few more stories from those years. I think Ava and I both enjoyed seeing Mrs. Cartwright lighten up for a while.

Eventually, to be polite, I returned the conversation to Ava. "I want to hear more about this transient thing. Where's home?"

"Home." She let out a smile, as if I'd rung the bell of her own inside joke. "Where is home?" she asked herself. She seriously thought about it, like she'd never considered the idea.

Speaking with her eyes on the ceiling, she said, "I was born in the Chicago burbs, but that's not home. We moved around, my mom and I. Traverse City for a minute, then Louisville, down to Pensacola, then to New Orleans and finally throwing somewhat of an anchor in Nashville." She returned her eyes to me. "My father left when I was young, so it was my mom and me, and she was an adventurer, always curious about what was on the other side. She used to say, 'Some people wonder what another life is like. You and me, we go find out.'"

It sounded way too much like my father, but I stopped before making the comparison out loud. "She sounds really special. Is she still in Nashville or . . . ?"

"No, she's gone now."

"I'm so sorry."

She shrugged. "Thanks. And you? What could possibly bring a man home after such a long time gone?"

"Three days ago, I would have said absolutely nothing. But . . ." I sat back and drew in a long breath. How to even gloss over an answer without showing how my return affected me? Still, I didn't want to be the phony one of the bunch. "My father is going through an existential crisis, so he bought a trailer and is fixing it up."

"As one does," Ava said. The way she seemed to care without judgment put my mind to ease.

Mrs. Cartwright appeared satisfied listening to us talk. It was extremely apparent she was doing nothing to bail me out. Was this her teaching again?

"Yeah, I guess. He's now filing for divorce and driving west on Wednesday."

"That's . . . so sad. I'm sorry."

"Yeah, thanks." They stared at me, waiting in silence for me to continue. "My mom wanted me to come home and talk some sense into him, but it's already feeling like I've wasted my time. I remember him being contemplative—always talking in these philosophical sound bites—but this has gone overboard." I felt the sadness of my parents' situation rise and redden my eyes, and I bit my lip hard. Mrs. Cartwright had already seen so much of me—the worst of me, and this Ava would never see me again, so who cared? At least, that was what I told myself.

"Have they tried counseling?" Mrs. Cartwright asked.

"I don't think so. I've been so concerned with trying to figure out what to say to them . . . but you're right. Counseling could help."

"Other than that," Mrs. Cartwright continued, "maybe some time apart."

Ava jumped in. "I'm old fashioned, but what about going back to where it began? Can you talk them into going out on a date? Where did they meet?"

I thought back to the stories my mother used to tell about when they'd fallen in love, the moment they first met eyes at Boston Garden, then my dad chasing her around for the rest of the time he was in town.

"I like that idea. But . . . I don't know if my dad is up for it. He seems to have made up his mind."

Ava let the idea go. "Isn't life tough enough without all the curveballs?"

"Don't get me started," I said. "What's funny is they love to give me a hard time about not wanting a relationship, but look at them. Why would I want that?"

Mrs. Cartwright softly giggled to herself—as if she enjoyed how we were learning the lessons she'd learned a long time ago. "I find that curveballs come our way when we need them most."

The way she'd said it came off like a mic drop, and neither Ava nor I would dare disagree.

"I read about you in the paper," Mrs. Cartwright said, going in a new direction. "What is this thing you've invented?"

I perked up. "You really want to know?" Asking about what I'd spent thousands of hours perfecting would always get me excited. I launched into the spiel I'd given more than a time or two. "The biggest orthopedic issue we run into with dogs is cranial cruciate ligament rupture in their knee, or as we all know it, an ACL tear. As I'm speaking, it occurs to me that you two are more knowledgeable than most when it comes to knee anatomy—especially you, Ava. But dog knees are slightly different. You would have thought evolution or God would have been able to come up with a better design, as opposed to clumsily lashing everything together with tendons and ligaments, but that's not the case. I came up with a surgical plating technique to repair the knee, which requires a specialized bone plate I designed. It sounds more impressive than it is."

They read right through my feeble attempt at humility. "How does one even begin to invent things?" Ava asked, lighting me up with her apparent enthusiasm. Either she was genuinely interested or one hell of a good actor.

"Necessity," I said, talking to both women. "I've been repairing cruciate tears for years with other techniques and figured there had to be a better way. When I came up with the plate design, I went to the metal shop down the road and worked on some prototypes, and it all blew up from there."

I wondered if that was pride in Mrs. Cartwright's eyes. I hoped so but I wasn't sure. Something about my life felt inadequate as I spoke about it, as if I could have done more, as if the CliffsNotes to Dr. Carver Livingston were missing a few pages.

＜

"A great woman, isn't she?" Mrs. Cartwright asked after Ava had left.

"Seems like it," I said. "From the little amount of time I've spent with her."

"Don't get too excited, though. She says you're not her type."

I turned defensive. "I wasn't getting excited."

"Okay, good." Oscar slept on Mrs. Cartwright's lap, and she stroked his back. "Yesterday I was telling her about you, what a fine young man you used to be. I told her you were both missing something in life."

"What's that?" I asked, pretending I was unfazed by her previous comment.

"Love."

I inclined my shoulders. "Ah. As if everyone needs it." I wasn't in the mood for a lecture about love. She and I knew what "love" had done to me.

"You see, she's the same way." Mrs. Cartwright craned her neck toward me. "You're both terrified of it."

I stopped short of rolling my eyes.

"When I look at you," she said, "I see the same wounded teenager who stumbled into my office his senior year. Who have you loved since Shannon?"

The mention of her name made me feel sick inside, and I froze.

"Who?" she asked again.

I stalled. There'd been a few women in my life, but certainly no one I'd actually *loved*. "It's not in my cards, not right now. Besides, ask Shakespeare about love. Or my parents. Or Jay Gatsby. It doesn't always work out so well. Not everyone needs it."

"You don't believe that for a second."

"I do, actually." She knew I did too. No one on Earth had heard me rant about love like Mrs. Cartwright. She was the only one I'd truly told how I felt back then, how the world had to be a devilishly evil place to set two destined souls together, only to tear them apart later.

She shook her head but didn't say a word. I remembered how she used to do that, as if her silence was enough to prove a point.

"Hey," I said, "you're the one who made us read *Wuthering Heights*."

"If I recall correctly," she said, "you hated that book."

How could she possibly remember that? But it was true. "Yes, but . . ."

"You are no Heathcliff, Carver. Love certainly comes with its risks, but the risk of living a life without love is far more dangerous."

"Who said that?" I asked.

"Yours truly." She exhaled slowly. "Carver, losing Tom has taken it all out of me, but I'd do it over a million times. Without love, what is life? You can't keep running from it. While we're at it, forgive me for saying so, but that might start with loving yourself."

I was there for her, *not* me, so I said, "What happened to him? To Tom?"

She let me derail her teaching moment. "Heart disease."

I felt a deep pain in my heart, thinking about how much love he'd shown me, stepping in where my father had fallen short. When I had first shaken his hand, the big man had nearly crushed mine with his.

"You know," I said, "it's not that I didn't appreciate your letters, or that I didn't care. I made the decision that I had to let it all go, every bit of my previous life. I had to disconnect. That was the only way I could become someone."

"You were always someone. Someone special."

"Thank you." The gushiness was too much, so I rose back to the surfacy stuff. "Do you keep in touch with your other students?"

"Of course." She tilted her head. "Do you remember those letters I had everyone write to their future selves? The ones I promised I'd send twenty years later? I still do that."

"Really?" I calculated the timing. "I guess you're about to send ours out. Oh God, what in the world did I write?"

She lowered her gaze to the rug between us. "I'll have to dig them up. I'm late this year."

"Understandably." My curiosity had gotten the best of me, and I tried to remember what I might have penned to myself. "Maybe I don't want to read mine anyway. When did we write them? Was it earlier in the year?"

"First week back, every single year."

Ah, the happy Carver time, when I was with Shannon and on top of the world. Or so I thought.

I'd attended a gifted camp hosted by the University of Vermont in Burlington in the weeks before school started. My mother had urged it on me, saying it was a great thing to add to my college résumé. Turned out Shannon was there, too, and I quickly realized she wasn't a clichéd blonde with nothing to say.

We connected, if only because we were the only ones from Teterbury. By the time we'd finished lunch that day in the cafeteria, I was purely and utterly in love, as only a teen can be. We chatted music and made fun of the jocks, and she talked about her older ex-boyfriend and how she'd never been in love. I hadn't, either, and even as we made the confession, we searched each other's eyes, certainly wondering if what brewed between us could be it. With us both staying in the dorms, I'd go to her window before lights out—fresh breathed from a swig of Scope—and we'd talk and laugh, and then I'd walk back to my room with the fullest heart I'd ever known.

Something occurred to me toward the end of that magical week, shortly after we'd kissed and made out. A fear that flickered with a darkness I would know far better in the months to come. Was this a camp fling, or would we continue when we returned? I was afraid she'd pretend nothing had ever happened.

I was never so happy to be wrong. She told me she loved me on the last day, and when we got back to Teterbury, we were an official couple. She held on to me tight when we saw the new *Halloween* movie in the theater, making our debut in Teterbury. That was the August that changed my world. My first week back to school was the best of my life. We'd make out by the lockers, and I could feel people watching us, maybe even wishing they were standing in our shoes.

"It's a lot to think about," I finally said to Mrs. Cartwright.

"You had a big year, didn't you? Does it still haunt you?"

I scratched my head, or more like dug into my scalp with my nails. "I have this awful feeling that what I did is why my parents don't love each other anymore."

Mrs. Cartwright pushed herself up and sat next to me—a book spine's width away from me. "Let me tell you something, Carver. Couples face challenges. Raising kids is certainly one. But if your parents are struggling right now, it has nothing to do with you. It has to do with them and only them."

The sudden intimacy was a lot for me—the way she spoke so tenderly, so I looked at her only out of the corner of my eye. "I know you're right. It's still jarring."

She patted my thigh. "I'm sure. We all have our younger selves inside of us, and we're all fragile. Losing Tom reminded me of that. To tell you the truth, there's probably nothing you can do to help. If you're seeking advice, I'd be there for them. Listen to them. Because as you get older, you lose your friends and your family. It's the loneliness that seems to kill us. Don't let your parents get lonely."

I turned all the way toward her this time. "You don't feel that way, do you?"

She considered the question. "It's nice to have visitors."

I nodded, glad that I'd felt compelled to come by.

"God should have taken me first," she said. "Not my Tom. But it's how it is, and now I'm waiting for the angels to take me to him."

"The one thing I know is that no man has ever loved a woman more than he loved you." My eyes watered. "He'll be waiting, and he'd agree with me when I say he'd happily wait for a long time."

She pressed her lips together.

I took her hand, which was something out of character for me, but she always brought the most out of me. "I still need you, Mrs. Cartwright."

She looked at me and paused. "You don't need me anymore. You're figuring it out."

"I've got everyone fooled," I whispered. She was the only one in the world to whom I would say such a thing.

Chapter 8

SWIMMING WITH PIRANHAS

"I've had about enough of this, Carver," my dad said a few hours later. "All this meddling is only going to cause problems, trust me."

What the hell did that mean?

My parents and I sat out back on the patio, where a six-foot wooden fence afforded us as much outdoor privacy as you could get in their neighborhood. I think we were all so frustrated we didn't even care if every neighbor in town was crouched on the other side of the fence, enjoying our argument.

The lawn was in good shape, which was my dad's doing. He'd always loved working in the yard—took great pride in it, and I supposed that hadn't changed, despite my mother's cleaning strike inside. The bird feeder was even full. A red bird currently ate the fallen seeds in the grass.

"It's counseling." I sat up and almost slammed my hand against the white table that stayed in the garage in the winters. "That's what you do when you're having marital problems." The way my tense jaws were moving, it must have looked like I was chewing marbles.

My dad dusted off the flecks of sawdust clinging to his flannel shirt. "Counseling is what you do when . . ." He stopped.

"What, Dad?"

He thought long and hard about what he wanted to say, and I could see he was holding something back. "Carver, I'm not doing this right now. I'd love to spend some time with you while you're home, but we're not going to waste another minute on this topic."

My mother sat on the other side of me and had stayed silent, like she'd done the best she could, and now I was the only hope. I turned to her, wishing I had more to offer. To think this woman had given me her all for my entire life, even more so after I'd slit my wrist, but when she finally needed me to step up, I was unable.

I tried to include her. "What do you think, Mom? Guys, you've been together for a long time. You don't go out without a fight."

As evident in her shrug, she had no fight left. "I don't know, Carver."

I could have screamed all the obscenities in the world. She didn't deserve what my dad was doing. For the first few months after I'd cut myself, he'd tried to be kind, tried to get me to do things with him. I appreciated it, but I didn't want to do anything with anyone. I hid in my room when I wasn't in school. When I was finally ready to spend time with him, nearer to the end of the school year, he turned on me. No longer was he even trying to be a good father, as if he'd decided I wasn't worth the trouble. I could hear my mom and him fighting, a new thing in our household. They did their best to keep it from me, but I could only assume it was about the fact that my mother was working extra hard, trying to keep it together, while my father fell into a steady decline, often doing nothing after coming home from the garage but sitting in his recliner in front of a sports game. Sometimes he wouldn't even join us for dinner. That was when my mom stopped cooking, and we started doing takeout.

Lashing out at him now wouldn't get me anywhere, though. With everything I had, I said peacefully, "Guys, do this for me."

"There we go," my father said. "How dare we rock Carver's boat. Just when things were going well, and he's building these new practices and cashing his big checks."

I let my eyes fall closed, trying so hard not to explode.

"I understand where he's coming from," my mom said, taking my side. "Ben, you're not only ruining our lives. It's his too. We're his parents. Your father left you when you were eight years old, and you still bring it up."

He jammed a finger at the table. "There's a difference between eight and thirty-eight." He must have seen the hurt in my eyes and backed down. "Look, Carver, I've already told you, it's not about you. It doesn't change how we feel about you. This is the way it's gonna be."

I mirrored his calmer demeanor. "I will accept that *after* you try counseling. You don't have to leave on Wednesday. Take a few extra days so that you and Mom can sit down with a marital specialist and try to save what you're losing."

"I'm not against it," my mom said, shaking her head. A sliver of hope clung to the edges of her words.

For a few seconds I had hope too.

My father stared off toward the fence. Was he reconsidering his position? Was he imagining a life without my mother? He started to stand, pressing his hands on the table so much it tilted. "I will not spend hundreds of dollars on some loon who thinks he can dissect a relationship I've been in for forty-three years."

Ava's suggestion came to mind. "You need to look back through the years and remember why you two love each other. Try to remember what it felt like when you two were in the heat of that first week together. Think of that spark. Not even two thousand miles could keep you away from each other after that."

My father rested his hands on the back of his chair. My mother looked so hard at the table she might bore a hole into it.

"You're right." My voice cracked, well aware I was arguing for them to fight for love when I certainly didn't believe in it myself. "This does mess me up."

"Oh, Carver," my mother said.

"I've tried to show you I'm better than the kid who"—I lowered my volume nearly all the way—"who tried to take the easy way out." I lost my train of thought, I was hurting so much. "Whether or not you realize it, the end of your marriage is because of what I did. It's because of me. If you're not willing to step up and try to save what I destroyed, then what the hell has it all been for? Why the . . ." I let out a long sigh, wishing I'd never come back to this town, never set foot back into this house.

I found my mother's weepy eyes, then lifted my head to my father. "Give it one more shot. For me. Counseling if that might work. Or do it the old-fashioned way. Dad, you somehow lucked out on the best woman in this state. Take her out on a date like you used to. Let her get dressed up. Take notice of how beautiful she is. Listen to that laugh. Listen to what she has to say. Don't wait until it's too late. What do you have to lose? If it's really over, then what's one date?"

My phone buzzed, and I glanced at it. A local Vermont number. "Who in the world knows I'm here? And how did they get my number?" I silenced the ring and returned to what I was saying. "You've made it this long. Don't give up now." With that, I rested my case and wiped away the evidence of my tears.

My dad stared at the fence behind me, as if he were waiting for something to break through it.

My mother and I watched and waited.

Don't go out without a fight, I thought.

He released his hands from the chair and put them into the back pockets of his Wrangler's. "I love you both, and I'm sorry."

I could see that—that he loved us both. I could also see his decision was firm. As my phone vibrated with a voice message alert, he left us—giving me a sense of what to expect Wednesday. My mom and I looked at each other with the realization that the family we'd known was truly over.

And it was on me, every bit of this hurt and pain, on me and me alone.

"I'm so sorry. I don't know what else to do."

"I don't either," she whispered. We held eye contact for a long time, and I felt so much love for her running through me. So much love and compassion, and sorrow too.

I sat back, exhausted. It looked like my mother had run out of both hope and tears, leaving her red eyed and pale. I took her hand to show her that at least I would never take her for granted.

A few minutes later, I reached for my phone. "Let me see who this is," I said. "I can't even imagine."

Once I'd pressed play, a familiar voice from twenty years earlier rose from the phone. "Dr. Livingston, I presume . . . I think this is your number. The voice mail message was vague. Long time no talk. It's your old pal Elliot. Rumor has it you've returned to Teterbury. If it's true, I'd love to see you."

A click signaled another giant silence in the backyard. His voice served the bitter past to me on a plate. I'd wronged all of them—my friends, my family, the Cartwrights.

Breathing out a long sigh, I asked my mother, "Did you tell anyone I was home?"

She sat back in the chair with her head turned up, looking so incredibly exposed, as if she were waiting for someone to take her away. Without moving a muscle, she said, "Of course not."

I nodded, believing her. My mother was one of those "my word is my bond" people. Like my dad, come to think about it.

"How about Dad?" I asked.

She sat up and looked at me with empty eyes, as if someone had plucked them from her, leaving only the sockets. "Does it look like I have my finger on the pulse of your father?"

I knew then that my father had been the one to get word to Elliot. Telling her I'd be right back, I moved through the house and out the front door to find him in his makeshift trailer park. Across the street, a neighbor pruned his hedges. One down from him, a mother watched from the stoop as her little girl played in the grass. My father sat in one of the Adirondack chairs, listening to Willie Nelson, sipping a Coke Zero, and staring at a map splayed out on his lap.

"What are you doing?" I asked, once again tempering my anger.

"Trying to decide whether to run south first," he said, not showing any signs of remorse for what had transpired in the backyard. "I'd love to see Texas before it gets too hot." Was my father a psychopath?

Standing over him, I crossed my arms like he had earlier, feeling distinctly like him today, like his genes were glowing inside of me. "Did you tell anyone I was coming home?"

He stopped what he was doing and looked at me. "Might have."

"Even though I asked you not to?"

Without a shred of shame, he returned his attention to the map. Several penciled routes ran west. "There's a good chance, yep. At the barbershop. Why? Someone find you?"

"Elliot called." I had an urge to swipe that map off his lap.

He nodded, as if his plan had come to fruition. "I hope you're going to make some time for him."

"I'm actually thinking about leaving this afternoon," I said, hoping that might jar him out of his annoyingly calm state.

He smiled that smile that used to sink my spirits when I was young, the one that made me feel like I was the disappointment of all disappointments. "I'll give you this," he said. "As much as I hate that you left, I probably should have followed suit. Maybe I've been jealous of you all these years."

I felt my head kick back. He'd never said any such thing before. I took a long look at the Shasta, at the metal wing on the end. "You think that's what's wrong between us?" I asked over my shoulder.

"Carver, there's nothing wrong between us. Not the way I see it. I was hurt you left us and never came back. Jesus, Carver, you haven't been home to see us *one* time. Not for a birthday or Christmas. My retirement party. Romo's funeral. But I've gotten over it."

My forearms burned with anger. "Have you?"

He sipped his soda, apparently absent of any anger at all. "Mostly."

"If it hurt so much, why would you do it to Mom?" Using his own rationale against him, I said, "Besides, I was a kid. You're in your sixties."

"You don't know the whole story."

"What is the whole story, dammit? At least look me in the eyes and tell me the damn truth."

He did me the kindness of looking in my eyes, but all he said was, "It would take a lifetime to tell."

I turned away and walked into the grass. "Jesus, you speak in these vague references with all these philosophical overtones. I don't know what you're saying."

"What I'm saying, son, is there is a difference between you and me leaving."

I gave a half bow. "Bestow your wisdom on me, Ben Livingston, before you depart for your homeland."

He took his time folding the map and setting it on the ground beside him. Willie Nelson began to sing "Whiskey River," and I hated that I knew all the words. He was my father's favorite, and I'd grown up listening to him, soaking up the lyrics with no choice in the matter. I could sing every word, but I sure as hell didn't want to. I never wanted to hear Willie again.

"You went running," my dad said, speaking over Willie. "Tail between your legs. You let that day beat you."

I gritted my teeth. "And you?"

He lifted his soda from the cup holder. "I finished what I started. I'm saying my goodbyes. I will leave with my head up."

Shaking my own, I said, "And the rest of us left in your dust."

He didn't argue.

I hated myself for ever leaving, letting that day get the best of me, and I hated him for hanging it over my head. Giving up, I walked toward the house.

"You should call him," he called out. "He could use a friend right now."

"Who?" I said, slowing some.

"Elliot. He needs you."

I stopped and turned. "Why? What's going on?"

"Go see him."

I was talking to a brick wall.

"Look, Dad. I know you've got it all figured out but do me a favor. Don't tell anyone else I'm home. I don't need you throwing me into the water to teach me how to swim. We're past that, okay? If you're going to leave Mom, I don't know what to say. I guess I'll try hard *not* to hate you for it. That's the best that I can do."

"I understand," he said.

I left him there with his Willie Nelson and his empty wisdom.

<hr />

Two hours later, my parents and I—my broken family—sat in front of the television, eating. I'd ordered pizza and a large Greek salad. No strangers to meals in front of the tube, I'd found the folding TV trays we'd used when I was younger and placed them in front of our places: my mother and I on the couch and my father in his hideously ugly La-Z-Boy.

In front of me I had a heaping serving of the salad and a slice of a spicy cauliflower and blue cheese that was about the best pizza I'd ever had. It was my third piece.

With the television playing a Sunday-night offering that had yet to make me laugh, I could feel the many conversations that weren't being had spinning around the room. Here we were, the three of us. I could remember our trips to Boston for Sox games and to Orlando to visit Disney World. The time we drove to Montreal in a snowstorm to catch the Stanley Cup finals. My dad had probably spent a month's salary on those three tickets. There were hard times, but we had some good ones too. My parents were good people.

The what-ifs dangling in my mind were hard to ignore. What if I'd never connected with Shannon? Where would we be now? Or what if I'd been a better boyfriend? What if she'd never left me? What if Trey had never entered the picture? Or what if I'd accepted the breakup and moved on? What if I hadn't pressed a razor blade into my skin?

Elliot's call was another thing coloring the room gray. I was still mad at my father for telling people I was home. That was as deliberate as anything he'd ever done. My mother hadn't said another word about it, but I know she wanted me to call Elliot too. It was the one thing with which they'd find common ground. They'd both loved Elliot, and for good reason.

Still, I wasn't ready to face him after all the wrongs I'd done to him. It seemed impossible that in my former best friend's presence I wouldn't crumble into the child who'd let a broken heart take the wheel of my and my parents' lives.

"You ever going to get another dog?" my mother asked.

I thought of the picture of Penelope that my mother kept on the fridge. "Not yet. I don't know."

"She was as good as they come, wasn't she?" my dad said.

"That's for sure." I wasn't in the headspace to talk about losing Penelope on top of it all. No way they could understand how badly it still hurt inside. I could see her racing with me through the mountains as I fought hard to keep up with her on my mountain bike. She'd always been with me, always by my side. Then, nothing. What an awful truism that dogs didn't live as long as or longer than humans. I would have killed to have her still by my side.

I chased the sadness away by asking my mother about work. She soon tossed the question back to me, and I told them how my radiology machine had crashed two weeks earlier and how I'd somehow managed to prevent my clients from taking their pets to a competing veterinarian while I had the equipment repaired.

My dad abruptly raised his finger to his lips and shushed me. "I like this one."

I looked at the television and saw the same Subaru commercial I'd seen before. We all watched in silence as the actor drove hard over a ravine in the mountains of somewhere out west. Ambient music played in the background. As he bumped his Subaru across a river, an elk appeared up higher, standing in the light of the falling sun. He cut through the trees, climbing in elevation, and then skidded to a stop only inches away from the edge of the cliff. The camera showed a wide shot through the windshield at the forested valley. In time-lapse, the sun dropped, and darkness fell like a blanket.

After stepping out and taking in the stars, the man pointed his finger at the camera. "What are the stars telling you?"

Silence as he let the audience ponder an answer.

My father chuckled and said with the man, "And remember . . . the stars don't lie." He laughed again. "That's a great one, isn't it? You seen it yet, Carv?"

His words barely reached me, as I was lost in my own world, trying to remember that feeling I'd had when I used to look up at the stars— per Mrs. Cartwright's suggestion. I don't know what had led my sad seventeen-year-old self to trust Mrs. Cartwright, but I did. I'd lie in bed hurting, consumed by the shatter of Shannon leaving me and the embarrassment of a whole town knowing how badly she'd knocked me down. When the hurt would ease enough, I would pick up one of the books Mrs. Cartwright had sent home with me, authors like Aurelius, Hemingway, Dickens, Woolf. She gave me less challenging works, too, stories by Raymond Carver, John D. MacDonald, and Ian Fleming. They became such a lovely escape for me, allowing me to step into another world, if only for a while.

Then at night, as my parents slept, I'd slip down the stairs and out into the backyard to take another spoonful of Mrs. Cartwright's medicine, her suggestion to spend time looking up at the sky. I'd sometimes see my parents peering out the window, making sure I was okay. That was in the spring, and the cold air still had a bite to it. I'd lie in the grass, shivering and yet captivated by the celestial splendor that waited for me each night. The door opened even wider when I first took in the wonders of our galaxy from the vantage point of the Cartwrights' farm, where there were no lights for miles.

I recalled a passage Mrs. Cartwright had underlined in *Meditations* by Marcus Aurelius that had fueled my search both upward and inward.

"Dwell on the beauty of life. Watch the stars and see yourself running with them." I was a long way away from understanding Stoicism, but I had liked the way those words settled into me and guided me. I'd imagined myself shooting up into the heavens, joining the other stars, escaping the hell in which I was living, going to a place where what I'd done didn't matter.

Twenty years later, and the concept of finding solace in the stars felt as foolish as believing in the Easter Bunny. I was a child worn raw by life back then, and those moments outside under the stars had done no more than hypnotize me, like a second-rate hypnotist at the fair.

"Carv, you seen that commercial yet?" he asked a second time.

I broke away from my thoughts and glanced at him. "Yeah, I saw it the other night."

"That guy . . . he makes me smile. *The stars don't lie.* That's clever."

I gave a weak smile, thinking my dad had certainly lost his mind.

Chapter 9

ONE MORE DAY

The next morning at Mrs. Cartwright's house, I glanced at a Red Sox player frozen on the television screen, caught halfway through a swing. "Eloise Cartwright watching baseball," I said. "Never would I have believed it."

She set the needles and afghan blanket she'd been knitting on the table beside her, then pulled off her glasses. "I can hardly believe it myself. I used to love watching Tom play, but I'd never watched games on the television until after he passed. Here I am keeping track of the stats."

Thunder grumbled angrily in the distance. My mother and I had sneaked in a quick thirty-minute run before a storm set in, but now it was dark outside, and the rain came down steadily. With my mother at work and my father lost in the world of his Shasta, I'd gotten restless. Visiting Mrs. Cartwright felt like the only thing I could do that would make a difference while I was back.

I sat in the same spot I had before, on one end of the couch. Oscar Wilde glared at me from his perch on Mrs. Cartwright's lap. Slightly distracted by my predicament with Elliot, I'd forgotten to bring the dog carrots, and he'd taken it personally.

"Remind me, what year did Tom play for the Sox?" I asked.

"Nineteen seventy-four." Saying the year aloud appeared to catapult her back in time. She was good at sitting still, I thought, remembering it had always been that way with her, especially when she became lost in thought.

I smiled at a memory of her late husband carrying his beat-up radio with him everywhere on the farm, following the Sox like a religion. We'd often work in complete silence until his boys made a big play. He'd rarely cheered. It was more of a casual, "There you go, boys."

That was how he cheered me on too. "There you go, Carver." When he said those words in his deep, resonant voice, I could have accomplished anything. In fact, that was all I had wanted my dad to say, but he'd already given up on me. He had barely made eye contact with me, for God's sake. Was it any wonder I'd hidden at the Cartwrights'? My mom had set a good example, working her tail off while holding it together at home, trying not to lose it at my father, who was blasting holes in the hull of our family ship.

I couldn't be in that house. I hated what they had become, and getting out of their way felt like the best gift I could give them. I'd caused enough damage, as every single time I saw my father reminded me.

Willing to do anything to be near Mrs. Cartwright, Tom had accepted a job as an accountant for a local building company, but he would have been a great teacher too. They both had a way of offering advice without ever preaching, and they were the only two who could get through to me. Perhaps because they mostly listened and offered their wisdom only when I sought it.

Not that reaching me had been easy for them. I'd barely gotten through my senior year, doing little more than showing up for my tests and exams, which meant I lost my scholarships, and subsequently any hope for a big life. Miraculously holding their faith in me, the Cartwrights urged me to keep working for them through the summer. Something about being around the animals made sense to me, and it was the only thing I wanted to do. I liked that I could be surrounded by so many beating hearts without feeling a need to explain or prove myself.

What no kid considering suicide could imagine is what it was like to return to school after such an episode. Everyone was involved, from my therapist to the principal. The teachers were instructed to take it easy on me, to give me a lighter workload. The guidance counselor, Mr. Sellars, had met with a lot of the kids to discuss what I had done, making sure they knew how to behave around me. When Elliot had told me that in confidence, I'd wanted to disappear.

I hated all the babying and the attention.

The Cartwrights didn't baby me. They simply treated me like they would have any other student helping them out. Besides sharing their favorite books and helping build me back up, they taught me about animals and how to take care of the land. In doing so, they somehow got me to realize on my own that I couldn't give up—that there were reasons to keep living. My destiny of becoming a vet grew stronger by the day over there, leaving me by the end of the summer with the drive to find a way back to the top. For the first time in my life, I knew what I wanted to do with my life, and the compass I'd found was enough to keep going.

The Cartwrights' spirit had stayed with me in community college, and I'd thought of them when I'd transferred to Davidson, but I'd neglected to report back. By then I'd learned that shutting out the past was the only way to move forward. I now knew that difficult choice had been the right one, because I felt like I was already backsliding, twenty years of progress evaporating in a matter of days.

Frowning, I looked back at Mrs. Cartwright. "I'm so sorry I didn't come back home to see you guys."

"He liked you, Carver." In her eyes, I could see that I'd cracked the shell of her sadness.

I clenched my teeth, trying not to tear up. "We had some great times."

She and I chitchatted for a while, recalling some of the better days, but I was distracted by my regret for abandoning them. "Though I didn't write you back, I've often thought of you. I'll never forget all those conversations we had, the way you'd challenge me on my spiritual and philosophical beliefs. All the talks we had about finding a way to contribute and to be happy, finding a calling and putting your all into it. I did that, Mrs. Cartwright. Because of you."

She petted Oscar's back. "You hear that, Oscar? Though it may not look it, there was a time when I served a purpose."

"You're still serving a purpose," I insisted.

"Don't be so sure." She gave a laugh and stared off to the side. "My impact has long been forgotten. If I were an appliance, they'd cart me out of the house and take me to the dump."

"Oh, c'mon, when did you become so jaded?"

"There wasn't an exact moment. It slowly comes over you like a poison you ingest. First, it was Principal Corey who ran me out. Then Tom getting sick and passing away. Then saying goodbye to the farm and the animals. Dealing with moving. Now my health."

I understood. "Where are all the animals, by the way?"

"Tom and I slowly said goodbye to them as he became sicker."

I recalled how much delight Mrs. Cartwright had in all the responsibilities of keeping life moving out there, cleaning out the chicken coop, collecting eggs, trimming sheep hooves, and I felt her pain in saying goodbye to them. I wished I had something valuable to say, but how do you offer up advice to someone who is so much wiser than you? Weren't people in their seventies supposed to have it all figured out? Considering my present company and the issues between my parents, apparently not.

I did have something to say, though, and if not now, I might never get another chance. Maybe I couldn't save my parents' marriage, but I could make sure Mrs. Cartwright knew the impact she'd had on me.

"Would you allow a student to offer some advice to his teacher?" I asked gently, as if I were clipping a questionable wire of a bomb.

She clasped her fingers together. "I can't wait for this. Hit me, Dr. Livingston."

I uncrossed my legs and leaned toward her. "I don't think your work is done here. Not only with me. I will always need your help. But others do too. I just know it."

To her credit, she didn't immediately react. She sat with what I'd said for a moment. Finally, she started to say something. "Carver, I . . ." She stopped and then said, "Thanks for thinking so."

"Seriously," I said, "Maybe we can take a page from my dad's book. He seems to have found a new lease on life. I don't agree with how he plans to live it, but I appreciate that he's not giving up. What kind of example are you setting for me, all this surrender talk? I hate to break it to you, but you may live twenty more years. Thirty, even."

"If that's the case," she said, "then I'm being punished."

She'd invited me into her office to talk a few days after I'd returned to school following my hospitalization. I thought it might be about a paper I'd written on Ralph Ellison's *Invisible Man*, but when I'd sat down across from her in her office, she'd pulled off her glasses and said something I'll never forget.

"You know what you told me when you first called me into your office, after the whole thing that happened?"

She braced herself, as if she hated to hear her own advice thrown back at her. "If you say something about how it isn't over until the fat lady sings, I'll—"

"No, it wasn't that." I tried to gift her a laugh, but my body had turned rigid at the memory of those days. "I don't think I've ever heard a cliché leave your mouth. Even today, I hear a cliché and cringe, thanks to you. Like a lot of people, you asked me how I was doing, how coming back to school after my time in the hospital had been. I told you what I'd been telling everyone, that I was fine."

I fell back into her office in 1999 so deeply I could smell the Gala apple she'd eaten moments before. "You sat up in your chair and shook your head. 'No, no, no, Carver Livingston. I'm asking. I'm really asking. How are you doing?'"

I lowered my voice. "There was a silence in that office while you let me process the question. Maybe what you were doing was showing me I was safe. I didn't have a lot of that in my life. Being at my house was like stewing in a pot of guilt and shame. My friends were all treating me so differently, as if I wasn't who they'd known all along. You guys and the farm, I . . . I was okay there. You know, it's funny. I can still feel the sense of safety that came over me." I paused and then whispered, "I still feel it now."

She frowned.

I closed my eyes and dove into that safety, feeling my lost seventeen-year-old self's feelings. I could remember exactly what had been on my mind when she'd called me into her room. Not exactly *Invisible Man*, that's for sure. The opposite. I'd felt like a zoo animal ever since I'd returned to school. I'd been back at school for a week, and I could sense everyone looking at me, talking about me. They all knew.

They all knew.

They all knew.

That was the toughest part. Had I not called Shannon, then she wouldn't have told her parents and her best friend, and then my egregious mistake would have been much easier to navigate. Instead, every single person in every class, every person walking past me in the hall, they *all* knew Shannon Bigsby had cut such a deep hole into my heart that it had driven me to attempt suicide.

When Mrs. Cartwright asked me into her office that day, I'd been questioning how much longer I could keep doing this. What was the point in even trying to return to normal? The only thing holding me back from a second attempt was that I didn't want to screw up again.

Back in the present, I must have been silent for two or three minutes. I looked over at Mrs. Cartwright, finding those eyes of compassion that were still as strong as ever.

Shivers came over me as I whispered, "I feel lost." Realizing I hadn't clarified whether I was speaking about way back when or in the present, I said, "That's what I told you in your office." It hit me that I felt lost now, too, unsure how to help my parents or Mrs. Cartwright—or me, for that matter. Being back was killing me.

"'I know you do,' you said. Then you said what gave me a flicker of hope, and I don't even know why." Doing my best impersonation of her, I repeated her words. "'You should spend some time looking up toward the sky.' You told me that, with some diligence, I'd figure out what you meant. Then you gave me a book. Do you remember what it was?"

She searched her memory. "I can't recall."

"William Styron. *Darkness Visible.*"

"That's right."

I raked my fingers across the back of my head. "Everyone else was so focused on lifting me up. My mother had covered the house in flowers and bright colors. My father kept talking about sports cars, trying to distract me. My friends wouldn't dare bring up anything sad. Other than the jerks who picked on me about what I had done, the rest of the world wanted to hide all the bad out there. You came along and gave me this book and showed me it was okay to feel trapped in the darkness. I read every word, and then I read it again and again. I read all your recommendations. And when I wasn't reading, I would go outside and lie on the ground and stare up at the sky, day or night. I didn't know what you meant by your suggestion, but I trusted you because, for some reason, you were the only one who understood me."

"You found it, didn't you?"

I knew exactly what she meant and nodded, unashamed by my tears. "Yeah. I couldn't have put it into words, but I found it. A reason to live. It was still dim, the reason, but it was enough to stop pondering the other way out, like a whisper of 'everything will be okay.' Shortly after I started working for you guys, the reason became apparent. Those animals, the majesty of them, and the way you and Tom cared for them. I wanted to do that for the rest of my life."

Mrs. Cartwright's eyes widened with pride. "He was the true teacher, wasn't he? My Tom."

"One of a kind. You're both so etched into my soul." I stopped. "But . . ."

"But what?" she asked, urging me on.

I felt self-conscious. "Here I am talking about myself again. This is all I did yesterday, and I told myself this morning I wanted to make this visit about you, not me. You've done enough for me and thousands of others. I want to help you this time. You deserve a break."

She almost laughed. "Every day, by being you, Carver, you're helping. Coming to see me, that's the greatest gift you could ever give."

"It was a long time overdue." I smiled at her, glad our reconnection meant something to her, glad I'd not hidden in my parents' house.

"How much time do you spend looking up these days?" she asked. I should have asked her the same thing. Oscar looked at me as if he wanted to know too.

"Close to none," I admitted.

"The advice still stands. And make sure you're looking through the correct end of the telescope while you're doing it."

I gave her a tiny smile. "Noted."

Mrs. Cartwright adjusted her glasses. "Do you remember the words I shared from Maria Mitchell, the first female astronomer?" She perked up, her voice finding sure ground. "Mingle the starlight with your lives and you won't be fretted by trifles."

"Ah, I suppose I do remember that quote."

"What she's going after is exactly why she became an astronomer in the first place, and why I have always impressed upon you and every other one of my students the importance of lifting one's chin. It's about experiencing awe, Carver. When you can put yourself in a state of awe, you see things for what they truly are. We're lifted out of the fragile cage in which our tiny minds are often trapped."

I could hear her getting on a roll, and it pleased me. "It's so good to hear you teach again, Mrs. Cartwright."

Judging by the way the excitement left her eyes, I seemed to have knocked her back to reality. She sat back and took a breath. "Anyway, what do I know?"

"C'mon. You're one of the wisest people I've ever met." Before she could brush off the compliment, I asked, "Why did you help me? I mean . . . I know you care about your students, and teaching is in your blood, but why me? I never knew that. Why did you take me on? I certainly wasn't the only one struggling."

She sat back in her chair, clearly considering my question. "I'd been there, Carver."

"What? You?"

"You didn't think I was without problems, did you?"

I raised my eyebrows. "Maybe."

"I'm no stranger to the darkness. Let's leave it at that."

This woman blew me away. Talk about safe. I felt so safe with her in that moment, as if everything was going to be okay, as if maybe I didn't have to keep beating myself up for what I'd done: causing my parents so much distress and running from everyone in my life.

"I could have used your friendship over the years," I said. "It's so nice talking to you again."

"I did have some good things to say back then. Seems so long ago."

"You don't think you're running out of words, do you?" I asked.

She thought about it. "I'm a fading light now, Carver."

"I don't believe that. Not about you."

We swayed into lighter topics for a while, but then Elliot's name came up. When I told her he had called me, I knew I was in trouble.

"I haven't seen him in a few months," she said. "How is he?"

"I . . . I don't know. I didn't answer."

She furrowed her brow but stopped herself before saying something.

"What?"

"I don't—"

"Please," I said. "I welcome some advice. Well, your advice. My father's, less so."

She sat up and I could see she was in pain.

"Are you okay?" I asked.

She brushed it off. "It's the same advice I gave you twenty years ago, Carver. You need to spend some time looking up at the sky."

I gave the weakest laugh in history. "I need to do a lot of things."

"Seriously," she said, "if we're sharing advice, let me have my say."

"Here it comes." I braced myself. Mrs. Cartwright had never been one to hold back.

She rolled her lips together. "Allowing yourself to be absorbed by the largeness of what's out there will put you in a different state of mind." She smiled and raised her eyes to the ceiling. "It's nothing short of magic, my dear boy."

She rested her hands on Oscar's back. "You've done a lot of good. Maybe the most successful man I know, and I've followed all my students. Certainly the richest. I think what you've done is great, becoming a vet. Giving back. But I still see a part of you that trudged into my office that day. The part that . . . needs to lighten up and not take yourself so seriously. Quit trying to prove to yourself and everyone else that you matter. You're still living like the entire world is judging you . . . waiting for you to fail."

There was no stopping her now. "So you attempted to take your life, and the whole town found out. If we all had to wear cards showing a list of our missteps, we'd be less judgmental. You don't have to explain yourself to anyone else. Everyone involved during that time in your life surely understands that you regret what happened and are grateful you're still alive."

Dammit if she couldn't get right to the core of things.

My heart rattled. "Maybe I have some baggage that still needs unpacking." It sounded so cliché when I said it. I was sidestepping her words. Backing up, I said, "If that day gave me the motivation to push myself, then maybe that isn't such a bad thing. Me not wanting to come home, why does that matter either? I've done well for myself. When I'm in Asheville, I don't think about the past."

"What's wrong with thinking about the past? Do you think it's healthier to bury it?"

"I think there's no one way when it comes to dealing with pain."

"Fair enough," she acquiesced. "But I don't think you need the memory of that day to keep pushing yourself," she said. "It can come from a better place. All the motivation you need is in the joy of realizing your full potential."

Slightly skeptical, I asked, "How do I find that place?"

Once again, she repeated, "Spend some time looking toward the sky."

Though I found none of this funny, I chuckled. "Because the stars don't lie." I said it in the same way the narrator did in the commercial.

Mrs. Cartwright smiled. "That's right. The stars don't lie."

The Subaru climbed a rocky grade in my mind's eye, chipping away at my desire to avoid this intimate conversation. "That commercial is haunting me right now."

"Isn't it funny how that works?" she asked.

My lack of a reply said more than anything else.

Oscar woke and hopped down off her lap. He found a bone and began to gnaw at it.

She picked off the fur he had shed from her lap as she said, "We're all carbon and water, Carver. A peek up high will settle that idea into your soul. Think of what Richard Carlson said. 'Don't sweat the small stuff . . . and it's all small stuff.'"

Oh, I remembered that book. My father kept it on the back of the toilet. All the fairy-tale talk was making it a little mushy in the room, and I decided we'd better slow down. "So . . . ," I started.

Mrs. Cartwright held up a finger. "One last thing before we abandon our talk. Don't you dare get on that plane without calling Elliot."

I wished she hadn't said that, and I offered my best reply. "I'll . . . I'll think on it."

That seemed to satisfy her.

Chapter 10

The Sanderton

Mrs. Cartwright's advice always lingered, like a melody from a nineties band you can't unhear. It was that way back when, and it was that way now. I was out of Teterbury in no time, and then it could all be left in the past, but I knew I had no choice now.

Walking through the light rain back to my parents' house, I drew in a sharp breath and finally returned Elliot's call.

"The rumors are true," he said.

Hearing his voice gave rise to a maelstrom of emotions. The most harmless guy in the world unknowingly launching an attack by simply answering the phone, reminding me of how piss-poor a friend I'd been, firing up guilt that lingered in my body like cancer in remission.

"The rumors are indeed true," I said.

"For a minute, I thought you might come in and out without saying anything."

Even after all these years, he knew me well. "Man, I'm sorry. I was going to call. I just . . ." What was I supposed to say?

He came in and rescued me. "I get it. No need to explain. I was happy to hear you were in town. It got me thinking about the good old days, the trouble we used to make."

"Yeah, I've had a few of those memories since I've been back." Along with the shame I felt in wronging him so many times, his voice did ignite some lovely feelings of what it had been like to have a best friend, someone who was always there for you. I recalled how cool he thought I was, despite my not being cool at all. That was probably why I was so attracted to him in the first place. From the first day we'd met, he looked up to me and made me feel like I mattered, that my thoughts mattered. We could throw a ball or play by the river or in the snow and talk for hours without running out of words. He even taught me how to be a friend in return, though I'd certainly forgotten what I'd learned the moment I'd met Shannon.

Before overthinking it any longer, I said, "We should catch up." The words nearly caught in my throat.

He apparently didn't realize how big a step I'd taken. "Yeah, for sure," he said casually. "How long are you in town?"

"I'm leaving Wednesday." As I said it, I hoped desperately that he would be busy and respond with, "We'll have to catch up next time." Whether burying the past was healthy, I certainly wasn't interested in excavating more of it now, and even having this conversation felt like the beginning of a painful archaeological dig into my psyche.

"We need to make something happen. Let's go get a beer."

His innocent suggestion was a kick in the ribs. "Not sure if I have time for that," I said. "I was thinking you could come by."

He laughed, like this was all a big joke to him. "Oh, c'mon. There's a new place called the Sanderton that I keep wanting to try. A beer . . . or two. You gotta see what this town has become."

There wasn't *one* effing excuse I could have offered Elliot without sounding like a complete jerk, and I'd done enough of that already.

Painted into a corner with no escape hatch in view, I said, "All right, let's do it."

"Perfect. We can catch up then."

I tried to pump my voice with enthusiasm. "Yeah, great. Can't wait."

Can't wait, I thought. I would show up for a speedy drink and then make my way toward the exit.

It took me all afternoon to gear myself up. I'd faced the fact that bailing on Elliot would solidify me as the biggest asshole to ever have come from Teterbury. Though I had no intention of returning, I far preferred that people in Teterbury look at me as someone they were proud to claim as their own, a man who'd gone on to be someone special.

Typically I loved a challenge. If you told me there was no better way to deal with a canine's cranial cruciate injury, I'd prove you wrong. If you told me a bird would never fly again, I found a way. If you brought me a cat nearing the end of its ninth life, I'd squeeze another one out of it. But put me in this type of situation, and I was a complete disaster.

It didn't help that my parents watched me get ready to leave the house, both wishing me luck in their own way, as if I were a shut-in. Need I remind them I was a doctor?

My mother placed her hands on my upper arms and met my eyes. "Go get 'em." It had been like I was about to step onto the tennis court to face my rival.

My dad, who was out by the fire, shared with me some of his classic advice. "Remember, Carv, everyone is too occupied with thinking about themselves to spend time thinking about you." He finished with, "I'm proud of you, kid." I felt him watching me all the way down the block until I disappeared, and I appreciated the pride that rose out of him.

When I walked by Mrs. Cartwright's house, I saw her through the window, sitting in her chair. Lights flashed from the television, probably watching more baseball. I said quietly, "This is all your fault."

Her voice popped in my head. *Look up at the sky.*

"Oh, what the hell," I said. I stopped right there on the sidewalk out in front of her house and lifted my gaze upward. The sun had dropped below the mountaintop, casting a fiery glow across the horizon. The dissipating gray clouds revealed a dense purple sky. I drew in a deep, deep breath, soaking up the post-rain air and attempting to take in the view: the colors, the vastness, the magic I'd once seen.

What had affected me so much when I'd first taken her advice? I could vaguely feel that sense of awe, of the bigger expanse taking me in with open arms. Those feelings felt as far away as remembering what it was like to be in love. Lowering my head, I chuckled at the ignorance of youth. Some of Mrs. Cartwright's lessons were better suited for teenagers and romantics.

Crossing the bridge with heavy legs, I tried to toss the shame into the rushing river that wound around the large rocks as it worked its way west to Lake Champlain. I tried desperately to appreciate the pastel colors that reflected off the water. I listened hard to the glorious and unparalleled New England birdsong, melodies so dazzling that as a young boy, I could get lost in them for hours as I lay by the shore, daydreaming with the clouds floating by. But I couldn't let go of the feeling of dread.

Dr. Carver Livingston, reduced to a fragile shell of himself—the senior who sat in the back of the classroom so no one could talk behind his back, the kid who endlessly stewed over his decision to cut himself . . . over a girl, for God's sake. No, I didn't want Elliot to see any of that boy. I wanted him to see the man I'd become.

In a perfect world, I would slide into the booth, say hello, and then move on as if we'd hung out only the day before. With that hope in my heart, I passed the first of what must have been a hundred new breweries in this town, only to be outdone by the art galleries and antique stores. Back in the late nineties, this place was a ghost town on Monday nights. That had certainly changed. Stylishly dressed people were gathered everywhere, and I could see what my parents had told me was true: Teterbury had become a destination. Who would have ever believed it?

There was something about old towns like Teterbury in New England, a rugged charm that had been waiting for the right minds to bring them to life. Having been renovated, the buildings oozed character. I noticed a fermented foods shop, a haberdashery, and a lively spot called Pottery and Wine—places that never could have survived the nineties. The Wayfair Hotel, where the reunion would take place a week from Saturday, stood on the other end of Main Street next to Advent Episcopal, which featured a steeple that rose above the town. That was where both my parents and Elliot and his wife had married, the latter being the one I dodged with a bald-faced lie.

Hopefully I'd make a good impression tonight, make peace with my old friend, and if people asked about me at the reunion, he'd say, "You just missed him. He was in town last week but had to get back for work. You read about him in the paper, right? He's busy crushing."

Crushing.

The neon-yellow sign of the Sanderton caught my attention. Strings of lights framed the sparkly windows that revealed a crowded bar, the likes of which terrified me. Shutting out my hesitation, I climbed the steps and pulled open the door. The speakers blasted the blues, a guitarist digging in deep with the drummer. Apparently people had been here since the beginning of happy hour, and the booze was working on them. Laughter and cheers and the sounds of people talking over one another bounced off the walls. I smelled the sweet tang of barbecue as a server passed by with a tray full of pulled pork sandwiches and creamy mac and cheese, reminding me of a place I frequented back home in Asheville.

Nerves firing, I scanned the room, not sure what I was looking for. I didn't even know if Elliot still had hair on his head, it had been so long. Nevertheless, I searched for familiar faces at the bar.

"Carver!"

The voice scared me, mostly because it did so well to cut through the noise, but also because it behaved like a big wooden spoon stirring the cauldron of my demons. I turned and saw my old best friend waving me down. His face softened me, reminding me of the good parts of the nineties, all the times he'd come over to my house to hang with my what-used-to-be-normal family. He'd even come with us to Disney World one year, and my parents had let us have the adjoining room. That might have been the most fun he and I had ever had.

"Look at you," I said, having fought through the crowd and wrapped my arms around his compact frame.

"And you," he said, letting go of me. "You got better looking, didn't you? Damn you." He looked a lot like his younger self, though now he wore glasses and a well-trimmed beard. He still parted his light-brown hair in the same spot on the right. Way back when, he dressed like a keyboardist for an eighties punk band, very much into making statements with funky attire, unafraid to don pink pants and white shoes at the same time. Noticing the pink socks beneath the hem of his khakis, I thought he seemed more dad-like now—more buttoned up. I imagined him with his colorful socks drinking dad beers around the grill as his boys jumped on the trampoline.

"What are you doing now?" I asked, not knowing where to even begin with a best friend lost to the storm of life. "Where do we even start after so long?"

"Still in software," he answered, smiling widely. He seemed genuinely happy to see me, and it was nice to think he hadn't held my disappearance against me. By the way he carried himself, he was living a good life. What had my dad been talking about, that I needed to go see him? A man couldn't have faked a smile like that.

Fighting over the volume, we caught up for a minute or two, and each second eased me. This wasn't so bad after all. To think I'd put so much worry into our reunion. Then he motioned for me to follow him to the back of the place. We passed a pool table where some younger guys were highly focused on a game like they had money on it. Beyond that, a thick wooden table offered a view out the back window to the terrace.

Familiar heads swiveled my way as Elliot said, "Look who I found."

Nineteen ninety-nine came at me like a fanged beast as I set my eyes on the faces of the past. There before me members of our old crew filled the table.

"I didn't realize . . ." The adrenaline racing through me made it hard to talk.

Elliot threw his arm around me. "I figured I'd get the gang back together."

"Yeah," I said with over-the-top excitement. "God, it's good to see everyone." If I wasn't careful, my knees were going to give way.

As I focused in on the faces staring me down, I saw Dali first. His real name was Aaron Dalio, but we'd turned it to Dali when he moved down from Burlington in middle school. It was the kind of nickname that would stick forever. Dali was the frat type through and through. He'd had shaggy hair in high school like the rest of us and still had it. Notably, he'd been the one to first bring a beer bong to a party, and he'd inevitably be the first one to shuck his clothes and jump into the river in the early mornings after those wild nights, even when in the clutches of the bitterly cold Vermont Januarys and Februarys. As I smiled at him, taking in his shaggy hair and wild eyes and slightly larger physique than what I'd remembered, I couldn't help but think he was probably still the exact same way, for better or worse.

Then there was Carlisle. He and I used to fight over girls, and he was especially shocked when he saw me for the first time with Shannon. I remember thinking I'd officially won for good.

Next to him sat Cassie. Her parents were big hippies who probably still lived in the same little cabin out west of town. We'd always joked that she and her family ate squirrels and bathed in the river. She was pretty good about taking the jokes and letting them brush by her. She hated the name Cassie, though, because she'd always been a few pounds overweight. One time someone had called her Mama Cass, and that single comment had broken her self-esteem for a while. What I recalled best about Cassie was that the girl could make you laugh harder than anyone else.

After going through and hugging everyone, I introduced myself to the one person I didn't recognize. Dale was apparently the newbie in our old posse of misfits, and Elliot was quick to say they'd upgraded from me. I made a dumb joke about how the bar wasn't set too high, and it landed flat due to my weak delivery.

I sat at the edge of the table, all eyes on me, and the edges of my anxiety flared. How could Elliot have done this to me? Had he no idea that such an ambush would be disastrous?

The excitement of my arrival died down, and the group waited for me to speak. We were a good bit away from the speakers playing the blues, and the quiet unnerved me. I dug my nails into my jeans, quickly getting the gist of how a guilty suspect feels when a sharp detective sits across from him. How could I possibly fool these guys?

For a second there I about confessed. How easy it might have been to say, *Guys, this is hard for me. Forgive me, but the anxiety is strong. I am still affected by what happened, and that's why I haven't been back—as if you don't know that. Bear with me.* That would have admitted defeat, though, and I'd spent the last twenty years winning. *Defeat* wasn't a word I allowed in my vocabulary. I told myself to toughen up. This was my moment to show them the man I'd become.

Cassie broke the silence by saying something about Asheville, and I jumped into the conversation, hoping to God my voice didn't come out as shaky as my emotions. Had she asked a question? I had no idea, but I treated it like she had. "Yeah, Asheville. After a stint in Raleigh, where I worked with a vet who was one of the best on the East Coast. He's who got me into looking at knees, you know, studying ways to fix them." Though my voice was shaky, I could also hear myself the way I am at cocktail parties, giving out my spiel in rote.

"Well, you're just the bee's knees, aren't you?" Elliot said, letting his humor show itself. "You know, knees and bees."

Everyone laughed . . . but me.

"Knees," Cassie said. "Isn't that a weird word?" She said *knees* five more times, and I wondered if she was trying to help lighten the situation for me. Or perhaps she'd already had a few beers.

My half smile was so cold and forced that I could have cracked the glass of the IPA in front of me. I went for a sip of it, and it dribbled down my chin. I felt my face redden as I wiped the beer off while they continued to look at me.

"How about your love life?" Cassie asked. Like Elliot, she'd always been so chill, probably because her parents were about as down to earth as one could get, and she always asked questions that were backed up by authentic care. "Who is the lucky girl that's enjoying you?"

Everyone laughed again while I wondered what shade of red my face had turned this time. Off behind me someone racked the pool balls, and then I heard the cue ball smack into them. I let it serve as a wake-up call.

"Love life," I said, trying to bring my brain back on track. "No love life to speak of." I thought of Erica, the last girl I'd dated—albeit only a few weeks. She'd told me it wasn't working, that I wasn't the dating type. I heard that as a compliment.

"How in the world are you not dating anyone?" Elliot asked. "They don't like rich Yankees down there?"

"I'm still waiting for the one," I said, feeling like the star of a Hallmark movie who'd recently returned home.

"You've been waiting for the one since you were ten years old," Cassie said.

Elliot followed her with, "Yeah, that's why Shannon cut so deep."

When he said that, I felt like the place had gone quiet. I set my eyes on the frosty glass in front of me and tried to find comfort in the brewery's logo. Then I sensed the staring. Not only from my table but from everyone within earshot. No, more than that, the whole town, thousands of eyes staring at me, trying to see the real me, wanting to know if my senior year still defined me.

"I'm so sorry," Elliot whispered. "You know I didn't mean it like that."

I think Cassie was trying to put out the fire by what she said next, but it worked in the opposite way. "Did you see her up behind the bar?"

I knew Cassie was talking to me. I lifted my face to answer her. "Who?" Of course I knew—and that scared the shit out of me.

"Shannon, dummy."

"Shannon's here?" I asked. Had there been an eject button, I would have pushed it. I looked at Elliot, wondering what he'd done to me. The last time I'd seen her was our high school graduation. Sitting beside Trey, she'd glanced at me. I'd quickly looked away and faked a laugh, as if I barely recalled her dumping me. Of course, I'd skipped the party that night and hid at the Cartwrights' for the rest of the summer before getting the hell out of Vermont.

He shrugged. "I had no idea she worked here."

"Behind the bar," Cassie clarified.

I screamed obscenities in my mind while pasting on my face the most casual smile I could, showing everyone that it was no big deal, that it was a long time ago. Through the chaos of the crowd, I thought I saw a flash of her blonde hair. This was the woman I had pictured myself marrying, my soulmate.

"You heard she divorced, right?" Carlisle asked.

I wanted to stand up and run, as I worried there would be no way to keep up this facade with her in the picture, but that would have made things even worse. I could hear people talking about me at the coming reunion: *Yeah, he up and bolted out the door when we told him Shannon was there. We never saw him again. He was at the Burlington Airport before the bill hit the table.*

"This just got interesting," Dali said, grabbing a potato chip and tossing it into his mouth like a moviegoer does with popcorn during a heated scene.

I gave a laugh, if it could be called that. More like a mouth fart.

Thank goodness the server appeared to take our order. I'm not sure there was any better gift in the world, my chance to pick up the big menu in front of me and hide behind it, as the others tossed in their orders. For the next three minutes my brain did this: *Wings? Hot, not too hot. Shannon is at the bar. No, not wings. Salad. Yeah, probably a salad. But then I won't have anything to soak up the beer, and I have a feeling the beers will flow tonight. Shannon. God, I don't want to see her. But I kind of do. I can't believe she divorced Trey. Appetizers, no. Salad, no. Burger. Ugh. I'll be dragging all night. Ah, no. Shannon. Dammit, get out of my mind.*

"For you?" the server asked, clicking his tongue ring between his teeth.

"Let's do the burger, no onion. Salad with whatever vinaigrette you have. No fries."

I looked back at my friends, wanting . . . no, *needing* them to see the man I'd become. When the server stepped away, I asked, "What's going on with you guys?"

As usual, it was Dali who spoke first. He was the guy who always picked up the conversation in the uncomfortable silence. "Let's see. Cassie's probably pregnant again. What's this, six now? I'm married to a supermodel and looking at becoming an astronaut. But NASA wants me to train over Christmas, and I'm not leaving the supermodel. She loves playing Mrs. Claus."

Dali always had a way of lightening me up, and tonight was no exception. The weight fell off me like a dog shaking water off his fur. "And Elliot?" I said, feeling like I was back in high school.

"Elliot," Dali said, taking a look over at our friend. "Journey asked him to be their new front man. They want him in for a second audition. But he's torn because his kids want him to be Scout leader." Dali raised his hands. "Journey or Scout leader. It's a tough call."

"Who says I can't do both?" Elliot joked.

Everyone at the table was laughing when Cassie whispered, "There she is."

I turned, and yep, there Shannon Bigsby was, working her way through the bar patrons toward the kitchen. No big deal, just the only person I'd ever loved romantically, the girl I had been so sure would be by my side forever.

Her beauty came at me like a tsunami. That hair, something about her long blonde hair. I wasn't even a hair person, was I? Not until I'd met her. It wasn't only the hair. Her profile showed she was still as jaw dropping as she'd ever been, hadn't aged much at all. She wore jeans and a revealing white shirt, and she moved with the same grace that I remembered, confident she was the prettiest girl in the room.

The others at the table were talking to me, but I wasn't listening. I could feel myself lifting out of the chair, a part of me wanting to go to her. Trying to get out of there without an encounter would be far worse.

The noises of the restaurant were still there, the clink of glasses, the hollering from the game on the television, the crack of the pool balls. The smells were there, too: roasted meat and hops and fried food. It was all faint, though, as I put my focus on Shannon's back, like she was a Russian MiG fighter jet I was trying to get into missile lock. I wanted nothing more than to get her attention and fall into an easy conversation, showing her I was a different man than back then.

She spoke through the window to someone in the kitchen, something about a problem with an allergy. I waited for her to finish, noticing she had some sass to her, giving the kitchen a talking-to. When she turned, she was shaking her head, and I quickly noticed that it was not the right time to interrupt her—she was pissed—but it was too late now.

"Hey, Shannon, is that you?" I was playing it like I'd been passing by and only just recognized her. I said to myself, *Take the upper hand.*

She looked at me, bounced her eyes up to my forehead and then down to my boots, as if she were making sure it was indeed me. "Well, look at you."

"Yeah."

I enjoyed one second of elation, but then my body turned on me. "I . . ." I started to speak but sounded like a dolphin instead: "I, I, I, I, I."

Shannon smiled, no doubt enjoying the reveal of my humanity. "You're back?"

Still in dolphin mode, I nodded like I was trying to fling a beach ball up in the air. "For a minute. You work here?"

This conversation was going nowhere. An exchange of the two most pointless questions in history.

She looked around, showing what I read as shame, as if she didn't want to be working here. "Yeah, as of a few weeks ago." She started to say something and then stopped herself. "Long story."

"I bet." *I bet.* Had I really said that?

More silence followed. Had I a pause button, I would have frozen the scene and taken myself outside for a good slap across the face. I'd been thinking about Shannon for years, and though I never thought we'd see each other again, I'd sort of been training for this moment. I could see the headline in the next article about me in the *Teterbury Times*: Dr. Livingston Blows It Again.

"You look great," I finally got out with a constricted throat.

"Thanks. You too."

Giving us both an out, I said speedily, "I know you're busy. I'm leaving in a couple of days and wanted to say hi. I hope you're well."

"Yeah, you too, Carver." She looked like she wanted to say more but didn't. That was what the entire exchange felt like, so much to say but none of it coming out.

I couldn't take another millisecond and took my retreat. Refusing to look back, I held my head high like my father had tried to teach me after my suicide attempt. I returned to the table with my mind reeling with regret and disappointment.

My friends looked at me like they couldn't wait to hear how it went. I smiled and tried to fake victory, praying inside they hadn't seen the truth of the moment.

Chapter 11

A String of Goodbyes

"Just like the old days," I said to Elliot as I navigated the steep dip that led down to the shore of the river. The underbelly of the iron bridge loomed overhead, haunted in the heavy mist. Over the steady whoosh of the water passing by came the calls of countless crickets and katydids sawing the music of the night on their wings.

I was in a strange place emotionally, stuck between the regret of screwing up my encounter with Shannon but also excited to be retracing the footsteps of my youth, reminded of our band of misfits crossing this bridge with our arms around one another, fearless because we didn't know any better.

"Just don't take a spill," he said, following behind me. "We break a little easier these days."

"Isn't that the truth." We'd both kicked off our shoes and rolled up our pants. Aside from twenty years gone by, it all felt the same. I'd even caught myself laughing some, and it was so nice to recall that it wasn't all darkness that had filled my childhood.

No, my times with Elliot were some of the best of my life. What in the world would have happened had he not moved to town? I was seven when I saw this strange boy swinging a lacrosse stick in the front yard of a recently purchased house. My mom pushed me off our lawn and forced me to go introduce myself. He was a shy kid, sad from being torn away from his friends in Buffalo, and I think I gave him hope for his new hometown when I said, "Hey, I'm Carver. What's your name?"

Like we'd known each other for years, we played that entire afternoon, then the next day, and the next day after that. It was on from there, two boys who together sought to find their place in the world. We put on ice skates together for the first time; we built our first forts, lit our first fires.

I jumped down to a small patch of beach peppered with river rocks and headed toward the boulders where we used to sit. All this time, and the same three were there, as if they waited for our return.

I took a seat and looked past the bridge to the half-moon, which projected a white light over the night sky. The beer and tequila shots had done a good job of loosening me up, and I found myself absorbed by the vastness of the universe in which we lived. How many best friends were reconnecting tonight? How many people sat on a rock by a river gazing up in search of something? How many people had run into their lost loves?

Elliot plonked down on the boulder next to me and slapped my back. "Though it may hurt tomorrow, a night like this is good for the soul."

"Yeah," I whispered. "It is, isn't it?" I sort of knew what he meant, to let loose, to feel young again. What a shame I hadn't thought of Elliot and me walking to school together, our big backpacks weighing us down as we figured out the universe, tossing out our first curse words, figuring out the details of reproduction, coming into puberty and talking more about girls than baseball and hockey.

"You know those time-lapse pictures?" Elliot asked. "Where they take a picture at the same spot every year? I'd love to see us over the years, sitting on these rocks."

"I would, too, buddy." I lowered my head, giving up on whatever spell I'd been under. My mind conjured up a series of such photos, and I saw what could have been had the two of us continued to be friends—our lives unfolding together, our families growing together. I had a lot of things in my life, but a good friend was not one of them.

"What was it like to see Shannon again?" Elliot asked. "I didn't mean to set you up like that. I mean, I did with the gang—I thought it would be fun—but I didn't know she'd be there."

"I know you didn't. Besides, I had to see her eventually."

How could I be upset with him? I could count on my fingers how many times I'd been mad at him, and it had been mostly over superficial stuff, like the time he said I'd been the one to throw the baseball through the Adleys' window, that kind of thing.

To answer his question, I said, "I feel like the last time we sat on these rocks, we were talking about her."

"That's possible," he said.

It would have been long after my suicide attempt in November, probably close to graduation. As he always did, Elliot had forgiven me for disappearing once I'd met Shannon, shaking him off like a dead limb on a tree. I was sure I had been going on and on about how something was wrong with the universe, how she and I were meant to be together, and how it was so fucked up she didn't see it. After all the dwelling on why she'd left me I was already concluding that I hadn't been worthy of such an angelic creature. Yes, I might have had superb grades and the fastest legs on the track team, but I was still a geek. Sitting on the rocks then, Elliot had probably told me not to give up, that we were young, and you never knew what could happen with our love lives. Maybe she'd come back to me one day.

"I'm sorry about what I said earlier, the cutting-so-deep thing," he said.

"Forget about it," I replied. I picked up a smooth pebble and skipped it along the river. It made it about halfway before breaking through the surface in a patch of white water.

"I'm sorry about a lot of things. Thinking I was too good for you after Shannon and I started dating, not putting any effort into staying in touch, skipping your wedding. How about we call it even?"

He sifted through the pebbles below him. "I feel like I'm getting the short end of the deal, but I'll take it."

"Seriously," I said. "I'm sorry for missing your wedding. I had so much going on, and—"

"Really, Carv," he interrupted. "I get it." He found a pebble to his liking and skipped it across the water.

I didn't want to stop apologizing, but I knew that he did get it. That was why I loved him. Changing topics, I asked, "Didn't you want to be a lawyer?"

"I guess I did, didn't I?" He shook his head. "I'm sure it sounds so boring to you, my whole life. I could spend ten minutes right now telling you what I do, and you'd walk away still wondering."

"C'mon. Try me."

He shrugged. "Let's just say it's software training and leave it at that. I don't want you dozing off on that rock."

I was truly curious. "And what is the software? Wow, when did you get so cryptic? Is this CIA stuff?" I stared him up and down. "You look like CIA, come to think of it, with your unassuming dad look."

He rewarded my poor joke with a smile. "Nah, it feels so small compared to what you're doing."

I felt like a jerk. "What's the software?"

He skipped another rock, and we watched it dance on the surface until it stopped. "You really want to know?"

"Of course I do."

"You asked for it," he said. "We do data analysis for insurance companies. I run a small team who walks our clients through our software, helping them determine accurate premiums, that kind of thing."

"It sounds important."

"It's not. But you know what? I love it. I mean, it's work, but it's enjoyable work. I like who I work with. The pay is good. Great benefits. I'm done at four every day, right after my boys get home. The best part is I don't have to take it with me. When I leave the office, I leave every work thought at the door. I cook three nights a week. Coach my boys in Little League."

He pressed his hands down on the rock and sat up excitedly. "You should come. We've got playoffs coming up this weekend. We're terrible, but I don't know if there's anything better in the entire world than watching your child step up to the plate. These guys are eight! Eight. Remember that, Carv? Trying to figure out what pitch to hit? Remember how wild the pitches were?"

"Oh, I do." I recalled the Little League of our youth with a chuckle. I could hear my team chanting as I stepped up to the plate, *Car-ver, Car-ver* . . .

"It's a shit show out there," Elliot said, obviously being swept away by the joy of it.

"Philip is catcher, and like all of them, he can't throw far enough to get to second base. So the base stealing is rampant. Jared plays right field, where no one ever hits. He sits out there and picks his nose. It's the *Bad News Bears* all over again."

The happiness beaming out of him took me aback. I had no choice but to smile. "You'll have to send me a video."

"Yeah, I will."

His enthusiasm for life was infectious, and I felt a late-night second wind coming over me. My work hadn't allowed me to nurture such a friendship, and it was obvious tonight how much I'd missed.

"Tell me about Alice," I said, feeling a sense of melancholy coming over me at the realization I'd not ever met his boys or his wife.

He hopped off the rock and walked ankle deep into the river, causing a ripple in the flow. "You wouldn't remember her, but she's from here. Just younger."

"How much younger?" I asked.

"Six years."

I let my jaw drop. "You dog."

"She's something, Carv."

"Tell me about her."

He lowered down and splashed water onto his face, hollering as the cold hit him. "Man, that's nice."

I was so mesmerized by his joy. Where could I get some of that?

He turned to me with river water dripping down his face. "Best mom in the world. I know all dads probably say it, but it's true. She makes everything seem okay, you know. I wake up and look over at her and feel like I've already made it. Like there's nothing else I ever need. I could lie in bed all day looking at her. Until my boys come running in, of course. She's taught me to be a better father, a better man. Things are . . . I don't know. I feel lucky."

He kissed his hand and held it up to the sky. "Incredibly lucky."

I smiled again and realized my facial muscles were getting a workout tonight. I ached to have more of him in my life, more of this way of living, the beautiful simplicity of it. What would it be like to not feel this constant need inside to prove myself? What would it be like to stop chasing?

When he returned to his seat, I said, "I'm so confused. My dad seemed to think you were having issues. He kept telling me I needed to call you."

"Nah," he said. "Everything is good. I mean, I'm not selling patents and shopping for airplanes, but I'm happy."

His happy was so different from my happy, his seemingly so much more real. No matter what I did, it was never enough, but I found joy in going after the next big thing anyway, occasionally experiencing what was most often a fleeting happiness. My mom was the same way. Of course that was where I'd gotten it from, the need to keep moving.

Elliot's happiness apparently existed without any attachments, as if he didn't need to do a thing and would still have a smile plastered on his face. I envied it, his contentment with his current situation. How nice it would be to know that feeling.

I stood from the rock and put my hand on his shoulder. "What if I told you I want what you have? And I'm not sure I knew it until now." Talk about honesty. That was exactly how I felt. Forget the patent and my ambitions involving work. I wanted to know what it felt like inside Elliot's skin—if only for a little while.

He smiled at me. "I want it for you too."

⌒

My condition in the morning reminded me why I'd given up late nights long ago. I rubbed my eyes and sat up, reaching for my phone. It was nine a.m. A slew of work thoughts cascaded over me as I peered groggily at my emails.

Then it hit me: my father was leaving tomorrow. Not for the first time, I wondered how I could possibly leave my mother on the same day.

I called Mary Beth to check in. Though I could tell a few things needed my attention, she told me not to worry and that I should put all my focus on family. I was too worn out to argue, so I let her off the phone without pressing.

Peeking out the window, I saw that my mom had already left for work. My father was out there shirtless and in jean cutoffs, washing the Shasta, prepping for his voyage. It looked like he was whistling as he dipped his rag into a bucket of soapy water and then spread it across the side. He and I used to do that sort of thing together, washing the cars, working in the yard. He hadn't been that bad a father, had he? Maybe a little distracted. But he worked hard and taught me right from wrong, annoyingly so. It was just that he'd never forgiven me for going to North Carolina. I could hear it in his voice on the phone, even when I told him I'd gotten into Davidson. His lack of enthusiasm hurt as much as anything.

"That's a long way away, isn't it?" my father had said when I had told him in early August I planned on attending Wake Tech Community College and then would fight my way into a better school.

The way he'd asked set the tone for the next twenty years. I remembered driving back home from the farm to tell them, fresh off the high of delivering that foal with Mrs. C, that I'd figured out what I wanted to do with the rest of my life. I'd assumed they'd be on top of the world, hearing the good news, knowing their son had bounced back. But they'd both seemed distracted, as if they didn't believe me or didn't care. Or maybe it had been too late. Maybe the damage had been done.

Accepting I was the cause, the only thing I had known to do was leave.

Not ready to speak to him, I knocked back a cup of coffee and unboxed and set up the Roomba. When I was done, I finally went out there. He held a terry cloth in his hand and wiped away the beads of water from the trailer. I was in no mood to appreciate the sparkle he'd put on her, but I could see the appeal of this new life he'd fallen into. I could understand the people who'd joined this community of vintage-Shasta-loving wanderers, including my father. I could still remember that feeling I had of driving away from it all—me and my beat-up Jeep, setting out on an adventure.

When he turned to me, I could see the excitement in his eyes, which saddened me, because he was doing all this at my mother's expense.

"What a day, huh?"

I glanced up for a second, noting the pure blue sky but more bothered by the sun in my eyes than anything else. "Yeah," I muttered.

"How was last night?" he asked.

Already charged, I wasn't about to give him the reward of telling him how nice it was to see Elliot and the rest of my buddies. "Pretty good," I said. "Elliot's fine, by the way. I don't know why you led me to think otherwise."

He cast a look upward. "I don't think I did. I wanted you to see him. He's in a good place, isn't he?"

My father had tricked me—a devious effort to teach me a lesson. What was it? That I should settle down and have children? That ambition bred disaster? That coming home was the only way? Considering he was leaving the next day, he was certainly not teaching me the latter.

Moving along, I said with some excitement, "The Roomba is charging. I just need to hook it up to Mom's phone. Want to come see how it works?"

He deflated me with, "Nah, you know me and technology. I'm best staying away."

An invisible wall kept us from loving each other, kept us from the relationship we'd had for so many years. I could remember so clearly the dad he'd once been, times like when he first taught me to cut the grass, how to be safe with the blade and create perfect lines. Or when we'd listen to Willie as we raked and bagged the fall leaves.

"You okay, Dad?" I asked. "Seriously. I won't see you for a while. You're not sick, are you?"

He tossed the terry cloth into the bucket. "I'm great. Never been healthier."

"All right." And like back in the old days, I said, "I'm going to go visit with Mrs. Cartwright. Be back shortly."

~

I caught my former teacher right in the middle of cooking spaghetti. She'd put Oscar in his kennel to keep him out of trouble. The smell of tomatoes hit me as she led me into her modest kitchen and offered me a cup of tea. Green-and-white-striped wallpaper covered the walls. A candy wrapper lay on the top of a large stack of dishes in the sink.

"I prep a bunch of single servings and freeze them in Tupperware," she said, walking toward the stove. "Makes life much easier."

I expected to see a butcher block covered with fresh vegetables. It wasn't that way at all, though. Next to the stove stood two empty jars of spaghetti sauce. The old Mrs. Cartwright *never* would have used canned sauce. In fact, she didn't even use canned tomatoes. She made her sauce with tomatoes from the garden—tomatoes I ate like apples the summer I worked for her. Even in the winter, she'd use the tomatoes she'd canned herself.

I asked her if I could help, but she declined and insisted I sit while she finished up.

"Take your time," I said, sitting at the small rectangular table in the corner to watch her work. "Is Ava coming by today?" I asked casually.

As she set the kettle on the stove, a grin I wasn't particularly fond of rose on her face. "She'll be here shortly."

I sat back and crossed my legs. "Just wondering."

"I bet."

"Hey," I said, fighting a blush, "don't go making assumptions. I was curious." I honestly don't know why I'd asked, just making conversation mostly.

"No assumptions here." She ambled to the sink and lifted out a strainer full of spaghetti and set it on the counter. Then she lined up a dozen Tupperware containers next to each other. Like she was in a factory line, she filled the bottom of each container with a generous portion of pasta and then ladled steaming sauce over each of them. I guessed she'd doctored up her jarred sauce with some ground chuck and maybe spices.

Though I'd been guilty of a similar style of cooking, her cooking this way was a crime. Where in the world was her garden? Where were the show tunes she used to play while she cooked? Where were the cookbooks she'd always have open on the counter? As far as questions went, where was her son? She needed someone in her life to take care of her right now.

She eventually sat down, and we made small talk for a while, speaking mostly about her prior students, what they were doing now. Once we were drinking our tea, the topic of Oscar came up. "If I may," I said, "it seems to me he's confused about his place in the pack. I'm a long way from Cesar Millan, but I've spent enough time around dogs to know it's important they know who the alpha is. You need to establish that you're the boss."

"How in the world do I do that?" she asked.

"A trainer would help. I used a prong collar with Penelope, but I don't know if that's still the best tool. Maybe a Halti would do. Your dog needs to learn the rules. You can't let him pull on the leash or jump up on you. You can't comfort him when he growls or jumps at strangers. You need to correct him. You need to show him, 'I am Mrs. Cartwright, the top dog.'"

She rolled her eyes at me.

"I'm serious. Don't let him run the show around here. I used a water bottle on Penelope too. It did wonders."

She gasped. "I never once used a prong collar or a water bottle on my dogs, and you remember how well behaved they were."

"Fair enough," I said, "but maybe Oscar needs a wake-up call. You mentioned he was attacked. He might have some other trauma in his history too. Trust me, with some work, he'll fall in line and be a treasure to have. You'll enjoy walking with him or having him outside while you garden."

"Garden?" she said.

"I'm assuming you're just late to planting. I see plenty of space out back."

"Carver, when you get my age, you will understand."

I dramatically set one elbow on the table and rested my chin in my hand. I stared at her for a while, not caring about the uncomfortable silence. "What can I do for you, Mrs. Cartwright?"

She sat back.

"Don't give up," I whispered. "That's what this feels like. You're too strong to give up."

Her eyes softened. "I appreciate you caring."

"More than you know."

"Tell me about you," she said. "Your father leaves tomorrow?"

She was maddening, avoiding talk about her plight. I didn't want to leave her this way. It might be the last time I ever saw her again, and I felt like I was abandoning her. Giving her a break, though, we talked about my parents for a while. I told her I'd called Elliot and how that had led to a late night of catching up. I stopped short of telling her about my encounter with Shannon, which was something I would have loved to stop stewing over.

Then I steered the conversation back her way, asking about her son in Chicago. She seemed frustrated by their relationship. "He keeps trying to fix me so I won't be in his way. First it's a dog. Now he's suggesting I look into a senior living facility."

Though I didn't totally disagree with his suggestion, I decided not to take his side. Instead, I said, "You need to find something to do, other than watch baseball. You need to get outside more. With Oscar. You both need the exercise. And gardening? Mrs. Cartwright belongs in the garden."

She cupped her hands over the steam rising from her cup, warming them. "Carver, I love that we've reconnected, but believe me, you don't need to fix me. I'm past my gardening phase."

I lifted the tea bag in and out of my mug. "You're never too old to garden. When I think of Mrs. Cartwright, even before I think of books and you standing up at the front of your classroom, I think of you and your stunning garden." I could hear myself pleading. I was damn near close to asking her to move down to Asheville with me. Something had to change.

"I'm not trying to fix you. I'm trying to remind you of the life you've lived."

She shook her head as if she didn't want reminding.

My phone came alive on the table. A local number but not Elliot's. I was pretty sure it was my mother calling from the bank, probably to check in. We hadn't spoken all morning. "One minute," I said to Mrs. Cartwright.

I put the phone to my ear. "Hello, Carver speaking."

"Carver, it's Shannon."

I'd never stood so quickly in my life. Almost knocking the chair over, I left the kitchen and raced down the hall toward the foyer. "Hey, there." The humiliation from the night before washed over me, but I didn't let her know that. "What's going on?"

"I got your number from Elliot," she said.

Speechless, I bathed in the silky sound of her voice as I paced back and forth on the runner covering the hardwoods.

"I was calling to . . ." She let her words trail off.

Yeah? I wondered. *To see if we could rekindle what we'd had?*

"I don't know . . . ," she continued. "I didn't know when you were leaving, but I thought it might be fun to catch up. Maybe a cup of coffee?"

I felt like all I'd been doing was drinking coffee since my return, but my heart tingled as I let her invitation settle. Was this really happening? "Yeah, I could do that. I'm leaving tomorrow, though. Do you have some time today?"

"I do," she said. "I have the day off."

Unconcerned whether Mrs. Cartwright had followed me into the living room and was spying on me, I raised a victorious fist in the air. The world was finally returning to orbit. We agreed on a place and time and said goodbye. Today would be different, I decided, and I would not screw up this time.

Nothing got by Mrs. Cartwright, even when she was not exactly herself. It didn't take her five seconds upon my return to ask me what "girl" had called. "I can see it all over your face," she said. "You men are no different than the boys you used to be."

"I don't want to tell you," I admitted.

She shrugged. "Suit yourself."

I let out a full-on grin. "Okay, okay, beat it out of me, why don't you. That was Shannon."

"I did no such thing as beat it out of you," she said, then added under her breath, "Sounds like a confession more than anything."

"What is that supposed to mean?"

"Be careful, Carver. Shannon is a good person, but I'm sure you know she comes with complicated emotions." She took hold of her mug. "Just an old woman's opinion."

I stopped before I said something like, "I've been waiting my whole life for this chance." Instead, I dialed back my response. "We're talking some, catching up. It's not like anything will come of it." Was that the first lie I'd ever told Mrs. Cartwright? "Hey," I said, "you're the one who claims I'm missing love in my life."

"I stand by that."

Twenty minutes later, Ava knocked on the front door. I seized my last opportunity alone with Mrs. Cartwright. "It's been so good to catch up," I said. "Please take care of yourself. You have done more with your life—impacted more souls—than any person I know. Don't forget that."

She faked a smile, and I called her on it. "No, no. I don't want to get on the plane remembering a fake smile. Give me more than that."

She raised her fingers to her lips and forced a smile by dragging the corners up. Even she couldn't avoid a laugh then, and we enjoyed one last wonderful moment.

With my lips still curled at the edges, I crossed the house to let Ava in.

"What are you so bubbly about?" she asked, standing in the doorway in her dark-blue scrubs.

"Mrs. Cartwright is in a particular mood today. But I got her to lighten up for a sec."

"Aw," she said. "I think she might have done the same to you. Look at you. You look . . . I don't know . . . you're glowing."

"Am I? Well, she means a lot to me, you know? It's good to see her lighten up."

"It doesn't happen that often," Ava said soberly.

"I can tell," I said. "Well, I'm so glad she has you. Let me know if I can do anything."

"I'll do that."

I stepped back into the foyer to let her enter. "And look me up if you ever end up in Asheville. It was nice to meet you."

"Likewise, Carver. You seem like a good guy."

"Nah, don't let me fool you."

She rolled her eyes at me, as if I was too predictable for her taste.

"Back in the Stone Age," Mrs. Cartwright said, appearing out of nowhere, "we used to play a game when we wanted to get to know someone quickly. Ever heard of eleven questions?"

I was instantly mortified by the idea—not to mention her intrusion. Was she attempting to play Cupid?

"Never heard of it," Ava said with a raised eyebrow.

"Me either."

Mrs. Cartwright directed us like we were her students. "Carver, you have thirty seconds to ask eleven questions. Ava, you must answer without hesitation."

"Okay." Ava looked less thrilled than I.

Saving us both, I said, "You know what . . . let's save it for next time. I do have to go. Mrs. Cartwright, all my love. Ava, good luck with her knee and the rest of her."

"Yeah, good luck with all your things back home."

"Yes, my things. Thank you."

Stepping toward the door, I looked back at Mrs. Cartwright. I patted my chest, wishing I could do more for her. "Bye, teach."

She waved and we shared a last smile. As I left her property, I once again questioned my decision to leave so soon. Damn you, Teterbury.

Chapter 12

Back to the Way It Used to Be

Busting into town like an outlaw looking for trouble, I came in the door of the coffee shop with my head held high. The exposed brick walls exhibited a collection of brightly colored abstracts. Pendant lights with Edison bulbs hung from the tall ceiling. People in headphones filled the bar along the window, tapping away at their laptops. Most of the tables were full with caffeinated people locked in lively conversation.

Shannon sat at a two-top pushed up against a window that offered a view of a busy Main Street. Her hair was pulled back, and she wore workout clothes: leggings and a Lululemon top. Within seconds we were wrapped into an embrace that was far from awkward. Her breath on my neck made my skin tingle. The parts where our skin touched radiated warmth. With the stars so much on my mind lately, it felt like they'd finally returned to their rightful places, everything finally in line again.

As we broke away, I said, "I'm glad you called." Her familiar scent dazzled me.

"Yeah, me too." She filled me up with the warm look in her eyes. "Just don't judge my outfit. I'm teaching barre at three."

"You look great," I said. She'd always had such electric-blue eyes. Long blonde hair and electric-blue eyes that carried enough of a charge to light up a city.

I felt myself strutting as we approached the counter and ordered cappuccinos. I insisted I pay. Then we chatted while a barista in a headband worked the shiny espresso machine. I asked about Shannon's parents, and she told me she'd lost her mother recently and that her father still lived in the same house she grew up in on Oakhurst. We played catch-up for a while, and with each passing minute I felt increasingly confident and composed, as if she'd renewed my faith in myself.

"So last night," she said. "Sorry I was so distracted. We have a new chef in the kitchen, and it's been a disaster."

I touched her arm for a moment, falling right back into the way we used to be. Our reunion felt like a dip in a hot spring, the most comfortable and wonderful feeling in the world. "No, no, I was distracted, too, seeing everyone after so long."

"You have been gone a long time, huh? How long?"

"Since the summer we graduated," I admitted, smothering a blush.

She overdid her shocked reaction. "What? You haven't been home in twenty years?"

I was ready to change the subject. It didn't take a detective to know why I'd not returned.

She didn't seem to hold it against me, though. "You haven't missed much. Things have changed, but at the same time, they haven't."

The conversation flowed easily until our drinks were called, and then we moved back to the table where she'd left her exercise bag. We sat face-to-face, nothing between us but the two drinks. It was only then we both seemed to take stock of our reunion. Our story wasn't finished. Even twenty years wasn't enough time to stamp out what we'd had. I wanted to say, "Just look at this, the fireworks between us. We haven't skipped a beat!"

A minute must have gone by as we each shook our heads and smiled at one another, allowing ourselves to enjoy what our reunion sparked. I liked lingering in the pocket of the quiet space we'd created. I enjoyed studying her face as she did the same to me. I would have killed to know her thoughts.

"God, we have some catching up to do," I said. "Where do we even start?"

She smirked as if she knew she'd won the silent game. Placing her hand on the paper cup stamped with the coffee shop's logo, she chewed on the question. "I know. You're not coming to the reunion?"

I let my head fall back dramatically. "Bree told you?"

"I'm on the committee with her."

"You are?" I tried to keep the curtain closed on my instant disappointment. Was she only here to do Bree's dirty work? "Don't tell me *this*"—I gestured to the two of us, trying to keep it light—"is all part of a mission to get me to attend."

She licked her lips. "You mean me inviting you? No. Though we would love for you to come, I'm not sure we're desperate to the point of begging." She hid a smile behind her cappuccino.

"So it's like that," I said, relieved. I leaned forward. "Don't tell me you have a better option."

"Listen to you." She let one corner of her lips curve upward. "Still sure of yourself, I see."

She was talking about the me I was while I was dating her. I'd never forget the lift she gave me when we were together, the way I felt like I finally mattered.

"No," I said, "not really. Well, okay, maybe a little." To play the game, I added, "I'm honored you guys would ask me. Wait, whose idea was it in the first place?" An enormous light bulb glowed in my head—or, perhaps, in my heart. "Yours?" Even the possibility of it being true made me as giddy as a NASA team safely launching a new shuttle. I could hear everyone in the control center of my mind giving high fives.

Her cheeks swelled pink, and I almost said, "Gotcha."

"I might have had something to do with it," she said with a shrewd grin.

"I see." Had I ever felt better in my entire life? Why hadn't she told me so or contacted me directly? If anyone had a chance at getting me home, it would have been her.

We locked eyes, both our heads bobbing slowly. Though I was a long way from understanding women, I was pretty sure she was making moves on me, which was one of the few blissful moments in my thirty-eight years when I thought, "Mission accomplished. I could die now."

"Okay," I said. "If your inviting me here wasn't a play to convince me to stick around until next weekend, why did you call me?" I asked gently, or at least, intended to do so. But she seemed to take offense to it.

"Carver Livingston, when did you get so serious? I remember you having an inflated sense of self, in an often-adorable way, but I don't remember you being so . . . I don't know . . . rigid."

That felt like an insult, but I held strong. "Am I really that rigid? I feel relaxed."

"You have this . . . I don't know . . . sharp edge to you now. Like you need acupuncture or something to restore the balance of your chi."

"My chi? I've been prescribed a lot of things, but no one has ever suggested that."

"And now someone has." She reached over and touched my hand. "You're still handsome, don't worry. You just need to lighten up a bit."

I inhaled like a yogi, my only answer to lightening up. "How's this?"

"There you go," she said, retracting her hand with a smirk. "I don't know why I called you this morning. It was nice to see you last night. A little awkward but . . ."

"It was awkward, wasn't it?"

She shrugged. "I suppose it's been building a long time. How could it not be?"

"What do you mean by *it*?" As the words left my mouth, I wanted to take them back.

"You know . . . the thing between us. What happened. I don't know that we've had a real conversation since."

I hated that I flushed hot. I'd expected we'd have to discuss our past but hoped the revisiting of it wouldn't hit so hard.

"Hey," she said, taking my hand again. "Deep breaths. All that's in the past, and we're here now."

I offered a chortle of the awkward variety.

Saving me, she jabbed her pointer finger at the table. "Back to the reunion. Why won't you go? Bree isn't giving up, you know."

I polished off my drink as a way to buy some time to collect myself. "She is nothing short of a bulldog. I'm having to screen my calls." My shoulders lowered as the tension inside of me waned.

Shannon didn't seem bothered by our uncomfortable moment. It was like she hadn't even noticed it. "But you're here," she said. "Why not hang around? It's going to be fun. A nineties theme. Catching up with all our old friends."

The idea didn't sound as threatening coming from her lovely lips. Still, I couldn't imagine myself walking through the doors with the feeling of everyone looking at me. "I just . . ."

"You just what, mister?"

I looked out the window and watched a woman and her poodle pass by. "I have work. I won't bore you with the details, but I have a lot going on back home."

Shannon nodded without hiding her skepticism. "In Asheville, right? I read about you in the paper. That's when I came up with the idea of you speaking."

Ah, that felt good. "Who else is speaking?" I asked. "I'm sure you guys will survive without me."

"It's a great lineup. Remember Maurice Tyler? He's talking about the dental work he does in Rwanda. And Christine Shore? She's out in LA producing movies." She named a couple more and then folded her arms and sat back. "Believe me, I don't want to go either."

"You don't?"

She made a disgusted look. "So I can be the cheerleader turned divorced bartender and barre teacher? No, thanks. But this is who I am now. I'm not a brain surgeon . . . or a dog surgeon—"

"A veterinary surgeon," I corrected her.

"Got it." Her eyes narrowed. "I'm no one special, just another girl trying to figure out her late thirties after an ugly divorce."

"You're so much more than that," I said, breathing her in.

"You don't know who I am now."

"Fair enough, but I don't know that I've ever met anyone since who knows how to have fun like you do. How many times did you talk me into cutting class? Which was difficult to do. You and your cigarettes and vodka shots. The way you used to stand up in my Jeep and yell into the wind like Braveheart. You've always been a 'give zero fucks' kind of girl, and I loved that about you."

She inclined an eyebrow. "Zero fucks? I gave you more than that."

Boy, did that knock me off center. "You know what I mean."

"I sure do." She flapped an eyelid at me, offering the sexiest smile I'd ever seen. Oh, she remembered. Just like I did.

A few topics later, once the temperature of the room had returned to normal, I asked, "What happened with you and Trey? Is he still . . . ?" I stopped because I didn't even know what I was asking.

She smoothed her ringless hand against the table and shut my question down. "We ran into roadblocks."

"I'm sorry." I didn't blame her for not opening up to me. She was right; I didn't know her that well now. Attempting to avoid being as serious as she'd accused me of, I offered a smile and said, "Elliot told me about the bartender teaching barre."

She closed her eyes for a second, as if wishing it weren't true. "It's mortifying, really. But it happened. My barre studio offered teacher classes, and I thought it would be a good time to do something different. I'm so over food and bev. So you're looking at Teterbury's only bartending barre instructor."

"I feel like there might be a business in there somewhere. You could call your place the Barretender—with the two *r*'s and an *e*."

"Barre-dy, barre, barre. I've heard them all."

She got me to laugh out loud. "I don't even know what barre is. You put your legs up on a rail or something?"

She gestured toward the street. "Why don't you come take a class? You could come today, or I'm teaching one tomorrow."

For about two seconds I thought it might be a good idea, but then the faceless people who might still judge me appeared in my mind. It was enough of a victory that Shannon had sought me out and that we'd been seen together around town.

"Definitely can't today, and I've got a flight out tomorrow, sadly."

She looked as let down as I felt. "Oh, well."

Was that the extent of our reconnection? What an awful, awful ending to what could have been so much more. No, I wanted more. I needed more.

"I might hang around. I don't know."

"You should," she said with enough excitement to make me feel like I was floating. I saw in her eyes the future we might have.

She asked me what brought me home, and I filled her in. "You probably remember about my mom. Whether I stay or go, she'll work the whole time."

"I do remember that." She sat back and did this thing she'd always done, resting her lips on her knuckles. "But she'll love that you're at home waiting for her. That's gotta be hard. Trust me, divorce is the worst. She could use a friendly ear."

"Yeah, I know." Mary Beth would be "tickled pink," as she liked to say, if I told her I was extending my trip.

"There's another reason I've been thinking about staying," I said. We talked about Mrs. Cartwright for a while, which led us down a whole slew of wonderful memories. I laughed like I hadn't in a long time. Something had been missing from my life, and it was Shannon.

I folded over and rested my elbows on the table. "I have a confession to make, by the way. I had the tattoo removed."

She frowned. "You did? You asshole."

I didn't think she would have been that mad, but I supposed I understood. We'd gotten the date we'd first kissed, etched in roman numerals, struck through with a bolt of lightning.

"Sorry, I didn't . . ." I definitely wasn't going to tell her I had it removed shortly after my mother had told me about Shannon and Trey's marriage. I'd held on to hope until then that maybe, just maybe, we'd cross paths again.

And here we were . . .

"So much for the past," she said, her face turning dark. "I guess it didn't mean that much."

I'd never understand women. "Are you really mad at me? I . . ."

She smiled. "I'm messing with you."

I couldn't believe it and shook my head at her, smiling with her.

"I had mine removed too," she confessed. "Trey made me."

"Ah, I see."

We grinned at each other. Then something brave came out of my mouth. "I don't like that I won't see you again." There was a lot to read between the lines in what I'd said, and I was slightly afraid she'd shut me down.

"It doesn't seem right, does it?" She glanced at the time on her phone and then reached toward me. For a moment I thought she was going to take my hand. Instead, she knocked on the wood. "You have my number. If you end up staying longer, let's connect. We still have a lot of catching up to do."

"Yeah, we do, don't we?" I loved that she'd given me a green light. It was all I needed. No matter what happened, I would see her again.

Just to see what might happen.

꿈

I couldn't have imagined a more dysfunctional situation than my parents and me eating dinner together on the last night before my father's departure. As he'd told us, he had the truck gassed up, air in all the tires, and he was ready for a sunrise liftoff.

To make the evening even stranger, I was texting back and forth with Shannon. Nothing serious, some harmless flirting. It was, in truth, the only thing keeping me sane. I'd sent her a picture of the three of us in the living room, accompanied with the text: My current situation.

We were having takeout. The whole house smelled like soy sauce. I'd given up on changing my father's mind. He appeared to hold back his excitement out of respect for us. My mother was so checked out she might as well have stayed at the office. All she'd been doing was stirring her moo goo gai pan with her chopsticks. She'd not taken a bite. On the television was the nightly news. I had become my parents, totally, wholly, and forever. This was what we Livingstons did now: Asian takeout in front of the television after a hard day's work.

Shannon texted back: My current situation. She sent me a picture of two drunk guys in sleeveless shirts tossing back shots.

I smiled. To simply converse this way felt so good inside.

She sent another text: If you get bored, come for a drink.

How could I ever get bored? I texted back.

True, she replied.

My smile put the cherry on top of all the dysfunction. My father was about to leave, my mother was heartbroken, and there I was striking it up with an old flame. And not just any old flame.

"What are you smiling about?" my mother asked.

My father turned to see too.

"Nothing. Just texting someone." The talking head on the TV was reporting on the rising crime in Boston.

She raised her eyebrows. "It's Shannon, isn't it?" I'd told them that we'd had coffee.

"It is," I said inaudibly.

"Carver, please be careful."

"Nothing will come of it, Mom. We're having fun reconnecting, that's all."

141

I could see she was biting her tongue, wanting to say something about how Shannon had once ruined me, and I shouldn't risk letting that happen again.

After we finished eating, I collected everybody's plate and cleaned the kitchen. Back in the living room, we watched cable news for another hour. At eight, my mother muttered that she was going to bed. Without making eye contact with either of us, she slipped out of the room.

"Good night, Lisa," my father called out. She ignored him.

I found myself angry at my father again, but we were well past the point of preaching. I could hear in his voice the sadness he felt. If so, then why was he doing it? Why was he leaving?

In what I thought was a very kind gesture, I stood and patted his shoulder. "I'm going to the Sanderton for a beer. Catch you in the morning before you leave."

"Yeah, okay, son. I suppose I need to hit the rack anyway." He clicked off the television. "You need to talk about anything?"

"No, I'm good."

He stood and stepped into his boots. "Okay, love ya, Carv."

"You too, Dad." At least he realized he was in no place to offer advice about Shannon. I was close to forty now, a long way from the boy who had slit his wrist. I could take care of myself.

As I walked away, sadness washed over me. I wished I could hold on to more of the good years. Though we lived a long way from each other now, it felt like him leaving my mother would only separate us further. No question, if there was a side to take, it would be hers. That crushed me inside, the way the last hope of us ever rekindling something was fading away.

I was glad for the escape of walking into the Sanderton. Shannon waved me over. I fell in love all over again upon seeing her. What a sight that had been missing from my life for entirely too long.

"I saved you a seat," she said. "What are we drinking?" I got the feeling she owned this bar, the way she commanded it.

"Whatever you're pouring." I settled in, noticing that I no longer felt any hesitation in being out in public. Now that Shannon and I had come full circle, were the rest of the pieces in my life coming into place?

"I make a mean mescal margarita, if that's your thing."

"Let's find out," I said.

I watched her make my drink, blown away that my whole life had led to me looking across a bar at my beautiful ex-girlfriend while the hours ticked down to my father leaving my mother. If that wasn't a reason to drink . . .

When she shook the cocktail shaker over her shoulder, she did it like she'd made thousands of drinks over the years. She poured the contents over a ball of ice and slid me the glass. With a wink, she said, "Enjoy."

I tried to strike up a conversation, but she'd already moved down the bar to help a thirsty couple. It was okay, though. As I sipped my frothy mescal, I enjoyed watching her work. She made good drinks. She was also good at walking that line of flirting with the men at the bar without going overboard, surely working for those extra tips. I couldn't blame her, but it did make me feel a bit less special.

When she had a lull, she came back over to me. "How is it?"

"Best I ever had."

She pointed a bottle opener at me and said with a smirk, "I don't mess around."

"Nope."

"So . . ." She leaned over the bar, her shirt falling open ever so slightly. I bit my lip, thinking of the last time we'd made love—a sneaky connection at her parents' house.

"Did you figure out if you're leaving?" she asked.

Actually, I'd been thinking about it a lot and come pretty close to a final decision. "I think I'm going to stay another night or so, to take care of my mom."

"Just for her?" she asked, smiling at me, knowing she was reeling me in.

I said confidently, "Well, I do have a couple of other things to take care of . . ."

She gave an impressed look, jutting out her lip. I was proud of myself for playing the game so well. "To take care of," she said. "I see. Well, I'm teaching barre at three tomorrow. Come take a class. Then maybe we could do something."

My eyes bulged. "You don't want me to come to your barre class. Trust me."

"Why not?"

"Isn't it for women?"

She rolled her eyes. "What do you care if you're the only man in there? Would that be a problem?"

"Hey, I've done my share of yoga with only women in the room. But I'm not sure I'm limber enough for whatever it is you do in there."

"I'll be easy on you. There are always a few beginners."

The drunk guy next to me who smelled like cigarettes muttered, "I'll go."

I ignored him.

"You want another one?" Shannon asked me.

I was a moment away from asking her what time she got off, but I resisted. She was putting on a full-court press, but I had to take a step back. Surely part of why I'd lost her the last time was that I had made it too easy on her, gushed over her too much. I couldn't be that rosy-eyed geek anymore.

"No," I said, "I should probably head back. Could I get the check?"

"This one's on me," she said. "I'll see you tomorrow at my class. Wear something loose fitting."

"I haven't even agreed to go," I said.

She leaned toward me again, close enough that I could see the texture of her lips. "You have something better to do?"

I looked at her, and I mean really looked at her. Ah, to step back into her world and have fun like we used to. I would have leaped onto her bar and barked like a dog if she'd asked.

Instead of doing that, I said, "Yeah, maybe I'll give it a shot, to see you in action." I pushed up from the bar, gave her one last wave, and walked back home. And by *walked*, I mean strutted like the peacock the Cartwrights used to have.

Chapter 13

HANDSHAKES AND DISTRACTIONS

For a second I wondered if my father was going to shake my mother's hand. Wouldn't that have been something, to say goodbye to your partner with a handshake? He had attached his Shasta Airflyte to the back of his big truck and parked it along the road. I held a tumbler of coffee in my hand, watching the two people who'd most impacted my life say goodbye to each other.

I never could have imagined how empty I felt. Divorce papers would surely follow in the next couple of weeks, and I'd be left knowing that it was me who caused their downfall. Had I held strong when Shannon dumped me, keeping faith that she'd eventually come back, then my parents would never be standing here in the awkward space between a handshake and a hug.

It could have been worse, I decided, perhaps convincing myself so. My mother could have left earlier in the morning to avoid seeing him. Or she could have moved out weeks ago. Instead, they both behaved in a way that still showed they loved each other—if only a little.

They did not shake hands, and I guess I was grateful to see them hug instead. More than anything, I was depressed down into the core of me. My mother looked strong—or, at least, determined to be strong. She even reached up to his cheek after they'd hugged.

"Ben," she said, "go have fun, okay?"

He touched her waist. "I love you very much, Lisa."

"I know," she whispered.

Then my father turned my way. I stepped forward onto the side-walk. We locked eyes. I was surprised I didn't hate him. Standing on the edge of our goodbye, my mind must have shifted toward empathy. Though I wasn't ready to cheer on his journey, I wanted him to find happiness. He'd been missing it for a long time. Maybe he was right to say goodbye.

"When will we see you again?" I asked, my voice a skeleton of its normal self.

He glanced back at the Shasta. "I don't know. Maybe we'll find North Carolina on our journey, a few months down the road." The "we," I assumed, meant Clementine and him. Or had it been a Freudian slip? Was there another woman?

Trying not to crack, I went for humor. "Yeah, okay, Cousin Eddie. I guess I'll let you park this thing in my driveway like in *Christmas Vacation*."

"Shitter's full, Carver," he said, tapping into his best Randy Quaid. He gave a soft chuckle as his shoulders rose and fell. Dammit, I loved him. Despite it all, I loved him, and I didn't want him to leave. I wanted things to go back to the way they'd been before I'd screwed it all up.

He stepped into my open arms, and I squeezed him tight. "I love you, Dad. Always will, no matter what you do." He'd said that to me a thousand times, and I know he recognized the words. A couple of tears came then, inching down my cheeks.

"Always will, that's right." He patted my back and let go. His eyes were wet too.

He looked at my mom one last time and blew her a kiss. She caught it and patted her heart. It was like they both still craved a life together but knew it was no longer possible.

Wiping his tears, he turned and climbed into the truck. I wrapped my arm around my mother. We watched as my father drove away from us, the vintage trailer bouncing behind.

"I'm going to stay for a bit, Mom."

She squeezed my shoulder. "You don't have to do that."

"I want to. Why don't you take a few days off? Let's spend some time together."

"I'd love to, but I can't, honey. You know how work gets. I'm in the depths of it right now." She wiped her face. "This is a new chapter, Carver. Don't worry about me. I'll figure it out."

The guilt of orchestrating this mess filled my veins, and I turned and pulled her into another hug. "You always do."

⁓

While I mused over the emptiness that befell the house—and, of course, the front yard—my mother went about her routine, showering and getting dressed, making herself a salad bowl for lunch. For a while, I was too befuddled to get anything done. Talk about the end of an era. Their marriage had been one of the few constants in my life. Even when they were bickering and falling apart during the end of my senior year and the following summer, I never considered they would get a divorce.

I stopped her to check in as she scurried out the door to work. She seemed surprisingly okay, considering. Much like with me, work was her safe space, and I was proud of her for moving on, staying busy, not letting herself be dragged down.

Finally breaking out of my fog, I spent the morning answering emails and knocking out other work-related items, such as pushing back a couple of surgeries until my return, interviewing a woman in Flat Rock about our receptionist opening, and walking through the calendar with Mary Beth. According to her, the relief veterinarian I'd hired was doing well, and the team hadn't run into any issues they couldn't handle.

It also came as no surprise that Mary Beth urged me to stay in Teterbury as long as needed. "I'm sure your mother appreciates it," she said. I told her I was thinking about doing something special for my mom, maybe cooking a big dinner, and Mary Beth said, "What's gotten into you? Not racing away from Teterbury. Wanting to cook dinner for someone else?"

My answer: "I have no idea. I think I've been bitten by something."

It felt good, though, and although a big part of me felt like I needed to get back to Asheville for work, I was proud of myself for taking a few days to step away from my ninety-mile-an-hour life. How many books had I read had insisted that taking time off made one more effective? It was sound advice, but something I'd not always heeded. Perhaps I was changing.

Heavy on my heart were my mother and Mrs. Cartwright, the two women who'd given the most to me in my life. Not that I was a savior, but I felt I could at least be there for them, show them they hadn't wasted their efforts.

Of course, there was another reason that sticking around wouldn't be too bad. The question that lingered on my mind as I worked all morning was: *Could I really pull off going to a barre class in the heart of the town I'd avoided most of my life?* Looking back to when I'd first arrived, the Carver hiding under a hood and behind dark sunglasses would have experienced a system overload at even a sniff of the idea. There was no telling who else I would run into. The truth was, though, that Shannon showing interest in me had pumped me with all the confidence I'd been missing. What was there to fear now?

Sure, I'd landed into town with a smoking engine and a missing wheel, followed by blowing my first meeting with my friends and then with Shannon. But that was over, and I was sure I'd be fine going forward. Considering the distance between our homes, the odds of something sticking between Shannon and me were slim, but who knew? Maybe there was such a thing as destiny. Our getting back together could make me a believer again.

Exclamation marks and big red heart emoji erupted in my mind in equal measure as we'd texted back and forth throughout the night and then in the morning. Shannon was all but admitting she'd made a huge mistake, and now she wanted me back in a big, big way. One more notch of happy and I would have done the MC Hammer slide on Main Street.

I'd sent her a message seeking guidance on male attire during barre class when I heard a vehicle pull up outside. By the time I'd opened the front door, Ava was hurrying my way with Oscar Wilde in one hand and his kennel in the other.

Knowing something bad had happened, I rushed down the steps. "What's going on?"

"Mrs. Cartwright is in the hospital."

"No," I said, my face tightening with concern. For a second, I imagined the worst. "Is she . . . is she okay?"

"She says she's fine, but she was in a car accident."

I sighed in relief, so glad she was alive. "What happened? Was anyone else hurt?"

"No injuries." Ava set the kennel in front of me. "She says she's got a bump on her head, but they're keeping her to run some precautionary tests."

Oscar panted in her arms. Such a tiny being, terrified without any idea why. "Everything's okay, Oscar," I said, offering to let him sniff my hand.

He sucked in his tongue and showed me his teeth, letting out a slow growl.

"Oscar," she said. "He's not going to hurt you."

"He's afraid and confused," I said.

She massaged his neck. "Mrs. Cartwright doesn't want me to leave him at home, and she said you might be able to help? I'd like to go up to the hospital for a while before my afternoon clients."

"Yes, certainly," I said quickly. "I'd like to come up there, too, though. Leave him with me, and I'll figure it out from there."

She set Oscar down on the grass as she blinked back tears. "She's not doing well, Carver. I've watched this fast decline lately, like in the last few weeks."

"It's killing me too," I said, the reality of Mrs. Cartwright's situation slapping me in the face. "The way she's giving up . . . she's not even hiding it."

Ava's brown eyes blazed with concern, showing a care about others that I may have never known for even a minute in my life. "She's so depressed."

I had no idea what came over me, but I stretched out an arm to offer a hug. "C'mere," I whispered. She looked surprised at first, as surprised as I was. But I held my arm suspended in the air, waiting. I even offered a caring smile, showing her we were in this together.

She eventually accepted and slipped her arms around me. As I held her, a firm determination to lift Mrs. Cartwright out of her own darkness came over me, stronger than ever before. This urge was no doubt sparked by Ava. It was nice to know I wasn't alone in wanting to help, and maybe she and I together could make a difference.

"Go take care of her," I said, "and I'll be there as soon as I can. We'll come up with a plan, I promise." Surprising even myself, I added, "I'm not leaving until we do."

"Yeah, okay."

I took the end of the leash from her. "Oscar and I will make fast friends, I'm sure."

The poor dog looked back up at her, as if pleading, *Don't leave me with this monster.*

"You be nice, Oscar Wilde," she said.

We exchanged telephone numbers, and then I waved as she drove away. Oscar watched her go, too, giving off a pitiful whimper when her truck disappeared.

I didn't want him to detect my escalating worry about Mrs. Cartwright, so I offered my most upbeat voice. "Oscar, I'm not that bad. Have you already forgotten all the snacks I've given you?" I gave him a tug to make him look at me.

When he did, I said, "I'm a veterinarian. Do you know what that is? I've spent my entire adult life helping animals. Give me a break."

He wasn't having it and turned back to the road.

It took some convincing, but I eventually got him to follow me into the house. A barrage of scents seemed to distract him from wanting to kill me. It bought me enough time to give him a bowl of water and cut up some carrots and radishes.

"I know it's not a bone, but it's the best we can do right now. When I go out, I'll pick up something at the store."

I ran through the thin mental Rolodex of my local contacts: Elliot, Shannon, and my mother. Shannon had barre class, so I knew she was out. My mom didn't know much about dogs, and she'd be mad if I made her leave work. Then again, a companion might be good for her. Wait, nope. That was exactly what Mrs. Cartwright's son had done, push a dog on someone.

That left me with Elliot. I dialed his number, and he picked up quickly. "I had a feeling Teterbury wouldn't let you go," he said. "Are you thirsty for more, Carv?"

Wasn't it nice to have a friend who, even with only his voice, could make you feel better inside? "Long story, but yeah. Actually, I do have a favor to ask. Mrs. Cartwright was in a car accident. She's okay, but she's in the hospital. Do you think Alice could watch her dog while I go see her?"

I explained the situation, and it took him all of two seconds to say, "Yeah, I think so. If not, I can figure something out. Let me get right back to you."

He phoned me a few minutes later and said he would come by to grab Oscar, that Alice was finishing up a hair appointment and would be happy to watch him.

I hung up, thinking I wanted to be a better friend, someone who would drop anything when called.

───

Teterbury Memorial had been remodeled since my stint in 1998. From what I could tell, they'd added two new wings—one dedicated to cardiology, the other to oncology, but it was still a small hospital, and any serious cases were sent to Lahey in Burlington.

At the end of a long white hall in a cramped room, Mrs. Cartwright lay on the bed, the thin wool blanket pulled up to her chest. A bandage covered a wound on her forehead. She had more color in her face than last I'd seen her. Probably due to the IV plugged into her arm. A steady bubbly hiss came from above her bed, where on the wall a flowmeter and humidifier fed oxygen to her nasal cannula. The screen of the mobile computer workstation by the side of the bed was black.

Ava sat on a love seat pushed up against a window that offered a view of a big grassy patch with a couple of bushy oaks. I smiled at her, feeling like the two of us were connected in this mission to help our friend.

Then I returned my attention to Mrs. Cartwright. The steady beep of her vitals monitor suggested that she was stable, and I couldn't help but do a confirmatory assessment of the numbers on the display. Attached to her IV line was a CRI of insulin and a syringe pump infusing fentanyl. What was the insulin all about? High potassium, or was there a diabetic issue of which I wasn't aware?

Mrs. Cartwright heard me moving around and peeled open her eyes. "Hi, Carver."

My heart nearly broke as I saw my once-strong mentor so very, very weak. "What are we going to do with you?"

"Don't you start," she said.

I held up a vase of chrysanthemums I'd picked up at a florist on the way over. "For you."

She thanked me as I set them on the small table in the corner. I approached the bed and took her hand. "What in the world?"

She cleared her throat. "I got confused and ran a red light on Riverview, ran into the mailman's truck."

"You hit the mailman?" A smile forced its way onto my face as I let go of her hand.

"The exact one who delivers my mail," she said. "Joseph Paisley."

"And he's okay?"

"He's fine," she said. "He was kind. I taught him in . . ." She thought for a moment. "It was a few classes after you. Maybe two thousand three." She gave a chuckle. "I taught the policeman who came to the scene too. Michael Testaverde. He was probably two thousand six."

I glanced at Ava. "That's small-town living, isn't it?"

She didn't seem as amused. What did Ava know that I didn't? I gave her my best sympathetic look, asking without asking what was going on.

Ava crossed her arms and looked at the patient. "And why did you get confused, Mrs. Cartwright?"

Mrs. Cartwright shot a nasty look at her and then stared at the ceiling.

"What?" I asked.

She attempted to derail the conversation. "How's Oscar?"

"He's with Elliot and his wife, doing fine. Tell me what's going on."

"You didn't tell them I was in the hospital, did you?"

"Of course I did."

Her eyebrows tightened. "I don't want people to know I'm here. I don't want them to see me like this. I don't even want you to tell my son."

"Okay." I could relate, so I didn't argue.

"Tell him," Ava insisted.

Mrs. Cartwright's jaw tightened. "I stopped taking my medicine, dammit."

"What medicine?" I'd asked too harshly and found her hand to show I truly cared.

"I'm taking metformin . . . to control my blood sugar."

"You're a diabetic?" I asked.

She gave a look that said how much she hated sharing this information. "Type two. It hit me hard after Tom died." She raised a finger. "I don't want a soul other than you two knowing."

"It's been two weeks since she had her last dose," Ava said. "The doctors said she had super low sodium and potassium. Very high sugar. They're loading her with fluids and insulin. She's going to be fine, but things are going to have to change, aren't they?"

"Why are you off it?" I asked.

Mrs. Cartwright lifted her faded blue eyes to me. They were the color of denim that had been washed a thousand times.

And I knew . . .

Tears pricked my eyes as the realization hit me like a hammer. I recognized the look because I'd seen it in the mirror years before. I knew *exactly* why, and it sent me sliding into the darkness. Much like I had done twenty years earlier, my former teacher was trying to end her life.

Mrs. Cartwright stared off into space, her eyes directed toward the window. I found myself unable to speak. How could anyone believe in God when such a perfect creature as Eloise Cartwright couldn't even find a reason to make it to the end? What kind of awful place was this we were living in?

My body heavy with worry, I squeezed her hand. "You're lucky you didn't hurt someone."

"I don't need a lecture." Her voice was an angry whisper.

I nodded, knowing she'd been through enough. We all sat there for a while, and I tried to think of what I could possibly say. If Tom had seen her this way, it would have crushed him. He would have expected me to do something, to be there for her.

Trying to bring some warmth into the room, I asked, "Is this all a ploy to get me to stay in town? Because I tell you what, it's working. If you want me to take up residence in your guest bedroom and dispense your medicine myself every morning, I will do it."

Mrs. Cartwright scowled at me.

Ava grabbed her fanny pack, which was clearly her version of a purse, and stood. "I'm going to find something to eat, let you guys talk. Can I bring anything back for you?"

"No, thanks," I said. "Can I do anything for you?"

She shook her head. "Just some fresh air."

I nodded as she disappeared down the hall.

When the door clicked shut, I stole her spot on the love seat. Mrs. Cartwright stared toward the ceiling like a child might while she waited for a scolding from her parents. I was mad, for sure. Angry and sad. Heartbroken. Frustrated. How awful it was to see someone you cared about lying in a hospital bed with an IV bag hanging above her head. Especially when I'd been on the other end of the situation, looking up at my parents and Elliot.

"So," she said to me. "I suppose you'll be giving me a lecture now."

"You have a lot of amazing people like Ava pulling for you, Mrs. C. I hate to put that burden on you, but all of us expect more out of you."

She didn't respond.

"I want to know why," I said. "Why would you stop taking your medicine?"

She looked at me like I'd asked the most absurd question on Earth.

"Because you want it to end?" I lost my breath saying it. "Is that what this was?" I closed my eyes for a moment to collect myself. When she didn't answer, I asked again, "Why?"

Her silence said it all.

"All the stuff you told me," I said. "All the reasons you gave me to keep living. Where is that woman? Where is that Mrs. Cartwright?"

A fire erupted in her eyes. "Carver, all bets are off when you get my age. I'm already on my way; it's my body holding on."

"That's not you." I thrust a finger toward the window. "What about looking up? What about the stars and all the lovely things you used to say? Don't you tell me we're allowed to just . . . to check out whenever we'd like. I don't believe that. I don't believe you believe it. Like I told you the other day, you're not done. And when did you last look up, by the way?"

"I've looked up plenty, and what I've learned . . . is that even stars go dark." She chewed on the thought. "Even stars go dark. And that's okay. I'm ready to say goodbye. I'm ready to join my Tom."

"What can I do?" I whispered. The question was more for me than her. I couldn't believe what I was hearing. She was family, and it felt like it was my turn to take the wheel in our relationship. Sure, she had a son, but she clearly wanted no help from him.

"Talk to me, Mrs. Cartwright," I said. "There are a thousand people in this town who would drop anything for you. Let us all help. What can *we* do?"

She coughed, her whole body shaking, and I gave her a cup of water. Once she'd had a sip, she said, "You can't know what it feels like in these bones, but I'm out of fight. That's all there is to it." Her eyes sharpened. "I'm serious when I say I don't want you to tell a soul. I never should have told Ava about the metformin."

We locked eyes. "Yes, you should have. Tell me what I can do."

She held eye contact, fiery determination glowing in her irises. "Let me go, Carver. Go back to Asheville and live your best life. I've lived mine."

Her words hurt me so deeply that I felt a nearly unbearable hollowness. "The world wouldn't be the same without you in it."

She gave a dark laugh. "The world will keep on spinning just fine without me."

Through the window, I saw a family strolling on a paved path. A little girl, her mom and dad. In the middle of them, an older man pushed a walker. Oh, the agony of mortality.

"No. I'm not buying it. You didn't let me go back then, and I'm not letting you go now." My words came out with conviction, and I sure as hell meant them. But inside, somewhere lodged in the fragile places, I wondered what I could do to make a difference. What would staying a few more days accomplish?

"I'm tired, Carver." Her words were barely audible, her lips sticking together.

"I know that. I can see that. But . . ." I rested my elbows on my thighs, leaning in. "You've lived too big a life to let it fizzle. You're bigger than this. Stronger than *this*."

Was I getting through to her at all?

She pulled her hands under the sheets. "I'm going to close my eyes for a while." Without looking at me, she turned the other way and curled up.

The question of how I could help was so strong in me that I found myself wandering the halls of the hospital, brushing by hospital staff and visitors, peeking around corners, as if I might find the answer there.

I stumbled upon Ava sitting at a table in the cafeteria. Though it was clean and decorated with some healthy plants, the lack of other decor and the poor choice in furniture and color accents made me feel like I'd walked into a newly built Holiday Inn. A line of people worked their way through a buffet that smelled like a . . . like a buffet, this hodgepodge of meats and vegetables all stirring up into the air.

Passing by the other tables, I was discouraged by the lack of smiles and laughter. This was a place no one wanted to be.

Ava stared out the window at a courtyard that glowed green in the last of the day's sun. She sat with her legs crossed and held a granola bar out in front of her, like a microphone.

"Can I join you?" I asked.

Lowering the granola bar, she turned to me. "Of course."

I joined her and blew out a breath. "I hate seeing her like this."

She bit her lip. "I should have been watching her more. I knew something was wrong, but I never would have thought she'd stop taking her medicine."

"You're not her nurse."

"I'm her friend." Ava set the half-eaten granola bar on the table. "I've told her to eat healthier. I see what's in the fridge. But she hates cooking for herself. I realize I'm eating a granola bar that's probably loaded with sugar, but . . . this is rare." The way she spoke, it was like she'd been so in her head, beating herself up, so frustrated with herself.

I pinched the bridge of my nose, remembering the woman who'd loved the kitchen, loved her garden, loved cooking for people. "You should have seen her garden at the farm. She'd take baskets of vegetables and fruits to give away at school. I bet she had forty or fifty tomato plants. The best I've ever tasted."

"Sometimes it's hard to believe she's the same woman," I concluded.

"Though I didn't know her back then," Ava said, "I can still see that side of her. She has her moments where she shines through."

I drummed my fingers on the table. "How can we bring more of that person back? She needs a wake-up call . . . or a reason to get out of bed in the morning. Becoming a widow isn't a death sentence. Nor is diabetes."

"I hate to say it," Ava said, "but I think her son is right. I think she needs to consider moving into a facility. She's lonely. She doesn't have anyone else. Tom is gone. Her friend Lyla has Alzheimer's. Of course, she has you and me while we're in town. That's it. She needs to find a new community."

I tried to imagine a jolly Eloise Cartwright playing bridge in the lobby of a nursing home. "I can't see it. I don't see her being happy like that. But maybe you're right. She definitely needs someone monitoring her medicine." An idea formed. "But I wonder if giving her a reason to fight would be the best." I didn't say that was what she and Tom had done for me.

"But what is that?" Ava asked.

"I wish she could go back to teaching," I said. "She's still sharp."

An image came to me, a gift from my subcortex, and I shared it with Ava. "I just remembered this particular day when I was working for them. Early in the summer after I'd graduated. Tom and I had mended a fence knocked down by a falling tree, and we were coming up to drink some of Mrs. Cartwright's lavender lemonade when we found her in between the rows in the garden. *Lying* on the ground, doing snow angels. She was covered in dirt and giggling like a little girl."

Ava came out of her shell and let out a guarded smile, one she seemed ashamed of showing.

"She had a smile like yours," I said, "so very contagious. I don't remember seeing it as much in the classroom, but when she was out there on the farm, she came into herself, like some dirt in her nails made her come alive."

Ava's smile rose through her cheeks and into her eyes. She could have raised the dead with all that light. "Snow angels," she said. "I love that image. What would you call them? Dirt angels? Doesn't have the same ring, does it?"

"Tom called her his earth angel."

"That's perfect."

"You know that song, right?" Considering my inability to carry a tune, I sang more than I should have of the chorus of the Penguins' song "Earth Angel." "Tom sang it to her all the time."

"Listen to your golden voice," Ava said, beaming.

I glared at her as she hit me again with that lovely smile.

"Please don't ever bring up my singing."

"I loved it."

"I'm sure you did. And anyway . . . ," I said, clearly drawing a line in the sand. "We will move on now. We need to get her back in the garden, Ava." I drew in a deep breath and exhaled out my frustration. "This whole thing about her not wanting anyone to know? I should ignore her and have the whole town show up with gifts. They'd line up all the way to the parking lot."

Ava sighed. "You can't do that. She doesn't like the way she looks. Especially not now, in the hospital bed. Trust me, she doesn't want a big surprise."

"Yeah, I know." I thought of everything I had going on back in Asheville, the things that were consuming my life. They were important, no doubt. I had people counting on our clinic. Animals that needed us. But right now Mrs. Cartwright was what mattered, and I was sure down to the core of me that there had to be a way to help.

A few minutes later, I stepped away to call Mary Beth.

"Dr. Livingston. I haven't heard from you in a couple of hours. That's a first. You really are changing." Her sarcasm sprang off her tongue.

"Yeah, some things have come up." Pacing in the hallway outside the cafeteria, I told her about Mrs. Cartwright—not about the medicine but about the car wreck.

"That's heartbreaking," she said.

"Tell me about it. Between my mom and her, there's no way I can leave right now."

"You're darn right there's not."

"So you can handle things without me a few more days? I guess I already know the answer to that question."

"Yes, you do."

We caught up on a few details before I returned to Ava in the cafeteria. We sat there in silence for a while. I needed to collect myself before going back in to see Mrs. Cartwright. I wanted to be at my absolute best. To do that, maybe a break from all the seriousness would be okay.

"Tell me something," I said. "What is the whole transient thing about? You don't own much more than your truck? Don't you have favorite electronics or . . . ? I don't know . . . family heirlooms. A bike? Pictures, paintings. No furniture?"

"I have a bike. It rides in the back of the truck."

"Of course it does."

"I've had a complicated life before," she said. "It didn't fit me well."

What did she know about a complicated life? I smiled at her take on one. "Will you do me a favor and talk to me about your complicated life? I could use the distraction."

She coughed up a laugh. "So you want to hear about my struggles to make yourself feel better? Do you know what that's called?"

"Sadism?"

"Nope," she said. "It's a German word. Schadenfreude."

"Schadenfreude? Is that truly a thing?"

"Look it up. I read about it somewhere, the experience of finding joy in other people's pain. You're not alone if there's a word for it."

"Well, that's comforting. And now I feel even worse."

She held up her hands.

"Okay," I said. "I don't want to hear about your struggles. I just want to hear you talk so I can stop thinking for one minute about Mrs. Cartwright deciding to end her life."

Ava's eyes filled with compassion. "Okay. I went to high school in Nashville—that's where my mom and I finally ended up. Attended Vanderbilt so I could stay close to her. She and I always had a turbulent relationship, but we were best friends too. Shortly after I graduated, she started having seizures. An MRI revealed a malignant tumor. Clichéd as it is, I fell in love with her surgeon."

"No."

"Yes." She rolled her eyes at herself. "She was gone only a few months later. By then, John and I were pretty serious. He was older. It was a tough time for me, losing my mom. I wasn't exactly sure what I wanted to do. Maybe a nurse. He was fun to be with, lifted me up. I moved in with him and gave up on a career for a minute. I was so young back then, I . . . I didn't know what I was doing."

She slapped the air. "I tried to be this person I wasn't for him. His family was so deeply embedded into Nashville, always hosting charity events and cocktail parties. I had a closet full of dresses I hated wearing.

He bought me a car and introduced me to women he thought I should know. One day I woke up and realized I wasn't ready for all that. I wanted simple. Or different."

She looked out toward the courtyard. "I broke up with him and moved back to Chicago. Served at a Rick Bayless restaurant to pay for PT school, and that was that. Now I guess I'm trying to find out where I do fit in. In the meantime, this kind of living suits me."

"Look at you," I said. "I served in college too. That's how I paid for some of it. That and some brutal loans."

"What kind of restaurant?" she asked.

"This fancy French place with the meanest chef in the world. The guy would throw things at us when we messed up. But the tips were great. Anyway, thanks for sharing. I feel like I get you so much more now."

"So your schadenfreude curiosities have been quenched?"

I couldn't *not* smile. "I am thoroughly satiated."

She shook her head at me, then looked away.

I wasn't sure what to make of her. For some strange reason, especially for a skeptic like me, I felt like we'd crossed paths for a reason. What that reason was, I had no idea.

Chapter 14

HEARTBREAKER

Nothing felt more reminiscent of the old days than Elliot coming over for dinner. I'd texted him to say I was staying in town longer, and he'd all but invited himself over, saying his wife was with her book club and his kids were with Grandma. I figured some Elliot time would be good for my mother. His parents were awful cooks, so he'd gotten used to hanging around our house at dinnertime. You wouldn't have known it now, but my parents could lay down an amazing meal when they wanted to and had inspired me to learn as I grew older.

He arrived while I was right in the middle of my preparations, a collection of small plates, which was how I most enjoyed cooking. My mother sat at the counter, making short work of a bottle of a pale-pink Provençal rosé. We'd been chatting about my father and then about Mrs. Cartwright's troubles. Mom had offered a few suggestions for how I might help her before I left. Of course, I hadn't told her about Mrs. Cartwright not taking her metformin. Any talk of suicide would hit way too close to home, and though my mother wasn't exactly showing it, I knew she was extra fragile tonight.

I'd stopped by a fantastic market that had recently opened up near the Sanderton and acquired some great finds, including this bottle I'd incorrectly thought might get us all the way to dinner. Candied beets and purple potatoes roasted in the oven. I'd soon top them with a feta whipped with fresh herbs and crushed pistachios. As I'd remembered about my hometown, the local mushrooms were out of this world. I'd chopped up some black trumpets, hen of the woods, and chanterelles and was about to sauté them with rainbow chard in some lovely Greek olive oil I'd found.

I wore my apron and was running a knife through a glorious loaf of local paesano bread when the bell rang. My mom went to the door and returned with Elliot and Oscar in tow. We were keeping Oscar tonight, and then I'd return him to Mrs. C after we brought her home from the hospital.

"My goodness, it smells good in here," Elliot said. He wore a green polo shirt and paisley socks hiding under chinos. The ultimate dad attire. He wore it so well.

I wiped my hands on my apron and gave him a fist bump. Then I looked at Oscar, on a leash. "And you," I said. "Are we ready to put our differences aside?"

The look he gave me in response was one that showed he was ready to launch into an attack at the slightest provocation.

I gave him some attitude. "I guess you don't want the surprise I picked up for you. Dare I say the word . . . *treat*?"

Oscar lightened up.

"Is that your tail wagging?" I asked. "Though I'm well aware that you're forcing me to buy our friendship, I procured a nice bone from the butcher." I reached for it on the counter and then held it up above him.

"Sit, Oscar Wilde."

He sat so fast he could have cracked a walnut underneath him.

"Do you shake? No, I didn't think so. We'll work on that one later. Here you go." I finally gave him the bone, and he nearly took my hand off going for it.

We circled around the island. Elliot looked at the stove. "I've been dreaming about eating your food, Mrs. Livingston."

"This is all Carver," my mother said. Because of the quick intake of wine, she'd come into a jolly mood. Good for her for figuring it out and staying positive, even if it did require lubrication.

Elliot regarded me with a look of being impressed. "Where does it stop with you? You've become a superhero."

"What are you talking about, become? Always have been." I smiled. "At least, Mom has always said so."

"That's right, dimple butt."

Never shy to try an early bite, Elliot reached for a slice of bread and moaned with delight.

"Alice doesn't feed you?" I asked.

He shook his head, not wanting to take his attention away from the bread yet. Once he'd properly finished it, he said, "Alice has us on this no-carb thing. I haven't even seen a piece of bread this month."

"By all means," I said, "have another. But don't tell her I gave it to you."

He helped himself to another slice and crammed it into his mouth. "I've lost seven pounds in two weeks."

"You do look good," my mother said to him.

"It's torture, Mrs. L. Torture." He grabbed his sides. "But she didn't marry me for my brains, if you know what I mean. I need to keep my muffin top in check."

My mom poured Elliot the rest of what was in the bottle and then went to the fridge to reload. "She's a lucky woman. I hope Carver gets a chance to meet her before he leaves."

"She was so sad to miss it, but she'd had plans with her girlfriends for a couple of weeks now. They've started a book club. Doesn't that sound like trouble?"

"The best kind," my mom said, returning with a bottle of chilled red and setting it on the counter. She produced one of those giant rabbit corkscrews and went to work. The cork came out cleanly, and she set it aside to refill her glass.

"You should join them," Elliot said, watching her. "They're all ages. A great bunch of women. I think they're reading a Kristin Hannah book right now."

"Maybe I will talk to her about it." My mom overpoured herself, filling it all the way to the top. "Oops," she said.

I felt embarrassed, but I knew Elliot understood. An impending divorce earned you a license to overindulge on occasion, though I hoped this behavior wouldn't turn into a habit.

"I'm so sorry about Mr. Livingston," Elliot said.

She waved her glass under her nose to enjoy the perfume. "Thank you, Elliot." For a second I could definitely see the toll my father's abandonment was taking on her, and I winced at how well I knew those same feelings, how we both knew them now.

They took seats on the stools opposite me at the island as I worked. Trying to time everything perfectly was my favorite part of cooking, making sure everything was the right temperature when it hit the plate. It was a source of pride.

We talked about Mrs. Cartwright, and I gave them the vaguest update I could, talking about only the car accident. Out of respect for Mrs. Cartwright, I hadn't told Shannon a thing when I'd called her to apologize about skipping the barre class.

Speaking of the one who almost got away, it didn't take long before my mother nudged Elliot and said, "What do you think of those two getting back together?"

"We're talking some." I attempted to smother my delight at the notion of Shannon and my grand recoupling.

"That is a door I'd keep closed if I were you," she said.

I transferred my beets and potatoes into a serving dish. "Noted, Mom."

"I think I'll plead the fifth on this one," Elliot said with a kind smile, showing he supported me either way. "Would be nice if she convinced you to move back."

I whipped my eyes to him like I was about to whip more feta.

My mom set her glass down so hard it nearly broke. "He won't move back for me. That's for sure."

I refrained from saying a word, knowing anything I said would only make things worse.

⌒

A while after our last bites, Elliot was taking the plates to the dishwasher when he said, "Hey, where'd Oscar run off to?"

I looked over to the corner where he'd been sleeping, comatose after all the food scraps we'd fed him. "No idea."

The three of us searched the house until Elliot called out from the third floor. I climbed both flights of stairs to find him in my room with Oscar in his arms, looking around as if he'd wandered into an undiscovered wing in a museum.

"They haven't changed your room?" he asked in a whisper.

"I know. Weird, right?"

"A little. I feel like I've opened up a time capsule." Carrying Oscar, Elliot went to the window. After a soft chuckle, he asked, "You remember Mrs. Adley?"

I stepped behind him, finding the neighbor's window that he and I had spent so much time staring through, hoping for a glimpse. Mrs. Cartwright was right. Men were only a step away from the boys they once were.

"That's one of those things you never forget," I said.

He turned to me. "Those tatas. They are indeed burned forever into my memory."

I grinned, seeing Elliot morph into his younger self and remembering how wide his eyes were when I'd first introduced him to that wonderful view. I gestured toward the bunk bed, the navy-blue comforters, and red pillowcases. "Remember spraying me with pee?"

"How could I not?" He heaved Oscar into the top bunk and then climbed up. "Holy shit, Carv. I'm a kid again."

I climbed into the lower bunk and stretched out. How strange to have Elliot up in my room in the bunk bed above me. He must have been thinking the same thing, because he said, "It has to be hard being up here, no?"

He didn't have to elaborate. "You could say that."

A tremendous amount of shame washed over me, and it manifested itself as a subtle burn under the band of my watch. The burn grew stronger as time pulled me back like someone was tugging at my limbs. I removed my watch and reached for the pain, massaging it like I'd removed handcuffs. There it was, the white scar that served as a not-so-gentle reminder.

I didn't notice until it was too late that Elliot had leaned over the top bunk and was looking at me. "Where'd you do it?" he asked. "Was it in the bed?"

"Yeah," I said, feeling a constriction in my throat. I'd slept in this bed a few nights, but I'd not let myself feel what it was like to be that kid holding the razor. Not until now.

"Right here," I whispered. "I couldn't take one more day of that empty feeling."

I was seventeen. Shirtless and shoeless wearing Red Sox sweatpants. I'd barely eaten since Shannon had dumped me two weeks prior, and it showed on my stomach and chest. I stared at the sharp edge of the razor blade. My father was at the garage. As always, my mother was at the bank.

"It was a whole thing trying to decide how to do it," I said, realizing I'd never talked to Elliot about the details. "It was before Google, but there was another search engine."

"Ask Jeeves or Yahoo maybe," Elliot said.

"Yeah, probably. I didn't want to mess up, so I searched for the most effective method. Remember my dad had a pistol back then, and I'd found the code to the safe in one of his tool drawers. I held the gun in my hand. A Smith and Wesson. It was terrifying. I didn't want to be one of those kids who puts a gun to his head and then wakes in the hospital with half a face. Something I read must have steered me toward a razor blade."

Elliot and Oscar were quiet above me.

My eyes were open to the bottom of the bunk, but I was seeing back through the years, blown wide open, so alone without the girl with whom I was supposed to spend forever.

"The blade was so much more intimidating, though. It wasn't as easy as pulling a trigger. Or maybe I didn't want to do it. My survivor instinct must have kicked in, a part of me that wouldn't let me put the blade to my wrist. I lay here forever, trying to find the courage. That's when the Jack Daniel's entered the equation. The entire cabinet was full of liquor bottles that you and I had watered down, but that bottle of Jack was brand-new, the plastic still on it. It did the trick. The room smelled like whiskey."

It occurred to me I'd not relived that day in a long, long time. Not even in the therapy sessions I'd briefly tried. I ran my finger over the scar, up and down, my whole life carved out by this small incision.

Shannon appeared in my mind. I could feel her fingernails as she drew pictures on my chest, the way she used to. Our origin story came alive in my head. "I remember calling you from Burlington. Remember I was in that gifted camp? I told you something between Shannon and me had sparked, and you laughed your ass off. Howled, even. When we first saw each other, I told you again, and I remember you saying, 'Quit dreaming, dude.'"

I smiled. "What I'll never forget is your face when you finally saw us together."

"I remember," Elliot said. "You two were all cuddled up in the corner over there, 'studying' together." Though I couldn't see him, I knew he had placed air quotes around the word *studying*.

I glanced over at the beanbag on the other side of the room. "Lots of 'studying' went down on that beanbag." Returning to the memory that was so vivid in my mind, I said, "Really, that face you had. You said something like, 'You gotta be shitting me.' Right in front of her. God, I want to go back to that first day of our senior year," I said, feeling the richness of it all over me. "We hit those double doors of the high school like we were smashing down the walls of the universe."

"You definitely changed," Elliot said. "You became the cool guy."

Shame coursed through me like a quick electric shock. "Yeah, maybe even too cool for you, huh?"

"Love makes you do strange things, brother. No hard feelings."

I heard him, but I was also riding a time machine, like my mother so often did. I had an old Jeep my dad had restored for me, and it was still warm enough in September where we could leave the top off and go for a long, breezy drive. Shannon and Carver, riding the world, our favorite songs blasting through the speakers. She'd throw her arms around me, her hair blowing back in the wind, and she'd kiss me with those luscious lips, and I felt like she'd given me wings. Then we'd find a quiet spot by the river, where we'd drink beer and swim naked and make love and talk until dark.

Did we love each other? Hell yes, we did. We planned to apply to the same schools. Her grades weren't as good as mine, but I was fine letting go of my Ivy League school ambitions. You sacrifice for the ones you love, right? Most high school loves didn't work out, but ours was different.

Then October came. The leaves had turned a fiery orange. When I picked her up one day in the Jeep that now had the top back on, she seemed like she didn't want to be there.

"What's on your mind?" I asked her.

"Nothing, why?" she said.

"You seem . . . I don't know . . . mad at me maybe?"

Those conversations continued until I felt like a pest bringing it up. But the seed was planted, and I had started to doubt myself. What had I done wrong? Was she over us?

The thing that made me the angriest was that she didn't tell me the truth. She'd been cheating on me for a couple of weeks and hadn't told me, probably to avoid such an adult conversation. I could see that. But we were different, or so I thought. We told each other everything. Why couldn't she have told me the truth? I wouldn't have taken it well, but it might not have crushed me like it did when Elliot ratted her out.

That had been a few days before Halloween. Shannon and I were going to be Mary and Ted from *There's Something about Mary*, a movie we'd loved that had come out in the summer. I remember the hollowness inside as I trudged around my room with a trash bag, cramming in the ugly taupe suit and ridiculous wig I'd planned on wearing, along with the pictures I had of the two of us, the cool watch she'd given me. If only I could have pulled it together from there.

"You know what's embarrassing to admit," I said, drawing a square on the bottom of the bunk above me.

"What's that?" Elliot asked. I was still barely aware that he was there, certainly not worried about oversharing.

"Even as recently as a few weeks ago, I catch myself wondering what happened to us . . . or what could have been. I remember you first telling me you'd seen them together, Trey and Shannon. That they were holding hands. She didn't even deny it when I confronted her about it at her house that afternoon. She said something like, 'It's over, Carver. I don't know what else to say.' From that moment on, I've spent so much time wondering what I could have done differently. Or what he had that I didn't."

"Jesus, Carver. High school love never lasts. You gotta quit beating yourself up; let it go."

"Believe me, I know. Maybe that's what this is, me letting it go." And it felt that way, a cathartic release to my friend. "It feels good to talk about it, I guess. Please . . . I know you wouldn't, but don't mention this to anyone."

He dropped his head down the side long enough to say, "You're right. I wouldn't." We held eye contact for a moment before he pulled himself back up.

My eyes had welled up with tears. I wiped them and then spotted the old landline on the table next to me. "The thing that most haunts me is that I called her right after I'd slit my wrist. I somehow thought that if she knew she was losing me, she'd wake up and realize what we'd had. God, the thought of me drunk and slurring words, mumbling that she was the only one for me and that if it was over between us, then it was over for me too . . .”

I cringed trying to recall what might have been said. “And I remember her being afraid, begging me not to hurt myself. I told her I already had and then I heard her screaming as the phone dropped.”

“If you hadn't called her, then the ambulance would have been too late.”

“I know,” I said, hearing the sirens that had filled the air. “It's just fucking embarrassing. All those people finding out, talking about me. Every teacher keeping an eye out for me. All the kids whispering about me, glancing down at my wrist, wanting to see the carnage. Shannon would turn the other way when she saw me coming down the hall. I feel like . . . all of them see me that way, even today.”

Elliot's legs appeared first as he set his shoes on the ladder of the bunk bed. With Oscar in his hands, he lowered to the ground. He set Oscar down and then offered me a hand.

“Come here, buddy.”

I sighed.

“Come get a hug from your best friend.”

I squeezed my eyes together, feeling both devastated and liberated. I took his hand. He pulled me up and into an embrace that invited me to let go of what I'd done. I wept into his neck, releasing all the shit that had been holding me back.

“I'm sorry,” I said, sniffling.

He patted my back. “You have nothing to be sorry for, my brother.” He pinched up high on my shoulders, finding a place where I held a lot of tension. “Just quit carrying it alone, man. You're not alone.”

“I know that.”

He stepped back to lock eyes with me. “Do you?”

I offered a brittle smile, wishing I could say yes.

Chapter 15

THE FATES

I woke at six the next morning feeling good, better than I'd felt in a long time. It wasn't exactly a mystery. Letting myself really feel what had happened had shaken something loose.

After reaching for my phone, I was delighted to see Shannon had continued to text me after I'd fallen asleep. I wasn't about to count them, but I'm guessing we'd texted about a hundred times back and forth, all the way until well after midnight. How miraculous that I'd not been wrong about us and that we had a chance together. Her decision to leave me and her relationship with Trey were to me glitches in the code of the universe. Apparently I should have kept the tattoo.

"Carver," my mother called out as I passed her bedroom on the way down the stairs.

"Yeah?" I opened the door to her room. Though she had the master, it wasn't any bigger than the other rooms on this floor. The only differences were the fancy bed and the nice crystal chandelier that hung over it.

What I found surprised me. Leaning against the elaborately carved wooden headboard, my mother held Oscar in her arms. She had the biggest smile on her face.

"Look who didn't want to sleep in his kennel last night," she said.

"I don't know what to say." I was thrilled to see her so happy and slightly amazed that my mother, who'd never wanted a dog in her life, held him so.

"He's adorable," my mom said. "He slept curled up against me the entire night."

"Oscar Wilde," I said sternly. "For your information, she doesn't even like dogs."

She covered his ears. "Don't you say that. I do like dogs." She kissed his head. "He's afraid, aren't you, Oscar?"

His tail whipped back and forth.

"You tell Eloise she can't have him back," she said.

"She might be okay with that. Seriously, Mom, how are you? I mean, with Dad leaving."

She considered her answer. "I'm . . . you know. Looking for the silver lining. I thought about putting the house up for sale, but Kara says it's always best to hold off on making any big decisions for a year or so after something like this happens. She's probably right." Kara had been her roommate at BU and now lived in Athens, Georgia. Even after all these years, they spoke frequently.

"In the meantime," my mom continued, "I'm going to work on me. If my ankle will stay out of the way, I'd love to do the half-marathon in Boston. There are big changes coming at work, a new CEO who is threatening to shake things up. I've got my hands full. And busy is good."

Relief came over me. "Isn't that the truth," I said. "Well, I'm here to talk, Mom. You seem like you're doing well, but if you want to, I'm here."

"Just knowing you're nearby is gift enough, my love."

"I wish you could give some of that strength to Mrs. Cartwright."

"Keep working on her, honey. She'll come around."

Over breakfast, I called Ava and offered her a ride to the hospital. Mrs. Cartwright was to be discharged at eight. Ava was right downtown, staying at an old mill that had been converted into high-end apartments. With Oscar in his kennel in the back seat, I pulled into the horseshoe-shaped drive and found her waiting for me. She wore a flowy purple dress and a band in her hair. She was a breath of fresh air, if I was being honest.

"How did Mrs. Cartwright seem last night?" I asked, turning down the music and hanging a right toward the hospital.

"Better, I think. I left about nine, shortly after she fell asleep. She'll be ready to go home."

"Hopefully with a different attitude."

"Yeah."

Coming to enjoy our time together, I asked, "How's your search for home going? Any big revelations since yesterday?"

"No, but I'm going to take a couple of weeks off. I'm feeling pretty spent. And then we'll see. Maybe it's time to settle down, own a house, all that." She sighed like a teakettle. "I don't know where."

"I could be of help," I said. "I've always overanalyzed everything. Even choosing North Carolina back when I was eighteen. I made charts. Can you believe that?"

She giggled.

"I'm serious. Same when I settled on Asheville. I could tell you the amount of dog parks, vet clinics. How many days of sunshine. The quality of the air. The average pollen count. How many bike trails. The bike safety index. The amount of good restaurants and breweries. Crime rates. What I missed was not studying future traffic patterns. Asheville is getting crowded, but it's the price one pays for living in a lovely spot."

I couldn't tell if she was laughing with me or at me, but she drew a smile out of me too.

"What's your idea of home?" I asked. "Mountains, beach? City, town? What is your ideal population?"

"That's the thing," she said. "I don't know yet. Teterbury's a delight. I like how everyone knows each other. I adore the mountains at the back door. I'm such a nature person, you know. I enjoy getting lost. But . . . something is not quite right here. Not sure how to put my finger on it."

"The winters?" I asked.

"Yeah, it does get cold, but I was in Chicago a long time. I love snow. Maybe it's that I haven't met my tribe, you know? The people are such a part of it. Of course, I love my clients, especially Mrs. C, but I don't have that many great friends . . . or a . . . you know . . . a partner. Not that I'm desperately seeking one."

"I hear you there." Had she talked to me about relationships a week ago, before Shannon had come back into my life, I would have told her I wasn't even remotely seeking one. Now I wasn't so sure. "Something tells me you would never have to desperately seek a partner. I'm betting a guy—or girl—will soon fight hard to tie you down."

She laughed back at me. "We'll see."

Speaking genuinely, I said, "You can't keep yourself all to yourself. That wouldn't be fair."

She turned to me, her hair whipping back. "Is this you giving compliments? That was very, oddly, sweet of you."

I stopped at a crosswalk to let someone pass. "I'm glad you think so highly of me," I said sarcastically.

"Actually," she said, "you're proving to be more oniony than I'd thought."

I gave a slow nod with my whole body, like I was doing the worm. "Boy, you're also so good at the compliment thing. Oniony?"

She touched my arm, and I'd be lying if I didn't take notice. "Just giving you a hard time," she said. "Somebody needs to."

Why did people say such things to me all the time? "I give myself a hard enough time. Nobody else needs to join in." I sounded more negative about it than I'd meant to.

She said in a pouty tone, like she was speaking to a baby, "You poor thing, it must be awful being a rich white man."

My jaw hit the steering wheel. "Wh . . . What? Did that just come out of your mouth?" Boy, had I dug a hole with my pity party.

I turned to find her grinning. "I'm joking, Carver." She hit me in the arm. "Gosh, you need to lighten up." Hadn't Shannon told me that too?

A car honked behind me. I'd frozen at the crosswalk. I pressed the gas. "The nerve of you," I said, still amazed she'd said the thing about the rich white man. "The feisty in you is like a wolf hiding in her den. She only comes out on occasion."

She held up her hands. "It was a joke. A teeny-weeny joke." She rolled down the window and stuck her hand out to enjoy the cool air. "How about you? Has your mother convinced you to move back?"

I shook my head, recalibrating after her rather deep dig. "Somehow I agreed to stay a few more days, but no, I'm not moving back. No, no, no."

"Something seems to want you here," she said. "A force has reeled you in."

Who was this woman? A psychic? "No question. I've failed so far in fighting it. Bree, the woman chairing our upcoming reunion, was coming after me, and I did everything I could to get rid of her. Then my parents with the divorce and Mrs. Cartwright. I didn't have a choice."

"You were meant to come home. Sounds like fate to me."

"Fate?" I said the word like it had no business in this conversation.

"Hold on," she said. "Are you a skeptic? You are, aren't you? The whole doctor thing, the metallurgist welding dog knees. You're a scientist, through and through."

"Guilty as charged," I said. Keeping it light, I asked in jest, "Do you know the one about the transient and the skeptic?"

She rewarded me with a small clap. "You're dodging the point. Is that what you do when you get uncomfortable?"

I smiled. "Another joke is coming to me . . . hold on . . ."

"Okay, we'll play games all afternoon." She pulled a foot up to her seat. "All I'm saying is that it's not a coincidence you're back here. You can hide behind all the science you want, but you'd better buckle up, because change is coming."

With my free hand, I tugged on my seat belt. "Way ahead of things."

"I know you're joking, but I'm serious. All the things that brought you home. You'd better lean into them. Don't you dare go home until you've heeded the call."

"Heeded the call?" I asked. "What is this, *Lord of the Rings*?"

"Look at you squirm," she said, apparently having fun with me. "I'm serious."

"Okay, Mrs. Serious, what is the call?"

Her mouth straightened. "Only you can know that. But it's big, like life-changing big."

Maybe she was referring to Shannon. Perhaps I was on a crusade to rescue my damsel, who had been stolen by the evil knight, Trey of Teterbury. Ava was the witch in the castle—an admittedly pretty one—staring into her crystal ball.

"You already know that, though," she said. "I can see it in you. You're different from when I first met you. Amazing what a few days home can do. All I saw at first was this guy with his fancy watch and his big-time job. Now you seem more human."

"You are a piece of work," I said. "Any more time with you, and I'll need a year of therapy."

"No. Your therapy is right here, right now. You've been tapped, my friend. You're going back a different person, whether you like it or not."

"Who are you?" I asked, feeling like someone was playing a trick on me. I was afraid she'd hit the mark even more than she knew. No matter what came of Shannon and me, or how much I could help my mother, I knew that cracking open the hard shell of my past had brought a fresh release that could have been only good for me.

She sat back, resting her case. In a much-less-animated tone, she said, "I know you think I'm silly, and that's fine. But trust me, there is some truth to what I said."

"No, I get it. I don't think you're silly. If anything, you scare me."

"Scare you?"

I switched hands on the wheel, finding myself leaning toward her. "I'm good at hiding from people. That's what I do. But I have this feeling you can see right through me, which throws me off guard."

"I'm sorry that I'm scary."

"Scary in the best ways." Seizing an opportunity to climb off the operating table, I said, "And speaking of therapy, I loved what you suggested about my parents revisiting what had given them their original spark. What if we took Mrs. Cartwright back to the beginning?"

I pulled into the crowded parking lot and searched for a spot. "She always talks about looking up to the sky, how important it is. Well, she never does that. She barely goes outside. I thought I'd go by her old farm today and see if the owners would let us come by tonight or sometime soon. Just to see her old place, her garden, and let her get a good look at the stars. As skeptical as I am, I've never seen the stars like I have on that farm." Realizing I was getting emotional, I wrapped up with, "Care to join us? I know she'd like you to be there."

"Look at Mr. Onion," she said. "Peeling off your little layers. Yes, I'd love to come."

As we climbed out of the car, I looked over at this woman, wondering when the surprises in learning about her ever ended. What she'd said earlier about a tribe and a partner. She might be right; home couldn't exist without them.

⌒

We came into Mrs. Cartwright's room to find her staring at her phone. A big crease lined her forehead. "You look so happy here," I said. "You sure you don't want to spend another night?"

She glared at me. "Get me out of here."

I had this funny thought of stealing her from the hospital, pushing her and her bed down the halls, like in a movie.

"You look chipper," Mrs. Cartwright said. "What's gotten into you?"

Shannon no doubt had a lot to do with it, but I hesitated to mention her. Why? Because my feelings for her made me feel like a kid about to confess to stealing a twenty out of his mother's purse.

To answer Mrs. Cartwright's question, I said, "It's been good to reconnect with everyone. I feel like the weight has left my shoulders."

"You look like that," she said. "Now we need to revisit my lessons on avoiding clichés."

"Always teaching," I said. "You ready to hit the road?"

She fired a finger at me. "Stop with the clichés."

I kept a straight face. "We'll put the pedal to the metal and see where the road takes us."

"Carver Livingston," she said, refusing to laugh at my awful humor.

Though we didn't bust her out, she was released within the hour. I retrieved the Audi while Ava pushed Mrs. C in the wheelchair to the exit.

Though we were attempting to keep it light, the mood in the car was unquestionably somber, as if we were driving to a funeral. There was no diluting the fact that Mrs. Cartwright had recently chosen to let her life come to an end.

I refused to let the silence bury us. I turned to the back seat, where she let Oscar lick her hand through the wire cage. He was too unruly to roam in the car freely. "I had to pry Oscar away, Mrs. Cartwright. You wouldn't believe my mom, taking to him like she did."

She seemed to have to work hard to jump into a conversation, as if she wanted to be alone. "I'm glad," she said. "Maybe she'd be better off with him."

"You don't mean that."

No response.

Ava and I looked at each other, and then Ava offered up an idea. "You know what I want to do today? What if we all go to your house and watch a movie? What do you say, Carver?"

"I have something I have to do at three, but I'm all in before then. How about you, Mrs. Cartwright?"

"You two don't need to do this. You have your own lives."

Ava twisted to her. "I'm going to watch a movie with or without you."

"What movie?" I asked.

"When's the last time you saw *Casablanca*?" Ava was asking us both.

"*Casablanca*?" I replied with more than a fair dose of disappointment. "Not once."

The women at the same time admonished me with, "You've never seen *Casablanca*?"

I slunk into my seat and said feebly, "I guess I know what we're going to watch."

That was what we did. As the clock ticked toward Shannon's barre class, the three of us sat in Mrs. Cartwright's living room and watched what I worried would be slow to the point of boring. I might have looked at the phone the whole time, but during my first attempt, early on when Rick and Ilsa first met, Ava hit my arm. "Don't you dare."

I gave her a playful salute and stuffed my phone back into my pocket. I hated to admit when I was wrong, but when the credits rolled, I wiped my moist eyes and turned back to Ava, "Okay, not as bad as I thought."

"Not as bad as you thought?" she asked in a defensive tone. "Why are you crying? Look at this grown man crying, Mrs. Cartwright."

"Crying?" I asked, noticing red eyes around the room. "The pollen gets me up here. It had nothing to do with the movie."

Ava jokingly clenched both fists. "You're impossible. You know that?"

"Me, impossible? It's women that are impossible. Look at poor Rick in the movie, running into an old flame, falling back in love. And she uses him."

"Oh, he had it coming," Mrs. Cartwright said. "She's married."

"You don't mess with married," Ava added.

I turned to Mrs. Cartwright, and she was fighting off a smile. Oscar, who had been at her feet the whole time, sprang up onto her lap. He must have sensed her change in mood.

I liked being with this crowd, and I found myself different when I was around them. Maybe these guys were part of my tribe. Then I realized the time. I had unfinished business with my own Ilsa Lund.

Chapter 16

Under a Spell

The question that screamed at me as I inched into the barre studio downtown was: What in the hell was I thinking?

Wasn't it amazing what a woman could do to a man? What was even worse was the surprise student who turned her head and smiled when I stepped through the door. None other than Bree Arsenault, the head of the reunion committee, the woman who had proved that she would have been a good bounty hunter if given the opportunity.

"Look at this," she said. "I never would have thought it."

I feigned my best smile. "Bree! So good to see you." Feeling like I'd repeated the same thing to everyone in Teterbury, I said, "You look better than ever."

"I do, don't I? It's Shannon's barre class. She's a tyrant in there." Bree had a swagger that I didn't remember. Maybe it was her new role.

Shannon came up behind us, radiant without trying. I didn't know whether to bow or kiss her on the cheek or hug her. Determined not to be indecisive, I thrust out my hand. Only after I had done so did it feel like I was standing in a conference room and sealing a business deal.

"We're shaking hands now?" she said.

Bree watched the exchange with interest.

"Sorry, I . . ." I opened my arms. "Hug?"

Shannon wrapped her arms around me and whispered, "That's more like it. Glad you came."

"Me too. I think." Boy, could she fill me up with her blatant and renewed interest in me.

To Bree, amping up my extroverted self, I said, "This is my first barre class. I'm gonna need you to avoid the urge to take pictures."

"You're going to love it," Bree replied.

"Love it" wasn't the phrase I'd use, but I didn't hate it, as I did most things when I wasn't good at them. I was unquestionably terrible at barre. I was indeed the only man, and I was also the only one who didn't know all the words to the pop playlist that thumped throughout the class. The one word I knew by the end of the session was *pulse*. I felt like all we'd done was pulse. *Pulse, pulse, pulse, pulse.* We'd get into these weird positions, like forming triangles with our legs, while holding the bar, and Shannon would say, "Pulse." The entire class would lift and then lower their hips.

I didn't do it right at first, and Shannon, of course, took the opportunity to embarrass me. "You can pulse better than that, Dr. Livingston." She came up behind me, grabbed my hips, and forced me to loosen up. "Tuck that tailbone," she said.

The collective giggle from the rest of the class was truly humiliating. But like all things, I got used to it. By the end, I was laughing out loud.

"I'm going to be sore for weeks," I said to Shannon and Bree, who'd cornered me after the class. I stood next to the shelf that offered stickers and books for sale.

"As long as you're able to dance next Saturday night," Bree said.

"Next Saturday night?" I asked naively. Then it hit me. "Do you mean the reunion?" I looked at Shannon, wondering if this was an ambush. Or to Ava's credit, was it fate playing out? I inched deeper into the corner, bumping into the rack of T-shirts.

"Yes, the reunion," Bree said. "Don't tell me you're not going to hang around. I've put together fun gift baskets for the speakers. It's gonna be the best night of the year."

Was she trying to lure me in with a gift basket?

Shannon approached me and put her hand on my arm. "I need a date anyway."

"A date?" I said, pondering the implications, a tingle running through me. Had I a therapist, he or she would have had a field day, because the thought of me missing prom struck a bell. No, I hadn't attended my senior prom. There had been no way in hell I was going to show my face while the new power couple of Teterbury, Shannon and Trey, pranced around the dance floor. Was I getting my chance now? This was when the therapist would have said, "You're really thinking about the prom you missed? You're thirty-eight years old, Dr. Livingston. Does this seem healthy to you?"

I would have answered, "It's not a question of healthy. It's the matter of restoring the balance to the universe. Shannon and I were always supposed to be together."

Shannon was killing me with her electric-blue eyes, waiting for me to surrender. Had Bree not been standing there, I think she might have kissed me.

"There you go," Bree said. "You have a date. And you're the last speaker of the night. Just think: Janet Jackson. MC Hammer. Garth Brooks. All the old goodies on the dance floor. Who wouldn't want to dance with this beautiful woman?"

"Aerosmith," Shannon said. "Remember?" She took my hand and pulled me into a slow dance. Bree watched as the two of us spun around the room like we used to.

I was reduced to a gushy little boy who would have done anything for Shannon right then. She had me right where she wanted me, and I couldn't believe it. All this time . . . and here we were, together at last.

"Fine," I said. "Count me in."

Shannon inched closer to me and, Marilyn Monroe–like, whispered, "Really?" The weight of her ensuing gaze made my insides quiver.

My next words came out like I was being controlled. "How could I turn you down?" In a distant galaxy of my rational mind, a voice chanted, *Shut your fucking mouth!*

"Now you get your gift bag," Bree added. I'd forgotten she was there. "You're in for the speech too?" she asked.

Shannon prodded me and I obeyed. "Okay, okay. The speech too."

Bree looked supremely satisfied, like she'd outsmarted me on the chessboard of life. "You've made my day. Thank you. I can finally print out the program."

I swallowed from a dry mouth. "Why don't we revisit this conversation tomorrow?"

"No, thank you," Bree said. "I have to run now. See you Saturday!" She went to the bench to collect her gym bag.

I turned to Shannon, who looked delighted by my choice. Deciding I'd better get something out of this, I said, "Don't make me wait until Saturday for a date. I'm thinking we go to dinner before then."

"Ah." She bit her lip and looked up into my eyes. "Where is this going?"

"I wouldn't mind finding out."

She flashed her eyebrows and inched toward me, our lips nearly touching. "Don't tease me."

"Tease you?" I said. "It's your teasing that somehow got me to agree to give a speech to my graduating class."

She pressed her finger to my lips. "I always get what I want."

Acknowledging for only a moment that warning lights were flashing, I turned and called out toward the door half-jokingly, "Bree, hold up. I've changed my mind." She'd already left.

When I turned back to Shannon, I said with the confidence that only Shannon could ever give me, "Seven, Saturday night. I'll pick you up."

⌒

After the barre class, I rolled down the windows of the Audi and cruised through downtown Teterbury. No hoodie, nor dark sunglasses. No riding low. I may have even released a howl or two as I stuck my head out the window. Ah, to be smitten in Vermont in the early summer, when the midseventies were the norm and the plants in the garden finally bore fruit; when everyone cleaned their grills and dusted off their outdoor furniture and spent most of their time on their porches or taking long walks; when it rained enough to wash away the pollen and polish the streets and turn every leaf a vibrant green; and when the misty air smelled like crushed mint.

Was there anything better?

Of course, not all was well, but I now felt equipped to fix it. I rode down Highway 3, leaving town and cutting between two mountains and then breaking into the valley where Mrs. Cartwright had once lived. A cluster of clouds gathered in the north, but most of the sky was a naked neon blue. The sugar maples and hemlocks seemed more alive out here, sparkling in the sun and dancing to the wind that siphoned through.

Once I came to the big bend in the road, I knew I'd reached it, the Cartwrights' former piece of paradise. Their white mailbox was still there, "56" in block numerals on the side. I hung a right onto the driveway that cut through a couple of acres of grain. A chipmunk scampered to safety.

"Make way," I said, feeling all kinds of goodness in my bones. No doubt a visit here would be good for my old teacher, but it was good for me too. I recalled that sense of resilience I'd discovered when I'd decided enough was enough. Even with a million things pulling me down, a morning spent slinging bales of hay for the animals would make it all go away.

The house looked the same as it always had, a charming country abode with a wraparound porch. It sat at the end of the driveway, framed by the mountains beyond. The stunning green barn that Tom had built had held up well. Wrapping the property was a wooden fence he'd put up too. Past the driveway, the garden looked as healthy as ever, a quarter acre planted with almost anything one could imagine. I was so happy to see that it had been maintained. No doubt this whole place had found its way to all the New England magazines over the years. It was hardly any wonder why it had crushed Mrs. Cartwright to say goodbye.

The car wheels chewing gravel must have alarmed the current residents, as a woman with a baby wrapped to her chest came out of the front door and shielded her eyes from the sun to make me out. Two border collies followed and dashed out ahead of her. I slowed to a stop and climbed out.

"Hey there." I introduced myself and then said, "I used to work out here and wanted to come back and see the place. I hope you don't mind."

She smiled, coming toward me. The dogs were young and excited, jumping up on me. The woman, Christine, was as nice as could be, saying she'd never had the pleasure of meeting Mrs. Cartwright but had heard the best teacher to have ever graced Vermont had lived there.

"I used to work for her and her husband. For a few months, anyway. Such a special place."

"It is," Christine said. "We feel lucky, though my husband is overwhelmed still. I'm pushing to get some animals, but one thing at a time, right?"

"He'll get the hang of it," I said. "From the stories I heard, the Cartwrights were overwhelmed at first too. But then things made sense." I gestured toward the barn. "We delivered a foal together in that barn. I'll never forget it." A smile stretched across my face, tasting the vitality I'd felt that day, that sense that anything was possible. Surely anyone who'd found their calling had experienced that one specific instance when everything fell in line, when they knew they'd found it, like a treasure hunter hearing the ping when his shovel hit something.

I looked at the baby, at his cherub cheeks and wild green eyes. "What a place for this little guy to grow up."

He smiled at me. I'd never paid much attention to babies before, but I had a feeling he'd leave an impression on me. One day he'd farm the same land I had. He'd go through the Teterbury school system. He'd fall in love. Find his calling. I hoped life would be easy on him.

I folded my hands. "The reason I came is that I wanted to bring Mrs. Cartwright one night. She's been down lately, and I thought it would be good for her to come back. She used to love looking at the stars out here, you know, away from town."

"They're something special," Christine said, glancing up into the blue where a flock of birds soared by.

"The garden too," I said. "I've been trying to convince her to plant a few things in town, but she's not interested. Maybe she'll find some inspiration."

Christine swayed to keep the baby calm. "Of course you can bring her by. And I'd love to help if I can. Maybe we could make it even more special. Would tomorrow night work?"

"Absolutely."

Back in the car, taking another look at the land, I recalled one night in the early summer of 1999. Sometimes, when I worked late, the Cartwrights would ask me to dinner. Once we'd finished up and I'd helped with the dishes, Mrs. Cartwright had led Tom and me out into the grass, where we had lain on our backs, so that, as she'd said, "we could break bread with the stars." On that particular evening, the sky had looked like it had been cracked open, revealing a glittery splash of stars amid the black canvas, a night so captivating it had made me wonder if my father was right in believing in God.

Mrs. Cartwright had said, "I'm not sure if it was Einstein who said it, but no matter. It does the trick. 'There are only two ways to live your life. One is as though nothing is a miracle. The other is as though everything is.' Which one do you choose, Carver?"

It was a question that required no response, and I remembered my worries—and there had been many back then—falling away. She had a way with words, always able to draw a quote out of her quiver or offer something of her own design at exactly the right moment.

Shifting the Audi into reverse, I let out a laugh at the gullibility of youth. As if life were so simple . . . so black and white. Still, like me, she'd found peace and meaning out here, and I intended to remind her of it tomorrow night.

From there, I went straight home to focus on my mother for the evening. I cooked for her, and then we spent the evening sitting next to each other on the couch, searching for furniture for the attic. If I ever was going to come back, it wouldn't be to sleep on my old bunk bed.

Though she was doing well, considering, she quickly declined my invitation for her to join us at the farm. "It's been a long few days, Carver. I appreciate the invitation, but I'd prefer to hide out for a while longer."

"Okay, Mom," I said. "Just be careful on the drinking, okay? It'll sneak up on you."

"I know, thank you."

I wasn't too worried about her drinking or her desire to isolate because I knew that, with some time, she could bounce back from anything.

Chapter 17

Fireflies and Other Stars

You would have thought I'd suggested the worst idea in the history of the world. At her place the next day, Mrs. Cartwright said, "I have no interest in going back there."

She sat in her chair with Oscar on her lap. A fresh bandage covered the bump on her head. Ava and I sat together on the couch and had been waiting for the right moment to bring it up.

"Don't pop my balloon," I said, trying to get a rise out of her with another cliché.

She knew it immediately and gave me the ol' Mrs. Cartwright stare.

"I've not stayed up late enough to see the stars in a long time."

"Then I'll load you up with caffeine," I said. I didn't tell her I'd spent the morning making a picnic. No way I was going to let that go to waste.

"Mrs. Cartwright," Ava said.

My mentor made a fist and shook it in the air. "Eloise. My name is Eloise. You two both have to stop calling me Mrs. Cartwright. I'm no longer a teacher, and I need no reminders of my age."

Ava and I looked at each other. It was nice to see some spunk in our friend.

"*Eloise,*" Ava said, "I've never seen your farm. Carver was nice enough to speak with them. Don't make us tie you up and throw you in the back of the car."

Mrs. Cartwright's head kicked back, in apparent awe of Ava's audacity. I have to say that I was surprised as well. When she looked at me, I raised my hands, saying I had nothing to do with that idea.

"Try me," Ava said.

I admired Ava for knowing when and how to push. Of course she was joking, but she was doing a fine job of convincing Mrs. Cartwright, who shook her head, clearly accepting that the two people in her living room weren't going to let her get out of it.

~

That evening I drove the three of us out of town. It was only a fifteen-minute journey, but even at night, the change in the land was evident. The blue sky had given way to a twilight purple as the sun kissed the mountain ridge and began its daily descent.

Mrs. Cartwright sat up front with me, and we were all completely silent, honoring this pilgrimage. When we turned into the driveway, she gasped. I did too. The owners had set out torches lining the drive. More torches bordered the garden. Christine had done that for Mrs. Cartwright. I teared up at the beauty of a stranger's kindness.

Once we'd parked, I ran around to Mrs. Cartwright's side and helped her out. She didn't swat me off like usual; she appeared preoccupied. I hoped she might be reconnecting with who she'd been while living here.

I held her cold hand as she stepped down onto the gravel. Her eyes were on the garden, lit up by the torches. Christine came out with her husband. "Welcome," she said, opening her arms. She raced to Mrs. Cartwright. "I'm so honored to finally meet you."

"You're so kind to let us come visit," Mrs. Cartwright said.

"It's the least we could do. This place, oh, this place. You guys made it special." She introduced her husband, Bill.

"Gosh, did you set the bar high," he said in a deep voice that reminded me of Tom. Funny, the circle of life.

"We'll get out of your way," Christine said, "but we wanted to say hi. Please make yourself at home."

Mrs. Cartwright didn't let them escape quickly, slowing them down with questions about their life. There she was, the woman I remembered. Within minutes, we were touring the garden. Mrs. Cartwright talked about when she'd first planted the asparagus and how she used to mow down the strawberries at the end of the year.

While they finished the tour, I retrieved the blankets and picnic basket from the Audi. Between the fenced-off pasture and the garden lay a patch of grass that could not have been more perfect for a picnic. As I laid down the blanket, the clarity of the sky dazzled me. The patch of clouds from earlier in the evening had dissipated, leaving only a palette of indigo fading to black.

A skeptic had no place here, and I questioned how much coincidence had been involved in my return. I happened to be home right when Mrs. Cartwright needed a boost. And vice versa. This happened to be perfect.

"Fate," I said out loud.

"What's that?" Ava asked, joining me to help with the red plaid blanket. She wore a formfitting sleeveless top and camouflage capri pants that stopped halfway down her shins, showing off her porcelain skin. It wasn't quite porcelain, though, was it? Because that would show a certain fragility of which she most certainly did not suffer. Seemingly carefree, yes. Fragile, no.

"You caught me talking to myself," I said. "I do that sometimes." I waited for her to find the corners of the big blanket.

"How adorable," she said as we lowered it to the ground.

"I suppose."

Mrs. Cartwright was still talking to the owners in the garden. Ava and I spread out the items I'd prepared. My mother had furnished me with fine china plates and crystal tumblers for wine. We put a turkey sandwich, a pickle spear, and a scoop of potato salad on each plate.

"Color me impressed," she said. "This looks delicious."

I pulled the cork on a sauvignon blanc from the Loire Valley and filled each tumbler. "I wanted to make it extra special."

"It's sweet."

Her approval meant more to me than she could know. Actually, it surprised me how much I wanted to impress her. Probably had something to do with her saying I wasn't her type.

By the time Mrs. Cartwright had joined, we were all set up, and she nearly tumbled over at the sight. "Are you kidding me?" she asked, her eyes watering and glistening in the last of the sunlight. "This is a dream."

"Come join us." I stood and helped her into the Crazy Creek chair I'd brought. She sat back and looked around, taking in her view of the farm, embraced by the mountains surrounding it.

"I wish I could take you up on the wine, but I'd best behave after what happened."

"That's right. I'm so sorry."

"No, please. Enjoy for me."

Once I'd filled her glass with water, I raised mine. Ava followed suit. "I am so grateful to have you in my life, Mrs. Cartwright, and I want you to know that, even when I go back to North Carolina, I am here for you. Gosh, I'm living a life that in so many ways is dedicated to you."

"Thank you, Carver."

"As if you haven't done enough, I'm going to ask something else of you."

"Oh dear," Mrs. Cartwright said. "Maybe I do need that glass of wine."

There was her humor. I waited until the laughter had left my body. "Don't lose sight of your power, Mrs. Cartwright. That's what matters to me most. You know the message on rearview mirrors, *Objects may be closer than they appear*? The person I knew, the incredibly talented leader and teacher, the amazing wife, the brilliant woman who gave so many students the love of reading and life . . . she's closer than she appears. Please don't let her go. Not yet. You fought for Tom and your son and for me and all of your students countless times. Now it's time you fight for yourself."

In the moonlight I could see her cheeks quiver.

"To you, Mrs. Cartwright," I said.

She gave me a wink and raised her glass back to me. "Thank you, my Carver."

"Hear, hear," Ava said.

We toasted and enjoyed our meal and had some wonderful conversation. She showed none of the new Mrs. Cartwright, the one who'd stopped taking her medicine. This being before me was the woman who'd been there for me and hundreds, if not thousands, of others.

The last of the light faded behind the mountains. The owners of the property walked up the driveway, extinguishing the torches. They came toward us and blew out the torches around the garden too. With every moment, the night grew blacker.

"Stay as long as you like," Christine called out when they'd finished their job. "We thought the stars might shine brighter this way."

We thanked her and watched as they returned to the house, shutting off those lights as well.

Then we were there, under the darkest night you could find in Vermont. I lowered onto my back, losing myself in a powdery crush of stars. To my great delight, Mrs. Cartwright shimmied out of her Crazy Creek chair and lay on the blanket beside me. Ava crawled toward us and took the other side of her.

"A taste of my own medicine," my former teacher said.

"That's right."

She took both our hands.

The stars twinkled back at us, staring at us like caring eyes. I embraced the music of the night, the birds signing off, the breeze blowing over the tall grass, a coyote off in the distance. It was there, like a name on the tip of my tongue. A reason. A message. A . . . a feeling down in the core of me. What was it?

That was when I saw them, the fireflies. The stars were coming to us! At least, that was what it felt like. "Look," I said, pointing to a cluster of them dancing above our heads. Chill bumps rose all over me, and the skeptic in me continued to shed its skin.

I sat up, because I wanted to see Ava's face. Her red hair was splayed across the checkered blanket, and she held a hand in the air, letting a firefly dance around it. It was an image I knew would never leave me.

Starting to speak but then holding back, Ava bathed me with a look of joy that was so infectious that I felt it to my toes.

I lay back down and twisted my head to Mrs. Cartwright. She was beaming, too, a smile without smiling, a glow like a halo hovering around her. Everything was going to be okay.

She turned to me and whispered, "Do you remember how to find Leo?"

Thinking back, I searched the constellations above. "I'm not going to lie, it's been a long time. I do see the Big Dipper, though."

"Well done, Galileo," she said. "Remember the pointer stars?"

"That's right." I did actually. I remembered her showing them to me around this same spot twenty years before.

She connected the dots with her finger. "Star hop upward to Polaris, which is part of Ursa Minor."

Tidbits of my astrology class in college came back to me. "The Little Dipper, right?"

"You see, you've still got it. Now follow the pointer stars the other way, and you'll run right into Leo. See the Sickle with Regulus at the base?"

"Regulus is that one?" I asked.

"That's right, the bright one."

"I'm sure there's an app that can show you all the constellations."

"An app?" She hit me. "You kids and your apps. Why not replace all our teachers with apps?"

"No," I said. "That will never happen."

"We'll see," Mrs. Cartwright said.

I peered past the stars to the darkness, and that revelation on the tip of my tongue came even more into the light, but it was a gem I couldn't get my fingers around. An undeniable magic shimmered up there above us and traveled through us, and I wanted to find a way to verbalize it, to bottle it, a way to recall it later.

I star hopped for a while, seeking answers. Something was missing in my life. What was holding me back? Why couldn't I let go and relax and live a life unencumbered by the need to . . . to what? To prove myself? My father and Mrs. Cartwright had suggested this idea. Was that all my life had been so far? A desperate effort to show the world I mattered? *No,* I told myself. It wasn't that simple. No matter what motivated me, I was doing what I should be doing, and I'd figured out the best way to do it—for me.

As if someone had pulled away the blanket of night, that feeling vanished. Replaced by thoughts of Shannon—a dose of fear of putting myself at risk once again—and of my father, who was running west. Replaced by knowing that my mother was alone and that Mrs. Cartwright wouldn't live forever. Ultimately replaced by thoughts of dread at the idea of standing up at a podium and facing my peers—the ones who all knew about the scar under my watch and what had led to it—and trying to show them I had gotten past it, that I was more than that scar and that night. That I was better than being dismantled by a high school breakup. That I was different now, far more than the boy who'd not been enough for Shannon back then.

Chapter 18

BIG SPEECHES AND LITTLE LEAGUE DADS

Outside my window, children played and lawn mowers buzzed as Saturday came to life. I was terribly sore from Shannon's barre class, so I sat on the floor of my room, stretching, trying to shake out the kinks. I'd opened up all the windows, and a cool breeze blew through, flipping up the pages of my notebook, which rested at my side.

It could have been and should have been a pleasant morning. The night before had been so fantastically magical, and I knew I'd never forget it. And yet . . . today I had to write a speech that I really, really didn't want to give. Part of me did, of course. How incredibly perfect and redeeming it would be to strut into that reunion with Shannon there to boost my confidence. Then I could take the stage and let everyone see that I had become so much more. Ah, that part felt good, so incredibly good, like warm water raining down on me.

The consequences of failing at the podium ate at me, though. What if I clammed up? Normally I was pretty good at giving a speech, and I'd done my fair share at various veterinary conferences. But the stakes were so much higher here, the emotional stakes.

"Failure can't be an option," I said to myself, crossing one leg over the other and twisting right.

How would I start it? What would be the theme? What would be the message? It wasn't about a powerful delivery. It was about dropping some great content and building up to a crescendo that left people feeling changed. Inspired even.

What had Bree wanted? For me to speak about my success. How do you do that without rubbing your success in people's faces? I probably needed to talk about the lessons I'd learned along the way. Resilience. Digging in. Not letting the other person work harder than you. Sleeping only when necessary. Avoiding distractions like social media and television. Putting one's eye on the prize. Where did that leave space to talk about relationships? Friends, colleagues, family? Maybe I'd leave that bit for someone more qualified.

Of course, I had no interest in talking about the past and what had happened, nor the year or two afterward. Elephant in the room or not, I didn't want to shine the light on that piece. I would start shortly after Wake Tech, when I attended Davidson, where I came in blazing, soaring back to the top of my class. I would talk about getting into vet school at NC State and then obtaining one of the most sought-after surgical residencies in the field. Of course I'd talk about how I became obsessed with solving a problem. There was no suitable solution to ACL repair, and I decided it was my calling to find an answer. Nothing was going to stop me.

I wanted to be Steve Jobs up there, someone who had truly made a difference. And I had. Until someone came up with a better idea, dogs that tore their ACL would have a much better life postsurgery. What I'd accomplished was something of which to be proud.

I grabbed the pen and notebook and committed to writing the first words of the speech.

Thank you for having me. As you probably know, I'm Dr. Carver Livingston. It's wild to see so many faces from my past. We all grew up together, didn't we? The good and the bad. And here we are. I'm so honored that Bree asked me to be here and say a few words. Since then I've pondered what it is I can say, what I can give to you that might be of some benefit.

No, I scratched through that last part. I didn't want to come off as pompous. But how could I talk about myself without sounding like a self-absorbed asshole? These were people with whom I'd grown up. These were people who had seen me fall on my face.

Holding the pen like a joystick, I scratched through everything I'd written. "No," I said. "You have to do better than that. Where's the humor? Dammit, why did I agree to do this thing?"

I heard movement and went down the stairs to see my mother. She was folding kitchen towels on the island. "How was it last night?" she asked.

"So good I wish you would have come. Mrs. Cartwright lit up." I told her about the torches.

"Sounds great. That was nice of you." My mother was less than thrilled. She wasn't jealous, was she? I'd asked her to go; what more could I do?

"You okay, Mom?"

"Honey, will you stop asking me if I'm okay?" She must have heard the defensiveness she'd thrown at me, because she took a step back with her tone. "Thank you for asking, but I'm fine. When you've made it as long as I have, you learn how to be resilient."

"I believe that about you, Mom. I love that about you." Leaning against the counter, I said, "Elliot's boys are playing baseball at eleven thirty. It's the playoffs. Wanna join?"

She sighed. "No . . . I . . ." What followed was a pitiful attempt at trying to manufacture an excuse. Her starting and stopping reminded me of the dolphin noise I sometimes made. "I, I, I . . ." Like mother, like son.

"It's okay," I said. "You don't have to. Just thought I'd ask. I'm trying to spend time with you."

"I know you are . . . and thank you. You being here is good for me."

I draped my arm around her shoulders. "I'm always here for you." Her body felt so rigid in that moment, like my touch had turned her to stone. If she was hurting more than she was letting on, I wasn't sure how to help her. How do you help anyone who is not receptive to it?

—

At eleven, I drove over to the Little League fields to catch Elliot's boys play. What caught me off guard was a bout of longing that hit me when I saw all the parents walking around the field, towing their little ones and toting bags spilling over with gloves and bats. I hadn't even found Elliot yet, but as I wandered up the hill, I wondered what I might be missing. How fantastic it must be to have a child that you get to follow, a little boy or girl who gets to dress up in a uniform. To learn how to play as a team. All while your dad and mom watch you.

When I passed by the first field, I had a clear vision of my father and mother sitting on those bleachers right next to Elliot's parents. He and I had always been on the same team. I could hear the four of them yelling from the bleachers when one of us would get a base hit.

Elliot had told me his boys were on the gold team, and I found their jerseys on one of the upper fields. Hiking up the hill, I smelled the hot dogs and fries from the "Snack Shed," the one the parent volunteers had been running for longer than I'd been alive. Wearing his gold jersey, Elliot stood at the mound, tossing pitches to a pint-size catcher in an oversize helmet and protector. I clung to the chain-link fence and watched him for a while. If I was being honest, I was truly jealous of this guy who'd found such peace with his place in the world. I'd never craved simplicity more in my life than in watching him pull the team into a huddle for a pep talk.

When they broke away, I called out to him. "Hey, Coach!"

"Get out of here," he said, running up to the fence. "You came."

"I couldn't go back without seeing this, c'mon." I didn't tell him that I needed to be here to show him I wasn't the worst friend in history.

"Come meet the boys," he said. "We still have a few minutes before the game starts."

I entered through the opening in the fence as Elliot called out for his two kids. They came out from the dugout, and we met between third and home.

Jared and Philip were identical twins. They were as kind and polite as could be and had firm handshakes. "Boys, your dad is one of the best men I've ever known. You have big shoes to fill."

They nodded together.

"Okay, let's get warmed up," their dad said, ushering them away. Elliot looked at me. "Welcome to my world."

"They're beautiful," I said. "Your world is beautiful, man."

He led me out to the bleachers, where a collection of parents used their kids' warm-up time as a social hour for themselves. A young and petite blonde stepped down and held out her arms. "You must be Carver." She reminded me a lot of a young Meg Ryan.

"That's me," I said, accepting her hug. "What a pleasure, Alice."

She wagged a finger at me. "You're the one who got him to break his diet, aren't you?"

I looked at Elliot, who put up his hands. "She busted me."

Alice pointed a finger at me. "I'm watching you, Carver Livingston."

We shared a smile, and I thought Elliot was probably lucky to have her in his life. "By the way, thanks for watching Oscar."

"Anytime. So I hear you have a hot date tonight."

"Yeah," I said, not wanting her to make a big deal of it. I'd already played it up big enough in my head.

"Where are you taking her?" she asked, clearly privy to everything going on in my world.

"The Lang House."

She cocked her head. "Nice choice. And Elliot says you're hanging around for the reunion."

"It's looking that way," I admitted. "Maybe we should all go together?"

"Sure!" Alice said. "A double date."

"Let's do it," Elliot said, clapping his hands together, possibly hiding his hesitation about Shannon from me. So much for keeping my nerves at bay.

Elliot soon returned to the field, and I sat down next to Alice, where we chatted for over two hours while we watched one of the most fun games I'd ever seen. Alice and I laughed to tears as the boys out there did their best to figure out the game of baseball. The base stealing was rampant. The attempts at throwing from home to second would cause only a debacle that always allowed at least one runner to make it home. Wasn't that how life was, figuring it out in the clumsiest of ways?

Despite the lovely morning, it left me torn in two. I was happy for Elliot. Unquestionably happy. No one deserved the good life more. I was jealous as well. All I'd done didn't touch what he'd done with his life. That smile he wore was so true. He should be the one speaking Saturday night. What was the secret? He and I both had gotten everything we wanted, but he seemed so much happier about it. In a way, he'd won. The grass was always greener, though, I told myself. I was sure a part of Elliot wanted to be in my shoes. In fact, I wondered if he ever spent time pondering the path he'd chosen, those crucial forks in the road. Did he have regrets like I did? Maybe not.

꿈

Shannon rented the carriage house of a large home that sat toward the edge of town on Main Street. It took me a moment to figure out how to get back there, but I eventually found a gate that opened to a courtyard with a concrete fountain trickling water. A cobblestone pathway led me under a patch of birch trees to the back corner of the property.

Her place was nothing short of adorable, a brick cottage with a blue door. I knocked, aware that the entire balance of the universe relied on how things went from here. When she appeared, it was like the light of the sun came at me. She wore a tight yellow dress that accentuated her long and slender body. The yellow blended with her hair like a sunflower would in a field of grain. Then there were her eyes, blue disks amid all that yellow, as if she'd reversed the color of the sun and sky. I recalled feeling this way when we'd last dated, not believing it, wondering how I was the one she'd chosen. Like I didn't belong.

"You look fabulous," I said.

"Thank you, mister." Her lips were shiny from a fresh application of gloss, and I wondered if they still tasted like they used to. She looked me up and down. "You sure have learned how to dress, haven't you? I'm glad to see something other than flannel. You're handsome."

Thanking her, I glanced down at my black jeans and Blundstone Chelsea boots, then tugged the bottom of my blazer. I did feel handsome.

Our faces moved toward each other. As if someone had pulled the trapdoor on my confidence, though, I moved left at the last moment and planted a quick kiss on her cheek. She smelled like wildflowers after a rain, and I wished I'd kissed her lips.

She invited me in for a drink. Her place was cozy and clean. Steps led up to a loft, where I assumed she slept. I hoped I might find out later.

"I moved here shortly after Trey and I ended," she said.

I should have figured we wouldn't get far without his name coming up. Pretending that I wasn't even fazed by the mention of her ex, I said too loudly, "I love it. Close walk to town. It feels peaceful. Lots of chi flowing in here."

"Aren't you funny tonight?"

She poured us glasses of an Italian white wine, and we walked back out the door to two wrought-iron chairs that faced out over the property. A tiny table rested between us.

"Who are they?" I asked, gazing through the trees at the enormous Federal-style home with no fewer than five chimneys. The kind of place that surely had a movie theater.

"A sweet older couple. Both retired. They're only here a few months out of the year. I keep an eye on the place for a discount in rent."

"So this is your life," I said, listening to the fountain drip water. "I like it."

"Yeah, it's a good place to figure out where to go from here. You asked about Trey before. I guess you should know."

I twisted toward her. "Don't feel like you need to tell me. It's not my business at all." Though I'd said that, I certainly wanted to know what had finally righted a twenty-year wrong.

Thankfully she felt compelled to tell me. "He wanted children, and I didn't."

I was confused. "You don't? I thought . . . we talked about them, didn't we?" I remembered clearly we had.

"Carver, that was in high school. We've all changed since then."

"Yeah, I know." Was she accusing me of something?

She set the glass down on her lap. "My mother had sickle cell anemia, and I'm a carrier, so there is no way I wanted to take the chance. I had a hysterectomy about ten years ago. I found out while we were trying to get pregnant, and I told him that was it, that I wanted to prevent a pregnancy."

"That had to be tough. I'm sorry."

"He'd always been so excited about children, and it drove a big wedge between us. He pretended to be supportive, but I knew he'd gone to pieces inside. And then the drinking, like during the day, sneaking vodka. I tried to call him on it, and that made things worse. Last February, I found out he'd been fired but hadn't told me."

I cocked my head. "What?"

"He'd lied and said he'd taken a job in Burlington, but he'd been going to a bar there."

"Oh, Shannon, I'm so sorry."

She shrugged. "He drained all our savings and used it to pay the mortgage and other bills so I wouldn't notice. We were broke before I even knew we were struggling."

"That's . . ." I stared into the white wine.

"Hard to believe," she said.

"Right out of a novel."

"Right out of a horror movie. I tried to keep us together, but he wouldn't get help. Now he's living with his mother in Stowe, drinking away all her money. I chose the wrong guy, didn't I?"

Ah, the sweet, sweet sound of her voice saying those words. It took me a moment to compose myself. "I'm sorry you had to go through that. So what now? You're a great barre teacher, by the way."

"I guess. I'd like to get out of here, really, but I don't have the money. He got us both into debt, running up credit cards."

I couldn't imagine. My first instinct was to offer to pay them off, but that felt like such a shallow thing to say.

We finished our glass of wine and strolled through town. She had her hand on my arm, and her heels clicked on the sidewalk. And I felt proud, so proud. Here she was, the woman who'd broken my heart, back in my life.

We passed the church and then the Wayfair Hotel, where the reunion would be. A bellhop in uniform loaded a cart with luggage. Up the red-carpeted stairs and through the golden doors I imagined my former classmates gathering before the dance. I wondered what it would feel like to stride up the stairs with this woman. Would everyone turn and stare? Would they whisper that we were back together?

"It's gonna be weird, isn't it?" Shannon asked, reading my mind.

"Hey, I'm the one who has to give the speech. You're in trouble, manipulating me so."

"You're going to kill it," she said. "I'll be right up front, cheering you on."

I liked that vision. "Can I ask you something?" I knew I was taking a risk, but I had to know. "Why did you break up with me? I know it was a long time ago, but . . . it would be nice to know."

"You sure are hung up on the old days, aren't you?"

I shrugged and then lied. "No. I just . . . I don't like leaving loose ends." I gestured to the crosswalk. "Let's cross here."

"Loose ends," she said, as we found our rhythm on the other side of the street. "Is that what we are? What I am?"

She was starting to make me feel like I had to be careful around her, careful about what I said. I didn't remember that about her. "Come on. That's not what I meant."

"I guess I do know why I broke up with you."

I slowed my breathing so that I wouldn't miss a word. Was she really about to extinguish the curiosity that had been following me around since high school? If so, was I ready to handle it?

"We ran our course, you know? We were teenagers. I had fun but it was . . . I don't know. I was curious what else was out there."

I felt sick to my stomach. "It was more than that, Shannon."

"Geez, Carver, don't get your briefs in a bunch. I don't remember. It's not like I think about it every day."

"I know that. But you have to remember. Good Lord, we got tattoos."

"As if that means anything. We were young and dumb. That definitely wasn't the only tattoo I got back then."

What the hell? Who else was she getting tattoos with? And young and dumb? What in the world was she talking about? Sure, young love could be naive, but we weren't that.

"I remember some things," she said, pulling her arm away from me. "I remember you never wanted to go out with everyone. You always wanted to stay home or do stuff, the two of us. I liked that some, but I also liked hanging out with everyone. Trey came along, and he was a little more fun than you."

A little more fun than me? Had she really said that? I felt like I was punishing myself by asking for more, but I was too deep now, the marrow of my soul spilled open.

"It was more than that," I muttered.

She crossed her arms and slowed. "Carver, you're the one asking, and I'm being honest. You were so different from the guys I usually dated, and it was a nice break. But that's all it was, a summer fling that bled into the school year. C'mon, I was a trophy on your arm; it's not like you actually knew me."

I stopped to face her. "Didn't know you?"

"No. You didn't."

"That's bullshit. I knew so much about you. The music and movies you liked—that we both liked. I knew what made you happy and sad. You wanted to live in Manhattan, then California—*if* you could put up with the earthquakes. I knew you had felt like a trophy before, and I'd tried hard not to let you feel that way again. You want your favorite color? Blue. Flower? Daisy. I could go on and on . . ."

She gave me this look like she'd been called on her bullshit. "I'm not going to have the answer you want. No matter what I say. Now I feel like I've ruined the night."

"No," I said. "You didn't ruin the night. I . . ." What was I to say? Maybe she had ruined the night. And even more than that.

We barely spoke the rest of the way to the Lang House. She'd done a pretty good job of making me feel damn small, and I was tempted to call the night early. The only reason I didn't was that I didn't believe her. I wasn't an idiot. I knew we'd had something.

The hostess sat us at a table with a view of the river that neither of us looked at for more than a flash. The restaurant had a Swedish feel, with light woods and modern curves. The couple next to us was uncomfortably close, which made the situation all the more edgy.

Wearing a thick leather apron, the petite server introduced herself and asked whether we'd like sparkling or still. Should I have been alarmed when Shannon and I blurted out different choices at the same time? Possibly.

Once the server left us to explore our menus, I leaned toward Shannon and offered my hand. "Let's move on," I whispered. "You're right. That was a long time ago. It doesn't matter."

She smiled and reluctantly took my hand. "Things are different now, Carver. You and I are different. It seems like we do still have our old connection. That's a good start."

The conversation warmed up from there, and by the time the salads arrived, we were back to good. Not great, but good. The walk back to Shannon's was a struggle. I didn't even bother holding her hand. I wished I hadn't asked her why she'd broken up with me. It had only exposed the ugly parts of the past. Something else gnawed at me. Why now? Why was she into me now?

When we reached the gate that led to her house, she said, "Thanks for dinner."

"Of course," I said. "I enjoyed it. A few bumpy spots, but I guess we had to get that out of the way eventually."

"I suppose so."

She stood there, clutching her purse and staring up into my eyes. Then she stood on her tiptoes and pressed her lips against mine. I hadn't seen that one coming.

"Do you want to come inside?" she asked.

On her lips I tasted the port we'd had to finish off the meal. I looked through the gate to the carriage house, imagining what it would be like to let her lead me inside. To follow her up the stairs to the loft bedroom. To see her . . .

No. It didn't feel right. The savage in me wanted her, but something was way off. If I'd been wrong about us, if she'd not felt the exact same way, then perhaps it wasn't destiny at all. Perhaps I was a fool. The spell in which she'd put me under lifted as I stood there facing her. All of a sudden the woman I'd craved my entire life turned into a stranger. What in the hell had I been thinking, chasing her around as if getting her back would heal all the hurt places inside me?

I said as politely as I could, "I don't think coming inside is a good idea."

She gave me an *Are you kidding me?* look, as if no one had ever turned her down. "You're not going to ask for a rain check to sleep with me, are you?" She shook her head in frustration.

"You said yourself that I don't know you. We need to take a big step back."

The woman who'd had the upper hand all night continued to shake her head ever so slightly, as her eyes stayed fixed on a spot back down the street toward town.

"Hey," I said. "Let's talk tomorrow, okay?"

She gave a *What's the point?* shrug, then turned to the gate. "Night, Carver."

"Good night," I whispered, watching her vanish into the darkness of the courtyard.

Chapter 19

THE WATER GUN THAT SHOT BULLETS

In the morning my mother slid a green smoothie my way as I posted up on a stool at the island. "Almond milk, kale, green apples, blueberries, bee pollen, and cacao nibs," she said proudly.

"Thanks, Mom." Groggy eyed from a rough night of sleep, I took a sip as I glanced at the cutting board where the apple core and the stems of the kale remained. "That is so good. I remember when you first made these. Back in the midnineties, right? I think you might have invented them."

"I doubt that."

"Either way, they taste much better than they used to."

She faked a smile. "Your father still won't drink them." The pain of losing him cast a shadow over her face.

Look what love does. It was more devastating and dangerous than any other emotion. I'd been up all night trying to make sense of how I'd read so wrongly what had happened to Shannon and me. She couldn't have played down our relationship any lower. And here was my mom, having fallen down the same well.

"He doesn't know what he's missing," I eventually said, knowing nothing I could say would make a difference.

"So how was your date?" It wasn't difficult to ascertain that she clearly hoped it had gone awry.

"Funny you ask," I said. "We set the bar at a new low last night."

She perked up like a flower after a summer rain. "Yeah?"

"Don't get too excited."

She reached for her smoothie while stifling a smile. "I want you to be happy, but . . ."

"I know. And maybe you were right about her." That was hard for me to admit, but I had to give her credit. "I think the spell is broken. For all this time, I've held our relationship up on this pedestal, thinking that . . . I don't know . . . that I'd been wronged somehow. I've spent twenty years thinking that we were supposed to be together and beating myself up for not being enough for her, like I didn't fulfill my part of the bargain—"

"I hope you know now that's not the case."

"Maybe. Twenty years I wasted." I stared into the granite of the counter, losing myself in the white space. "Turns out I wasn't much more than a fling. I figured she had to have thought about me some, wondered what could have been. I had this stupid fantasy that she'd even questioned marrying Trey." A sharp maniacal laugh, almost a cackle, jumped out of me. "She couldn't even remember why she broke up with me."

"I'm so sorry."

"I know, I know. You told me so."

"I wasn't going to say that."

I took another sip of the smoothie. "I wonder if there's such a thing as soul chafing. I feel rubbed raw right now, so worn down. Somehow I agreed to a barre class and then to speak at the reunion. She completely brainwashed me without even meaning to. Twenty years I've been trying to become better than that kid she dumped. Twenty freaking years I've been thinking that my soulmate had been taken from me. And she's barely given me a second thought."

"I'm sure that's an exaggeration."

"Not that she doesn't want anything from me," I said. "I think she's fully interested now, but I'm not feeling it after what she said. I don't know. I feel wronged and turned off. Not only by her but by love."

"I know a thing or two about that." Was she thinking about my father driving away from her, one mile at a time?

"You know, though," I said, "it was good to get her out of my system. Now I can go back to Asheville and get back to work with no distractions. No offense to you, but this town is wearing me out."

She replied all too quickly with, "Or you can go back and find someone to love."

I chuckled. "Yeah, I'm okay. Been there, done that."

"Have you, though?"

I watched the condensation collect at the base of my glass as I thought about how awful relationships could be. Considering someone had to die first in every relationship, even the good ones ended in loss.

"Don't take your father and me as an example of what can go wrong. He and I had other . . ." She stopped.

"What, Mom?"

She shook it off and changed direction. "Carver, there's someone out there for you."

"Hold on, let's back up. What is it you're not telling me?"

She wrapped her fingers around the glass and pulled it to her. "What I haven't told you . . . is that it's worth taking the risk. Even for what I'm going through now, I wouldn't trade anything for your father and the good years we had. What I haven't told you enough is that you need to find someone and love them. When things get rocky, love them even harder."

She peeled her eyes away from the glass and looked at me directly. "Maybe I didn't do that."

I launched from the stool and rounded the counter. Slipping my arm around her, I said, "Don't take the blame for what he did. I was there, Mom."

She shook her head.

I faced her and waited until she looked at me. "I will never forget how you were there for me, the entire time. You, Lisa Livingston, are an amazing mother."

"Thank you."

"I'm serious."

"I need to get ready," she muttered as she stepped away and left the kitchen.

"What about your smoothie?" I called out.

"I'll take it to go." She disappeared down the hallway.

At ten I managed to get Mrs. Cartwright and Oscar out of the house. A lovely breeze danced off my skin, fighting the sun-warmed air. In one hand I held the end of Oscar's leash, and in the other a spray bottle. He'd been fighting me, but a quick spray and a tug on the Halti helped me communicate directions. Still slow from her knee surgery, Mrs. Cartwright set the pace, inching along in her tennis shoes at half my usual stride. I was no expert, but I thought she might have spent some extra time today on her appearance.

Referring to my mother, I said, "I can't figure her out. She seems okay one day, and then this morning, she's a disaster."

Mrs. Cartwright slid her eyes toward me as she twisted her head.

"Give her a few days, Carver. The end to a forty-three-year marriage is not something that you can scoot by without facing head-on."

"She was certainly happy that my date with Shannon didn't go well."

I caught Mrs. Cartwright up, and she replied, "Shannon may have not felt the same way, but that doesn't mean your feelings weren't real. Don't beat yourself up over them."

"What should I do? Give up on us or . . . give it a shot now? She's interested, that's for sure. I feel like, after what she said . . . is there anything worth exploring . . . and is it worth the risk?"

Mrs. Cartwright shook off my question. "I learned a long time ago that it's best if I don't insert too many opinions when it comes to matters of the heart."

"I hardly believe that," I said. "C'mon, speak freely."

"I will not choose which woman you should pursue, if that's what you want."

"Which woman?"

"You know what I mean."

"I don't." Then I did. "You mean Ava?"

"Perhaps."

Though Ava was an extraordinary woman, a person anyone would be lucky to have in their life, I hadn't considered anything with her. That I wasn't her type wasn't helping things. Even if I was, what would be the point?

"I'm not looking for a relationship, that's for sure."

The slightest chortle fell out of her. "I think you've already mentioned that."

"It's that this thing with Shannon happened, and I got caught up in it."

"Shannon is right. You *don't* know each other."

"Yeah, but we were super close. At least I thought so. She said something about how I didn't know her back then. I guess that's why she broke up with me. But she's wrong. I did get her." I caught myself. "Okay, Mrs. C, I am fully aware that I'm psychoanalyzing a relationship I had twenty years ago, but this matters."

I slowed to walk with her in parallel.

She looked my way for a second. "I think this might be one of those times when the answer is screaming in your ear, but you refuse to listen."

"I don't hear a thing." I noticed the houses we passed by, remembering the people who'd once lived there. The German man—was his name Boris?—who would get so angry when Elliot and I would cut through his yard on our bikes. Mr. and Mrs. McCarter, who had always won the best yard in the neighborhood. By the looks of the yard now, they'd certainly moved.

Oscar pulled hard to sniff the next tree. I gave a tug, sprayed his back with water, and snapped a sharp, "No." He gave up and kept walking. It was working.

I knelt down to pet him but he avoided my hand. "Here's a hint. If you're easier to walk, she'll take you out more often."

"The thing that's confusing me most," I said as we got moving again, "is that Shannon seems all in. Even after last night. If she doesn't remember what we had, why go after me now? Is she lying for some reason? This is why I will never understand women."

She found that to be hilarious. "You are not the only one."

We meandered along the river. On the other side was one last line of houses before the buildings of downtown began. Rising high over Main Street, the gold tip of the church's spire sparkled in the sun.

"If you're asking me to say something negative about Shannon, I won't."

I pulled my eyes from the two loons who bobbed for fish in the calm center of the river. If only life were so easy, floating and bobbing and flying. "No, that's not what I'm trying to do. But I wouldn't mind your thoughts."

Oscar must have sniffed something, as he jerked toward the water and put his nose into the grass. I corrected him again, and he obeyed. "Good boy, Oscar. You make me proud."

He looked up at me, as if he understood.

"Look at that, Mrs. Cartwright. He's learning. Wanna give it another go?"

"I don't think he likes it."

"That's the point," I said. "This is permission-based training. He can't go after a smell unless you let him. Give it another go, trust me."

She reluctantly took the leash and water bottle, and I advised her as she tried to get Oscar to walk in line with her. I kept telling her to be sterner—hit him with more water—but she resisted.

"How would you like it if you'd come into my office when you were younger and I'd beamed you with water?" she asked me.

"That's different."

"Is it?"

A fellow younger than I passed by and waved, saying, "Hi, Mrs. Cartwright." She waved back and called him out by name, but a shade of embarrassment washed over her face. I hated that she didn't like who she'd become.

She pointed to a bench ahead. "I need to rest my knee."

We sat facing the river, our feet resting on the stretch of grass that bent down into the shore. "So you want my advice?" she asked.

I watched Oscar curl up at her feet. "Yes, yes, I do. I was sure for a lot of years that if Shannon and I ever had another chance, it would make right a lot of wrongs in my life. Here she is fully open to something with me, and . . . I don't know. I thought I'd feel better inside."

She took her time responding, lost in the river's beauty. "If you want my opinion, I think you need to take that one foot that's still stuck in the nineties and pry it out. If there's a relationship to be had between you and Shannon, it should be based on the here and now. For God's sake, she's not a prize, Carver."

Her words stung. "Only you can cut close to the quick and get away with it."

She liked the compliment. "Just stop running your mouth and listen. *Listen . . .*"

Taking her advice, I clasped my hands together and closed my eyes and listened, as if a voice were out there trying to say something. *As if.* The river was now barely audible, only the slightest stir from a patch of rippling whitewater closer to the bridge. The rising cadence of a car engine rose and fell behind us.

What I knew was that answers didn't blossom in silence. I'd never liked the quiet anyway, because the darkness waited for me there. Sometimes it showed itself through my thoughts, these invading enemies carrying flags of guilt and shame that dispersed only when I was hard at work. Other times, like now, it was this edgy feeling rising, a sickness inside, something so bone deep that I couldn't have cut it out with my scalpel.

"What is it you hear?" Mrs. Cartwright asked.

Her question sounded eerily familiar, like the Subaru commercial.

I lifted my head and saw a lone cloud blocking the sun. It hovered above me as ridiculously as one might see in a cartoon.

What did I hear? The darkness, that was what. The whispers and screams that I'd spent a lifetime shutting out. The agonizing echo from the cavernous space growing between my mother and father, all a result of my attempted suicide. I heard the sound of Mrs. Cartwright's heart monitor in the hospital, reminding me that even she was fragile. I heard Willie Nelson and the rumble of my father's truck and trailer as it sped away from us. Then Shannon's words as she shattered what I thought we'd had between us, then my lust-blinded self promising Bree and Shannon that I'd give a speech I'd give anything to get out of now. And how could I not hear the ancient chatter of all of Teterbury after I'd cut myself at seventeen, over nothing more than a girl dumping me?

"What do I hear?" I asked out loud. I looked down at Oscar and then up to his owner. "I hear a voice telling me to go home. Get out of this mess. There's no fucking point in trying to make sense of it."

Mrs. Cartwright lowered her head.

When she finally turned to me, I asked rather harshly, "What? This is me freely discussing my feelings. This is what everyone accuses me of not doing."

"You need to extract your cranium from your posterior, Carver. See how my words are so much more interesting than your three- and four-letter blockheaded ones?" She raised the water bottle and sprayed me right in the heart. The look on her face was one of frustration and determination, the latter a part of the teacher who'd not once tolerated a student disrupting her lessons.

My mouth fell open, waiting for an explanation.

Her eyes darkened to the color of blueberries, reminding me of how she looked at students who refused to participate in class discussions. "One thing I will not hesitate to tell you is that running away isn't the answer, Carver. You shouldn't leave this place until you've come to peace with it. Otherwise you'll return to Asheville with the same festering splinter that's been embedded in you all along. This trip is your chance to finally set yourself free. Speaking at the reunion will be good for you. Another week in Teterbury will be good for you. Look at it like one giant pair of tweezers."

I touched the wet spot on my shirt like it was a wound from a gunshot. *Get me out of here,* I thought.

She held up the bottle like she was going to spray me again.

I put my hands up in defense and looked away.

"It's okay to be human," she whispered.

I was too embarrassed and exposed to look back at her.

She shot me with another stream of water. "When are you going to realize you're wonderful? How many university degrees or patents do you need to add to your résumé before you accept it? What dollar amount in your bank account will finally convince you? Guess what. You're amazing just the way you are, *even if* you didn't accomplish all those things. You deserve someone equally wonderful. Be it Shannon or Ava or another fortunate girl."

I spun my head around, making sure no one was within earshot.

"But you know where it starts?" Mrs. Cartwright pressed the nozzle of the spray bottle against my chest and then said in a quiet voice, "It starts with loving yourself."

Fire burned in her irises. "That's something no one has ever accused me of, not loving myself."

She ignored my attempt to lighten the situation. With a look so straight and stern that she could have sawed down a tree with it, she lowered the water bottle and said, "You're enough as you are."

With that, she stood and gestured for me to follow. Oscar popped up and trailed behind her. She was in complete control now.

I sat there for a moment, feeling like coals smoldering in the fire she'd left me burning in. She was wrong, actually. I wasn't enough as I was. That was why I'd spent my life trying to be better.

Catching up with her, I said, "You know, you're one to talk. All this 'love yourself' BS. If loving yourself is the answer, you're doing a pretty shoddy job."

She gave a dark laugh.

"What you're doing isn't even living," I said, "let alone loving yourself. You don't go outside. You're not doing anything to take care of yourself. You've given up on everything you love. You're digging your grave but then trying to tell me how I do things is wrong. I'd much rather avoid coming home and all the shit that lingers back here than give up on life."

Oscar pulled, trying to get at another smell. She jerked him by the leash, a bit too sharply. "No," she hissed. He obeyed like a foot soldier and fell back in step with her.

A message became clear in the following silence: I'd said far more than I should have.

I gently put my hand on her arm. "I'm sorry. That was uncalled for." I'd lost her. I'd upset her and possibly broken her heart.

"I'm sorry," I pleaded, wanting to leave town now more than ever. All these people were better off without me. It had always been that way.

"It's fine." She sped up, like she was trying to get away from me.

"It's strange to see you as lost as I am."

"I'm not lost," she said. "I know where I'm going." She was marching now.

"But you don't. You don't know where you're going, and you don't know when either. What if you sit in your house bumping heads with Oscar and avoiding the sunlight and eating your terrible food for twenty more years?"

"It won't be that long," she said.

I looked around, so frustrated. "You don't know that. How can I snap you out of it?"

She cast me an angry look. "I should ask the same to you."

I raised my voice, frustration coating the tone. "Then we do it together, if that's what it takes. Let me build you some damned garden boxes. It will make me feel better. How about that?"

She tightened the leash on Oscar and crossed the street, headed back home. "Ah, I see. So you want me to garden again to make you feel better?"

"Don't be my father," I said, chasing her to where the sidewalk passed by the house of the former mayor, whom everyone praised for fighting off the chain stores from invading.

"The garden boxes are a sweet gesture," she said, "but it would be a waste of time. A waste of wood and soil. That part of me is already dead."

I could have cried. Why the hell had I come home? As far as I was concerned, my decision to avoid this toxic place for twenty years was among my wisest.

I threw up my hands. "Okay, suit yourself."

Staring at Oscar, she said, "We'll say goodbye now."

She never looked back at me, and I decided I'd show her the respect of leaving her alone. "Okay, have a good day. I'm sorry."

"Don't be sorry," she called out. "Stop being sorry. Stop trying to pay me back. We all have our battles, and we can't fight each other's."

I chose not to respond and turned away from her.

It was a long walk home. Twenty-four hours earlier I'd been on top of the world, and now I felt utterly worthless and knocked down to my knees. As a further blow, I noticed I'd missed a call from my father. How I desperately wanted to talk to him. *Pfft.* Please. That was the last thing I wanted to do.

I listened to his message as their house came into view.

"Carv, just checking in. You still in Teterbury? How's your mother?"

I stopped the message before he continued. "As if you care."

Chapter 20

LIKE MOTHER, LIKE SON

Considering my mother's apparent turn for the worse, I resisted the incredibly delectable urge to get the hell out of Teterbury. Instead, I spent the day working.

Mary Beth attempted to stop me from plugging in with the occasional We got this or You're on vacation text, to which I replied with such snarky responses as A vacation this is not or I'm still the boss. Then she would attack me with emoji.

Nonetheless, I sat at the kitchen table, a pot of green tea next to me, and worked through the afternoon. It was so nice to let all the drama around me go and fall back into my routine. I had patients I wanted to check in on, a relief vet who had questions, bills that needed to be paid, emails that needed to be read and responded to. To no surprise, the contractor was already asking for more money.

Not even when Shannon texted midday did I stop working. No doubt I'd caught myself thinking about her earlier, though. During a conference call with the leads for the Greenville clinic, I wondered what in the world I was going to say. That I wasn't exactly feeling it between us? I loathed such conversations.

At three, the guilt set in. I could hear Mrs. Cartwright berating me, and I knew what she'd tell me to do. To face the fire and call Shannon and not drag her along another minute.

Closing my laptop, I reached for my phone and texted her. Wanna go for a walk?

It took her all of two minutes to reply with Just got to work. Come see me.

—

I found Shannon behind the bar, cutting limes. They didn't open until five, so it was only the staff running around getting ready. The smell of oil from the deep fryers heating up trickled into the bar area. A man in an apron cleaned the window where it read THE SANDERTON in gold lettering. The ceiling speakers let out a Tom Petty song.

I sidled up to the bar in front of a condiment caddy full of cocktail garnishes. "I'm sorry I didn't call you back. There's been a lot going on."

"It's okay, Carver." The woman had a way of squeezing more attitude into a few words than some could in a lifetime. She sliced through a lime, and I wondered if she was imagining me under that blade.

The sleeves of her T-shirt were rolled up, showing a maple leaf. I wondered how many other tattoos she had and if any of them had to do with Trey.

"How goes it?" I asked, hesitating to jump right in.

She dropped the knife on the cutting board, set her elbows on the shiny wooden bar, and leaned toward me. She was the queen of her bar, her realm. "I don't know, Carver. You come into town, act like you want something between us. You come to my barre class and embarrass yourself for me. You take me out to dinner. Then nothing. Barely a text. What do you want from me?"

"I should ask you the same thing."

She broke eye contact and stood tall. "I don't know. I'm available, obviously. You're clearly not interested, so I don't even know why I'm bothering."

I placed my hand on the bar as a kind of peace offering. "Hey, what happened to Ms. Confident?"

"Don't fucking placate me, Carver." She picked up the knife and grabbed another lime.

"I'm not . . ." I sighed, knowing it was time to be real. "I'm not placating you. I haven't called you because I'm a mess inside." I glanced around to see if anyone else was listening. "Coming home was even worse than I thought it could be. Seeing you . . . it's dredged up a lot of stuff. It occurred to me I'd better process it before I drag you down with me. What you said the other night is true. We don't know each other."

How honest did I want to be? I would have preferred to be on the way to the airport, texting her that I had to get back and eventually letting the two of us fizzle. And yet that wouldn't have been right. If I could give her anything, it would be what I'd wanted for far too long: an explanation.

"I don't want to use you." Once I'd said it, I realized I could get in trouble by saying such a thing. I also felt relief, though. Honesty always did the heavy lifting.

"Use me? What do you mean? To get me back, after I left you?"

"Bingo," I said, as if it were the most obvious consideration in the world.

"Carver, are you nine years old? What was this, some plan to get me back so you could feel less sorry for yourself? Or so you could feel like you won?"

"No, Shannon." An icy chill came over me. "Maybe some of that."

She slid the knife into the next lime, halving it. It was an angry motion. "Well, guess what, Carver. You won, okay? You don't need to lure me into your amazing life to win. You have the money, the recognition. Probably a big house and a fancy car. Everything in your life seems so good." A tear rushed down her cheek. "I'm just picking up the pieces of my broken life."

I was no stranger to feeling like an asshole, but this moment was certainly the most defining in my development as a world-class fuckface.

"Shannon," I whispered, "don't—"

"No," she said, moving to the next lime, avoiding looking up at me. "You don't get to console me. I'm not some girl you get to use in order to . . . I don't know . . . get past your own demons."

She was making my point for me. "That's exactly what I'm trying to say," I said, hoping she'd see I was trying to be my best self here. I drew in a long breath, seeing myself in the reflection of the mirror in front of me. "You and I had a totally different read on what was going on between us. All this time I thought what we'd had was one of a kind. Seeing you, hearing that you were single . . . I thought it meant that it was finally our time. But you made me realize we can't jump back into what we had . . . which, as you said, was nothing special. Maybe I got it all wrong."

She rapidly wiped her eyes.

"I'm so sorry you're going through things," I said. "You're such an amazing woman—"

She dropped the knife hard on the cutting board and stared me down. "Jesus, Carver. An amazing woman? That's all you got? I'm no idiot. This is you breaking up with me in your very Carver way, by not getting right to the point. Maybe you haven't changed." She shook her head in frustration. "I'm not a charity case."

"I know that." So much for helping her with her debt.

"Carver, here's a tip. If you're going to break up with someone, say it and move on. Quit trying to polish it."

Noted.

She slid all the limes she'd chopped into a white bucket and then topped the container in front of me. "I'm a big girl, and I've been through a lot lately. Trust me, I can handle it."

"Okay. But . . ."

She set the bucket down on her workstation. "Don't, Carver. Let's say goodbye, and maybe I'll see you before you go."

"I don't want it to be like that."

She laughed, a sad laugh. "It *is* like that. I need to get back to work. And this . . ." She made a motion that circled all of me. "I don't need it."

Way to go, Carver. What was I to do? I'd been honest with her. "All right, I'll get out of your way. Just know that . . ."

She held up a finger. "Don't tell me what I need to know. Have a nice life."

Ouch. I stood and started out of the restaurant. When I turned, she was polishing a glass. What more was there to say? Breakups or whatever this was were ugly. She was right: no sense trying to polish it like the two of us were glasses in a rack.

—

About five thirty, my mother came in the door nearly limping. The day had beaten her up properly.

"Hey there," I said, watching her come into the kitchen and drop her Louis Vuitton tote and keys onto the counter.

"Hi." The word came out so weak it barely reached my ear.

"What's going on?"

She shook her head. "Long day but I'm okay. I'm going to take a bath."

"I thought I'd cook dinner tonight," I said.

"Yeah, okay."

"That's one too many okays." Much like Mrs. Cartwright, she avoided eye contact and left the kitchen before I could press her.

As I listened to her climb the stairs, I wondered if her grief had only now set in. I worked on dinner while trying to figure out how the hell I was ever going to return to Asheville with my mother's declining emotional state.

An hour later, I walked up the steps and knocked on the door. "Mom, dinner's ready."

She didn't answer.

"Hey, Mom." I tried to open the door, but it was locked.

In the following seconds, the darkness poured over me, terrifying me with what I might find on the other side of the door. I got a taste of how my mother had felt when she'd raced up the steps after Shannon's mother had called. I jiggled the handle and called out to her again. Still no response. Stepping back, I raised my foot to kick in the door.

"I'm here," she finally said.

A gasp of air left me. "You scared me. Will you open up?"

The lock clicked, and I waited for her to pull it open. Instead, she said, "Come in."

When I opened the door, I found her crawling back into the covers. "What is going on? You can't keep hiding in here."

She pulled the covers up high, only her face showing. Her red and watery face. Her mascara marked the white sheet and duvet cover. The blinds were drawn on the windows. A stale smell hovered in the air, probably from the dirty clothes overflowing out of the basket in the corner. It mixed with the scent of the dinner I'd prepared, the garlic and olive oil.

I stood about halfway into the room, slightly freaked out by the scene. "Mom, what in the . . . ?"

"I'm okay, just a long day."

I noted another *okay*; she was setting records. "Yeah, it looks like it. What can I do?"

She began to sob.

I sat on the edge of the bed. "Everything is going to be okay."

"It's not, Carver. It's not."

"I've been there. I've had my heart broken. It does get better."

That only made her cry worse.

I put my hand up near her shoulder, resting it on the covers. "I made dinner. Some polenta and kale and squash. A beautiful piece of trout. Why don't we eat together and talk?"

She rubbed her face.

"He tried to call me," I said.

"Who, your dad?"

I nodded. "I didn't answer. Has he called you?"

"Of course not."

"He asked about you, though. On the voice mail, I mean."

She shut her eyes, so much pain all over her. How stupid I'd compared my little high school fling to this woman who'd put forty-three years of life into loving someone. I once again found myself hating my father, wondering what kind of selfish it took to break someone's heart like that. It didn't matter that I didn't know the details of why he'd left. No excuse could justify abandoning his wife for what I considered the second time in their marriage.

I held out my hand. "You can't lie in bed and let him win. Come downstairs. Let's talk, like really talk."

She eventually drew her hand out from under the covers and let me lead her out of the bed. Tightening her robe, she said, "Let me clean myself up and I'll be down."

I turned and hugged her, then left the room.

She looked better when she came into the kitchen, though I could see she was still mired in sadness. "Looks delicious," she said, seeing the two place settings.

Thinking it best she didn't drink, I poured her a glass of sparkling water and asked her to sit at the kitchen table. I'd played a dinner jazz playlist and we ate and talked. I mostly asked questions and listened, let her recount how much fun she and my father used to have together, how strange life felt without her partner, and then more about what she might do going forward.

"You should talk to Mrs. Cartwright," I suggested, "spend some time with her. It would be good for you both. She's going through the same stuff."

"Yeah, maybe," she said dismissively as she stabbed a zucchini.

My mom changed whenever we talked about Mrs. Cartwright. I wondered if my disappearing to the Cartwrights' farm had hurt her. Of course it had. I'd been in the worst spot of my life, and instead of leaning on my mother, who'd always been there for me, I'd left her for Mr. and Mrs. Cartwright, as if I'd replaced my mom and dad.

My mother caught me off guard when she said, "Go build her the garden boxes. Sometimes it's better to ask for permission later. We get stubborn at our age. We don't want to listen to anyone. Don't give her a choice."

I squeezed some lemon juice on my last couple of bites of trout. A lemon seed shot out unexpectedly. "Just show up and get to work?"

"Exactly," she said. "Build the boxes, fill them with dirt, get her some plants, and push it on her. She might appreciate it."

I moved the seed to the side of the plate with my fork. "If she doesn't bite my head off. Wait, why don't you help?"

"Me?"

"Yes, you," I said. "Take a day off tomorrow. You still haven't even visited her since I've been back. She'd like to say hi."

"Honey, we're right in the middle of switching software at work."

I finished chewing. "Do I need to sic Mary Beth on you? I'm only home for a little while. When's the last time you took some vacation time?"

"When we came to see you last year."

"All right, that's ridiculous. Even I take more vacation than you. That's saying a lot. Take a day. Let's do something nice for someone else and then go have lunch. We both need the distraction."

She looked like she was wrestling with the decision, but when she finally lifted her head, I knew she was in.

"The only problem," she said, "how are you going to transfer the dirt and supplies?"

"No problem. We can rent a truck from . . ." I stopped as the idea hit me. "Wait, I know someone with a truck."

Chapter 21

A Family That Dines Together

In the morning my mother and I went to Billy's Diner, an institution in Teterbury. It was a few miles outside of downtown, on a two-lane road that led to the highway. Stepping inside instantly took one to the fifties and sixties. The floors were black-and-white checkered, and the cracked and worn booths were red. In the center of each table was a napkin dispenser, a chilled steel pitcher of cream, and a basket that held red and yellow squeeze bottles of ketchup and mustard and packets of honey and blueberry jam. Toward the back, a dusty trophy case featured some old sports memorabilia—mostly Boston teams. Behind the bar where white-haired men sipped their coffee, a stout woman in a hairnet worked a flat grill with the occasional shake of her hips.

Mom and I were both morning people and rarely ever allowed ourselves time to sit down for a long breakfast. Neither of us could stand the idea of others getting a leg up on us. So this was special, and I think she felt it too.

While we perused the menu, I caught her drifting away and falling into the melodies of the tunes coming out of the old jukebox, some voices I recognized from when my mother had played them when I was a child, like Sam Cooke and the Everly Brothers. I kept looking at a group of retirees who'd pulled several tables together. They looked like they were having the time of their lives, catching up and talking about old times.

"I should do this more often," I said, "play hooky from work. Is this what people do, sit around and chat over a couple of cups of coffee? I can sort of see the appeal. The magic of doing nothing."

"I don't know whether or not to get pancakes. That's what I used to get here."

"Yes, get the pancakes," I said.

She set the menu to the side. "I should do this, too, play hooky. You know, Carver, life passes you by, and you'll wish you could remember more of it. And savor more of it."

"Yeah, I suppose so. Wait, it's wild imagining you as a kid coming here."

She laughed. "Our senior year, we'd sit over there in that corner booth before school on Fridays. Those of us who were cheerleaders wore our uniforms, getting ready for the morning pep rallies. I was dating Nicholas Records, the most handsome boy that had ever graced Teterbury High. Until you, of course."

"Thanks, Mom," I said dutifully.

"We'd hold hands and share drinks with two straws." The memory stole her away. "I was sure we would be together forever."

I knew the feeling. "What happened?"

She looked up to the ceiling. "You know how teenage relationships are . . . well . . ." She stopped abruptly as she realized what she was saying.

I brushed a hand through the air, surprised I wasn't more bothered by her fumble. "It's okay. I held on to mine tighter than I should have."

She let out a breath of relief. "I hope you don't let what happened between you two scare you off love forever. 'The one' is going to walk into your life when you least expect it, and I hope you'll let her in. That's all I'll say about that."

"I appreciate you caring," I said.

The server came by and took our order. Then my mom said, "There's one more thing, actually, that I'd like to say to you. If you'll allow me to do some momming for a moment."

"Mom away," I said, knowing there was no stopping her.

"I need you to do me a favor."

"Yeah, anything."

She looked like she was about to divulge a secret, hesitating before finally getting out, "I need you to let your father off the hook."

So much for a nice and easy breakfast. "What? Why?"

"Honey, he . . ." She reached for a napkin from the dispenser and wiped away a drop of cream from the table. "I know you're protecting me, and I know you feel like he let you down before you left. But there was more to it than that; let's leave it there."

"What do you mean, more to it?"

She rolled her lips, like she'd applied lipstick. "Just know that he was never disappointed in you. He was always your cheerleader, always pulling for you. He hit a bad streak back then, a depression. You thought you failed us. That's how we felt. Ben took it especially hard."

It was nice to hear her say those things. "Mom, I don't want to hate him, but I think he could have been stronger for you back then and definitely now."

So much seemed to be on her mind, and she worked hard to meet my eyes. "I could have been stronger for him too. It goes both ways."

"I don't know that I believe it. You don't need to be a martyr for him."

"Trust me, I'm not being a martyr. Take my word for it. Your dad is a great man, still the same great man I married and who raised you. I'm begging you, please don't hold anything against him. Just because he and I are divorcing doesn't mean you have to take sides. I think it's time you two reconnected. Invite him down to Asheville; show him you're ready to move on. That's the favor I want to ask."

And what a big ask it was. Wasn't being the bigger person a parent's job? Still, I knew she was right, and she must have caught me at a good time, because I was surprisingly open-minded to the idea. Or was it more than that? In that moment I knew I wanted more out of the relationship between my father and me. Maybe it was I who would have to take the first step.

I couldn't believe the relief that came over me when I said, "Yeah, sure. I'll reach out and try to mend things. I know it's not always simple."

"Isn't that right?"

When the food came, we talked about less-penetrating topics, like the current argument over the renovation of the elementary and middle schools.

I'd ordered scrambled eggs and hash browns, like I used to do as a kid. With the taste of Tabasco and eggs on my tongue, I said, "Are we at least going to knock on the door of Mrs. Cartwright's house or just start putting things together?" I'd loaded my father's toolbox, circular saw, and drill into the back of the BMW.

"Let's see how far we get before she comes out. Are you thinking we put it in the front or backyard?"

"Front. That way it will make her take care of it."

My mother gave me a nod of approval. "Good thinking." She set her fork down and went for her coffee. "This Ava. Tell me about her."

I could see in my mother's eyes that all-too-familiar need for me to grow a family. "Ava's good people," I said, "but don't go thinking she and I are a thing. It's not like that. She's a woman with a truck, that's all."

"Uh-huh." My mother gave me a smirk.

I felt myself blushing. "I told you, she's a traveling PT. Even if we wanted a relationship, there'd be no point." I was glad my mother didn't bring up how my father had moved across the country for her. We knew how that had worked out.

She must have been thinking the same thing, because she appeared to trail off down a darker path of thinking, her face vacant.

"Ava's a really caring person, not a selfish bone in her body. I don't even know how she has the motivation to be ambitious, but she is. Her whole thing is a mystery. A wanderer who doesn't have a home. Leaves every few months. Goes around helping people. Doesn't even have a storage unit. I can't imagine."

"Sounds like a guardian angel to me."

"Something like that. For Mrs. Cartwright, for sure."

I took a bite of the hash browns, enjoying the saltiness. "I should eat more potatoes. It's a shame they're so carby."

"I know. Same way with pancakes. I won't touch a carb for a week after this."

"You and I both," I said, considering for the thousandth time that I was my mother in so many ways.

As if I'd woken her from a dream and she'd realized how naughty she was being, she pushed the plate away from her, the last bites of pancake becoming orphans. "Ava's meeting us at Home Depot at what time? We'd better get the check."

We finished up and I tipped big. I didn't let my mom see it, and I got us out of there before the server had returned. Only as we were driving away did I see the woman staring at us through the window. She blew me a kiss, and I smiled like I hadn't in a long time.

In the parking lot of Home Depot, Ava climbed out of her turquoise truck and waved.

"Oh my, she's a looker," my mom said.

"I hadn't noticed."

"Right."

We pulled up beside her and stepped out. I shoved my hands into my pockets. "Shall we do this?"

We walked the aisles, filling three carts. Ava apparently got a kick out of my mother chatting her up about me as a child, my dimple butt, and the way I used to climb on the counter and eat sugar from the jar. I tuned them out and focused on my shopping list.

While we were in line, my mother said—right in front of Ava— "She's a find, isn't she?"

"Who, me?" Ava said.

"Absolutely," my mom said with a jovial lilt I'd not heard since I'd been back.

Mortified is the word I'd used to describe my reaction to my mother's overt matchmaking. She was worse than Mrs. Cartwright.

Once we'd loaded up, my mother suggested I ride with Ava, an attempt so blatant that she might as well have said, "Spend enough time with him and he'll grow on you. I insist you two procreate by the afternoon. That way I can start painting the nursery."

I climbed inside of Ava's Chevy truck. She'd told me earlier it was an '85. It was big and roomy inside. Spotless. An open can of kombucha stood in the cup holder. A pine tree air freshener dangled from the mirror, faintly giving off the last of its scent. As she cranked the engine, an AM radio station played. How fitting.

She turned down the music. "Your mother is struggling, isn't she?"

I clicked my buckle and turned to her. "She was trying to hide it. I guess not too successfully."

"It's understandable. We've all been there."

Ava made no attempt to keep up with my mother. I swear we caught every red light, but she seemed to focus more on our conversation than the road. I wasn't complaining.

When we were about halfway to Mrs. Cartwright's, I couldn't help but laugh at how slowly we were moving.

"What?" she said.

"You're funny."

She putted across an intersection so slow I expected someone to honk. "How am I funny?"

I took in her side profile, her easygoing smile. "Look at you. It must be nice not to be in a rush."

"What's the point?"

"I guess there's not. It must be in my DNA. Look at how my mother drives." By then she was far ahead of us.

Ava switched lanes, a process that took a full minute to accomplish. "True. But DNA or not, if you want to slow things down, slow them down."

Not that we would be in the same town long enough for her to teach me anything, but I said, "I'd love for you to teach me how to do that."

She gave me a quick glance before setting her eyes back on the road. "Unlike our Mrs. Cartwright, I was not born to be a teacher."

"I don't know about that," I said. "You seem to be super intuitive and certainly opened my eyes the other day. All that stuff you were saying about heeding the call. It hit home. Are you sure physical therapy is your calling?"

Teterbury's modest skyline came into view. "It's all connected, isn't it? The body and the mind? I'm fascinated by all kinds of healing—holistic healing."

"How about the intuition, though? Where does that come from?"

She made a big wide turn, the truck moving like an old Cadillac. "Probably as a survival instinct. My father wasn't a great man, and growing up, I had to be aware of who was coming in the door, what to expect from him. He had a drug problem, but even when he was sober, he could be mean."

I'd guessed wrongly that she'd glided through life. "I'm sorry . . . I didn't mean to . . ."

"It's okay. I'm at peace with him."

"Is he still alive? Do you talk to him?"

"I have no idea. My mom kicked him out of the house regularly, but one time he never came back. The police came looking for him a few days later, telling us they thought he might have held some people up at gunpoint. We never saw him again."

"Wow, Ava. And here I am complaining about my parents."

She shrugged. "Our challenges are what sculpt us, you know? I had to grow up quickly."

"And then you lost your mom. You don't deserve that."

"I don't know that anyone gets a free ride out of life." She looked over at me. "What can you do?"

What can you do? I pondered her words as I watched the traffic move around us. Was that the answer to everything? Trying it on for size, I said to myself, *You fell for a girl that you wrongly thought was your soulmate. She dumped you, breaking you into pieces. So you attempted to kill yourself, and everyone in town found out.*

What can you do?

I actually laughed out loud for the second time in a few minutes. Was it that easy? Was it as simple as a choice to come to peace with your past?

I could have kept talking to her forever, but we had a job to do. When we rolled up to Mrs. Cartwright's house, it felt like we were volunteering for Habitat for Humanity, brandishing materials and invading a property. My mother climbed out of her BMW. She'd probably been waiting on us for ten minutes.

We unloaded and discussed where we'd build the garden. A busted-up walkway led to Mrs. Cartwright's house from the street. A monstrous sugar maple that must have been a half-century old cast a swatch of shade onto the western side of the lawn, so we picked a spot on the right side, near the hedges that lined the porch. That way she'd still have some grass. It wasn't much of a thing, though, taking up part of the lawn. Most of the neighbors had sacrificed bits of their small yards for garden boxes. Grass didn't seem to be as important in Vermont as it was in other parts of the country.

I set up a sawhorse and cut four-foot pieces. On the third piece, I heard Oscar barking, and then Mrs. Cartwright swung open the door. I let go of the trigger and waved. When the saw stopped spinning, I said, "Good morning."

"What's going on here?" she asked, straightening her glasses. Her hair was in curlers, and she looked like she was in no mood for company. The way I'd spoken to her the day before, was it any shock seeing my face didn't lighten her day?

"We're surprising you," I said, stepping next to Ava, who waved too.

My mother came forward as well, making us three criminals with good intent, ready to commence our sentence. "Hi, Eloise."

Mrs. Cartwright's look of annoyance fell away at the sight of my mother. "Lisa, how nice to see you."

My mother ascended the steps to greet her. "Forgive me for not visiting earlier. It's been a strange week."

"Yes, Carver told me about it. I'm so sorry."

After an embrace, my mother gestured back toward Ava and me. "We thought we might help you build some garden boxes. I had the day off, and Carver and I are spending some time together."

Mrs. Cartwright looked down at the materials and then at me. "A garden? Carver, I told you I didn't want a garden." She was failing to keep her tone light.

Leaning on my mother's wisdom, I said, "You know what, Mrs. Cartwright, we're giving you one anyway." I stared up at her, saying with my eyes, *So sue me.*

"I think it's a sweet gesture," Ava said.

My former teacher forgot her manners and that my mother was there. "Ava, I'm sure this was your idea too."

Ava had no problem sticking up for herself. "That's right. And guess what I got you? A seat so you can take care of your knee while you're gardening." She walked to the back of the truck and pulled out the contraption she'd found at the store. "You can use it like a stool," she called out, walking back toward us, "or if you're feeling extra limber, flip it over and use it as a kneeler, so you don't have to put your knees on the hard ground. Pretty neat, right? It has little pockets for your trowel and your hand rake."

Mrs. Cartwright's face tightened. For a moment, I thought she might snap at all of us, even tell us to get off her property. We let her stew in her own anger long enough for three cars to pass.

She finally said, "If you have nothing better to do, then so be it. But I won't promise to use it."

I pointed to the plants we'd bought, the squash and zucchini, the pole beans and snap peas, the cucumbers and tomatoes. "We'll get these in the ground today, and I'll find a landscaper later who will install a sprinkler system for you. All you have to do is give the plants some love. Read them some Jane Austen or something. Can you do that?"

She could have ripped my head off from thirty feet away. I held strong.

Raising a finger at me, she said, "You're incorrigible, Carver Livingston. A real hardhead."

"Takes one to know one."

She shook her head at me and then found my mom, as if she was the culprit. "You've raised a heck of a stubborn young man, haven't you?"

My mom, who'd been watching from the sidelines from the side of the porch, had teared up for some reason. "I sure did."

Mrs. Cartwright sighed. "Let me put some clothes on. If Carver and Ava think this will make them feel better about themselves, then I suppose I'll go along with it. But you're not putting anything anywhere without my approval." She looked up. "My pole beans and snap peas don't like that much sun." She pointed farther toward the driveway. "That's where I want the boxes."

There she was. My teacher. I looked over at my mom, wanting to say thanks for suggesting that I push the limits, but her face was frozen with a frown.

"Lisa," Mrs. C said, "thank you for taking care of Oscar the other day. I've been meaning to come by and say hello."

My mom had to shake herself out of wherever she'd gone. "Me too. Ben and I didn't even know you were here until Carver said something."

"I'm barely here."

"That makes two of us," my mother said.

"Why don't you come in for a cup of tea? Let's let the youngsters work, and we can complain about life for a while."

They left Ava and me to work. We did so in silence, and I turned to see her making marks with a pencil on the board I was about to cut. We had three more to go. She was focused on the task and as eagerly devoted to helping Mrs. Cartwright as I. That was our common ground. Was there anything else to it? Thank goodness others couldn't hear my thoughts.

She held a board as I ran the saw over it with a *zing*. We both laughed when we noticed how crooked I'd cut it.

"I question your skills as a surgeon," she said.

I grinned at her. "I work with far more precise tools back home."

"Ah." How nice it was I didn't have to pretend to be someone I wasn't.

Twenty minutes passed, and then the ladies came back out from the house. Mrs. Cartwright had put on clogs and descended the steps to inspect our work.

"What do you think about putting them here?" I pointed at the two four-by-four boxes Ava and I had constructed. We'd placed them next to each other about three feet from the shrubbery that abutted the house.

"Move that one farther apart," she said. "They'll need to be able to get the lawn mower in between them."

"Spoken like a seasoned pro," Ava said. She turned to me and whispered, "I think she's excited."

I hoped so.

Mrs. Cartwright and my mother sat in the two rocking chairs on the porch and watched us work. At one point, they made plans to go shopping together, which was promising. Actually, when my mother asked her, Mrs. Cartwright had replied, "You know, I might like that. It seems I'm going to be around here longer than I thought, so perhaps it's time I put more effort into my appearance."

I heard that and glanced over at Ava, who shared a hopeful smile with me. She and I emptied bags of soil into each box until they were nearly full. By the end, we were both covered in dirt and laughing, having a good time doing this, being out there, helping someone.

As Ava and I began to clean up our mess, my mother mentioned my favorite hiking spot, a lookout six miles up Moose Mountain. "The top of Moose was always your favorite place, wasn't it?" my mother said. "It's a good workout, going up there."

"But so worth it," I said. I could still see the Moose lookout in my mind, could still hear our footfalls as my parents and I climbed up there every few weeks in the warmer months.

"Ava, do you hike?" my mother asked. I knew instantly what my mother was trying to do. The world stopped moving as the dread of how this might play out hit me.

"I've been getting out a little," Ava replied.

My mother continued her ploy. "You should have Carver take you up there. It's the best view anywhere around, south of Stowe."

I should have been happy to see my mom caring so much about me. Despite her troubles, she was putting me first as always. Still, I was a wreck inside. And it wasn't due to a lack of interest in Ava; it was my fear of rejection. Having resisted relationships for twenty years, even the idea of wanting one was akin to walking out on a frozen lake.

"You two *should* go," Mrs. Cartwright interjected. Wait, had they hatched this plan together while they were drinking tea?

Giving my teacher a hard-and-fast look, I almost said, "I see what you're doing," but I couldn't bear to.

Ava still hadn't said anything, which forced me to fill the silence. "I'm sure Ava has better things to do than go hiking with me."

"No, I'd love to."

Wait, what? Though one voice in my head warned me not to get my hopes up, the other voice told it to shut up. "Then it would be my honor to take you up Moose Mountain. You know, as a representative of Teterbury."

That was how Ava and I had been played, the two puppeteers up on the porch steering us toward each other.

Chapter 22

THE VIEW

I met Elliot the next morning for breakfast, catching him up on the madness surrounding my life. He listened and laughed and made me feel less alone. It was nice to have him back in my life, and as we were leaving, I suggested he bring his family down to Asheville in the fall. The last thing he said to me was, "Good luck with Ava. She sounds like a good one." I gave him a thumbs-up as the jitters tingled my abdomen. What in the world had I gotten myself into? Or, more accurately, what had I let Mrs. C and my mother concoct?

Ava and I left the trailhead at eleven. I carried a backpack with water bottles, a couple of apples, and a bag of trail mix. It was overcast, the cumulus clouds thick and low, but the meteorologist doubted we would see any rain. We both wore shorts, wool socks, and hiking shoes, a couple right out of an REI catalog.

The first leg of the trail ran along a creek where I used to catch crayfish in the summers. The water made a trickling sound as it crept toward the Tye River. Rich smells of mushrooms and wet earth and fragrant June blooms filled the forest.

We fell into a steady stride, talking nonstop. I loved the rhythmic tennis match of conversation. She attempted to steer topics away from her and direct them to me, but I hit them right back to her, slowly getting her to reveal herself as she talked about what made her tick and what she believed in. She had a way of swaying this skeptic toward some sort of faith. Faith that we weren't alone; faith that there was something beyond what we saw; that there was a purpose to these lives we were living. A woman who could do that . . . man, oh man. I couldn't imagine letting her go without at least taking a chance at telling her how I felt about her. Even if the idea scared the hell out of me.

The trail crossed over the creek before the ascent up the mountain began. Farther up, a waterfall splashed down into a pool.

"How has no one mentioned this place?" she asked. "It's so, so magical."

"Yeah, it is . . . magical." I felt the same way about her.

I pointed to a pathway of four moss-covered stones in the shallow creek. "We need to cross here. Be careful, they're slippery. I've eaten it more than once." Showing the way, I leaped from stone to stone until I came to the rocky bank.

When I turned, she was just getting started. She leaped gracefully, and I reached out my hand to help her on the last jump. As she reached the bank, we came dangerously close to each other. She met my eyes long enough to bend her lips into a smile before continuing past me. I would have paid a lot more than a penny for her thoughts. She wouldn't have come if she wasn't interested in me, right?

We tackled the first healthy grade up the mountain, a switchback that never failed to get my heart racing. The mustiness of the valley floor gave way to a scent reminiscent of dried herbs.

"What do you do with your days off?" I asked. "It must be nice always being in a new place. So much to discover."

"It never gets boring. Getting to know the different microcultures, the different ways of life. Meeting new people. I'm pretty simple, though. I like going to the museums and learning about each place. I'm a sponge for useless knowledge. I love reading. That's probably what I do most."

"Yeah, what kind of reading?"

"I'm all over the place. Mrs. Cartwright has been my guide lately, sending me home with more than I could ever keep up with."

"I'm assuming you've read *Outlander* like the rest of the female population on Earth? Even Mrs. C had those on her shelves."

"Twice," she said.

"Twice? That is quite the undertaking." My heart rate elevated, and my shins burned as we took on the steepest slope yet.

"I don't know that there's anything more fun in the whole world," she said, her breath getting heavy.

"The world?"

"The universe! They're literary but page turning. To me, she's nothing short of a genius, that Diana Gabaldon. They're perfect novels, every single one. I might read them a third time soon, to be ready for the next one."

I peered up through the trees, noticing a cloud had blocked the sun, throwing a shadow over the forest. "Supposedly there's a guy named Jamie that everyone talks about."

"I don't remember that specific character."

"No?" I didn't pick up that she was joking until I saw her face. "Ah, I see. He must be a real minx."

"He falls into the category of *extremely hot*."

"Hot. Hmm. But he's in a book. You don't know what he looks like. I mean, unless you watch the show."

"He was hot before I saw the show, trust me. In fact, he was hotter."

"I see." For an iota of a second, I found myself jealous of a character in a fantasy series. "The women in my office talk about the wedding episode. It seems they're in a competition to see who's watched it more."

"I bet I could beat them," she said, lighting up.

When we reached the flatter stretch, we took a water break. Through an opening in the trees, we could see most of Teterbury. My hometown looked so gentle from up high.

I took a long swig of the water from a Nalgene bottle. "That hits the spot."

She did the same and then looked at me. Her freckled forehead glistened. "You didn't warn me we were climbing Kilimanjaro."

"It used to be a lot easier," I said. "I think the mountain got higher."

She laughed at that one. "Yeah, that must be what it is."

Once I'd packed the bottles back into the pack, we continued up the switchback. The trail narrowed even more, so I let her walk ahead of me. She looked incredibly attractive, her long white legs tucked into those hiking boots, her hips so beautifully feminine in her shorts.

We continued on toward the summit, and I tried to make sense of the two of us. All I knew for sure was that I enjoyed every moment we were together. *If* she had perhaps come around on me, detecting the same spark I wasn't able to ignore, would I be able to open myself up to something?

I certainly had to consider the timing relative to Shannon. I wasn't acting out of desperation, was I? This most certainly wasn't a rebound. If anything, I was letting myself feel something for Ava *despite* what had happened with Shannon.

Not too far from the top, she brought up my speech for the reunion. "I want to come, just to hear it."

"I bet you do. I'm going to change a lot of lives while I'm up there."

She stopped and gave me a dramatic eye roll. I was glad she got me, at least enough to know I'd been joking.

"You know what keeps niggling its way into my mind," I said. "I've been trying to write this darn speech that I've somehow agreed to. It's silly, this idea that a few of us get up and talk. When I was first asked, a part of me liked the idea that I was one of the chosen ones. Kind of like I'd won, you know."

"Because it's always a competition," she said, clearly poking at me.

"Right. It is. And this idea of giving the speech—it's mortifying." I raised the pitch of my voice. "Oh, look at me. I'm a doctor now. I did this and this and this. You are so lucky to have known me. I will allow you to wash my feet now."

She laughed at my ridiculousness that we both knew wasn't far off the mark. Maybe I'd been too open to her. "You must have the lowest opinion of me."

"No, not at all. In fact, you're adorable with all your stuff going on. I can see you with your hands white knuckling the wheel, trying to steer your life in exactly the way you want it to go."

"That's what we're supposed to do, right?"

"Maybe, but it seems exhausting not to let go every once in a while, see where you end up."

I let out a laugh that might have scared the birds. "I can verify that my life is definitely exhausting. Hey, I'd like to see you get up there and give a speech."

"Please. I'm perfectly fine not trying to prove anything to anyone."

"Ouch," I said. "You really know how to throw a punch."

She touched my arm. "Sorry, that may have been harsh."

I looked down at her hand on my arm, enjoying the moment despite the way she had me cut open like I would one of my patients. "What I'm trying to say, though, is that I *don't* want to get up there and prove anything to anyone. I mean, okay, I do, but . . . let's be honest. Who wants to hear from me?"

"I think it would be interesting to hear other people talk about their lives. Maybe you're overanalyzing, taking it too seriously. It's not like CNN is going to do a postbreakdown analysis of every word. Besides, it's not about teaching them. They're not coming for a motivational speech. They want to hear what you've been up to. Maybe the great things you remember about growing up here."

"The great things . . . ," I said, hearing the hilarity of that concept in my tone.

"Why don't you tell stories about Mrs. Cartwright? Sounds like you have more than a few."

"I like that." I tried to imagine my classmates and what they expected of me. An idea came, a spidering crack in shatterproof glass. "Especially if she was there. I wonder if I could convince her to go. I think seeing so many former students in one place would give her the lift she needs. What if we did something to honor her?"

"I love this idea," Ava said.

"But she'd never go for it. She doesn't seem to want to see anyone."

Ava shrugged. "She was up for shopping with your mom. Maybe she's having a change of heart."

"True." I chewed on the thought. "How would I get her there? Surprise her? And I don't know what Bree would say."

"Bree?" Ava asked.

"The organizer. She's militant about this reunion. She might think I'm hijacking it."

"Hijacking a reunion by honoring a teacher?"

"Okay, fair point. Maybe I'll call her." In fact, Bree had texted me earlier, saying that the reunion committees were meeting in the morning to run over logistics. Those of us speaking were welcome to come by to get a feel for the room. I'd initially texted back an I'll try, thinking there was no need to suffer twice, being immersed in my old peers, but maybe it would be a good way to ease into seeing more people while also presenting the idea of honoring Mrs. Cartwright in some way.

I was high on the idea as we neared the top. I barely even noticed that my legs were burning. Maybe Bree would bite. If so, perhaps I could convince Mrs. Cartwright to attend.

We came to the top of Moose Mountain through two towering pine trees that opened to a giant rock face, giving us a sensational three-hundred-and-sixty-degree view. The mountains stretched as far as one could see. The only sign of life was Teterbury, resting quiet and easy in the valley. Bearing witness to such grandeur, how could I not feel pride to be a Vermonter?

Ava stood close to the edge, where she could see the river winding through the trees. She raised her arms as if recharging her soul. "This place is a treasure," she said with infectious joy.

Coming up behind her, I said, "I must have hiked up here fifty times over the years, and it always takes my breath away. Well, the last of my breath. That hike is a doozy."

Ava looked like she'd had a huge revelation. "I think I've made up my mind. I'm a mountains person."

"Wait, you've just made up your mind?"

"Right here, right now. I have to live in a place where I can hike like this. I love it."

I took in the view again. "That's why Asheville reeled me in. You have to see it."

"I definitely will one day."

What I wanted to tell her was that she had to come to see *me*. Maybe I could lure her into taking an assignment down there. Hold on, what was I saying? Yes, it was true. I would love to spend time with her back home, to share with her the views I'd found in my three years of hiking and biking the Blue Ridge Mountains.

We looked toward Teterbury, and I helped her find her bearings, pointing out my parents' neighborhood first. Because of the tree cover, you couldn't see the house in which I'd grown up, but I found Mrs. Cartwright's roof. Stepping close to Ava, I let her follow my finger as I pointed toward it. From there I gave her a tour of the parts of Teterbury that mattered to me. I ended with an unassuming collection of buildings surrounded by athletic fields on the edge of town.

I peered down the length of my arm. "And that's Teterbury High." I'd driven by it, but something about looking at it from up here made the memories of my high school years weigh that much heavier.

"Aw, I can see younger Carver now," Ava said. "Sitting at the front of your class, throwing up your hand, being a know-it-all, flexing that big brain of yours."

Her accuracy sparked a snicker out of me. "You're not far off." Other than my senior year, I thought, where the back row by the window became my refuge.

A need to tell her about my demons came over me. It felt like a prerequisite to getting to know me, and I wanted that from her. I couldn't believe I was thinking it, but I was . . . I wanted to see if the two of us had something. Even the idea of a long-distance relationship didn't scare me off.

I found a good spot to take a seat and she followed suit. I dug into my backpack, found the bag of trail mix, and handed it to her. "Did Mrs. Cartwright tell you how we came to know each other? I mean, more than me being in her class."

"No." Ava popped a handful of nuts and raisins in her mouth.

"Something happened to me years ago." I took a moment to gather myself. "There was a reason I didn't come back."

"I figured," she said with her mouth full.

"Yeah, it wasn't good. I tried to kill myself." Fresh pain burned my wrist. I took off my watch and showed her the scar. As I did so, I couldn't believe the wave of shame that pounded me.

She set down the bag of trail mix and took my hand and dragged a finger along the scar. "I . . . I'm so sorry. That must have been an awful time."

"Yeah. It was over a girl who broke up with me. Shannon Bigsby. She messed up my world pretty badly." I told Ava the overview of my collapse, how I'd come out of the hospital and lost all the fight my mother had instilled in me. "Then Mrs. Cartwright happened. She and her husband snapped me out of it, and I clawed my way back." I talked about how I'd worked my way to Davidson and NC State, eventually landing a surgical residency. "Somewhere in all of that, I found a way to fight back the demons. I don't know if it was the best way, but it was a way."

"But it still hurts," she whispered, glancing at my wrist again as I pulled my watch back over it.

"That's why I haven't been back."

"I get that," she said, and I could hear in her sympathetic tone that she did get it. She got *me*, even. "Thanks for telling me. So this Shannon, have you seen her since you've been back? That's got to be tough."

"The short answer is yes. For a long time, I thought getting her back would make me feel whole." I told her about Shannon's divorce and how we ran into each other and what happened from there. "I'm glad it happened. She was lingering for entirely too long in my head, you know. Finally, I was able to find closure."

"Good for you."

It didn't feel right, asking Ava out now. Not after I'd told her about my suicide attempt and then about Shannon and me. But if I didn't ask Ava out now, I might not ever, and something felt wrong about that.

I swallowed, gearing up. "Other than wanting to share with you, there's another reason I wanted to tell you."

Her eyebrows curled in confusion. "What's that?"

"I . . ." I took a deep breath. Dating Shannon had been one thing, the evolution of something a long time coming. Taking a leap toward Ava would be something else entirely. It would require me shutting out twenty years of avoiding exactly this kind of vulnerability. And yet something soul deep was telling me not to leave without coming clean and telling her about these feelings rising within me.

Out with it, you twit!

I found her eyes and thought that if I was going to take a chance, this was the woman. "Ava, the reason I wanted you to know all that is because . . . I want you to know the real me, not some facade of me. Because I keep thinking maybe you and I . . . we could be great together."

She gave a look like I'd thrown a wadded-up piece of paper at her, which wasn't the best fuel for my self-esteem. I'd taken the leap, only to now be free-falling down into a canyon.

I tried to pull a parachute that wasn't there. "I know Mrs. Cartwright says I'm not your type and that we're both afraid of love and all that, but . . ."

I met her dead clean in the eyes, her soft and safe eyes. "I know we're both about to leave, and you don't even know where you're going, but what if we both go on with our lives and regret not exploring what's between us?"

She looked away, and I felt a need to explain myself further. "I like the way you make me feel, who you are. I like that you have such a big heart. I like your truck and the way you drive, how you are around Mrs. Cartwright. I like who I am around you."

I stopped running my mouth and ended with, "Would you go out with me?"

She kept her eyes set on the horizon. I could see the word *no* rising like the sun. She finally turned to me. "This, coming from a guy who says he's not looking for a relationship."

"I know. It's bizarre, but . . ."

"*Not even remotely interested*, I think is what you said."

"I know what I said."

"I'm so sorry, Carver. No. You were chasing your ex from high school. You've mentioned your distaste for love multiple times. You're all over the place. And you're right; we might not ever see each other again. I don't even know where I'm going next." She blew out a breath in exasperation. "I'm sorry if I gave you the wrong impression, and maybe I shouldn't have agreed to come. I know your mom and Mrs. Cartwright were hoping for more, but I wanted to go on a hike."

Rejection. Full stop. Finally, *finally*, I had taken a chance, and this was where it landed me, right back into the gutter of a broken heart. To add insult to injury, I felt a raindrop. Was there any doubt about why I'd had a mixed relationship with the sky? Get me back to frigging Asheville.

The only thing I had left at that point was my dignity. I wanted to be the guy who had casually asked her, not really caring one way or another. "You didn't give me any impression," I said. "Seriously, don't sweat it. I thought I'd ask. I'm headed back to North Carolina anyway. It would be a terrible idea."

The only way I could handle the situation was to stand up and get walking again, so I did just that. "We should probably head back; that rain might get worse." I held out my hand, wishing for the fucking bottom to drop out of the sky.

She pressed up and whispered, "Yeah."

We didn't say much on the decline, only a quick comment or question. My head was a raceway for thoughts, though, most of them incredibly self-destructive. I hadn't been enough for Shannon when I'd first opened up my heart, and I still wasn't enough now, even after everything I'd done.

Only as we were almost back to the trailhead did she say, "Carver, there is no way we are going to part with all this awkwardness."

"It's fine."

She cast a soft gaze in my direction.

"It's okay, really. It wouldn't have worked out." I hated how I sounded like I was backpedaling, like I didn't care. But I couldn't stop. "I'm super busy. You don't seem like someone who would put up with a workaholic."

"It's not that," she said. "It's not you. I'm still trying to find me. There's no room for someone else yet."

I wanted to say, *You think you're lost? That leaves no hope for the rest of us.* I didn't, though. "Yeah, I get it."

And I made a mental note to never let myself feel this way again.

Chapter 23

THE REHEARSAL

I had not been into the Wayfair Hotel since I'd parked cars there as a valet when I was sixteen. Though the hotel had always possessed a certain New England charm, it had gotten a much-needed facelift and now would have passed for high class about anywhere. It was six stories high and mostly brick, and it probably had about fifty rooms. US and Vermont flags flanking the impressive entrance whipped in the wind. A revolving door at the top of the stairs ushered people into the lobby.

It had been a long eighteen hours since Ava had rejected my invitation, and I'd done everything under the sun to shake the thought from my head. No matter what, though, it acted like a hammer striking my self-esteem.

Still, I had hope for today. I wondered if Bree—and maybe even the others—would indeed join me in honoring Mrs. Cartwright. Every time I thought about the idea, it grew bigger in my head. Part of it was surely that I had something to prove, not only to myself and to my classmates, but to Ava now too. I wanted her to see I could make things happen. That she should have given me a chance.

The hotel had clearly hit their busy season, the hustle of the staff causing beads of sweat on their foreheads as they tried to appease their many guests. A bellhop with a cart full of luggage nearly ran me over as he raced to the elevator. A family of four followed closely behind, clearly eager to kick off their Teterbury vacation. That was something I never thought I'd say, *a Teterbury vacation*. I supposed people from all over had this romantic idea of small-town New England, the cool summers, the windows always open, the quaint ice-cream shops and antique stores, the peddlers of maple syrup and honey. If only they knew how dangerous this small town could be.

I continued through the lobby over the recently polished tile floors, past several seating areas, where guests sat in plush leather chairs and couches, thumbing through their devices. At the doorway into one of the conference rooms toward the back, Bree stood at the center of a group of people, spinning around, addressing everyone like she was Lincoln giving a stump speech, drumming up support for a vote. All she needed was a beard and a top hat and another foot of height.

"There he is," she said. Maybe she needed a more distinguished accent as well.

"Hi there."

The whole group turned, ten of them.

In an instant, I came close to having a panic attack, my vision blurring, the room spinning. This was a lot of the past staring at me at one time. I drew in a sharp breath, telling myself to pull it together. They were all faces I knew, including Shannon's, who looked north of ravishing. So many of the names I'd forgotten.

Resisting the urge to check my fly, I smiled wide. They probably hadn't seen so much white since their bedsheets that morning. "What's going on, folks? How nice to see you."

The collective responded with hellos and handshakes.

"We're waiting on one more," Bree said, as I worked my way to Shannon, hoping to extinguish some of the awkwardness.

"Hi there," I said.

"Hi," she whispered back. I was surprised at how immune to her I felt. What a far cry from the me that had first seen her at the Sanderton.

In my peripheral vision, I thought I saw Christopher Campbell, who'd been class president, eyeing Shannon and me together, possibly thinking back to what had happened. Could he see that I was stronger than I used to be? If he only knew that I was the one to end things with her this time.

We all made small talk, laughing about the past. Lance Poitier talked about the time the seniors pranked Mrs. Jones, our science teacher, filling her car with shaving cream. That one hadn't gone over well and had resulted in three students' suspensions. Marissa Jackson told the story of the time they caught another teacher smoking cigarettes in her car. I laughed with the rest of them, though every anecdote cut dangerously close to the November of our senior year.

"I had an idea, Bree." Of course I directed the suggestion to her, as our fearless leader. "Not to invade on the program, but I ran into Mrs. Cartwright the other day and have spent some time with her. Maybe we could do something for her Saturday night? Something to show her how much of an impact she had on us."

The collection of positive nods was encouraging.

"What do you think, Bree?"

"Certainly," she said, "if you think she'd be up for it."

"That's the thing," I said. "I thought we could surprise her. I'll get her here, one way or another. That will be my job. Then maybe I could introduce her as part of my speech. I wondered if maybe all the speakers might say something about her. We could invite her up and give her flowers. Nothing too embarrassing." I looked around the room. "I don't know about you guys, but I feel strange making it all about me up there."

"I feel the same way," Maurice Tyler said.

"I think it's a great idea," Bree said. "A bit of a curveball for me, but that's okay."

"Awesome." Hopefully Mrs. Cartwright wouldn't kill me. I could already feel this thing gaining momentum. What I knew was that such a night would be so good for her.

When the last of the party came, Bree led us into the conference room she'd rented out for the reunion. It could have held about 150 people comfortably, but according to Bree, there would be only 120 attendees.

"There will be a few who back out at the last minute," she said. "And, yes, they will pay later, when I hunt them down for a donation for the foundation." She began to point and show her vision. This was her big moment. "We'll have some high tables on one side with easy-to-eat food. Then the dance floor in the middle. We'll keep the podium over there. That makes the most sense."

She drew out a fancy electronic notebook and began to go through the program, how we'd start with booze to loosen everyone up. Then the band would play a set. Between sets, Bree would talk first, then introduce the speakers. I would go last and introduce Mrs. Cartwright.

"If I can pull off getting her here," I said. "Just to set expectations."

"Would you like me to get involved?" Bree asked.

"I don't think so. Let's save the big guns for when we need them."

She got right back to business. "Great, okay. Then we'll have the band play one last set, do the requests bit, and call it a night. I'm sure people will want to break into their cliques from the old days and take over the town."

Thirty minutes later, as everyone exited the conference room, I beelined it to Shannon. She didn't look too pleased.

"Are you mad at me?"

"No." By no, she clearly meant yes.

"Wanna go for a walk?" I asked.

She shrugged. I think that meant yes too.

A host of memories came flooding in as we meandered by Advent Episcopal with its impressive columns and the steeple that marked the skyline. I couldn't remember exactly when, but this church was one of the first buildings the founders of Teterbury had constructed. Other than the impressive stained-glass windows, the entire structure had been painted a stark white—even the two big doors that led its parishioners to salvation. I could barely look at all that wood without wondering how it had managed to avoid a fire over the years. Maybe there had been something holy at work.

I'd certainly seen an angel every Sunday in the form of Shannon Bigsby. "You probably never knew," I said, "but I used to watch you in church. I remember you guys always sat up front on the left. We would sit on the other side about four rows back. I'd wait for you to turn my way."

"Would I?"

"On rare occasion. Of course you were nervous. Hopelessly in love with me and desperately nervous."

"I'm sure," she said, allowing me to get a faint smile out of her.

"You're the only reason I would agree to go to church in the first place."

"At least I gave you religion then."

Behind an impressive iron fence was a graveyard that had been hosting Teterbury's finest dead men and women since the mid-1800s. If I weren't careful, they'd bury our friendship in there too.

We stalled in front of a bakery that smelled like cinnamon buns. A rainbow flag hung above the door. A dog bowl spilling over with water sat under a chalkboard sign that read ALL DOGS WELCOME. Through the polished glass were baskets of baguettes and sourdough loaves. "Shannon, there's something I need to ask."

She crossed her arms harshly. "What now?"

"We'd talked about going together to the reunion."

Her electric eyes narrowed as she gave me a nasty look. "No, you don't have to cancel our date, Carver. We already decided our fate. I'm not sure if I'm even going now."

"Don't do that." Last week's me would have loved to have taken the upper hand, but I didn't want it now. "It's just . . . I would like to take Mrs. Cartwright, and I thought we'd best talk about it first. I think it's the only way I'm going to convince her to come."

"Well, aren't you a saint?" she asked snidely.

Had I been digging a hole, I would have been jabbing my shovel up through western Australia soil about then.

A guy stepped out of the bakery toting a bag of goodies. Once it was the two of us again, I said, "C'mon, Shannon."

"It's fine," she said. "It's sweet, what you're doing."

We smiled at one another. Was there a path to being friends? I didn't know. But I was glad that we were at least talking.

My dad called as I walked back home. It was a picture-perfect day, and diners occupied every outdoor table in sight.

"What, Dad?" I asked.

"I'm checking in." His mood was as chipper as ever, as if he'd set free every string attached in his life. I could see him driving down the highway, towing that god-awful trailer, singing "On the Road Again" along with Willie.

"We're still here," I said, hearing the impatience in my tone.

"Bravo. I didn't think you'd last this long."

"Somebody needs to be here."

He sighed. "How is she?"

"How do you think?" I wasn't sure that he even had the right to ask, but then I remembered my mother's request at the diner. *Go easy on him.*

"Carver, I love the heck out of your mom, and I want to know how she's faring."

I turned a right down an alley to avoid the crowds. "What do you want me to say? That she's drinking too much and stays in bed? Or that she's already found someone and forgotten you?"

"I can hear that you're mad," he said.

"No shit, I'm still mad."

A cat gnawed on something that had fallen out of a trash bin ahead.

"She's not answering my calls. I want to hear that she's okay. Is there anything I can do for her? Or for you?"

I could think of a million things. Trying to be somewhat cordial for my mom's sake, I said as kindly as possible, "No, we're going to be fine."

Cold silence as I watched my feet move across the pavement back toward the house he'd abandoned. The cat didn't even bother looking up as I passed by.

"I know you don't care, but I'm in New Mexico. Santa Fe is a heck of a place."

"That's great, Dad." What did he want from me? A cheerleading routine? Though I had made my mother a promise of sorts to mend things, it wasn't going to happen quickly.

"Call me sometime when you want to chat."

"Don't hold your breath, all right?" I hated that I kept throwing jabs at him. What rankled me was that I still loved him. Although he'd walked out on my mother, a part of me did want to call him and chat. Considering the current state of my life, I could have used some advice.

"I get it, son. Take care of her for me."

I ended the call and crammed the phone back into my pocket. Had someone been watching me march back through town and over the bridge toward my parents', they would have seen a man not only repeatedly shaking his head in disgust but talking to himself all the while. Why was he so different from the dad I remembered for most of my youth? Was it solely because I'd dragged a blade across my wrist?

I stopped at Mrs. Cartwright's house to see when she wanted me to take her to Hannaford, the grocery store she preferred. She was still days away from getting her car back from the shop.

I scooped Oscar up into my arms after she opened the door. "Are we finally becoming friends?" He sniffed around my hands, having gotten used to the treats. "I'll bring you back something from the store, okay?"

She invited me in, and I set Oscar down in the foyer near the coatrack. "First off, I wanted to say that I'm sorry for speaking to you the way I did two days ago. I had no right to—"

"You don't need to apologize, Carver."

"No, I do."

"No, you don't," she insisted. "Because you're right and you're right and you're right. I could do better."

I certainly wasn't going to argue. "Me too," I said. "Why don't we do better together?" I wasn't exactly sure how we could do it together, but I'd find a way. We could stay in touch and have weekly check-ins. Cheer each other on.

She gave a kind nod. "Yeah, okay. I'd like that."

That made me happy. "So I came by to see when you'd like to go shopping."

"That's right. Let me get my list together. I lost track of time watching the Orioles beat my Red Sox. I swear, that Mookie Betts couldn't hit a hanging slider creeping in at sixty miles an hour."

"I don't know if I'll ever get used to you talking baseball."

She pulled the glasses off her face and cleaned them with her shirt. "Life is full of surprises, isn't it?"

"Indeed. Speaking of . . ." I put my hands on my waist. "This reunion coming up on Saturday. Would you come as my date?"

She set her glasses back and looked at me through the polished lenses. "Don't you have enough women in your triangle, or are you trying to make a square?"

I laughed. "My triangle has turned back into one single point."

"Ah," she said. "So I'm the last resort?"

I gave her a sharp look. "Don't even."

"It's kind of you to ask, but I will politely decline."

"Why?" As if I didn't know.

She didn't move a muscle. "Because I already told you. I don't want to be seen like this. All of those students there. No. I'm sorry, but there's no way I'm walking into that reunion." She finally glanced down at herself. "Look at me. I'm overweight, slow, and . . . I'm not who I used to be."

I held eye contact. "You look the same as you ever did."

"Let's hope not."

"You're beautiful, Mrs. Cartwright. Just the way you are."

"I appreciate your dishonesty, but you're going to have to find another date."

How could I convince her? As hardheaded as she could be, her *no* was strong. "Do I need to threaten to leave and skip the reunion? Bail on my speech?"

"That would hurt you more than me."

I scratched my head. "Look, I know you've done enough for me. But I need one more favor. I need you there. This is going to be hard for me, to see all these people and to get up and give that speech. To pretend I haven't thought about what I did since it happened. To pretend . . ."

She let her head fall back in an Oscar-worthy performance of frustration. "My goodness, you're persistent."

I directed my gaze toward the framed photograph of Tom swinging at a ball at Fenway Park. "I think Tom taught me that. If I remember correctly, it was his persistence that won you over. He even left his team to move here. Surely you admire such a trait."

She looked at Tom and then gave me a "not fair" look. "I do. Much more than I admire pretending." She all but winked. "The last thing you need to do is get up there and pretend."

"You know what I mean," I said. "Not pretend, exactly, just showing my best foot forward."

"Best foot forward?" She shook her head. "My God, I need to usher all of you kids back into my class. Surely you can think of a more creative way to say things than resort to such apathetic use of the English language."

"This is why I need more of you in my life, Mrs. Cartwright."

"Will you please stop calling me Mrs. Cartwright? And Mrs. C is no better."

I lowered to one knee and held out my hand. "Eloise, would you do me the honor of accompanying me to the reunion?"

"You can't charm me into going."

I lowered my head in defeat.

"Stop it, Carver Livingston."

I peered up at her. "I need you there."

She looked toward the living room as she chewed on the idea. "I don't know. I suppose it would be nice to see my former students."

"I think that's a *yes*."

She met my eyes. "It's an 'I will consider it.' I suppose I owe you after all the help you've given me. Or the trouble. I don't know which. My back about gave out on me this morning while I was trying to train the tomato plants."

"Look at you, getting out there. I'm so proud of you." A sense of pride filled me, thinking of what Ava, my mother, and I had done. Even our mentors needed a lift from time to time.

"Don't try to play me."

"I wouldn't dare."

Her cheeks swelled, and I could tell she was fighting off a smile.

I bit my lip. "God, I missed having you in my life."

Chapter 24

About That Speech

"Ladies and gentlemen, I oft think of you when I'm in my mansion in Asheville, pondering my empire. It is through my humble beginnings in this shithole town of Teterbury that I found myself. It is where I found my calling as a lover of animals, a savior *to* animals. It is here I have returned to gift you with my presence. As if that were not enough, I have decided I will start a new charity that we will call the Livingston Foundation. I will personally fund scholarships for two students each year to any college in the country. Heck, why not make it four? We all know I'm loaded! Muhahhahhahhaha!"

I thrust my hand into the air in triumph, hearing the cheers. "Not only that, ladies and gentlemen. *Not. Only. That.* I will also match every dollar each of you small peons contribute. This I will do in perpetuity, as a way to pay back this town for all that I've become. All that I ask is you erect a statue of me—thirty feet tall and bronze. Right in the center of town. I'll have to think of what I'd like it to say on the epitaph. Words such as *leader*, *motivator*, *achiever*, and *winner* come to mind."

I made a sound like throngs of people were going wild for me, as if I were the Beatles returning home to Liverpool. The people bowed, and Bree raised her fists, knowing she'd chosen the perfect speaker. Shannon eyed me from her place in the crowd, wanting me more than ever. Ava slid beside her, pulled her hair, and clamored for me, saying, "He's all mine!"

That was when, in the present, I glanced to my left. Two young men sitting in the adjacent car were laughing at me. Though tempted to ram them off the road, I pulled my foot from the gas in defeat.

"You wait," I said through gritted teeth. "The world's coming for you. It might all be roses now, but the skulls are coming. The darkness takes no prisoners."

I realized I'd growled out the words. Good God, what had gotten into me?

According to the last sign, I was twenty miles from Burlington, where I was en route to find something to wear for Saturday night. I had plenty of appropriate attire back in North Carolina, but I certainly hadn't prepared to stay so long in Teterbury, let alone attend this reunion.

There weren't a lot of options in Burlington, as I'd found after a Google search, but I certainly wasn't about to fly to Boston. Even I didn't take myself that seriously. I decided Banana Republic could get the job done. After putting together an outfit, I beat it down the street to a men's barber, where a nice woman covered in tattoos started me with a neck massage.

My typical MO with hairstylists was to close my eyes and fall into my thoughts, working out any lingering work issues, but the tattooed woman, named Melanie, was a first-degree talker and had little awareness of her clients' needs. By the time I got into the chair for a cut, I was exhausted by the chatter.

To the snip, snip, snip of the scissors, she said, "My daughter, she's finally talking now, and you wouldn't believe the words she's saying. Her first word was *daddy*, which is the most ridiculous thing in the world. How many diapers has he changed? Now, she's . . ."

I tuned her out until she asked me where I was from.

"Teterbury."

"Get out." She slapped my back, which wasn't the most professional move for someone demanding sixty bucks for a haircut.

"Guilty as charged," I said. Mrs. Cartwright would have written those words on the board and circled them. Then she would have made me get up there and repeat twenty-five times, "Clichés are for boring people, and I'm not boring."

"You went through the Teterbury system?" she asked.

"I did. Class of ninety-nine."

"You're so much older. I was oh four."

"Oh four," I said, thinking I wanted a haircut, not a cocktail party.

As we conversed, I decided Vermont as a whole was as small town as Teterbury. What was the population, seven hundred? Couldn't I find one corner of this state where I could enjoy some privacy?

Melanie couldn't have been more thrilled by our connection—as if we'd discovered we shared the same family. "Did you have Mr. Bates? You heard what happened to him, right?"

"No." I finally surrendered and accepted that Melanie and I were doomed to talk until she was finished. All I could hope for was a decent trim.

"He got busted for a car theft in DC. They came and arrested him during class."

"What?" I remembered Bates. He taught physics. Had one of the worst comb-overs in the history of partially bald men.

"You can't make this stuff up, right? You live there now or what's the four-one-one?" She made a cut and followed it with, "Oops."

I instantly froze. "Everything all right up there?"

"Yeah, honey. It's looking good."

I became worried, but what was I going to do now? Resuming our conversation, I played dodgeball as she assaulted me with questions to which I responded as shortly as possible. She wasn't having it, though, and kept hacking away at me like I was a tree she was cutting down. It didn't take long before she knew where I lived, what I did for a living, and why I was back.

As an act of charity, I relented and offered up my own launch point for a conversation. Anything to make her stop talking about her cockapoo named Nico. I love a good cockapoo, but there was only so much I wanted to hear about his bowel movement issues while I was in the hot seat.

I gave her my best diagnosis and then asked, "Did you have Mrs. Cartwright?"

Melanie lit up so much she might burst her bulb. "Didn't everyone? I credit her with my love of reading. She was awesome, wasn't she?"

"So good."

"I wonder what she's doing now," Melanie mused, the purr of the razor scaring me to death.

I sat up straighter. She sure was spending a lot of time back there around my neck. I wasn't a Chia Pet, for God's sake. I'd had a trim two weeks earlier.

"I've spent some time with her lately," I said. "She's retired and trying not to get bored. Loves baseball and knitting. Her husband passed away two years ago."

"That's so sad."

"It is," I said. "But we're having a reunion, our twentieth, on Saturday, and I've asked her to be my date."

She cut off the razor. "Aren't you a doll?"

"Not really," I said over my shoulder. "She means a lot to me, that's all. We're doing something special, surprising her, so don't say anything."

Melanie came around to face me. "No way, my class should have thought of that."

Nope, I'd thought about it first.

"People are already talking about our twentieth," she said. "I don't know if I want to go." Someone came in the front door, and she called out for them to sign up on the sheet. "Give me about ten more minutes," she told them.

Ten minutes? I wasn't going to have any hair left.

"That's so nice of you guys," she continued. "Is there anything I can do? I wish I could come."

"I know." I wished the whole world would come. Wait a minute . . . couldn't they?

Finishing up, she snapped the apron in the air, knocking the hair off it. I stood and looked at the mirror cautiously. What I saw made me gasp. She'd done way more than clean it up. She'd given me a new do, something dramatically higher and tighter than I wanted. I felt like I was in the military fashion show.

"What do you think?"

"Superb," I said. "Simply superb." How foolish of me to trust a stranger with the hair I'd be taking to the reunion.

Recovering as best as I could, I fished a card out of my pocket. "If you felt like recording a quick video, we could use it. I know she'd appreciate it."

"I will definitely do that."

My smile couldn't quite match her enthusiasm. "Good luck with your cockapoo."

I barely got out of town before my mind started turning over what Melanie had said, how she'd wanted to help. What if I could get more people involved? I was selling myself short by only having a couple of us mention her. What if we did a video with her students from all over the world saying something? It was Wednesday, though, not a lot of time.

But there was *enough* time, wasn't there? If God could create in seven, Dr. Carver Livingston could pull off a miracle or two in four. What that miracle was, I wasn't so sure.

I picked up the phone and dialed Bree.

⌒

I was surprised to see my mother's BMW in the driveway. Had she taken *another* day off? The concept was hard for me to wrap my head around.

As I searched the house, I heard her call for me upstairs. When I pushed open the door to her bedroom, my worry skyrocketed. Three cups and an empty glass of wine rested on her bedside table next to an army of wadded tissues. She'd neglected to put up her clothes. The blinds were drawn. The shopping network played on the tube.

She looked at me with dark eyes, eyes embarrassed to see me. "I'm taking a mental health day."

"Those are good," I said, entering the room cautiously. "Do I need to confiscate your credit card?"

"Funny," she said.

"How was work?"

She gave a quick headshake. "I pulled into the parking lot but never went in."

I sidestepped a pile of clothes. "That's okay. You have the time; take it." I didn't like what I was seeing, and it hit me hard that I'd been more focused on Mrs. C than on my own mother.

I put my hand on her foot, which was covered by her comforter. "What can I do for you, Mom?"

Her mouth was covered by the sheet, her voice muffled as she answered, "You don't need to worry about me. I need a few more days and I'll be back at it."

"Mom, I am going to worry about you. How many diapers did you change on my little dimple butt? How many times were you there for me? Let me take care of you. Do you want to go for a walk? A movie? I could turn on the grill."

She pulled the sheet away. "You don't turn on a grill, you light one."

"Fair point. That shows you how many barbecues I host down south."

Something I said caused her to sob.

"What, Mom. What?"

"Your father will never grill for me again," she said in a whimper.

I could barely believe what I was seeing, my mother crumbling so. Desperate to bring her out of it, I joked, "If you're not careful, I'm going to buy you a dog."

She pressed the heels of her palms into her eyes. "Buy me a dog?"

"I saw how you came alive. Maybe that's what you need."

She said the following with a pause between each word. "Don't buy me a dog, Carver."

"Then what? What can I do?"

"You've done everything. You're the perfect son. Just keep . . ." She stopped and pressed her eyes together. "I don't deserve how good you are to me."

What was she talking about? "Will you quit beating yourself up? This was all him. He's the jerk here."

She shook her head, as fragile as a child. "I worked too hard and wasn't always there for you . . . or him."

I sat on the bed. "You were, Mom. In your own way, you were. Don't you dare accept blame for what he's done." I pointed west so quickly that I almost flung off my index finger. "He's the one who deserted you."

She cried harder. "It's not all his fault."

"Yes, it is, dammit." How in the world did she have anything to do with my father abandoning her? So what if she was working too much. Boo-hoo.

I was desperate to fix her. "Why don't you grab a shower and let me cook dinner. I only have a few more nights. Besides, I have something exciting to tell you."

She pretended to show a little light on her face. "What?"

I touched her cheek, pressing down on a tear with my thumb. "I'll tell you downstairs."

My father had tried me several times while I was driving, but I wasn't in the mood to call him until I left my mother lying there. Downstairs, I said in a hiss, "Do you know what you've done? Do you know what she's going through?"

"Whoa, big boy. Did you miss your Wheaties this morning?"

"What the hell does that mean, Dad? While you're over there chasing Sitting Bull and Custer, I am trying to pick up the pieces that you left behind. Including the love of your life. What am I supposed to do?

I have to be back by Monday, or my business will collapse. She won't come back with me. Hell, she won't even get out of bed."

"Damn." Then nothing.

"*Damn.* That's all you have to say."

I paced so hard I'd leave the kitchen floor polished by the end of it. "I didn't think it would upset her so much, me leaving."

"You didn't think her husband leaving would bother her?"

"Not enough to put her in the bed."

I wanted to sling my phone against the wall. "Forty-three years. Jesus, Dad. You have lost it. They shouldn't even let you drive."

"Maybe she should see somebody."

"Maybe she should see somebody? That's your answer?" I was vaguely aware that I kept repeating his words. I also knew that I'd thrown my mother's request to be kind to him out the window.

"I don't know what else to say, Carv. I'm pulling into Billings. Decided I'd better come see my family before moving on." I had a quick flash of what he had left for family. My great-aunt Morgan, who refused to die. My three cousins who always picked on me. I didn't bother saying, *Tell them I said hi.*

"All right, I gotta go. Don't worry about calling for a while. We both need some time."

"Okay, son. I understand."

I leaned into the following silence, wanting to say a billion things.

"Carv, one day you'll understand."

"That helps," I said. "Thanks for being there for me, as always." I ended the call by mashing the button with such force that my thumb turned white.

Chapter 25

I Should Have Seen That Coming

The next morning I dragged my mother out of bed for a run, but that didn't seem to help. She barely spoke to me. After breakfast, she called into the bank and told them she was working from home, then disappeared back into her room. Trying to distract myself, I worked on the video and several other ideas for Saturday night. I had so much work to do that I'd even let the speech go to the wayside. Maybe Mrs. Cartwright could help me with it later, but I was honestly a bit hesitant to go see her, in fear Ava might be there.

I took my mother a tray of food for lunch, an avocado and hummus sandwich with some crisp alfalfa sprouts I'd found at the store. I put a lot of care into the tray, including some homemade lemonade sweetened with stevia—my mother's way of managing her sugar intake. I even picked a flower from the garden and put it in a small vase that I squeezed onto the corner of the tray.

Injecting a healthy dose of happiness into my voice, I announced, "Lunch is served, my dear."

"I'm not hungry, Carver." Her voice barely made it through the crack at the foot of the door.

"You have to eat, Mom."

It took her a while to respond. Was this one of those times when I should barge in? "I need some time today, okay?"

I let her be.

She didn't come down all day, though I tried several more times. At eight, unable to keep stewing in my failure to help her, I climbed the stairs and tapped on the door. "That's it. We're done doing this." Through the hallway window that looked out to the neighborhood, the streetlights glowed, showering the bushy oaks with an orange light.

I started to barge in, but the door was locked. That same shivery feeling in my belly I'd had a few days earlier set in. "Mom?"

I had never considered that my mother might kill herself. And yet love could make one do unthinkable things. I kicked open the door, and it flew open with a loud crash. A crack ran up the side of the doorframe.

My mother was on the floor, her back against the bed.

"Mom." I rushed to her.

I would never be so thankful as the moment when she twisted my way. Tears rushed down her cheeks; her hair was wet from them. "Oh God, Carver, I can't do this."

I fell to the floor and wrapped her in my arms. She smelled of wine and a lack of hygiene. "What's going on?" I asked. She'd never been so brittle, and it scared the shit out of me. She cried into my shoulder, and I let her, gently patting her back.

When she raised her head, I pushed the hair from her face. "Everything is going to be okay."

"No," she said. She studied my face. Her shoulders slumped. "It's not."

"We all think that sometimes."

Her cheeks quivered as she blinked at me. "I have to tell you something, and you're going to hate me."

I pulled back a bit. What I knew was that my entire life was about to change. I didn't know if it was the heaviness in her eyes or the way the room inched down in temperature, as if someone had lowered the thermostat.

"What is it?" I braced myself, wondering if she was sick. Why would I hate her for that, though? Then it hit me. There was indeed more to my father leaving than some sort of crisis.

She diverted her gaze to the white wall. Never could I remember a moment like this with my mom, the way she folded into herself, the way her skin paled in front of me, the way the tears came down her face. I saw in her so much pain, as if it were visible and pressing down on her.

Her eyes locked on the wall. "I cheated on your father."

It was a whisper that screamed, lodging itself in the core of me. Staying low to the floor, I backed away several feet, as if she'd drawn a knife.

She looked toward me, showing me her broken face, the way it seemed to melt, as if her entire life were fading away. "I . . . Carver, I had an affair."

I looked into her eyes, searching for the same woman who'd raised me, the woman who'd pushed me to be my best. The woman I would always tell people was my hero. I couldn't see her.

Question marks spun in my mind, sparking anger and guilt and a thousand other emotions. I stood and crossed my arms, looking down at her. "What are you talking about? When?"

She sat with one leg to her side and one folded in front of her. "I was hurting, Carver. After you . . . after what happened, I was broken. I thought I lost you. I couldn't stop replaying in my head what would have happened if you'd died—if Shannon's mother hadn't called. You can't ever understand the pain of a mother losing her son, and I thought I'd lost you. I thought I'd failed you. It was too much, all of it. And then . . ."

She began to cry, and it took her a minute to collect herself. I slowly lowered myself to the edge of the bed, keeping my eyes on her. She rested against the wall.

"Your father . . . he . . ." She sniffled hard and wiped her face dry with her shirt. "He tried so hard to be there for you, despite how much he was hurting. But he wasn't there for me. We barely looked at each other, barely spoke. He was dealing with his pain differently than me. And I . . ."

She breathed deeply and let it out, clearly trying to find the courage—or gall—to continue. "I met someone."

"You mean you had an affair twenty years ago? How am I finding this out now?"

"We weren't going to tell you, honey. You were so fragile."

I couldn't believe it. They'd hidden my mother's affair to protect me because I was too fragile to handle it? How about fifteen years ago or ten years ago?

My mouth was dry, and I tried to drum up some saliva with my tongue. "With who?" I could barely ask the question, but I had to know. In some ways, that felt like the worst part. Never in my life had I imagined my parents would get a divorce. Maybe they didn't have the best marriage, but a divorce? Still, that was far more digestible than this woman meeting someone else. She'd always preached honesty and loyalty and family and love. And yet . . . she had cheated on my father. Not only cheated, had an affair.

"It doesn't matter," my mother finally said.

My voice curdled into a roar. "It matters. Who did you have an affair with? For how long, goddamn it?"

"No," she said. "Let's not do this."

"We're doing this." In no way did her vulnerable position there against the wall or her feeble look deter my fury. For a long time, I blamed my father for being who he was. I had felt so much hate for him for leaving her. And I'd stuck up for her countless times. "I don't get it. Dad leaves twenty years after you did this?"

"We got past it, mostly. Or learned to live with what I'd done. I ended the relationship."

"With who did you end the relationship?" I asked, returning to my original query. I hoped that it wasn't someone I knew, as I wasn't prepared for such a blow.

"Someone who no longer lives here. He . . . he was married too. He worked at the bank."

I attempted to compute this atrocity.

"The whole thing was ugly, Carver. The man's name was Gerry. He was one of our financial advisers for a couple of years. We had lunch occasionally and had martinis one time. Gerry listened in a way that your father hadn't been able. He helped me grieve."

"Grieve?"

Her speech sharpened. "Yes, grieve, and he let me talk about it. It all happened from there."

"When was this?"

"We started seeing each other in February of your senior year. Ended it in May. Just a few months."

Somehow she'd managed to look me in the eyes ever since then without letting it show at all. They'd come to see me in North Carolina maybe twenty times over the years and completely hidden what must have been pulling them apart inside.

"And Dad found out when? Recently? Is that why he left?"

She shook her head, her face still slippery with tears. "Gerry's wife busted us right before you graduated. She'd hired a private detective, who took pictures. She sent the pictures to your father."

I had this awful flash of seeing my mother and this man all over each other after they locked the door of their hotel room. How much did I want to know? "Pictures of . . ."

"Gerry and I . . . we took weekends together, most often to Montreal. I told your father I needed to get away."

Part of me wanted to get up and walk away myself, but I needed to know more before I got the hell out of there. I felt a dreadful guilt for hating my father. Oh, how I'd read things so incredibly wrong. He'd found out about my mother's affair right about the time he'd changed. I thought it had been because of me—well, it had been, but not in the way I'd thought. He'd found out his wife was cheating on him, and I'd misread it to be that he'd given up on me.

"I don't understand," I said. "Dad knew for what? Nineteen years? Only now he decides to leave."

She looked like she might collapse if she kept talking. I waited for more until she continued. "He confronted me after he found out, said he was going to leave me. The first thing I thought of was you. You were spending all that time with the Cartwrights, and we saw how much better you were doing. I didn't want you to see us go through a divorce. I didn't want you to know I'd made that awful mistake. So I begged him to let it go, to forget what I'd done."

She gathered herself for a moment. "He knew I was right, that we had to protect you. I immediately stopped seeing Gerry, and your father sucked it up. Tried to pretend he still loved me. All for you."

Tears pricked my eyes. He'd suffered so much, living a lie for twenty years—for me.

For me.

"Why now?" I asked.

She rubbed her eyes. "The whole thing with Romo dying. Your father came home from the funeral and told me he couldn't keep pretending any longer, that life was too short. We'd figured out how to live with each other, but we never figured out how to love each other again. I mean, I loved him always, and I always will, but I . . . I treated him like I was punishing him. Like he was the one at fault. I guess I kept blaming him for not being there for me. I blamed him for so long that it became the only truth I knew."

She let her head fall back against the wall. "Then the other day, the morning after your date with Shannon, you said that thing about wasting twenty years. That hit me hard for some reason, made me realize I'd wasted the same twenty years—and maybe your father did too. Not only did I not accept responsibility with your father, but I kept the whole thing from you. I let you be so angry at him for so long. You thought he abandoned you. He didn't, sweetie. He was heartbroken. What I did almost killed him, but he swallowed it and tried to move on."

She jutted out her lip. "Neither one of us ever moved on, and he finally got sick of living a lie."

I looked at the closed blinds covering the windows, wanting out of that house. "I have to go. I need to process this."

"No," she said, her brow furrowing. "No, Carver, don't leave me."

I stood and stared down at her. "I have to go."

She crawled toward me and wrapped her hands around my foot, and then wrapped her whole arm around my leg. "Don't leave me, Carver. You have to understand."

"What do I have to understand?" I asked. "You had an affair. It sounds like it would have gone on longer if you weren't caught. You made me hate my father. What I don't understand is why you asked me to come home. You knew why he was leaving. What did you want me to do?"

Her eyes hollowed; her voice cracked. "I just needed you. I don't know. I needed you home."

I tugged my foot away, but she held strong.

"Why didn't you tell me why he was leaving in the first place? I can understand you hiding it from me twenty years ago, but not now."

Her cheeks tightened. "As if that day doesn't still cling to you, Carver. You haven't come home since."

This was a bad novel about the most screwed-up family in the world. How embarrassing that we were so broken. How many people in this town had found out about the affair? I didn't even want to know. Not only had everyone in Teterbury seen me publicly fall apart, but they'd surely seen what I'd done to my parents too.

In my head, a bass line from a Tool song began to pound, quaking my insides. I didn't know what song, and it didn't matter, but I felt the heavy metallic throngs of Tool's thrashing hit me, fueling a fury that filled my insides. They were the band I listened to in high school when I felt like I wasn't being understood, and they were the band I returned to when I woke from the hospital and realized I'd not bled enough to die.

I pulled away from her, and she tried desperately not to let me go, crying, "Please, Carver, don't go. Please."

"I have to."

I broke free and exited her bedroom, shooting straight up the stairs. She called for me, weeping like she'd lost someone. I flung my clothes into a bag and came down the stairs. In the guest bathroom, I collected the items on the sink and shoved them into my travel kit. Downstairs, I jammed my laptop into my briefcase, followed by several legal pads and a host of different chargers.

My mother tried to block me at the front door. She wore a nightgown smeared with tears and mascara. Tool played in my head, loud like someone screaming, loud like the dial was cranked to max, the speakers in my mind breaking up.

"I'm sorry," she said.

"I know," I muttered, ready to push past her.

"It's all my fault," she said. "You have to know that. He . . . he did nothing wrong. He tried to save us so many times. He'd asked me for years to travel with him, but I wouldn't leave work and . . . ugh, I failed him."

She grabbed my arm, apologizing over and over, as if one of her desperate pleas might sneak past my anger. She tried to stop me, but I pulled open the door and started out.

"Where are you going?" she cried.

I did not grant her an answer. I flung my bags into the back of the Audi and then climbed in. I didn't know where I was going and didn't give a blue-bloody hell. I sped past Mrs. Cartwright's house and over the river and through the town, like that Thanksgiving song—over the river and through the woods—but it wasn't fucking Thanksgiving, and I sure as hell wasn't going to Grandmother's house. I wanted away from all family, even my father, a saint who'd hidden the truth for my entire life. Come to think of it, that didn't make him much of a saint at all.

I didn't take the highway. I wanted the curved roads of the mountains. And I didn't care if a cop pulled me over. I'd take my ticket and get the hell out of there. The night fell down over me, every bit of light being soaked up by the black. All that was left were the beams of my headlights, giving me the only direction in my life.

The one thing that gave me a modicum of peace was the green sign in the rearview mirror indicating Teterbury was three miles away. It shrank in the mirror and drew my pain away with it. Never had I ever felt so all alone. Even when I was cutting myself, saying goodbye, I knew that my mother loved me. Maybe she had been my last thought. She'd been the only one I was afraid to hurt.

There on the road, hitting a curve at seventy miles an hour, I felt the blade in my hand again, and I could feel the sharpness as it pressed against my skin. I could see that first bit of blood.

Yes, it had been my mother whom I'd thought about, how she might find me, how she would hurt so badly as she pulled my limp body onto her lap. But it wasn't enough, was it? What I felt inside was so painful that even the thought of crushing her hadn't prevented me from digging into my wrist with that blade. I thought I'd escaped from this darkness, but it was here now, and this time I didn't even have my mother to worry about.

Would anyone miss me if I were gone? Why did it matter anyway?

The dark form of a giant animal rose before me on the road, straddling the yellow line and looking at me, bracing for its own demise. It was an immense stag, with incredibly impressive antlers that a hunter would have certainly killed for. And those eyes. Eyes so white in my headlights.

I slammed my foot down on the brake pedal. The car shifted as I hiked the wheel to the left. I barely missed the deer as the car slid and rose on one wheel before settling down at the edge of the road.

Everything came to a sudden stop: the sounds of Tool in my head, the noise of the car sliding across the road, the screaming in my head from the devastating news my mother had just shot into my soul.

It took me a moment to collect myself, to realize I was alive. My heart pounded. I smelled burned rubber from the tires. The deer still stood there. His eyes blazed, glowing big and bright and beautiful there in the darkness. Behind him rows of trees ran west to nowhere. We held eye contact for a long time, long enough for me to find a steady rhythm to my breathing.

Then he turned and wandered off into the forest, a creature elegant and proud. I wasn't sure I had a place in a world so beautiful.

Chapter 26

Don't Know How to Die

I climbed out of my car and looked to where I'd last seen the deer. A bird screeched from up high. A band of crickets filled the spaces between each of its cries. The deer was nowhere in sight, and I was thankful I hadn't hit him. In fact, it may have been that feeling of gratitude that alleviated my emotional pain. Still, what my mother had done lingered inside of me.

The man she'd had an affair with . . . his name was Gerry.

Gerry.

Had she loved him? How had my father felt when he'd found out? How had they managed to stay together so long afterward? All for me. Was that an incredible gesture of love or a foolhardy act that had made their lives only worse?

In the stillness of the night, though, the sharp pain that had been stabbing at me dulled. After I rounded the car, I saw that the tire was halfway off the edge of the road. Another couple of feet and I would have rolled down the embankment. For a man who'd once attempted to take his life, it was strange to feel thankful, but that was what simmered inside of me. I was glad to be alive.

There wasn't a car in sight. I was maybe twenty miles south of town, out in the middle of nowhere. Something caused me to look upward, and the vision nearly buckled me. The hazy band of the Milky Way shot across the night sky in an explosion of color. Before a canvas of deep black, countless stars pulsed with life. And as if it had a sense of humor, the fingernail moon was turned up into a sideways smile.

Though the view was limited due to the soaring trees swaying above me, it was enough to act like a hand reaching into my chest and cupping my heart in what felt to me like an incredibly loving embrace.

Wanting to see more, I scrambled down the hill that I almost tumbled down in the Audi. There was a possible opening in the forest ahead. My feet slid as I grabbed for purchase on the heavy branches and small trees. Once I'd reached the bottom, I raced toward the opening, worried clouds might come to take away the majesty of what I'd seen. I ran through one hundred yards of thick forest. Pine needles crunched under my feet. The crickets sawed harder with their wings. The faint moonlight revealed a meadow in the valley. I could hear the Tye River running, and I ran harder, racing through the trees and then into the tall grass of the meadow.

She was still there, this night sky, this elegant gown woven with diamonds. There was no place for cynics here, and I could feel all the doubt inside of me break away, the pieces disappearing into the tall grass.

I fell to my knees.

Up there above me was an eruption of a million lights dancing in the blackest black I'd ever seen. A shooting star darted across the sky, sparking a sense of awe I hadn't known in a long time. How marvelous that there were more stars than grains of sand on Earth? How many of those stars had planets like ours circling them, planets that could have beings like us going through the same struggles of mortality?

I lay down in the grass and let my eyes feast on this bit of heaven, my awe drawing me upward, allowing me to run with the stars, to mingle with them. I wasn't alone—didn't have to be alone; didn't have to keep hiding. I'd kept people at a distance for so long because I was afraid they'd see me for the flawed person that I really was. I'd hidden from myself by creating this facade that didn't even matter.

A seed of forgiveness was planted in my heart, and it spread through my blood and organs and across my skin. So my parents were flawed. Wasn't I equally so? Weren't Mrs. Cartwright and Shannon and even Ava?

I didn't know where this was coming from, all these revelations, but the sky fueled what I hoped I would never forget. Something about peering upward—perhaps simply the awe of it—made it okay, made everything okay. It gave me the perspective I'd missed all my life. It was okay that I wasn't perfect, because I was so far from perfect.

Just like everyone else.

I didn't need to pretend anymore. I could hear Mrs. Cartwright urging me to find a way to love myself. Had I never before? Not with all of me, that was for sure.

I connected the dots as I bounced from star to star. Mrs. Cartwright had called it star hopping. What a marvelous concept.

When was the last time I'd paused to take a breath? When was the last time I'd actually lived? I'd raced my whole life because it had been the best way to distract myself from actually living.

Something had to change. When would I ever be enough? Mrs. C had asked me how much I had to do before I realized I was worthy as I was. When would it ever stop?

I didn't have all the answers right then, but I knew tonight was the night when I drew a line in the sand. No more pretending, no more putting Band-Aids on the wounds of my soul. No more chasing.

Most importantly, it was time to let go of what I'd done. Time to forgive myself for falling apart back then and to forgive myself for ruining my parents' marriage. It wasn't about blame, was it? Nor was it about punishing myself. It was about accepting that it had happened and letting it be. We were all together, all flawed beings trying to find our ways, and it was okay to make mistakes, because we were all making them—we were destined to make them. It was okay to laugh at ourselves.

I smiled, settling into the grass.

No more taking me or life so seriously.

With those last thoughts, my mind quieted, as if I'd finished a poem and gotten out what had needed to be expressed. I took a deep breath and let out the last ashes of the dead part of me, blowing them up there toward the sky, thinking I'd finally, after all these years, found the answers in the stars.

That was when it hit me, and my smile stretched to my toes. Wasn't it funny how the world worked? Glancing again at the moon's smile, I said to no one in particular, "You've been playing me, haven't you? That commercial. Forcing me to come home. Running into Mrs. Cartwright. This is the climax of your symphony, isn't it? A night sky that can't be denied."

A barred owl hooted, and I felt it was calling to me, acknowledging me, validating me. In the sky, I saw the eyes of the deer. He'd been trying to tell me something. The stars pulsed up there in the blackness, waiting for me to continue, waiting for me to get it.

"What do the stars say to you?" I said. "Is that the question? Are you going to make me say it out loud?"

Another star shot across the sky, tingling my skin.

"I get it," I said. "As small and as insignificant as I am, I'm a part of you. And it's one big, beautiful thing that we make, this living and breathing and ever-flawed oneness."

I felt a richness in my heart. I was Carver Livingston, one of the nearly eight billion people on Earth. How many stars were out there? How many other planets? How many countless people or beings trying to find their way? I was nothing . . . and yet I was everything.

I felt like I belonged for the first time, like I was a part of the great magic. The shame and guilt I'd carried most of my life drifted up into the black, being absorbed into it as if it had never existed.

Then I heard a voice from within. My voice. *Like every single star up there, you're perfect just the way you are, Carver.* I burst into tears, as if that was the heaviness that had been pushing me down for all my life.

Pressing up to a seated position, I looked back at the sky as if it were a dream. I thought of the man in the commercial and his question, "What do the stars say to you?"

And I knew. I finally knew what they were saying. I didn't know where it had come from. My subconscious maybe? It was as if the stars were above me but also inside me, speaking to me.

I said out loud this time, "You're perfect just the way you are." I could have said it a thousand times, it felt so good, the relief of finally knowing I could slow down and quit trying to prove to myself and others that I mattered. Mrs. Cartwright had been right all along.

Then I laughed. Ava had said I'd been tapped; she was right. I would walk out of those woods a new man, eager to live for the first time in my life.

I also knew something else . . .

The stars don't lie.

Chapter 27

The Mess of Life and Lessons in Cleaning

The lights were still on in the driveway. I couldn't have summoned my earlier anger at my mother if I'd tried. I felt so sorry for her, if anything. I wished she'd been out there in the meadow with me, because she was like me, wasn't she? She never paused to look up or to even breathe. She had lived her whole life with something to prove, breaking through the glass ceiling of the banking industry. No matter what she'd done, it had never been enough. She'd never been enough. Only now that I'd pulled my cranium out of my posterior could I see that.

It was such a sad, sad way to live.

I found her on the couch in the living room. The television was black. She sat on her legs and looked over at me as if I were a ghost.

"You came back?" she asked.

I stood in the doorway for a few seconds. "I'm sorry, Mom. I shouldn't have run out on you."

"No, I'm sorry."

I crossed the room, sat down, and hugged my mother, leaning into the undeniable fact that we were both flawed, just like every other person we knew. I had tried to kill myself when I was seventeen years old. That day had kicked off a hard twenty years for my parents. But what can you do? *What can you do?* It was over and we'd survived.

We eventually broke apart and sat next to each other, as if we'd survived a hurricane, as if the windows were shattered, leaving glass at our feet. "Did you love him? The man, Gerry? That's the worst name, by the way."

She looked incredibly worn down. "No. Not really. I cared about him. I was sad when we lost each other. But I never loved him like I loved your father. He was just there for me. He'd lost his daughter when she was eight, and he understood the pain. For so long after that I worried you'd try again, and there was nothing I could do. I wanted to be by your side at every moment, but you didn't want to be here in this house. You wanted to be out at Eloise's farm."

That last piece came out with a lot of pain. It must have been tough on her, me running to the Cartwrights. "Mom, please know that you had nothing to do with me attempting suicide. You did everything you could to support me afterward. You sacrificed your lives, as I now know. I went to the Cartwrights, and I went to North Carolina, because I'd done enough damage and wanted to get out of the way."

"You didn't have to run from us."

"I thought I did."

"You didn't."

I patted her hand, which rested on her thigh. "I know that now. Something happened tonight, something so incredibly powerful. I almost hit this deer and pulled over and looked up at the sky. Right there. Right *there* were all the answers I needed. It sounds so silly saying it out loud."

"No, it doesn't."

I crossed my leg and twisted toward her. "I don't know how to describe it, but I saw something. No. I *felt* something tonight that I haven't in many, many years. I don't know that I'll ever unfeel it. It's like I've cracked the code. For the first time in my entire life, I feel still inside."

She put her hand on my cheek; her wedding rings were still on. "I can see it in you." She let go of me. "I called your father tonight after you left."

"You did?" I didn't know why her news injected hope into me.

"I told him I'd told you and that I was so sorry for forcing him to carry my lie. Maybe one day he'll forgive me, I don't know."

I sat back. "I'll call him first thing in the morning. I owe him such a huge apology." Sadness and remorse came over me. "I can't believe I . . ."

"Stop," my mother said. "Let's move forward now."

We talked for another hour, until the yawns beat out the talking, and that was when we called it a night. As she closed the door to her bedroom, I said, "Run tomorrow? To shake off the cobwebs."

"You're on. Maybe later than usual?"

"Definitely. And tomorrow's a new day."

"Yeah. I hope so."

Chapter 28

SECOND CHANCES

We made it out of the house by seven for a run. It definitely felt like a new day. I'd already been up for two hours, chasing down students in Europe for the video tribute. The secretary at the high school had sent me the school directory. Surprisingly, I enjoyed the calls. The conversations ballooned as we shared our love for a teacher who'd become an institution in Teterbury and a fixture in the hearts of her students. One woman told me it was Mrs. Cartwright who'd encouraged her to take the chance and move to Amsterdam, an experience she said had changed her forever. Of course we couldn't show all the dedications Saturday night, but I thought Mrs. Cartwright might enjoy watching them on her own time later.

I had other ideas that were working out, too, and after I'd caught my mother up on my plans, I said, "You never told me about your reunions. Did you and Dad go to any of them?"

We had already crossed the bridge at the halfway mark. I could have kept going forever, enjoying this glorious feeling of being light as a feather.

She laughed at my question. "I took your father to my twentieth. I didn't love all the small talk, but it was definitely entertaining, all the posturing and seeing who everyone had become. Evelyn Wycoff married a plastic surgeon, and it couldn't have been more obvious that she got the family discount. It looked like someone had plugged an air pump into her. These huge boobs and lips, a stretched smile plastered on her face. He was this dweeby little guy, and there she was bursting out of her dress. And then Bill Hitchcock. We found out later that he rented the Maserati he showed up in. He was the talk of the town for a while."

Having been the talk of the town at one point, too, I empathized. "I guess it is tough walking into a room with everyone from your past, basically saying, 'This is who I am, who I've become. An entire life of trying and here's what you get.'"

"Yeah, exactly. And you have to admire the people who don't mind being themselves. No compulsion to impress, just happy to see everyone."

I dodged a branch protruding into the path. "Elliot will be like that. I feel like he could walk in naked and not care."

"Yeah, your father is like that too," my mom said. "Even though he didn't make a lot of money, he was always so proud of the work he did at the garage."

I planned on calling him shortly to offer the first of many apologies due his way.

Turned out I wouldn't have to make that call at all . . .

When we came around the last corner, my mom and I almost tripped over each other. My father had returned. His truck was parked out front; Clementine was attached to the hitch.

We stared in amazement.

"Did he tell you he was coming back?" I asked, settling into a walk.

"No!" she said, her delight causing her to chirp out the word. "He was in Billings when I talked to him."

My father opened up the front door of the house and gave a smile that soothed the heck out of me. "Look at you two carpe-ing the diem," he said. With his jeans and boots and a short-sleeved button-up, he looked a lot like a trucker. Eschewing the shame of having judged him wrongly, I focused on how spectacular it was that I had a chance to make it up to him.

My mom and I walked his way, both of us panting. "What are you doing here, Ben?" she asked.

"I told you both I was in Billings, but the truth is that I was on my way back. Wanted to surprise you."

My mother actually snorted. "Why? I . . . I don't understand."

He offered me a warm smile that made me realize all he'd ever given me was love and grace. Then he came down the steps and stopped a foot from my mother. "Lisa, this is my home. You are my home. I've been hanging this thing over your head for too long. It's time we move on and find a way to heal."

She spontaneously combusted into a cry, and I wasn't far behind her. "I'm so sorry," she said. "Please, let's never break apart for another minute. I'm nothing without you."

He pulled her in. "It's all good, my baby. It's all good."

They held each other for a while. Then my mother said, "I can't believe you were on your way home before I even called you."

"Yeah, but I put the pedal to the metal once you did. Drove through the night last night to catch you before you went to work."

She reached up and fiddled with the button of his shirt. "I haven't been to work in days."

"I don't know if that's a bad thing or a miracle."

"Me either." She sighed, still sobbing. "Ben. I screwed up so badly. And I hate that I made you bury it for so long. I'm such an awful—"

My dad lifted her hand from his chest and kissed it. "I forgive you. I forgive every bit of you." He kissed her hand again and then grabbed her waist and kissed her lips. "It's time you and I get back to the way things were."

She squeezed her eyes together. "I can't believe I'm hearing you say that. Are you sure?"

"Darn right, I'm sure."

They embraced, making a pretty fine argument for what love could be. Maybe it wasn't all peaches and cream, but the good moments made it all worth it.

Without a care for who might be listening, my father began to hum. He wasn't one who could carry a tune well, but it was enough that I could make out the melody of the first song they'd ever danced to: "We've Only Just Begun" by the Carpenters.

He placed his hands on my mother's waist and swayed his hips, encouraging her to dance with him. She didn't think twice about it. Bewildered, I watched them move to the rhythm of his out-of-tune rendition.

When they stopped, I said, "You guys need to find a better song."

They both turned to me like I'd burned a picture of the pope. In unison, they said, "Are you kidding me?"

My mother donned a smile that could have melted the snow of a Vermont blizzard. "That's one of my favorite songs in the entire world. And, Ben, I think you do it better than the Carpenters." She kissed him again.

I laughed. Had we taken a complete one-eighty from our trajectory days before? "So this is us, huh? The Livingstons."

We smiled at each other.

"I guess it's my turn now," I said to my dad.

"Oh, you wanna dance?" he joked.

"Ha ha. No. But I do want to apologize." I paused to make sure I did it right. "Dad, I'm sorry. Sorry for judging you, doubting you. All these years . . . I messed up."

He offered a close-lipped smile. "How could you have known, son? We were all doing our best." He approached and opened his arms. "We have a lot of life ahead of us. Let's do it right from now on."

"I'd love a second chance, that's for sure." I squeezed him hard.

My mother joined in. "My two boys."

We moved the party inside and talked for a while about my father's trip and what had been going on in Teterbury since he'd left. While I was telling him about Shannon, a text came in. I read it and then said, "I ran into a snag with tomorrow night I need to go deal with."

"Everything okay?" my dad asked.

"Yeah, a lot of moving pieces. I need to run out. Can we spend some time together later? I'm sure you and Mom have some catching up to do."

"You're darn right we can. You know where to find me."

⌒

That afternoon I found my father and mother having lunch together on the back patio. They were all smiles and laughter.

"Look at you two, on a date."

My dad reached for a chip. "We did that Uber Eats thing. Your mom did. They got it figured out. All the sauces were wrapped up well. Decent portions. This could be the way of the future."

I looked down at their spread, a couple of Italian hoagies and a bag of potato chips from a place that had been around longer than me. "It's nice to step into the twenty-first century."

"There's hope for us yet," my mother said. She seemed so full inside, as if her secret had been pinning her down for twenty years.

I set my hand on my father's shoulder, the flannel of his shirt. "Do you know I never saw the inside of your trailer, Dad? I wanted to see if you'd give me the grand tour."

He turned to me. "Really?"

I have seen some excited people in my life, especially the owners of my patients after a successful surgery, but I don't know that I'd seen more elation in someone like I saw in my father then. It was enough to fill me up too.

"Who knows?" I said. "Maybe you'll convince me to go on a trip with you one day."

His grin widened even more. "Now I know you're yanking my chain."

"Not at all, Pops. It might even be fun."

If he sprang up any faster, he might have hurt his back. Dusting off his mouth with a napkin, he said to my mom, "Lisa, do you mind?"

"Are you kidding me? Go show him what you did." She looked at me. "I got the tour earlier. I have to say it's adorable in there."

I followed him through the house and out the front door. "She held up on the drive," he said. "Blew a tire on Route 80 in Nebraska, but other than that, she was a dream to pull."

I looked at his 1962 Shasta from a different perspective than I had before he'd left. The baby blue on the bottom half, the white up top, the silver wing hanging off the back. No doubt the whole thing beckoned back to a simpler time, a lot like the diner where my mother and I had gone.

"She really is a beaut. Did you get any compliments?"

He whipped open the door and waved me in. "Are you kidding me? I couldn't stop for five minutes without someone coming up to ask questions about her."

Inside, the trailer smelled like Old Spice aftershave. "I don't know what it is, Carver, but this thing spoke to me. I've had a ball working on her, showing her off."

I looked around, from the checkered floors to the seating area, then to the kitchen and the bed. "I bet it was fun out there on the open road, meeting people."

"Yeah," he said, resting a hand against the counter next to the sink. "Only thing missing was your mom. Nothing like highway time to make you realize what matters."

"I bet."

"But . . ." He held up a finger. "She says she wants to go next time, next summer."

"No kidding?"

"I'm as in shock as you. She says she's going to retire."

"Retire? Now you're yanking *my* chain."

"That's what she told me."

I couldn't believe it. Had we somehow found our way out of the darkness after twenty years?

"Dad," I said, finding his eyes, "I'm sorry."

He turned up one corner of his mouth, as if it were no big deal.

It was, though, and I wanted him to see I knew that. "Seriously, you were one hell of a good dad, and I let everything I was going through cloud my vision of you. I'm . . . I'm sorry. You're the one who makes us whole, and I somehow thought you'd given up on me."

He sucked in a big breath. "Carver, I'd never give up on you. You can't know how great love is until you're in it, and you can't know the heartache either. We all hit a rough patch and dealt with it the best we could. Nobody is perfect, and that especially includes me."

I couldn't have admired this man any more than I did. He was not only forgiving me but also somehow gifting me the ability to forgive myself.

"Well, if anyone is measuring, you're more perfect than me."

"Nobody is measuring. And it doesn't matter if they were."

I guess he was right about that. I stuck out my hand to shake his. "Let's make up for some lost time, Dad. All three of us."

He pulled me into a hug. "That's exactly what we're going to do. Starting right now."

Chapter 29

THE BIG NIGHT

I had the jitters when the limo picked me up the next night, mostly because I didn't want to screw up. I hoped I hadn't already made a mistake by simply putting the event together.

What had come to me in recent hours was that I'd been working toward something Mrs. Cartwright had warned against. She'd said you couldn't save other people, that you had to worry about yourself. Was that what I was doing tonight by helping honor my teacher? Was I trying to fix her?

I also worried about another motivation, one I hated to admit even to myself. Was I still making tonight about me? Was it important that people saw what I was doing for Mrs. Cartwright? That *I* was the one who'd had this idea and had pushed it through?

Though I wondered what Ava would think, that stuff didn't feel as important in this moment. It hadn't since I'd walked out of the woods and driven back to Teterbury. It was indeed too late to change things now. So many pieces had already been put into motion, including this limo that now felt slightly absurd, like I wanted everyone to make sure they saw *me* as I arrived.

All I could do now was be real up there onstage. Tonight was about all of us getting a chance to honor a woman who somehow thought we'd forgotten about her. If I never did another thing, it would be okay, but I wanted this night to matter. I wanted her to see the impact she'd made on all of us.

In front of her house, I stepped out of the limo and straightened my blazer. A few days in and I could already see the love she'd put into her garden. My mom had said not to give her a choice. Maybe sometimes we needed a push.

When Mrs. Cartwright answered the door, I said, "Look at you. A stunner as always."

She blushed, but she didn't deny it. She wore pearl earrings that matched the necklace Tom had given her, and a dark-blue dress with matching heels. Every inch of her glowed.

"I don't know if you remember," I said, "but I never went to prom."

One corner of her mouth turned up. "Of course I remember that. And . . . I remember trying to convince you to go."

"I've decided that this is my makeup prom, and I am so honored to have you as my date, Mrs. Cartwright."

"You're not going to call me Mrs. Cartwright all night, are you? For heaven's sake."

"Eloise, excuse me. So is Oscar all taken care of?"

"The neighbors are watching him."

"Good. My mother felt bad she had to cancel."

"It's perfectly fine."

What Mrs. Cartwright didn't know was that my mother had canceled because she and my dad wanted to be a part of tonight's festivities.

Mrs. Cartwright thrust up her elbow for me to take it, and I loved seeing her subtle attitude. I wondered if she'd been thinking about tonight all day, preparing herself for it, preparing to face her past. I certainly had.

Only as we went down the steps did she see the limo. "Get out of here."

"Hey, this is my prom. I wanted to do it right."

She patted my arm. "That's sweet."

I helped her inside and then climbed in after her. Duke Ellington and his band played from the speakers as we set out to pick up Elliot and Alice.

"I have to tell you," I said, sitting across from her, "I've had a big couple of days."

"Is that right?"

I didn't tell her about my mother's affair, but I told her how I'd seen the stars like I never had before, and I told her about my father coming home.

"Isn't it nice when the stars align?" she asked.

"It is, but I'd not be a worthy pupil of Mrs. Eloise Cartwright if I didn't point out the cliché that you let slip out of your mouth."

She smiled wider and leaned over and patted my knee. "I was just testing you, my dear pupil."

Elliot and Alice brought their boys out to say hello, a visit Mrs. Cartwright got a clear kick out of. Once the babysitter had reeled the kids back to the house, my best friend and his wife climbed inside to join us, sitting opposite Mrs. Cartwright and me. Elliot wore blue slacks with a twill blazer featuring a red handkerchief poking out of the pocket that matched exactly the red of Alice's dress.

"Mrs. Cartwright," Alice said, "you look wonderful. I was so excited to hear you were coming with us."

"Me too," Elliot said. "I feel like I'm in the queen's caravan."

Mrs. Cartwright nearly coughed a laugh. "That's a bit of a stretch, but I will say I was equally delighted. You both were two of my favorite students."

"Hey," I said, "you told me the same thing."

"All three of you were," she said sincerely, enough of a smile rising on her face to say that we weren't the only favorites.

Once we were moving again, I reached for the bottle of Duval-Leroy rosé champagne waiting in an ice bucket and popped the cork. I poured us each a glass and then raised a toast. "To the best date I'll ever have."

"Let's hope not."

Everyone laughed.

Letting my smile fade, I said, "In all seriousness, I want to say thanks to you, Mrs. Cartwright, and to you, Elliot, for always being there. My life is richer with you in it, and I promise I won't disappear again. And to you, Alice. I'm so glad he found you, and I'm excited to get to know you and the boys more. You guys are an inspiration to me." I raised my glass higher. "To family and friends."

"Hear, hear," everyone said, clinking glasses.

When we arrived at the hotel and I saw my old classmates climbing the steps with their partners, I hoped that the evening would work out the way I'd planned. It had been a lot to coordinate. Then again, whatever happened would be fine. All I knew was that an army of people had shown their love for her, and she would feel it tonight all the way to her essence.

Nothing appeared out of the ordinary as we pulled up, which was how I'd attempted to design it. I wanted her to walk into the hotel thinking she was merely here to support me as my date, there for me when I took the stage to give a speech I'd been working on for a week now. The index cards weighed heavily in my pocket.

Darn it if everyone didn't swarm her, though, as we tried to get up the red-carpeted steps. For a guy who wasn't exactly excited about small talk, I got drowned in it while people pried and pulled at my date. I held her steady, to make sure she didn't fall. We quickly lost Elliot and Alice in the zoo of people.

Mrs. Cartwright hadn't forgotten one face and said each of their names as they came to give her a hug. She was so sharp that she didn't miss a chance to ask about their children or their pets or their new careers. I'd known she kept up with her students, but seeing her in action interacting with them made me love her even more, if that was possible. I eventually got her up the steps and inside. Dragging Mrs. Cartwright through the lobby wasn't any easier.

We came into the conference room, where maybe eighty people had already gathered, collecting in groups that were surely the same as the ones they'd been a part of in our formative years. The band had set up on the stage dead ahead and played a U2 song. Above them was a banner that read: WELCOME, TETERBURY HIGH CLASS OF 1999! Something about reading those words brought the thunder, making me realize what I'd committed to. The storm windows of my soul shook when I put my eyes on the podium in the center of the stage, where I'd soon stand. A round of jitters came over me. Not that I had something to prove. Maybe it was more intimidating because I *didn't* have anything to prove now. I wanted to be real, and being real wasn't always easy.

Spotlights shone down on the dance floor in front of the stage, and I imagined even I would make it there eventually. The band would play nineties music most of the night, but I'd spoken to the bandleader and asked that they learn one particular tune for me. Beyond the busy bar were several long rectangular tables filled with food. More tables toward the back offered a place to sit and eat.

Mrs. Cartwright's former students surrounded her, nearly pushing me out of the way. So much for spoiling the surprise. Couldn't they wait? She didn't seem to mind, though, and was stable enough on her feet, so I let her be and went toward the bar, where Elliot and Alice had already beaten me.

A mustachioed man in a fedora handed me a glass of red, and I stood there with my friends, making light and enjoyable conversation as we looked across the crowd, stepping back to the late nineties. Soon enough, the rest of our gang of misfits had joined us, and I found surprising and considerable joy in meeting their spouses and learning more about their lives since I'd last seen them.

Once the majority of people had arrived, the band paused, and Bree stepped up to the microphone. "Thank you all for coming. Holy cow, what a ride the past few months have been, trying to corral all of you. People get squeamish about coming home, don't they?"

A mix of nervous laughter rose into the air.

"Yeah, I see you out there," Bree said. "You're all beautiful. Every single one of you." She leaned into the awkward before continuing. "Give me a moment to say thanks to some people and then we'll get this party started."

As Bree addressed the contributors, I saw Shannon come in. I waved and was glad when she headed my way. Considering I'd be back far more often now, I would have loved that we be okay around each other. In fact, I was ready to be in a place to pull for her, to hope that she found what she sought in love and life.

"Most important," Bree continued, "I wanted to say that we have raised more than any class in the history of Teterbury High reunions for the Teterbury Foundation. Thanks to all of you—well, most of you"— she paused to eye the stingy—"we will be paying for *three* scholarships to college for the class of twenty nineteen. How about that? Let's give each other a round of applause."

Everyone clapped.

"I especially want to thank the person who made an extremely generous anonymous donation. Whomever you are, you've changed a couple of lives, for sure."

I wondered who that was . . .

Actually, I'd written a check earlier in the week and had thankfully neglected to send it in. The day prior, I'd torn it up and wired over an anonymous donation instead. Teterbury was my hometown, and even though I'd left for Asheville, I wanted to be a part of it going forward.

"Have fun, everyone. Don't be shy. Get on the dance floor. Reconnect with old flames. Eat this amazing food and drink all the cocktails and wine. They're free!"

Everyone clapped again and returned to their conversations. Shannon cautiously approached me.

Once she was close, I said, "I know you're going to hear it all night, but I'm gonna say it. You look absolutely beautiful."

"Thanks. You too."

A silence followed that I was determined to break. I gestured toward the table. "Great crackers."

"Nice," she said, rolling her eyes.

"No, they really are. Sesame on top."

She sighed. "You're going to have to up your game if you're ever going to find anyone. You know that?"

We both smiled. I felt like that moment was the one we'd been waiting for, the moment when we both fully accepted that we could move on and both find love and be happy for each other in doing so.

"How is this for you?" she asked. "Being here, I mean."

"I'm working through it. It's a lot revisiting the old days."

"So much," she said.

"I have to admit, I'm still miffed by what you said, that I made more of our relationship than there had been. We had a good time together."

"I know," she said. "Maybe I played it down more than is true."

"Ah, to knock me down some?"

"You need it sometimes." She gave a half wink.

"Everybody seems to think that, but I swear it's not true. I do enough knocking me down for everyone in this room."

She looked around. "We all have our pasts, Carver."

"Isn't that the truth." I was finally accepting the fact that my old friends and the other people of Teterbury hadn't frozen in time, waiting for my return. They'd moved on. Sure, they had read about me in the newspaper and knew that I'd caused a few ripples, but they'd gone on and were living their own special lives. They weren't spending their days thinking about what I'd done in high school, and they weren't all sitting around watching the highway in hopes I might one day return. I thought of the whole *don't take yourself so seriously* thing that Mrs. Cartwright had said. She was oh so right.

"Where to from here?" Shannon asked. "You're leaving tomorrow?"

"Yeah, I have to be back for work Monday. Would you believe I've not taken two weeks off since I graduated college?"

"I would totally believe it. Even back in school, you didn't stop."

"Never stop chasing," I said.

"What?"

"Never stop chasing. That's what I have written on the whiteboard in my home office. That's been my thing. Never stopping. The relentless pursuit of . . . I don't know what." I laughed at myself.

She dipped her chin and said with a healthy dose of sass, "I know one thing you're no longer chasing."

Ouch. I think she was mostly kidding. "There's a guy out there, Shannon. He's searching for you. His whole life, he's been searching for you. Give him time."

"I appreciate that, Carver."

"I mean it." Maybe a woman was waiting out there for me, but I wasn't so sure.

We both turned with wide eyes to the stage when the band kicked off Aerosmith's "I Don't Want to Miss a Thing." Of all the songs in the world, they chose this one, the one that Shannon and I had danced to countless times, in this moment.

"Our song," I said.

She smiled vulnerably, and I relived our relationship in the following seconds as we held each other's gaze. Maybe ours had been small and perhaps even insignificant, but she and those moments had been a part of my growing up, and I was grateful for every one of them, even the ones that hurt.

I held out my hand. "Wanna dance?"

"Yes, of course." She let me lead her to the dance floor. We pulled each other close and fell into the song's rhythm.

She whispered into my ear, "So *who* or what are you going to chase now?"

"I'm done chasing," I said. "I want to slow it all down. How about you? What's next?"

She sighed. "I want to speed it all up, if you know what I mean. Fast-forward to a better place."

I pulled back to meet her eyes. "You're gonna get your break. Don't lose heart."

"We'll see."

When the song finished, I kissed her on the cheek. I don't know if she felt the same way as I, but I think she did. That dance would be our last, but it was a nice way to say goodbye. Our story ended exactly as it should, and I hoped she felt as full as I did inside.

She glanced over her shoulder. "You'd better go rescue your date. The men are all over her."

Mrs. Cartwright had just finished a dance of her own. With none other than Elliot. I should have known. He flashed the most wonderful smile as I approached.

"Don't tell me you're coming to steal her."

"You know I am." I looked at Mrs. Cartwright. "I hope I don't have to get in a fight over you tonight."

Her smile indicated she knew what I was up to. But she didn't. Not at all. I had things in motion, and I couldn't wait to get up on that stage.

I glanced over at the band. The timing could not have been more perfect. The lead singer, whom I'd spoken to earlier in the week, saw me and nodded. He wrapped his wiry fingers around the microphone. "We want to do a song we've never done before, but it was a special request. It's a fine one too. Enjoy." The drummer counted off the tune, and the band broke into the beginnings of the Penguins' song "Earth Angel."

"Would you let me have this dance?" I asked, offering my hand to Mrs. Cartwright.

Recognizing the song, Mrs. Cartwright's eyes sprang to life. "Don't you dare make me cry, young man."

"Make you cry?" I said. "Never."

I pulled her in, this woman who had not only changed my life but changed this town. For forty years she'd sent good people out into the world, readying them to make Earth a better place.

My earth angel. She was as imperfect as the rest of us, doing her best to shine her light to fight the darkness.

We found ourselves in the center of the dance floor, only us, falling back through the years. I thought of the first time she'd called me into her office, the first time I went out to the farm. Then Tom and me, watching her do her earth angels in the garden. What a special woman.

So special that another classmate stole her from me halfway through the song. As he pulled her hand, she whispered, "Thank you, Carver."

I survived the band's first set, catching up with some old friends and circling up with my crew. We watched Bree take the stage again and invite up the first speaker, Maurice the dentist. Everyone stood in his or her circles, and most people listened. The line to the alcohol grew longer. He was a good man, Maurice, and he'd done some good in the world. Next up was the film producer and then a woman named Meg Porter, who'd swum in the Olympics. She didn't once mention that fact, which was a lesson unto itself.

By the time Bree came back up to introduce me, I was ready to go. "We all know about Dr. Carver Livingston from the paper. He's done some good down in North Carolina. We have to forgive him for not doing it here. Something tells me we haven't seen the last of him, though. As a sidenote, you should have seen him join our barre class the other day. Let's hope he's a better speaker than barre student." She placed her hand on her forehead in a dramatic fashion. "Let's say . . . awkward. Hashtag, not graceful."

The whole room laughed, and oddly, I felt okay with it. Who cared if they were laughing with me *or* at me? Truth was, I could use being laughed at. Because it was funny, wasn't it? My life was funny. Their lives were funny too. Being a human was funny, when it came down to it.

"Let's give it up for Dr. Carver Livingston."

As I took the stage, all I heard was my crew howling, supporting and being there for me like I'd never left. My God, was there a better feeling in the world than being loved despite all your flaws? Once I stood behind the podium, I raised the microphone and looked out over the people who, in my imagination, had turned into sharks circling around me for twenty years.

They didn't look so intimidating now. I pulled out the index cards that I'd prepared with and glanced at the first one.

Thank you to Bree and everyone on the committee. It's such a . . .

Blah.

It all felt like blah.

I stacked the index cards and then pushed them back into the inside pocket of my blazer. "I had this whole thing prepared, but I know what I want to say." I drew in a breath, taking in all the eyes in the room, knowing that they knew everything about me. I was okay with it.

"You may not know this, like if you were on the moon or doing a stint in Siberia in the late nineties, but I had a rough go." I happened upon Shannon's eyes glowing out in the crowd, and I smiled at her before continuing. "I haven't been home in twenty years because I've been running from all that. It was tough, guys. But I've learned a lot in the two weeks since I've been back. One is that you had your tough times too. I wasn't the headline in your lives, though I thought I was. Coming back, I thought I had to prove something after all that, living this big life. Having recently reconnected with so many of you, like my best friend, Elliot, if he'd still allow me to call him that, I've learned that I had the wrong definition of 'living a big life.' Ten minutes with Elliot and you know who won the game of life."

I pointed at my amigo. "That guy."

With one hand, he waved me off, saying, "Stop it, stop it," but with the other, he motioned for more praise, that beautiful juxtaposition we all knew so well, that desperate need to hear every once in a while that we mattered.

To Elliot, I said, "I love you, buddy. I'm sorry I didn't keep in touch, but I'm going to make it up to you. I'm so honored to finally know your wife. And your kids . . . boy, it makes me desperate to be a father."

He wrapped his arm around his wife's waist and whispered a thanks.

I paused to look around the room. "Anyway, I've been nervous about getting up here all week, thinking about what to say. For a while I had decided you were all desperate to hear about my growing practice in North Carolina and all the great things I was doing . . ." I rolled my eyes. "I know, give me a break, Carver."

I raised my hand. "Forget about me. Instead, I wanted to take a moment to recognize someone who had a major impact on all our lives. Where would we be without the teachers out there who dedicate their lives to making the world better, one student at a time? *They* are the ones we should be talking about."

Mrs. Cartwright stood amid a few others several rows back. She looked both appreciative and slightly embarrassed, saying with her eyes, *Don't you do it, Carver.*

Oh, the comedy of life, the push and pull.

Holding eye contact with her, I said, "She doesn't want me to put her in the spotlight. Sorry, my friend. I'm doing it. We had this idea that we wanted to recognize you tonight, to make sure you know how appreciative we all are."

Her eyes grew wide, and I could see the nerves hitting her.

"But we ran into a couple of problems." I paused for effect, settling in up there. It's amazing how easy life is when you have nothing left to prove. "Word spread to other classes that we were honoring you tonight, so we came up with the idea of a video, Teterbury grads from all over the world saying hi. The first problem was that the video's run time was rivaling a James Cameron film. The other issue was one of capacity. This room only holds a hundred and fifty. Turns out you taught most of the people in this town, and they all wanted to be a part of it."

I paused. She really was going to kill me, and I smiled wide, thinking she deserved every bit of what was coming. "So I had to find a bigger room."

Question marks appeared in her eyes. I felt so much elation inside that I could have levitated.

"With your permission, Mrs. Cartwright, I'd like to escort you down the street to the church. Some others want to say hi and give you a hug. Would that be okay?"

Everyone watched her, moist eyes all around, many people holding their hand to their hearts.

Mrs. Cartwright seemed too shocked to answer.

"I'm going to come get you and walk you over there, all right?"

She shook her head at me, like she had when I'd hidden her chalk during the spicier part of my senior year, when Shannon and I were still together.

I left the podium, jumped down from the stage, and weaved through the crowd. People clapped me on the back, and I smiled back at them, showing them that it felt nice to be seen.

I took Mrs. Cartwright's arm, and we walked our way through the crowd, who began to follow us. People from other classes had filled the lobby. They smacked their hands together and cheered when we appeared.

"I can't believe you," Mrs. Cartwright said.

I patted her arm, her reception sending me spinning with delight. "I hope you're feeling the love."

"You know I am."

It was only beginning to get good, though. I led her through the sea of her former students. She gave hugs and shook hands and waved and came alive in a way that surely mirrored Mrs. Cartwright when she was at the absolute peak of her teaching game.

When we descended the steps of the hotel, we looked left and saw yet another crowd. Close to five hundred people formed a walkway that led to the entrance of the church. They erupted with cheers when they saw us. People even had signs. One read WE LOVE YOU, MRS. CARTWRIGHT. She fought hard to keep from crying. Somehow all of Teterbury had worked together to pull this off, and we'd done it.

At the end of the line and up the steps of the church stood Father Bryan, the priest whom I'd talked to two days prior when I realized this thing had snowballed. He was a tall guy, probably six five.

Mrs. Cartwright squeezed my arm. "Don't let go of me, okay?"

"You know I won't." I guided her through the gathering of people. They reached for her and offered her hugs and blew kisses as if she were royalty. I gently moved her along like I was her bodyguard.

I was finally able to pry her away and lead her up the stairs to the church. Father Bryan welcomed us. Though he had distractingly bushy eyebrows, he carried himself like a holy man: upright and calm. As if he knew something I didn't.

We came through the church doors to find every single pew packed with people of all ages. At the front, a trio of stained-glass windows framed an elaborate altar decorated with bright flowers. An impressive gold cross sparkled in the light coming through. A quick flash of my parents up there saying their vows came to me. Putting my eyes back on the crowd, I couldn't believe the turnout and felt bad for everyone behind us who wouldn't be able to fit inside. How could we have known to expect such a response?

As Mrs. Cartwright and I made our way down the aisle, her fans turned toward us and clapped so hard that the chandeliers dangling from the vaulted ceilings could have crashed down. When we reached the front, I was beyond pleased to see that her son, Jack, had made it. She broke down with happy tears as they hugged. I looked past them to my parents, who'd been sitting with him in the first pew. My mother and father had dressed up nicely. We shared in that moment a sense of acceptance, that no matter what any of us did, the intentions were always right.

Beyond them I saw Ava wearing a cream-colored dress and clapping. We met eyes. I suppose she was the one piece in my life that didn't make sense to me. Something between Ava and me resonated so deeply . . . but what can you do? She would no doubt be the one that got away.

I gave her an unobtrusive wave.

"Hi," she whispered back.

The cheers continued as I led Mrs. Cartwright to a chair by the podium. I stood and put my face in front of the microphone. Everyone kept cheering for her. I clapped, too, and it must have gone on for three minutes.

When I decided it was turning to punishment for her, I raised my hand and tapped the microphone. It took a moment, but people quieted. Those in the back pushed in to take a peek. Behind me was a large screen to show the video we'd prepared. We'd had to leave most of the submissions out because we received over three hundred. What I loved most was that so many people I'd reached out to had said they were booking last-minute plane tickets. What I'd also heard is that every single bed-and-breakfast and inn and hotel within twenty miles was fully booked.

How about that to speak to the love of a teacher?

"We did it, guys," I said. "Somehow this whole town pulled together what I think is the most remarkable tribute I could imagine for this legendary teacher. She would never want me to embarrass her, but I think it's a little late for that."

Everyone thought that was funny.

I looked to the back, where people were trying to squeeze in for a look. "I thought we would have enough room, but apparently we should have moved this to the memorial auditorium in Burlington. My apologies to everyone who is stuck outside."

I glanced at Mrs. Cartwright and then said, "What I had started to say in that teeny conference room that wouldn't hold enough people is . . . Mrs. Cartwright left a mark on me I will carry forever. As we can see by this turnout and by the tribute we're about to show, I'm not the only one by a long shot." I took a moment to let my roaring heart regulate. "Mrs. Cartwright . . . I mean, Eloise, thank you for being you."

She kissed her palm and then blew it to me. I did the same right back as I left the stage and joined my parents, who'd saved me a seat and glowed with pride. It so happened my spot was right next to Ava.

She took my hand. "All of this is pretty amazing."

"It is, isn't it?" I was trying to get past her holding my hand. What was that all about? She wasn't allowed to send me mixed signals. I was still too smitten with her.

Father Bryan took the podium and asked that the lights be dimmed from the back. As they were, he said, "I think Carver put it well. How do I add to it, other than I think this night and this gesture is a testament to every great teacher out there in the world. We are a product of our teachers. Mrs. Cartwright, thank you for showing all of us how it's done. And now, let's all enjoy this video put together by people from all over the world."

The projector splashed light onto the large screen, and a severely condensed ten-minute version of the movie began. First up was a woman who was in charge of Jeep tours in Dubai. "Mrs. Cartwright, sending you all my love from Dubai. Know that I think of you often." Then Melanie, the hairstylist, appeared on the screen. Remembering what a talker she was, we'd be there all night.

"Mrs. Cartwright, I'm so glad I get to do this. You were the best teacher I ever had. And you'd better come to Burlington so I can do your hair."

Ava squeezed my hand. "I'm curious about something," she said. "You still not looking for a relationship?"

I didn't even bother playing it cool, instead letting out a very real smile. "I can't believe I ever said that to you."

"And I'm sorry that I may have misjudged you. You're not exactly the man I thought you were."

"I warned you, didn't I?"

"No, I mean in a good way." She dragged a finger along my palm. "I can't believe I'm saying this, but I think I like you."

"Was there a question mark at the end of that statement?" I felt like the earth had fallen off its axis—in a good way.

"I'm trying to make sense of it," she said.

I nodded. "Okay. I don't know what to say. Would you like me to help you make sense of it?"

She leaned over and whispered into my ear, "The thing is . . . I keep hearing about all this persistence you have, but you seem to have given up on asking me out."

I pinched my chin. "Was I not supposed to?"

She shrugged. "I don't know."

My mother leaned over to show us we were being loud. Ava let go of my hand and put her focus back on the screen. I did the same, sort of. Most of me was still thinking about what had happened. Did we have a chance? There was no distance I wouldn't travel to take her out to dinner.

Students continued to show up on the screen, saying their piece. Though Mrs. Cartwright's back was to us as she watched, I could feel how full she must have felt inside.

Applause rattled the church as the movie came to an end ten minutes later. Father Bryan returned to the podium and covered the microphone to ask if Mrs. Cartwright wanted to say anything. She gave a thumbs-up and stood. I leaped to my feet to help her. I guided her to the podium and then took the chair where she'd been sitting, in case she needed support.

She stood up there like she was at the front of her class, chalk in hand. Everyone silenced seconds before she spoke.

"To say that I am humbled and grateful and overwhelmed would not do justice to this moment. I don't know that I deserve it, but I'll take all this love. I'll take it on behalf of every teacher out there. Thank you all for being my students and for caring for me and making it out tonight. I had no idea this was going to happen." She rubbed her eyes. "I told Carver not to make me cry, and he's still not listening to his teachers."

After a collective laugh, she said, "I don't have a lot to say. Please know that I am grateful." She looked over at me. "Hold on. I'd like to say something to Carver and Ava, who have been my friends, taking care of an old lady who's fading away. That's exactly how I've felt lately. It's not easy getting old. I'm sure many of you can testify to that fact. Losing my husband cut me off at the knees. There is no feeling in the world like love, and I thought I'd lost it forever, like a star burning out."

I noticed my mother and father share a loving look before Mrs. Cartwright continued. "There's a term out there among astrologists, a phenomenon that's very rare and wonderful. Resurrected stars. They are stars that fade to black only to come back to life again. Thanks to Carver and Ava and the rest of you, I am a resurrected star. And I promise you I will wake up tomorrow morning so full of love and life that the good Lord himself will have to drag me kicking and screaming when he's ready." She hit the podium with her fist and then looked back to the large cross at the altar.

The church exploded again in cheers. I looked to Ava, who was bawling, and we held eyes for a moment. We'd found a way to help our friend.

A resurrected star. Never had I heard anything more beautiful.

Mrs. Cartwright left the podium, and I rose to help her. Like my father had taught me, I held my head high as I guided her down the aisle toward the exit.

"You're in big trouble with me," she called out over the commotion.

I laughed. "I accept full responsibility."

Chapter 30

GOING HOME

The next morning, my dad stood in the grass with his arm around my mom. "Let's not make it so long before you're back, huh?"

I flung my bag into the back seat of the Audi. "I'll be back in a flash, I'm sure. What's better than summertime in Vermont?"

"That's my boy," he said. "By the way, your mom showed me the Roomba this morning. I'll be damned. The thing's a robot."

"Yeah, that's the idea."

"I'm serious. Your mom pushes a button on her iPad and the thing goes about its business. Best invention I've ever seen in my life."

My mom and I smiled at each other. What a character, my dad. I suppose we all come to terms with obstacles in our own sweet way.

Once I'd gotten in the Audi, I rolled down the window. "By the way, don't forget the furniture shipment coming in tomorrow. I'm done sleeping on bunk beds."

My mother gave a thumbs-up.

I stopped at Mrs. Cartwright's on the way out of town. I shouldn't have been surprised that an old turquoise truck was parked in the driveway. Actually, I'd texted Ava earlier to see if she would meet me there.

Mrs. Cartwright sat on her stool in front of a garden box, her hands digging in the dirt. Tom's old Sox cap held down her hair. Oscar was attached by a leash to a pole next to her, and he lay in the grass, enjoying the sun. She turned when she heard me pull up and then began to stand. "Look who it is." She gifted me a smile that could have fertilized the whole world.

Ava came out of the garage barefooted and carrying a bucket. "Hi there," she said.

"Hi." I held my gaze on her for a moment, hoping I would indeed have more of her in my life. "I like your overalls." I turned to Mrs. Cartwright. "And look at this garden. I'll have to come back in August to check your progress. Do you think your tomatoes will be as good as the ones in the old days?"

"They'll be better," she said with the authority I remembered so well.

Ava and I shared a look, surely both of us feeling the same way, that Mrs. Cartwright was going to be fine.

"You know what they do down south with them?" I asked. "They make white bread sandwiches, using this mayonnaise called Duke's. Ava probably had them down in Nashville."

"I have and I miss them. I miss all that good southern food."

Then she would love Asheville.

"You'll have to make me one in August then," Mrs. Cartwright said.

"It would be my honor. I'll bring a jar of Duke's with your name on it."

She gathered her hands together and took on a more serious tone. "Carver, thank you again. I don't know how I'm going to get you back but . . ."

"I feel like you're about to follow that statement up with a threat."

"Wait until next time."

I cut to Ava. "That's the feisty we all know and love."

"She's full of it this morning," she replied.

I went to pet Oscar, who was far more receptive than he used to be. "Hey, buddy. You take care of these ladies, okay?" Coming back to a stand, I said, "I'm off to catch a plane home. Bags are in the car. I wanted to come by and get one last hug."

"From whom?" Mrs. Cartwright said. "Me or the transient?"

I took time to look into the eyes of each of them, feeling very much like I was going to miss this tribe we'd formed. "I'll take one from each."

Mrs. Cartwright patted me on the cheek, which I loved. "You be a good boy, okay?"

"I will." I hugged her.

When I looked at Ava, the sadness of my departure hit me the hardest. "I know I'm late for this, but remember that game Mrs. C tried to get us to play? Eleven questions?"

She perked up, a smile that would last for days in my mind. "Yeah?"

"Wanna play now?"

"Sure."

Interacting with her was too much fun. Was this what a real relationship could be like? She made me feel young again. The good kind of young.

"So, thirty seconds, right, Mrs. C?"

She fired a finger at me. "Call me Eloise, and yes, thirty seconds."

"And what are the consequences if we don't get through it?" Ava asked.

"Oh, I don't know," I said. "Missing out on the chance of a lifetime."

Ava's eyes expanded. "Well, we can't risk that, can we?"

I looked at my watch. "Ready."

She took a big step toward me. "Let's do it."

Feeling Mrs. Cartwright smiling at us as if she was finally getting what she wanted, finally getting two people to let go of their fear of love, I waited until the second hand hit twelve, and then, "Favorite food?"

"Umm, salad."

"Salad? Are you kidding? You can have anything in the world and you want lettuce?"

"Are you supposed to question my answers?"

"Okay, favorite dressing . . ."

"Lemon and olive oil," she rattled out.

"What about blue cheese . . . or ranch?"

She made a disgusted face. "Eew. You're terrible at this, by the way."

"Yeah, you're right. I think we should start over." I couldn't remember having more fun in months. Both our cheeks swelled as we read each other. "Thirty seconds, starting . . . now. Ketchup or mustard?"

"Why all the condiment questions? Is this the best you have?"

"Fine, how do you feel about decorating for Halloween?"

"That it may be *the most* important holiday for decorating."

"Look at you. Favorite place you've ever traveled."

"Egypt."

"Favorite . . ." I paused. "Favorite color."

"Really?"

"Yes, really. You can't know someone without knowing their favorite color."

"Fine. Orange. How many questions was that?"

I laughed. "I have no idea."

She tapped her wrist. "Five seconds."

"Will I ever see you again?" That was the big question, wasn't it? I wanted a yes more than I wanted about anything in the world.

"How do I know?" she asked matter-of-factly. She grabbed my wrist and turned it so that she could see the time. "Oh no, time's up!"

We were both smiling widely, though I noted how she'd dodged the question. "Now I know everything about you."

"With your eleven questions that were probably only five."

I held eye contact. "One's choice in condiments says everything about a person. As does one's avoiding of a particular question."

She smiled even wider, this big, beautiful waterfall of good energy hitting me. "I wasn't avoiding your question."

"No?" Jumping in with all of me, I said, "So about that date then . . ."

She shuffled her bare feet in the grass. "I thought you might have forgotten."

"Not a chance," I said.

"Actually, I was looking at Airbnbs in Asheville this morning," she admitted, setting my heart into a dance. "I thought I'd spend my free time there before getting back to work."

"Is that right?" I said, inching toward her this time.

She shrugged. "Seems like a place I should check out on my never-ending pursuit of home."

I flapped my hand in the air. "Let's not say *never-ending*. Home is waiting somewhere."

"Fair enough."

"I'd love to show you around," I said more seriously.

"I'd like that. I keep hearing about all the good food."

"Some of the best. Even for salad eaters."

She burst into a laugh. Though she was better at reading energy than me, I could feel the sizzle in the air.

I opened my arms. "Well, until then . . ." I laughed as our cheeks pressed together.

"What?" she whispered.

"Life, Ava. Just life." I squeezed her and then let her go.

"Carver, I have something for you," Mrs. Cartwright said. She approached me and handed over a package wrapped in newspaper with a bow made of the green tape she used for gardening. "Don't open it until you've left town."

"Thank you, Mrs. Cartwright."

"Eloise, Carver. Both of you, call me Eloise."

"I don't know that I could ever stop calling you Mrs. Cartwright. But I'll try."

We hugged, and she kissed my cheek.

I waved one last time and then walked toward the car. I turned back and locked eyes with Ava. Maybe for the first time in my life,

I was ready to love. Because for the first time in my life, I loved myself.

I drove through town, falling back into all the good that had come during my childhood years. At risk of Mrs. Cartwright chasing after me for my use of a cliché, there was no doubt that what doesn't kill you makes you stronger.

When the green sign for Teterbury faded in my rearview mirror, I remembered the gift Mrs. Cartwright had given me. Still three miles from the highway, I pulled over into the parking lot of a nail salon and peeled open the package. It was two books. The one on top was *Outlander*. I belted out a laugh. Was there room enough in my world for Jamie and me?

The second book was Oscar Wilde's *Lady Windermere's Fan*. A bookmark stuck out of the middle. Wait, it wasn't a bookmark; it was a letter. I had begun to pull it out when I noticed a highlighted section on one of the open pages.

I read Oscar's words out loud. "We are all in the gutter, but some of us are looking at the stars." I read it again and then set the book down on the passenger seat. "Always teaching, aren't you, Mrs. Cartwright? Who and where would I be without you?"

That was when I looked back at the letter. "I'll be damned." There in the center of the envelope was my writing:

Future Carver Livingston, Whereabouts Unknown

Anxious to see what kind of wisdom my seventeen-year-old self—the one who was dating Shannon at the time—had shared, I tore open the envelope and began to read.

> Dear Future Carver,
> Man, you're old. Are you showing any gray hairs yet? Whatever it is you're doing, let's hope you're rich. I'm surely setting you up for it with this 4.0 coming your way. If you married Shannon, then . . .

I threw back my head and laughed at myself. How could any of us take ourselves so seriously? Deciding to save the rest for later, I folded the letter and tossed it onto the passenger-side seat with the books.

As I pulled back out to the road, I said to myself in the most loving of ways, "What a putz you were, Carver Livingston."

It was a relief to know I no longer had to live my life with one eye on the rearview mirror.

In the airplane I took my window seat next to a pimple-faced kid with a hat turned backward and a right leg that shook so hard I could feel it through the floor. Other travelers raced to push their bags into the overhead bins and get situated in their seats. A flight attendant welcomed us aboard via the cabin speakers.

I clicked my seat belt and asked my neighbor, "How's it going?"

He turned to me with clueless eyes and pulled out the earbuds that I didn't see a moment ago. "What's that?"

"Just saying hi."

"Hi." He put his earbuds back in and locked his eyes on the back of the seat in front of him.

I waved to get his attention again.

He pulled his earbuds back out with a modicum of annoyance.

"What are you, a senior in high school?" I asked.

"Junior."

I smirked, feeling like I had something to offer—knowing that I did. "It'll be okay, whatever comes. I wish someone had told me that. But I guess sometimes we learn the hard way. Know that there will be broken hearts and sad things that happen and times when you think you're not worthy of the air you're breathing. But hold on to the good stuff and know it'll be okay. Your place is out there in the world, and you'll eventually find it."

He looked at me like I'd eaten an edible earlier. "Yeah, all right," he said dismissively, probably the same way I would have responded to a stranger on the plane.

We rose high over Vermont, and I pressed my face to the window, taking in what would always and forever be my home. I was proud to be a Vermonter, proud to be from Teterbury, proud to be the son of Ben and Lisa Livingston.

Epilogue

A Full House

One Year Later

"Carver Livingston, I know you're not calling me on a Saturday." Mary Beth's voice spilled out of the speaker on my phone.

"Is it Saturday?" I asked jokingly. "I forget sometimes."

"I figured Ava would have knocked some sense into you by now."

Ava was cuddled up with me on the couch. A fleece blanket covered us. She held the latest Diana Gabaldon in her hands, a thousand-page-plus tome that would take her three days maximum.

"These things take time, Mary Beth," Ava said, a grin coming to life.

"Hey, Ava. Please keep him straight over there."

"I'm trying," Ava called out.

"It takes a village," I said, setting down on the table beside me the first in the Outlander series—the one Mrs. C had given me. She'd written *Resistance is futile, Carver* on the title page. When I'd spoken to her the day before, calling to wish her bon voyage, she'd been delighted to hear I was finally taking the plunge into the lives of Claire and Jamie. And she was glad I'd finally found her inscription.

"If you can't beat 'em, join 'em," I'd said.

She'd replied, "Had I a water bottle with long-distance range, I would hit you square in the forehead for that horrible cliché. Please find more creative ways to make your point."

Back in the present, Mary Beth cleared her throat. "Okay, out with it. What can't wait until Monday?"

I looked through the sliding glass windows to the deck and the mountains. "Actually, I was calling to see if you wanted to come over for dinner tonight. My parents are arriving shortly, and I thought it would be fun to cook some hamburgers and hot dogs on the grill."

She let out a laugh. "How beautifully American of you. And you don't have to sugarcoat it. I know you want me over there to show you how to light a grill. Lord knows that thing hasn't seen one lick of a flame."

Ava and I looked at each other and grinned. "You caught me there. I haven't even taken the tags off yet."

"Ava, he's helpless. No wonder he needs a whole team of women trying to clean him up."

"Hey," I said, "at least I'm trying."

"There is that, sweetie," Mary Beth said. "What time do you want me over?"

We worked out the details, and when I hung up, I reached for Ava's thigh under the blanket. "I'm not going to lie. I get excited about this house being full of people."

Ava put her hand on my hand and squeezed. "Me too."

$\backsim$

We stood with our arms together in the driveway, waiting for my parents to come around the corner. They'd texted they were close.

"How do you feel?" Ava asked me.

"Really, really good," I said. "How about you? Can you handle a week with them?"

"Are you kidding me? I love your parents. Your mom and I are going to find every single boutique in this city, not to mention a spa day at Grove Park."

"You're speaking her language."

They appeared through the trees. My father honked the horn of his big truck as it dragged Clementine up the driveway. They came to a stop right in front of us, and the first thing I noticed was that my mom was still growing out her hair. I'd been back to Teterbury three times since I'd left in June, once on my own and twice with Ava. My mother seemed to be coming alive more and more as she learned to embrace retirement.

When she stepped out of the truck, she had Oscar Wilde in her hands. "Look who we brought."

"Hey, Oscar," I said, reaching for him. He even licked my face. Holding him to my chest, I said, "Look at you, Mom! You look great."

She pulled back her now-long blonde hair and showed me a smile that assured me she'd found peace with the past. "Thank you, dear. I feel great." She let go of me and took Ava into a hug. "My future daughter-in-law, how could I be so lucky? Congratulations, you two."

She let go of Ava and took her hand to inspect the ring with which I'd proposed in April. "I want to hear the whole story again, guys. What better way to propose than at the top of a mountain."

"Lisa, he was so romantic and sweet. His fingers were shaking when he took to one knee and asked."

I smiled, remembering how she'd said yes ten times as I slipped the ring onto her finger.

"I'm the lucky one," Ava said, and I was pretty sure she meant it. "How's camper life?"

My mom let go of Ava's hand and clipped a leash to Oscar's collar. "Would you believe I'm having the time of my life? I'm even falling in love with Willie Nelson after all this time. And having Oscar is a dream. I don't want to give him back."

"Somebody say Willie Nelson?" My father came around his side of the truck and gave us hugs and offered congratulations. "Boy, it's nice to be here. I can already smell the barbecue joints."

"No shortage of those down here, Pops. So how did Mrs. Cartwright seem when she dropped off Oscar?" She was embarking on a two-week European cruise on Cunard's *Queen Mary 2*.

"She looked like a new woman," my mom said. "I took her shopping, and we had our hair done. I think she's going to have the time of her life."

"I'm sure of it. She says she hadn't left Teterbury since Tom passed. And she's promised to visit us next."

"We can't wait," Ava said.

My mother clapped her hands. "Okay, I can't take it another moment. Where is my grand puppy?"

Ava gestured with her thumb. "He's in his kennel sleeping. Let's go wake him."

My father and I carried up their bags, and we all moved into the living room, where Ava introduced Syd, our eight-week-old German shepherd mix, who yawned as he came to life. Agreeing it was time to bring a dog into our lives, we'd visited the animal rescue near my house a week earlier. All the dogs were adorable, but when we both came upon Syd, our hearts melted. He had a black face with rims of brown above his eyes. The person who'd brought him in had found Syd hiding behind a dumpster in Black Mountain. The poor pup had worms and was malnourished, but they'd nursed him back to health, and he was ready to find a home.

His paws were entirely too big for him, and he had stumbled on them as he first came to say hello to Ava and me through the wire gate. He'd been both curious and timid, taking his time to ensure that we were not a threat. They'd set us up in a room together, and we sat on the floor, gave him treats, and slowly earned his trust. In a matter of minutes, he was climbing on top of us and licking our faces. Ava had turned to me and said exactly what I'd been thinking: "I'm not leaving without this dog."

Standing alongside my parents, we watched Oscar and Syd get to know each other, their tails wagging as they sniffed around. Then Syd took on a playful attack position. He slapped those big paws down in front of his new friend, taunting him. Oscar took on a similar stance. After a dance around the carpet, they eventually launched into a happy bout of wrestling.

"Have you ever seen anything more adorable?" My mom lowered to her knees to get her hands on him. Both dogs raced to her and jumped up on her. My mom giggled and closed her eyes and let them lick her face. If I could have bottled joy, that would have been the time to do it.

"Ben, you better get ready," she said. "I see a puppy in our future."

My dad's eyes grew wide as he let slip a sly grin. "I know better than to say a darn thing."

Smiles rounded the room.

Taking my fiancée's hand, I took a moment to breathe in what this house had become, a home full of love and life. I was so thankful I'd taken that trip to Teterbury, and that everything had happened the way it had. Mrs. Cartwright and my mother had been right: love is worth the risk, because a life without love isn't a life at all.

Author's Note

About ten years ago, I had the great pleasure of connecting with the fabulous author, proud Texan, and supremely talented English teacher Leila Meacham. For some reason, she decided to take me on as her student, and we established a lovely relationship, communicating via the phone and email for many years.

Early on, I told her my ambitions and that I was thinking about writing something other than thrillers. I said that I had these wild characters in my head who lived in wine country in eastern Washington State and that I felt pulled to tell their stories. The thing was, unlike my thrillers, the story wouldn't have the added horsepower of unsolved crimes, loaded guns, and car chases to propel the plot. Though they were colorful, these were just everyday people trying to figure their way in the world. Leila read some of my stuff and encouraged me to follow my heart and switch genres. I'm so thankful I listened to her.

She also told me that despite how much work I had ahead of me to hone my craft—and she assured me that in my case it was daunting—I had the thing even she couldn't teach: talent. Her words were all the validation I needed and continue to motivate me to this day.

All the way until she was issued her wings, she pushed my development as a novelist and coached my writing career. She had this extraordinary ability to critique me heavily while at the same time firing me up to keep chasing my dream. Even into her final months of life, *even* while she recovered from seemingly endless radiation treatments, she continued to share her writing wisdom with me, long emails on topics such as honing one's style, zapping qualifiers, finding the exact word, building the perfect character arc, limiting passive voice, and avoiding clichés. That, my friends, is what being a teacher is all about.

In our last exchange, I mentioned that I was going to write a novel inspired by her. At that time, the title was *We Love You, Mrs. Cartwright*. I told her that, for drama's sake, I'd have to give her character flaws so that I would have somewhere to go with her arc. I would have been hard pressed to find a flaw with the real-life Leila. Of course, being an author herself, she understood, and I think she was maybe even tickled by the idea.

I'm sad she's not here to read what I did with the story. Then again, maybe she is. She will certainly always and forever be in my heart. May we all live such a rich, graceful, giving, and beautiful life as my friend, mentor, and sage.

We love you, Mrs. Meacham.

Acknowledgments

I don't know the words to accurately convey how grateful I am for the team that surrounds me, strengthening my stories and making me a better writer. How could I be so lucky?

Danielle Marshall, thank you for taking a big chance on me, encouraging me to write from my soul, and pulling all the right strings in the background to help me grow as a writer and find my readers. You are a rock star. To the whole Lake Union team, thank you for being flat-out amazing—every single one of you.

Andrea Hurst, my agent and creative partner, you and I have something that comes only a few times in a lifetime, if an artist is lucky. Where would I be without you? Thank you for teaching me and creating with me and coaching me. Your talent for understanding story is truly remarkable. Our work together will always be one of the highlights of my creative endeavors.

Tiffany Yates Martin, how absolutely beautiful that you and I could work on this story together, as I know how much Leila Meacham meant to you as well. Coincidence? I think not. You and your extraordinary mind have become an integral part of my process. Somehow you always know what I'm trying to put on the page, even if what I've done in a draft is far from it. Thank you for putting your whole heart into my books and finding every which way to poke holes in them. Your efforts hurt in the best of ways. Know I will always chase the goal of having you one day respond with, "Wow, that was perfect, Boo. I have nothing to offer." In the meantime, I will embrace your ocean of red ink with open arms.

To my beta readers, I am forever grateful. I hope you see, book after book, how your contributions lift my stories up much higher than they'd be without you. You better know how much you mean to me.

I don't know that I could have pulled this story off without having my good friend and very skilled surgical vet, Dr. John Pierce, helping me along the way. Thank you for taking time out of your busy schedule to help me make Carver sound much more professional. What you do for animals is nothing short of extraordinary.

Ruth Chiles, my guru, you are like the finest Formula One pit stop team. Thank you for always making sure my engine is running well. I've no idea how I survived without you, and I hope that, on occasion, I make you proud. Your teachings run through all my stories.

Speaking of gurus, Lisa Gianvito, thank you for offering up a Reiki session as a gift for speaking at your book club. I'll make that trade any day. You came at the right moment and gave me the lift I needed. I won't soon forget our exchange.

Drew Breakey, my bandmate for life, thank you for being at the ready whenever I had physical therapy questions. It was a joy to create with you once again. Your idea to give Mrs. Cartwright a gardening stool was priceless.

Dr. Susan Satterfield, thank you for jumping in with your expertise and helping me bring some verisimilitude to Mrs. Cartwright's troubles. Love that we've connected with you and Sattie, and we look forward to the Newport Folk Festival!

Marieta Warnstedt, thank you for putting us up in your lovely home in Waterbury, Vermont. Can you tell I stole a little of your beautiful town as the setting? Can't wait to see you again, friend.

As those who knew me way back when are well aware, I was no easy student, but I had some amazing teachers and mentors who believed in me and encouraged me. You know who you are. Thank you, truly.

Because of you, I always keep an eye out for any kid still searching for his purpose.

Riggs and Mikella, you are my world, and what an extraordinary world it is. Thank you for loving me even in the depths of my deadlines. It gets hairy, doesn't it? As always, every word is for you. Mikey, my readers don't know how lucky they are to have you pulling the strings in the background, demanding I rework the first page for the thousandth time and offering a suggestion to make an average line or even scene far more intoxicating. Anything great in the first few pages is always your handiwork. And, Riggs, you're the fuel that keeps the engine running, the best story your mom and I will ever write. But will you stop telling everyone your daddy lies for a living?

Finally, to my readers, those of you who show me endless support by taking a chance with my stories, sharing them with friends and family and fellow book club members. I send you a soul-deep thank-you. I am humbled and grateful that you allow me to tell stories for a living and to express myself so openly. You lift me up, friends. And if you're not careful, I'm gonna keep doing this until my last breath.

Book Club Questions

1. Who was your favorite teacher and how did they leave their mark on you?

2. Did any events from your youth affect the rest of your life? Do you have wounds that need healing?

3. Do you go to your high school reunions? Did you feel like you had something to prove?

4. Are you still in touch with your best friend from high school?

5. Do you know anyone who married their high school sweetheart? Did it last? Does it take a unique couple to make that work?

6. Did Mary Beth remind you of Mrs. Cartwright? Did they play similar roles in Carver's life?

7. How did Carver's experience on the Cartwright farm affect his life?

8. Can a couple survive infidelity?

9. Discuss Elliot, his life, and his impact on Carver. Carver's father suggested the two previous best friends reconnect. Was he pushing it so Carver could see that happiness is not defined by accomplishments?

10. One of the themes is that you are perfect as you are. Discuss.

11. How far away from your hometown do you live? How often do you return? Do you feel hesitation in doing so? Why?

12. Do you have or have you had pets in your life? How much of an effect have they had on you?

13. When was the last time you looked up to the stars?

14. When you need inspiration, where do you go and why?

15. What, if any, misconceptions did you have against your parents? Have your opinions about them changed over the years?

16. If you were to write a letter to your seventeen-year-old self, what would it say?

17. Carver Livingston has worked hard to overcome his past. He is a success in his field of veterinary medicine, yet he still seems to need emotional approval on all levels, especially his own. Have you ever felt this way? Why do you think we are most often our own worst critics?

About the Author

Photo © 2018 Brandi Morris

Boo Walker is the bestselling author of *A Spanish Sunrise*, *The Singing Trees*, *An Unfinished Story*, and the Red Mountain Chronicles. He initially tapped his creative muse as a songwriter and banjoist in Nashville before working his way west to Washington State, where he bought a gentleman's farm on the Yakima River. It was there, among the grapevines and wine barrels, that he fell in love with telling high-impact stories that now resonate with book clubs around the world. Rich with colorful characters and boundless soul, his novels will leave you with an open heart and a lifted spirit. Always a wanderer, Boo currently lives in Cape Elizabeth, Maine, with his wife, son, and two rambunctious dogs. He also writes thrillers under the pen name Benjamin Blackmore. You can find him at www.boowalker.com and www.benjaminblackmore.com.